DARK ENCHANTMENT

To Winifred Nerney

DARK ENCHANTMENT

Dorothy Macardle

With an introduction by Caroline B Heafey

TRAMPPRESS

First published by Doubleday in 1953

Dark Enchantment © copyright The Beneficiaries of
the Literary Estate of Dorothy Macardle, 1953, 2019

This edition published 2019 by Tramp Press
www.tramppress.com

Introduction © copyright Caroline B Heafey 2019

A CIP record for this title is
available from The British Library.

1 3 5 7 9 10 8 6 4 2

ISBN print: 978-1-9164342-3-3
ISBN ebook: 978-1-9164342-4-0

Tramp Press gratefully acknowledges
the financial support of the Arts Council/
An Chomhairle Ealaíon.

Thank you for supporting independent publishing.

Set in 10.5 pt on 14 pt Minion by Marsha Swan
Printed in Sweden by ScandBook

Dark Enchantment: An Introduction

Caroline B Heafey

'This is witchcraft; we have the right to kill.'

NESTLED IN THE FICTIONAL TOWN of Saint Jacques in the French Alps, Dorothy Macardle's 1953 novel *Dark Enchantment* is a stand-alone story as well as a spiritual sequel to her two previous novels *The Uninvited* (1942) and *The Unforeseen* (1945). A third story about supernatural forces, *Dark Enchantment* is foremost a narrative that considers women's independence in post-war Europe. Whereas *The Uninvited* and *The Unforeseen* are set in England and Ireland respectively, *Dark Enchantment*'s setting focuses on continental Europe, evoking the supernatural in a decade already haunted by ghosts from battlefields of the Second World War. As the title suggests, the story is positioned in a French fairy-tale tradition, complete with a sorceress and an enchanting town. Saint Jacques is quaint and charming, encapsulating the facets of fairy-tale France one might expect: buildings constructed of carved stone and wrought iron, fountains, squares lined by pepper trees, and an old church, centred as the town's focus. Juliet, the novel's protagonist, finds Saint Jacques idyllic and romantic, as if plucked from the pages of a storybook. Yet once she becomes further acquainted with the community, Juliet uncovers its ugly and violent history. The dark past of Saint Jacques centres around a woman called Terka, labelled a gypsy, a criminal, and a pariah by the townspeople. At first Juliet mistrusts their superstition and hostility, and regards Terka with sympathy. That is, until strange events start to overwhelm even her sensible mind. Fundamentally, the novel asks the reader to consider what it is to be an outsider, and what social systems determine an individual as an outcast, and why.

Born in 1889 to the affluent Macardle Brewing family of Dundalk, Dorothy Macardle had access to education and a global worldview from an early age. The family travelled to the Continent and to England, as her mother was English. She later attended Alexandra College in Dublin before going on to University College Dublin. Trained in both history and literature, Macardle published research on Spenser and Shakespeare, and began writing plays for the Abbey and the Gate Theatres. She lectured in a series that included WB Yeats, and later lived with Maude Gonne. She was firmly grounded in the Irish literary social and academic circles of her time. While in prison, she demonstrated her own *sangfroid* under truly abhorrent conditions by writing *Earth-Bound: Nine Stories of Ireland*, published in 1924. These short stories are rooted in an Irish revolutionary literary tradition and culminate with 'A Story Without an End', which concludes by envisioning the violence of the Civil War and the romanticised united Ireland utterly divided. For many years she has been best known for her history of the Anglo-Irish and Civil Wars, *The Irish Republic* (1937).

Upon its release in 1953, *Dark Enchantment* was marketed as a kind of 'book club' novel, aimed primarily at a female readership. In Ireland, review coverage was surprisingly sparse. Evelyn Eaton wrote for *The New York Times* that the novel 'is perfect escape literature, especially for those who have at any time (preferably years ago) turned a tourist's eye on the south of France'. We understand Eaton's reading to position the novel as an ideal escape for a bourgeois housewife, eager to take her mind back to the European tours of her youth. There is a charm that the reader sees upon encountering the novel; however, Eaton's comments do not age well. While Macardle's writing indeed indulges the reader with a kind of nostalgic depiction of a small French village, a deeper reading of *Dark Enchantment* provides a critical commentary on the opportunities for women during this historical moment with regard to socioeconomic mobility and agency.

The novel begins with the problem of what to do with a woman. Recently reunited father and daughter, Frith and Juliet, make their way through France. Frith, a well-known actor on hard times, is constantly reminded of his daughter's precarious financial circumstance. Juliet is introduced as a burden to her father as he considers how to manage her financial status and fiscal sustainability. The young woman has been left in financial ruin by her mother, who divorced Frith after the War and accumulated gambling debts in Monte Carlo. Furthermore, Juliet abhors teaching, one of the few respectable working positions for women of Juliet's class status, leaving her with no means to support herself. Frith ultimately decides that his daughter is well-suited to work in the inn where they are staying in Saint Jacques, under the supervision of its keepers, René and Martine, who are expecting their first child. Before long, Juliet meets Michael Faulkner, a handsome and charming young Englishman with ample knowledge of the village and the people who live there. Michael confides to Juliet that he expresses sympathies with the ostracised 'gypsy' woman called Terka, whose livelihood comes from selling brooms in the market, and, as we later learn, from selling remedies and reading fortunes. Terka's independence extends beyond the regional economy. She is a self-sustaining woman, though at the expense of acceptance from the townspeople within the village. Saint Jacques, not unlike Juliet, seems also to be coming of age in the aftermath of Nazi Occupation and grappling with the subsequent shifts in socio-economic gender dynamics. In addition, Terka is said to have had an affair with a married man, for which she has been maimed.

Macardle's contrasts between female characters in the novel demonstrate the limited options available to women during this post-War period. In Saint Jacques, a woman can either maintain financial independence and live a life of solitude as an and outcast, or she can marry and relinquish all economic agency and social mobility to her husband. We see these themes presented primarily through Juliet, Terka, Martine, and Alison, Michael's elegant and independent mother. Juliet is the protagonist here, and the character through whom we as readers access the narrative. While the story is told in third person, Macardle situates the novel's perspective and the reader's gaze with Juliet and how she navigates Saint Jacques. In contrast, Martine wholeheartedly embodies the domestic. She is a paragon of expectant motherhood and of economic agency that she derives through her business of running a small inn with her husband. All of Martine's identity revolves around the coming of her child, and their business which provides a source of income within the home. Terka is the foil to Martine in many ways. Childless, marked by adultery, and a social pariah both in her Romany community and in Saint Jacques, she is the only woman in the novel who functions as fiscally independent from any man or marriage. She counters the marriage plot through each broom that she sells in town and each fortune that she tells. Michael's mother Alison is affluent, elegant, and financially solvent because she is a widow. She has learned to navigate her world independent of her marriage, but still through the economic resources she has gained in it. Her role in the novel is to offer a portrait of women's independence, but one that still maintains a bourgeois dependence on marriage. By considering the roles of each of these characters, Macardle demands her reader question what choices are available to women, and by what means.

Terka is one of the more perplexing characters in *Dark Enchantment*. She is doubly ostracised by having been cast out by her community and unaccepted by the French townspeople because of her Romany origins and the salacious gossip that she is a witch. She is shunned as adulterous, whether or not such rumours are true. Furthermore, her body bears the markings of her trauma as a pariah. The townspeople recount a story that when Terka disappeared with a married man some years prior, his wife and other women physically attacked her with torches, causing the loss of her eye. In this way, she functions as a physical reminder of the inequitable blame toward women for their sexuality and the destructive potential of a mob. For 1953 France, having only recently experienced Nazi Occupation, the horror of that human potential to scapegoat and comply with violence is not lost on readers. The outcast woman is marked physically and socially specifically by violence that is gendered. Despite these hardships, Terka is financially independent and refuses to sacrifice her agency in exchange for social acceptance, which ultimately places her at odds with the influential Roman Catholic Church. Terka is thus the antithesis of the domesticated married woman. Though her body wears its trauma, she is frequently regarded as beautiful – a beauty that comes from stoicism and agency. She survives abuse, isolation, and the village gossip that ever encircles her whereabouts and constructs her identity as an outsider. There is something alluring to Juliet about Terka, even if she ultimately rejects these impulses.

When Juliet first meets Terka, the woman with one eye reads her palms and tells Juliet not to go away from Saint Jacques. Juliet's decision to stay ultimately secures her in marriage and provides her with financial stability. Later, when she reads the Tarot cards, Terka advises Juliet to leave Saint Jacques, warning that she is in danger staying there. Michael and Juliet eventually leave the village, but together as a married couple. Terka says that the card of St. Michael, which Juliet interprets to be Michael Faulkner, is leading her 'into darkness'. We might understand that Terka advises Juliet to secure independence in contrast to marriage. While the reading in general is upsetting to Juliet, she notes that she believes Terka to be exiled and regarded as suspicious because of the woman's knowledge. It is as if a knowledgeable and financially independent woman cannot exist in the society of the novel. Any disappointment one might feel in Juliet's tidy and neat conclusion seems to mirror the disillusionment Macardle felt with the expectations of women at this time.

Terka is a suitable sort of villain to the typical marriage plot and the fairy-tale 'happily ever after' ending that is the novel's conclusion. She is an outcast because of the suspicions that married men in particular succumb to her advances. Martine accuses Terka of cursing her and her unborn child, another foil to the reverence of motherhood. In the end, despite initial sympathies, Juliet does not take Terka's side in the social conflict and instead chooses to marry Michael Faulkner, answering the question of her financial future. The contemporary reader might consider Macardle's depiction of Terka and her engagement with the occult and the supernatural as an exploration of power, and a critique of the systems of authority present within the novel.

While perhaps disappointing that Juliet chooses not to resist social and fiscal pressures, her decision is unsurprising. Juliet might be read as a product of her circumstance, privileged by education and affluence that afford her class expectations. She does not express a desire to live entirely independently, and instead makes the active choice to marry Michael Faulkner, knowing well what other options might be available to her. She is complicit in the ostracisation of Terka as it relates to the overall social systems available for women in this moment, which seem to be the larger critique of the novel. Juliet enacts her own agency in that her decision is an active choice – one that she makes with careful consideration. She makes no assumption that Michael will ask her to leave with him and instead begins plans to move to London, to live in a boarding house with other women. Indeed, her attraction to Michael is only heightened when she meets his mother. To marry him is to also secure herself with a strong maternal figure whom she can look to for guidance in navigating a society that is not conducive to women's independence outside the home.

Macardle positions the female characters of *Dark Enchantment* in one of two categories: alone and financially independent, or married and dependent on a partner while also primarily confined to the home. The novel thus poses domesticity and social mobility as binary opposites. The setting depicted here is one that aesthetically evokes the nostalgic memories of pre-War France. Saint Jacques is also a town ruled by gossip, and hungry to condemn women who are seen as threatening to the fairy tale the townspeople and the Catholic Church seek to restore. Macardle makes brief references to Terka's roles in the French Resistance during the War, and we might read these moments in the text as inferences to a social distrust in women who participate in social unrest. Macardle, through her incarceration during the Irish Civil War, understood and experienced wartime violence first-hand. Terka as an outcast cannot find a life within the home and even more so refuses to give '[...] to the State a support without which the common good cannot be achieved', as the 1937 Irish Constitution outlines. Macardle invites her readers to ask what is the 'common good'? And what is a women's relationship to it in this context? How might societies in Europe and abroad position themselves to resist authorities that oppress certain members of their populations? Who are the global powers legislating society and what groups move in the margins of these environs? In *Dark Enchantment*, the dark and the dangerous lifestyles are also the most liberating, albeit painful and difficult.

In the novel, France, having experienced governance by force, is a country grappling with its position in the aftermath of violence and Nazi occupation. Questions posed about the roles of women in Ireland, France, the United Kingdom, and the United States during the post-War years. Women, having entered the workforce, are suddenly finding themselves back in the home, their husbands having returned from war. (Sixteen years earlier, in 1937, Ireland had legislated a woman's place into the home once she marries through Article 41.2 of the Irish Constitution and it is worth noting that this article still exists today.) The United Kingdom, Europe, and the United States are struggling to reorganise social structures in the workforce that largely revolve around marriage and family life. In *Dark Enchantment*, Juliet's father Frith remarks how his career has been changed and how his marriage ultimately ended because of the domesticity imposed on his wife: 'It was the War. How many actors had found their careers in pieces when it was over? How many wives, returning to London, had found themselves reduced to domestic bondage in dilapidated flats?"' Within the first few pages of the novel, Macardle outlines how imposed domestic roles ultimately become the ruin of marriage and the idealised family life that these roles are meant to uphold.

Dorothy Macardle would have been well aware of the limitations imposed upon women in Ireland and the United Kingdom. Having been arrested and imprisoned during the Irish Civil War for her opposition to the Free State Treaty, she radically fought for an

Irish Republic that would recognise both Irishmen and Irishwomen equally, as declared in the Proclamation. While in prison, she developed lessons in Irish Republican literature and history to continue to exercise her mind, and to provide education to women prisoners who had not been afforded the academic advantages that she had enjoyed. From her early writing onward, Macardle was interested and preoccupied by experiences of violence, trauma, and specifically those of gendered oppression. *Dark Enchantment* is a novel that allowed her to explore her own disappointment with a world that had not changed enough and where, despite her socioeconomic and educational advantage, she often found herself to be an outsider, unable to succumb to the pressures imposed on women during her time.

Curiously little was written about *Dark Enchantment* leading up to its publication and release in Ireland. Whereas *The Uninvited* and *The Unforeseen* received publication announcements, *Dark Enchantment* only made it into the papers upon review. Perhaps as a result, any mention of the novel tends to be absent from her obituaries. Notably, Benedict Kiely reviewed the first UK edition of *Dark Enchantment*, crediting Macardle with a 'steady descriptive power' as she 'studies the whole business of supposed diabolic power against the backcloth of faith and law and reason'. Kiely's cautiously positive review concludes by naming Juliet as 'a lovely study' but fails to give a more nuanced reading of the text. If Kiely refrained from interrogating the novel further, critic 'W. L.' seemed to miss its purpose entirely in reviewing the novel for the *Irish Independent*. Our second reviewer finds the novel's greatest flaw in a sense of disbelief that 'a whole village community should be so superstitious' as to turn to gun violence for fear of witchcraft or deviousness. One might conclude that W. L. may not have been so aware of the human potential to scapegoat, which Macardle had witnessed on the Continent during the Second World War.

Macardle's outspokenness about her own disillusionment with the Republic of Ireland – and its journalism – in the early 1950s may have coloured some reviewers' approaches to her work. In December 1950, Macardle openly criticised the Dublin press at a symposium stating that 'dramatic criticism in this country was not criticism, but a handing out of bouquets. The newspapers should show more rage at bad plays.' The Ireland Macardle lived in during the last decade of her life was not the one she envisioned from her Mountjoy prison cell (she died in 1958, just five years after the publication of *Dark Enchantment*). Her more direct criticism seems to indicate growing frustration with the limited available opportunities for women and the social structures that eclipsed women's agency. In her radio address published posthumously in *The Shaping of Modern Ireland* by Conor Cruise O'Brien, Macardle expresses that frustration hearkening to the myths of ancient Ireland but likened for her present. In her broadcast she begins, 'the Ireland of legend was haunted by mystical beings, "shape-changers", who would delude the senses by appearing at one moment radiant and beneficent but ugly and menacing the next. I sometimes think Ireland is itself a shape-changer – so captivating, yet so enraging this nation's ways can be.' We might read Macardle's attention to the haunting shape-changers into her writing. Terka is in one moment beautiful and captivating, and another terrifyingly dark. The complexity of social mores embodied through her character seems to function to undermine the otherwise heralded Mother Ireland figure in that she was once celebrated in the Maquis and transforms into the fallen woman. Ultimately, it is Terka who remains outside social constructs and is incarcerated through hospitalisation, a practice that was steadily increasing in Ireland at this time. Macardle's voice does not falter here both in her social activism and in the content of her novels. She continuously invites readers to consider the options available to women and underrepresented identities and champion for more power.

•

I first encountered Dorothy Macardle's writing in autumn of 2013. At that time, the awareness of her contribution to Irish literature was minimal, as she was largely associated with Éamon de Valera and her tome *The Irish Republic*, for which he wrote a preface. Six years later, in large part because of the efforts by Tramp Press to recognise quality writing and the ways in which biases and publishing trends can silence narrative, Macardle is receiving recognition that is long overdue and from a new generation of readers. The Recovered Voices series has proven that readers are willing and able to consider writers and works of the past, examine what becomes lost in the present, and look toward the future. Irish readers of 2019 live in an era of #WakingTheFeminists, #RepealTheEighth, and #MeToo. These movements are demonstrations that women have had enough of inequitable representation in the arts, in legislation, and in society's expectations about women's bodies. The voices that have risen out of frustration and anger have been powerful in affecting change. There is a new and welcome challenge in the mainstream to consider what voices have not been heard enough, and which identities underrepresented historically. The world has changed since 1953 and indeed since 2013. Readers are hungry for literature that is different, unknown, or underacknowledged. Who do we think of when we reflect on Irish writing? Who are the writers that come to mind? Who speaks for Ireland? Recovered Voices prompts us to push back against a canon that is not comprehensive enough. The novel you will read in the following pages fills one of many gaps and is part of an effort to shape a new canon of Irish writers: one that is more dynamic and inclusive.

Author's Foreword

ALTHOUGH SET AMONG well-known mountains, the village of St Jacques is imaginary, and the people of this story are equally fictional. Some of the incidents, nevertheless, had their origin in actual events, while the curious beliefs recorded survived in remoter parts of those mountains at no very distant time.

Contents

DARK ENCHANTMENT

Chapter I

THE DARK WOMAN

ZIG-ZAGGING UP from the coast, swerving at high speed round dizzying bends, pausing at bridges and crossroads to let burdened, perspiring women descend, the bus climbed in less than an hour from parched August to fresh September, leaving the pavements and shops of the Riviera for the vines and olive orchards of the Maritime Alps.

A sharp turn, and St Jacques appeared, crowning a mass of rock high up on the right – a pile of stone-built houses and towers hugged by an ancient wall.

Juliet turned to her father with an excited, 'Look!' then gazed up again, half incredulous to see a five-year-old dream come true. It looked scarcely real, hanging there in the golden air. She thought of all the times her childish wish to spend a whole day in one of the mountain villages had been almost granted, then disappointed. To do it now, and with him, would be the supreme delight of the unimagined, astonishing holiday.

Frith's response to his daughter's elation was a grimace.

'They call that a village?'

3

'A *village perché*,' she explained.

'"Perched" is the word.'

For another ten minutes the vision was one and trees lined the road, then the planes on the right gave place to a towering wall, the bus came to a halt, and passengers for St Jacques cumbrously hoisted themselves, their baskets and one another down. Only a few excursionists kept their seats, bound for the high pine-woods and the *Gorge du Cheval Mort*.

Did the bus, then, not enter the village? Frith demanded of the conductor in his utility French, and Juliet translated the reply which was poured forth in the *patois* of the frontier with Italian vowels all over the place.

'The gate is too narrow. One walks by an easy gradient up to the right or one takes a short cut through the wall.'

The bus grunted, lurched and went boisterously off again by the tarred motor-route on the left while the local people proceeded towards the village at a steady, accustomed pace. Juliet and her father stood looking about them, taking deep breaths of the pure mountain air, glad to be free of the stifling heat and the crowd.

'I saw the steps,' Frith said and began to walk back by the way they had come.

Juliet chuckled.

'You and your short cuts!'

His experiment was a *raccourci* from Castellar down to Menton, and yesterday had brought them out at the wrong end of the town. This narrow passage, however, looked promising. Cut in the thickness of the fortifications, it rose by a flight of steps to a little platform and turned to the right.

'It must come out on the ramparts,' Frith surmised.

'A wide walk,' Juliet suggested eagerly, 'and a breeze and a gorgeous view ... But I'm afraid,' she added in a small voice. Her father did not hear, and she did not persist. Saying, 'Well it's a gamble, but here goes,' he addressed himself with energy to the climb.

Frith Cunningham, after ten days of strolling, swimming and sight-seeing, was in good walking form. He was in good spirits, too.

Forty-eight years old and feeling it, in London, he had dropped a year or two, he told himself, in Paris; sunk a few in the Mediterranean and, next week, in Corsica, in the best of company, making this crazy film and earning money, he would back himself to shed ten more. Life might get underway again after years in the doldrums – if he only could think what the devil to do with the girl.

The girl was hoping he would not look around. She had done a stupid thing, attempting this short cut. Her heart was behaving like a battering-ram. Each step was too high; the only way was to stand for a moment on one before taking the next. Pretending to be interested in the small flowers that grew in chinks in the wall, she advanced slowly, thankful to see her father's long legs striding ahead and relieved when he reached the top. He stood there, like Hamlet on the battlements, staring around him. Juliet, the last step achieved, sat down on it and kept still until the breathlessness passed. She was pleased with herself. A week ago she could not have done that. The station steps at Marseilles had defeated her. In another week she would be perfectly fit. And then? She shook her head, dismissing all the problem and speculations that might dim the radiance of today; pulled her hat off, adjusted the scarf so that it would hang over the brim and protect her neck from the midday sun, put the hat on again and stood up.

'Well, I'm certainly jiggered,' her father said. 'You'd think some child of a giant had spilled a box of toys on a head of rocks. I supposed the place is a thousand years old.'

It was. Juliet had read about it, and marvelled at all that the small remote village had survived, but she kept her information to herself. Her father detested what he called 'guide-book stuff', as she had learnt during this wandering holiday.

'I dare say you're used to these crazy places?' he said.

'Only to seeing them up in the air and longing to explore them,' she answered. 'Several times we drove to St Paul and Vence, but only had tea and poked into antique shops. Mother didn't like steep hills. I want to explore every inch of it.'

'Well, that could be done in half an hour, I imagine, and we've got all day – but it's going to be hot.'

'It's cooler than Menton: there's even a breeze.'

They turned their backs on the village and gazed south-eastwards, along the valet through which they had come.

'Not a glimpse of the sea,' Frith complained.

Juliet laughed.

'You want everything all at once.'

She sat down on the parched grass that edged the wide rampart; the landscape, saturated with summer, radiating heat and light, flickered like an image in water. She wished a cloud would draw over the sun, but there wasn't a cloud to be seen in the sky. Now her father was frowning down at her, tall and lean, handsome and aquiline, his skin bronzed by the south. She gave him a mischievous grin.

'Well, Mephistopheles?'

'Didn't the doctor say something about not climbing hills?'

'I didn't. I only walked up stairs.'

'You've gone whey-faced.'

'I'm not. I managed it. I'm a hundred times better. I'm not the person the doctor said that to.'

He continued to glower out of his brown eyes.

'Why didn't we go round by the road?' he demanded, vexed. 'You can't expect me to keep thinking of these things. You're twenty: you've got to look after yourself, you know. I can't be a mother to you.'

Juliet flushed.

'I do. You don't have to! Nobody has.' She heard the hurt in her own voice and said lightly, 'Every day in every way I'm getting better and better.'

'Are you?'

He took a seat on the crest of the wall, facing her, more than willing to be convinced.

A little teasing smile curled her mouth.

'If you fuss about me I'll call you "Daddy",' she threatened.

'I'll drop you over the battlement if you do.'

She became serious, meeting his eyes with a blue, candid regard.

'Look Frith: forget Dr du Bois. My heart's perfectly sound: he said so. What's a little anaemia? I'm sure more than half the children have it. How could they not?'

His nostrils pinched at the recollection of the stuffy school in Rouen.

'How, indeed? ... But he definitely told you ...'

'He said', Juliet broke in, '"sun and air" – and aren't you sunning me and airing me all day and every day? I bet you, in three days I'll be completely well.'

Every crease on her father's expressive face was reversed by his sudden smile. He crinkled his eyes at her, saying, with approbation, 'Quick work.'

Juliet pursued her advantage.

'Besides, Frith, you can't take that doctor thing literally. He *had* to say that something was wrong. To give Madame Regnier a pretext, don't you see?'

The blush that was such a trouble to her; that her pupils had loved to provoke and made her feel like a Miss out of Jane Austen, rushed to her cheeks again.

'That is why Madame sent for him,' she went on, breaking into the painful topic that must, some time, be discussed. 'She had to get rid of me and she didn't want to give the real reason, and besides ...'

Frith silenced her with a jerk of his head.

'Oh, I know. They were obviously saving faces all round.'

'That was just it, I wasn't ill really. Not enough to justify her writing to you like that.'

'I'm glad she did. It has worked out very well. It's fun, having a run-around with you like this, and tomorrow is another day.'

His tone, easy and light, brought complete assuagement. His daughter returned his smile with a glowing look. He rose, stretched himself and glanced right and left, seeking shade. There was none to be found. Away to the west, where the village escaped the wall, there were orange gardens and olive fields, the country rising in terraces up the hill, but the gardens just under the ramparts were parched strips and belonged to the tall, narrow houses that stood looking out, with other houses peering over their roofs and buildings towering over those again.

'I'd get claustrophobia in this place,' Frith said.

He badly wanted a drink but it would presently be time to go prowling amongst those streets looking for lunch. He supposed he'd better let Juliet rest. He sat down and lit a cigarette.

JULIET RESTED, surveying the world below. It was a quiet world, wide and serene. Up on the right, rocks cut into the sky: the jagged crests of the Alpes Maritimes. From a gap between them the long valley ran down, widening out and winding away to the left, the river that had made it seeking the sea. The shadowed slopes on the far side of the valley were terraced with beautiful symmetry right up to the forest belt. Lovely, the dim coolness must be, under those pines with their resinous scent … Somewhere up there, to the west, where the motor road disappeared in the woods, must be the mysterious gorge where the river raced through a ravine and where, in legendary times, a rider and his horse had been lost. The scene with its soft greens and tawny browns, so smoothly composed under the blue dome, made her think of the *Très Riches Heures du Duc de Berry*. 'And,' she thought, 'this is a very rich hour of Juliet Cunningham.'

Contemplating his daughter's clear profile, watching her smile deepen, Frith wondered what was going on in her head. The child had no right to look as she did at the minute, almost translucent with happiness. What did she imagine? That this interlude could go on and on? That an endless holiday had begun? Didn't she realise she was on a spot?

A pity, in a way, that he couldn't support her. She was a pretty thing – graceful and quick and companionable. If he had happened to require a daughter Juliet would do. But he didn't. On the contrary.

And one thing was certain: neither of them would ever see her mother again. As surely and as finally as last year's snow, Linda had gone out of their lives. Forzelli and the Argentine had her now. After six years tangled in snarls by Linda's delicate fingers, he and the girl had to make new beginnings, and, after one week from tomorrow, their ways would part again. Oh, well, no use getting tense about it. Millions of girls were in the same kind of fix. She'd be all right when

8

her health recovered. The thing, now, was to give her a good week with plenty of food and wine – red wine.

Wine was the answer, also, to his own gloomy mood. He stood up. 'Come along: let's hunt lunch.'

FRITH QUICKLY FOUND another short cut. From within the ramparts the chemin des Arquebusiers ran straight uphill, cramped between houses that would surely have toppled together from decrepitude had not earthquake arches high up held them apart. Down the middle, among big cobbles, a gutter ran. Smells of cooking issued from dark doorways but otherwise the street seemed asleep, given over to somnolent cats and dogs. Heat beat up from the cobbles and out from the walls. A great clock somewhere struck twelve and then, echoed among the little streets, they heard the clanging of the angelus bell. As they came out on the level *place* they could see the bell swinging in one of the two towers that rose up beyond the roofs.

While Frith wandered about Juliet rested, leaning against a palm. The scene, with its odd perspectives, its sharp contrasts and charming harmonies, held her entranced. She stood gazing at ridged roofs and stairways, arcades and wrought-iron balconies until two chattering, black-clad women bumped into her with their bulging reticules. Smiles and apologies were exchanged and they crossed the square. On the far side, in a green triangle, grew three fine chestnuts. A troop of children came running from a road behind the trees, schoolbags on their backs. They dashed away on all sides, racing and chasing, little ones borne on the shoulders of tall boys, greeted and smiled upon by the passersby. A few of them stopped in their tracks to say a polite *bonjour* to the foreign lady. One eyed her cheekily and said 'Good morning, Mees,' with a grin. Quickly Juliet asked him, in English, where she could find a hotel. Not to betray lack of language, he replied with gestures, pointing to a sign just behind her which displayed a gilded clock. Her father joined her while she was reading the promises of the Coq d'Or: its menu of four hundred francs; its good wine; its dining-room of the tenth century and its courtyard with an ancient tree. It was to be found in the marketplace.

'Right-about-turn,' Frith commanded, but halted in his stride, stood back and motioned Juliet to wait.

The woman who had caught his attention was not well dressed: her long, full skirt was threadbare and patched. She had come from the *chemin* behind them and was crossing the square with such freedom and vigour and grace in her walk, such poise, so airy a tilt of her head, that Juliet at once understood her father's interest. He was seeing her in a play or in a film. Frith was always declaring that not one woman in fifty knew how to walk. This was a peasant woman – Italian, perhaps; her bare arms and ankles were tanned by the sun; the narrow scarf tied round her head revealed glossy black hair and gold ear-rings dangled from her ears.

Frith jerked his head, his eyes narrowed and bright.

'Come on. I want to see if her face comes up to that magnificent walk.'

Close in pursuit of the tall woman, they crossed the *place*, turned left by the chestnuts and walked uphill along the rue de la Pompe. This was a pleasant road with few houses, where the air flowed scented and fresh. The path they were on ran under high garden walls and on the other side of the road were little modern villas and a school. It seemed, however, an unlikely place in which to find a restaurant and Juliet began to hang back. She had climbed a good deal and walked much too fast. Frith's long legs kept pace with his quarry and when he stopped it was because the woman had vanished, turning in through a small iron gate that stood open in a garden wall. Juliet burst out laughing at his disconcerted stare and enquired, 'Well, did you see her face?'

'About one-third of it,' he replied ruefully, 'and there was not satisfaction in that. She has a bandage or something over one eye.'

'You have been spared another disillusionment,' his daughter said solemnly, making him grin. 'And now, please, may we eat?'

'We may, I hope, and drink, also; but where?'

They looked ahead. The road opened fanwise about a fountain, to divide on either side of a low wall with washing troughs and water spouts under it and send branches away into the olive-clad hills. Facing the fountain, above crescent-shaped steps that rose from the path on which they hesitated, stood a doorway in the gable end of a house – the house, it seemed, to which the garden belonged, and a sign hung over the door. Hopefully, they walked on.

It was only the side of the house that gave on the road: a stone wall; small windows; an old, heavy, wide-open door. Above hung a picture of two birds in profile bowing to one another, with a scroll on which was inscribed *Auberge des Colómbes*.

'Nothing much to look at,' Frith commented, 'but I, for one, am too droughty to wait. Let's risk it.'

So they climbed up the steps and entered the Inn of the Doves.

Chapter II

THE INN OF THE DOVES

JULIET, HALF AWAKE, kept her eyes shut, playing a childish game. She knew where she was – in a pet of a room, in the nicest, friendliest inn one could imagine, on the edge of a village out of a fairy tale. She pretended that was still at the school.

Eyes shut, breathing uneven and every muscle tense, she awaited the hateful clang of the bell. It would peal and clamour, wresting the girls from their beds.

'Elise, Elise, must you *always* lose your hair-ribbon? … Ask for a slide nicely and don't squeal. Oh, Annette, your stocking laddered again! … No, you can't! Get out another pair.' Not one of them would wash properly. They were all cross and headachy from sleeping with the windows closed and so was she … Hurry, hurry, hurry! The breakfast bell! Weak coffee and bread in the basement. Pained glances from Madame Regnier because collars were rumpled or stockings twisted or hair untidy. And all the faults of all the eleven were Juliet's fault.

The game stopped there. Imagination, seduced by the low, throaty gurgle of doves canoodling on the roods, let in the present, with its full, sweet astonishment. Juliet opened her eyes.

There it was, the small white and yellow room; the open window; far off, the wooded mountain behind which, yesterday, lying in bed, she had watched the sun going down like a golden wheel. A breeze was blowing the muslin curtains inward. The hands of her big watch were at twenty past seven. It was usually slow. She had slept enormously and all tiredness was gone.

Never again, Juliet vowed, would she let any fraction of her mind consent when people declared that all men were selfish and called her father 'a charming egoist'. An egoist would have been furious with her. To make him come all this way and then to flop in a faint over the table and have to spend the day lying down! Even his 'I warned you, didn't I?' had been not really cross, and he'd uttered not another reproachful word. Instead, he had made terms with the Loubiers, booked rooms here for the rest of their holiday, and gone all the way to Menton to return with their suitcases. Not a word about the expense.

Now, down below, doors were opened; buckets clattered on cobbles and water gushed. A quavering bleat rose, piteously repeated, and a girl's voice mimicked it – 'Mireille! Mireille!'

A step brought Juliet to her open window. She pulled her coolie coat on and stood unnoticed looking down. Young Madame Loubier was at work in a setting that Pieter de Hooch might have painted – everything was so trim and the colours were so soft and pure in the early light. The house and the wing built out from it on the south shadowed most of the yard, but the olive orchard beyond it, on the far side of a low wall and a lane, was flooded with the sunlight. A higher wall separated the yard from the street and in the far corner between the walls stood the dovecote where grey doves were fussing in and out. The goat had her stable in a wired-in cell that, with two others, composed the ground floor of the wing. Over them was an attic with curtained windows and a door from which an outside staircase ran down.

The young woman let the goat out, called to her to be milked, and sat waiting on the base of the pump. One could see that Mireille, with her silky, snow-white coat, was a spoilt and conceited pet. She greeted her mistress with playful buttings and curvettings and, during the milking, rested her head on the girl's shoulder with a comical look of patience on her sentimental face. Juliet watched, enjoying the comedy. When the goat, protesting, was shut in again, Madame Loubier placed a bucket under the spout and began to work the handle of the pump. From the attic a voice, low but imperious, ordered her to stop. Her husband, in shirt and trousers, his black hair tousled, came dashing down the suitcase like a bird of prey on a songbird, Juliet thought. His wife laughed, pretending to disobey, and he seized the handle, scolding her. Juliet listened, amused by the vehemence of his gesture, the urgency of his tirade. Never, never, must Martine attempt it! How could she forget? Was he a peasant that his wife should be permitted to injure herself with such heavy work?

He seized the handle and pumped with excessive energy, showing off, so that the bucket immediately overflowed. His wife, to tease him, made as if to lift it; he caught her by both elbows, held firmly and began to rebuke her and plead with her in tones so earnest and tender that Juliet turned away. Here was something nobody ought to spy on: something she had never before seen.

'Le ciel est, par-dessus le toit, si bleu, si calme—' Juliet sang to herself in her deep, luxurious bath. Since childhood, her heart had not been so light. She made her bed, spread the white muslin cover over the yellow quilt, and then unpacked the two suitcases which contained every single thing she possessed. Now, with her books on the window-sill, her photographs and the postcards from the Louvre on the shelf, her hand-glass and brushes set out on the chest, the room was her own domain. She put on a white-and-green cotton frock and was whitening her sandals when there was a tap on the door and her hostess came in with frothing chocolate, rolls and butter on a tray. She wore a rose-coloured apron over her brown dress and looked, Juliet thought, like a robin, with her bright, dark eyes. Her brown hair was worn like a little girl's in a thick plait round her head. She looked three or four years older than Juliet, not more, but could put on a managing, matronly little air.

'Up and dressed already, Mademoiselle? You slept well then? You find it not too bad, this little room? All the others look out on the terrace and receive the morning sun. It is a pity that only these two were free.'

Juliet reassured her.

'I like better to look out over the yard. The mountain is beautiful and so is your goat.'

'Ah, Mireille! She plays the coquette, that one! My husband she will not suffer to milk her, and every day she must graze in a new place, and in summer, when the grass is burnt ...' Her voice changed. 'But, Mademoiselle, you should not have deranged yourself to make your bed!'

'I have the habit, and yesterday I gave you so much trouble. You were very kind.'

'But naturally!'

She rested large, dark eyes on Juliet's face.

'Is it not rouge? No! You have a colour! Already it works, our fine, pure air. Here you will regain health rapidly. You will see!'

Juliet sat on her bed, the tray before her on a stool. The chocolate was delicious; so were the bread and fresh butter. She was hungry.

'I think I have regained it already,' she said.

The other did not respond to her gay mood. A little reproachfully, she shook her head.

'One does not recover in a night. You are a little anaemic, I think. I, too, when I lived in Toulon. Please, Mademoiselle, do not make too much haste. Do not try to climb our steep streets. Always there are easier ways around. You will remember, will you not, to repose yourself?' Juliet could not help smiling when the girl added, 'I know it is not easy when one is young.'

She promised to take the roundabout roads. It was impossible not to respond. No one had talked to her in just that way before, with an almost sisterly, wise concern. She would have liked to detain this girl and talk with her about all sorts of things – tell her what a new and joyous this week and the inn was going to be; but she said, only, that the room was *mignonne* and the bed the softest she had slept on for years.

'Ah yes! René will buy only the finest,' his wife declared proudly. 'He says ...' Her laughter gurgled like the chuckling of her doves.

'He says that he will have nothing but the best in the things that are important: a dog, a gun and a wife.'

She reddened, bent her head and made for the door.

'I'll bring Monsieur Cunningham his tea.'

She was gone, running downstairs. How busy she must be, with a houseful of guests to wait on, Juliet thought, yet she was light-hearted.

Oh, what a *waste* they had been, those years in Rouen! And even, yes, even the years on the Riviera, with their tensions, their anxieties about money and parties and people who didn't really matter at all. If only, she thought, her mother had known how to be simple, and kind, and serene! But she hadn't, and everything had gone wrong.

Well, it was over. Probably she was happy now. Alberto had money and property out there and she would be popular.

No more tears. There had been tears enough. She and Frith were going to have seven perfect days.

And next week? Next year? Going out to work every morning? But, from where? Not a London flat. It was too late for Frith to hope for West End engagements now. They had labelled him 'unreliable' and that, as she'd heard him say, was a 'sentence of exile'. But perhaps, with a daughter to come home to …?

Vexed with herself, she checked that train of thought. For years she had tried to teach herself not to dream. It was weakening. That wouldn't happen. There had never been the least, minutest reason for imagining that it would.

So violently Juliet shook her head in the effort to shake wish-thoughts out of it that her light, short hair became a wild mop and she had to brush and comb it over again.

It would be another hour before Frith was down. She decided to take herself for a walk.

FRITH ROSE EARLY and breakfasted on the terrace. He had the place to himself; the air was exhilarating; the clear sky promised a brilliant day and in the distance glimmered the sea. He was uneasy, nevertheless. His problem teased him, more difficult than ever to solve. A girl who fainted for nothing would not, for quite some time, be able to hold down a job. There wasn't a soul he could send her to, as things were. What a mess Lydia had made – not only of her own life, but of his too, and the child's! Well, all her misfortunes had flowed from her own temperament: certainly *he* hadn't been to blame.

Frith smoked his pipe while his memory unreeled the whole wretched sequence in detail, and nowhere did he see that he could reasonably have been expected to do anything other than what he had done.

It was the War. How many actors had found their careers in pieces when it was over? How many wives, returning to London, had found themselves reduced to domestic bondage in dilapidated flats? Most of them had stuck it, but Lydia couldn't: she had been a sky-lark in a cage. He'd have been selfish to ask her to.

So when, in the November of '46, her aunt Isabel, rich and widowed and lonely in her villa in Nice, had begged for a long visit, he had quite properly let Lydia go, on condition that the child went too. He couldn't afford a decent boarding school, and it was a thrill for Juliet, at fourteen.

And how, when they'd settled down there so happily, costing him nothing, could he insist on dragging them back? Besides, Aunt Isabel was ill – dying, as it turned out, and it wouldn't have done for Lydia to desert her – from any point of view. Then, he had to let the flat. He wasn't in a position to keep up a home.

But it hadn't turned out well for Lydia – inheriting the villa without enough money to run it. As a gambler she was always unlucky, and the sharks had gathered, of course. It was then that Forzelli had got his hold on her: acting as friendly advisor; persuading her to become officially resident in France; involving her in his black-market racket and his jugglings with foreign exchange.

How old was Juliet – about seventeen – when Lydia began to ask for a divorce? One couldn't refuse, there'd have been no point. Nothing would have brought Lydia home. All Frith had worried about was extricating Juliet, and that he had managed to do.

That had been the one stroke of luck, the way the solution fell out of the blue. The letter, he remembered, had followed him from theatre to theatre and caught up with him at last in Bath. Damned impertinent, though damned opportune, too. He recalled its suave phrases with distaste. The good lady, Madame Regnier, appeared to have scraped acquaintance with Juliet in a Monte Carlo hotel and had somehow secured an address which would find him. She ventured to suggest to him that his daughter, so amiable and intelligent, was not receiving an education conformable to her aptitudes, and she had a proposal to put before him. With her sister, she directed, at Rouen, a school for young ladies whose parents were abroad. They were prepared to offer Miss Cunningham the post of English assistant. She would receive a small salary and would be enabled to attend courses and qualify for the profession of teaching in her free time. They had not thought it right to open the question with the young girl until they had ascertained his views, as he might, naturally, have other projects concerning her.

School-teaching! It hadn't seemed the likeliest future for a child of himself and Lydia. He had thrust the letter into his dressing-gown pocket, intending to think it over, though hoping something better might turn up. It had been there still when Juliet's sober little letter came.

'Oughtn't I to be doing something about earning my living?' she had written. She was 'an awful problem' for her mother and was learning nothing practical. Might she come back to England and train as a hospital nurse? Would the training cost more than he could afford?

There had obviously been plenty behind that letter that the child preferred to keep to herself. What a relief to find she had that much sense! But nursing wasn't the answer: she was too young and, although he would continue to give her occasional presents, he couldn't, as things were, do more. All the same, he had used no pressure whatever – not by a single word. Simply, he had pulled out Madame Regnier's letter, scrawled across it 'What do you think of this?' and posted it to Juliet. Next thing he heard, she was on her way to Rouen.

He had supposed she would go to her mother for holidays but, after the first year, that hadn't happened. She'd stayed on at the school. It had seemed too bad. He'd felt sorry for the girl and had given her sprees in Paris two or three times.

Odd, he reflected, what a wash-out those meetings had been! Disappointing. Juliet had changed. Her grooming and clothes were all right – Lydia sent her dresses and so on from time to time, but she was *gauche*. The loving, impulsive child had become a prickly, inhibited adolescent; too self-effacing, over-anxious to please, nervously afraid of being in the way. They had made no real contact at all.

It was astounding, what this final rescue had done for her: how she had responded, revived, expanded, like a butterfly breaking out of the chrysalis. He had a notion that Lydia's final escapade – her flight to South America with Forzelli, had snapped the last link that bound the girl emotionally to her mother and set her affections free to return to him. Anyway, it had brought them together again.

The school mistresses hadn't behaved badly, on the whole, when Forzelli's racket blew open, for the scandal-mongers hadn't missed their opportunity and the well-publicised story of the absconding racketeer and the elegant *divorcée* must have been embarrassing for the school. They had kept her all through the summer until a decent pretext presented itself and then Madame Regnier had written him a silky letter expressing concern about Juliet's health and doubts whether teaching was the girl's true vocation, after all.

He had fitted everything in rather neatly: the two-and-a-half weeks left before work was to begin in Corsica could very well be spent in the south of France, giving his daughter a break and fixing her up in some sort of post there. If necessary, he'd collect her when he returned in November; but, by then, something regular might have turned up for her.

Promptitude paid: he had wired to Juliet – 'What is wrong write fully'– and, for the first time, had received an unreserved letter from her. She told him she was a failure at the school and not very well and *Mesdames* clearly wished to get rid of her, 'and', she had concluded, 'if I've got to be a burden on somebody for a bit, I suppose you are the unfortunate somebody'.

'I am definitely somebody prepare travel south next week', had been his telegraphed reply.

Well, when he'd seen the place, he had understood the girl's becoming anaemic. Those putty-coloured women and their putty-coloured rooms! The stink of petrol; the clang of rails carted past on the cobbled street.

All the same, there had been tears, leaving it. Juliet apologised for them in the train.

'It's heaven to escape. I just can't tell you how glad and grateful I am. It is only that some of the children are darlings, and rather lonely, poor little things. It really is a stone-cold place.'

'Why on earth', he demanded, impatiently, 'did you stick it for three years?'

'I wouldn't have, much longer', she replied and proceeded to inform him that she had been secretly answering advertisements – advertisements for kitchen hands, of all things, with the notion of learning to be a cook. When he exclaimed, 'Shade of my grand-mother Cunningham!' Juliet retorted, cheekily, 'The one who made the famous mince-pies?'

That had been about the first sign of a remarkably sudden, rapid and complete thaw.

Yes, Frith told himself: from first to last, no one could say he had been to blame, and Juliet, he believed, appreciated that fact. Affection shone out of her. She was all right; but the question remained: next Wednesday, when he would be on way to Calvi, where, in the name of all that was problematical, would Juliet be?

AT THE MOMENT she was crossing the terrace, hatless, her cap of light-brown hair bright in the sun. That razor-cut he'd treated her to at Nice was definitely a success – showed the good shape of her head. She was flushed with sunshine and pleasure. She looked well. Moreover, she had bought him a newspaper and cigarettes.

'Good girl! Feeling all right?'

'Tipsy with the air; aren't you? And there's your eternal sea! Are you pleased, Frith? Are you really going to like it, up here?'

'Fine. It's an uncommonly good little inn.'

She chattered, telling him about the yard, the goat, the dovecote and the garden that belonged to the inn. That small gate below on the road led into it; then you walked uphill inside the wall and a short flight of steps brought you up to the terrace. Below the orange trees there were beds of herbs and vegetables; no lawn; very few flowers. The tall hedge of tamarisk that gave shade on the south of the terrace ran all the way down, separating the garden from the back lane. There was a garage at the end of the lane.

'I have been orienting us,' Juliet said. 'Here we are really outside the village beyond where the wall stops. The rock sticks out of the mountain like a clenched fist and we are on the back of the wrist. The village is just two streets and little passages squiggling about. It is sort of built up on the knuckles with the church like a thumb sticking up.'

Frith, who was more interested in people than in places, was observing with amusement the fussy exodus from the inn of a family party slung round with picnic baskets, flasks and cameras. They were followed by a lanky, bearded Frenchman laden with easel, canvas and box. The long front of the two-storey house looked over the terrace and they came out by a deep, recessed porch with a rounded arch; crossed the terrace, the painter bowing politely to Juliet and Frith as he went by, and descended the steps and went down by the garden path. A little old woman who was slowly and methodically dusting tables and setting out cane chairs greeted one and all with a toothless smile. René Loubier, who was busy in the dining-room, came to one of the windows and whistled.

'All are out now, Marie. Go up and help Madame,' he called, but the old woman failed to hear. Looking round when a pebble, neatly aimed by Frith, struck the table she was wiping, she observed her young master's eloquent gestures, gathered up her cloths, and went in. Presently the inn-keeper came out, lithe and swift, like an athletic boy. At closer range one saw that experience and authority had given a resolute set to his lips and jaw. A man close on thirty, Frith conjectured, who had seen military service or had been active in the Maquis. His French had only a slight trace of the local accent – less than his wife's. One was able to follow him.

'I thank you, Monsieur. Old Marie grows more deaf every day; also more slow. If there is anything you desire it becomes necessary to ring the bell in the porch.' He turned to Juliet with an expression of satisfaction on his dark, intelligent face.

'I do not need to enquire for the health of Mademoiselle! She has slept like an angel, one can see! … The sun is not yet too strong? Presently I will pull down the awning … Something to drink a little later? A Pernod, and, perhaps, an ice? Then if you should wish to walk in our olive orchard, one can enter it by crossing our yard.'

'You seem to leave all doors open to the world,' Frith remarked. 'Is everybody virtuous in St Jacques?'

'Oh, yes, here we are honest,' was the boastful answer.

'We do not even need police. One man, the *Garde Champêtre*, is sufficient, and he has an easy life. Only five times in two years has it been necessary for him to telephone to Menton for help.'

Frith observed that he hadn't seen a dog about and Juliet asked, laughing, 'Does the beautiful Mireille guard the house?'

René Loubier was delighted.

'Is she not a beauty, Mireille? She is a princess among goats – so delicate, so fastidious! … No, Monsieur, I do not keep my dog here. He is a gun-dog of the first class and I leave him with my uncle up in the forest. Hotel life ruins a good dog: his sense of smell becomes confused and weak; also, with so many strangers making a friend of him he ceases to know who is his master or at whom he should bark, or else he barks at everyone, and they complain. My father took his old sheep-dog with him, three years ago, when he handed the inn over to me, and we are better without one, I find.' He turned to Juliet, asking, 'You like the terrace? Is not the view magnificent?'

Juliet spoke with admiration of the view, the air and the village. He was clearly a young man who thought well of his surroundings and liked to hear them praised.

'You will find,' he assured them both, 'that although St Jacques is small it contains more of interest than all the other hill-villages. It has an older history than Eze; finer views than Cagnes; better restaurants and shops than Roquebrune. Vence is too high and St Paul too expensive. Here, there is pleasure without cost. On Sunday, if the fine weather continues, there will be dancing in the marketplace – the old dances in costume: some of our young people have studied in Cannes at the Académie Provençale; and on Monday the September market will be held. Very soon St Jacques will be famous. For that, we work hard. When my son is grown this inn will be a valuable property for him.'

'I haven't seen your son,' Juliet said, with interest.

René Loubier's smile flashed wide and his black eyes twinkled.

'Nobody has seen him yet,' he replied and then, afraid that he had committed an indelicacy, turned and hurried indoors, leaving Frith convulsed.

'Gosh,' said Juliet, somewhat abashed, 'ought I to have noticed?'

Frith was half inarticulate with laughter at his daughter's *faux pas*.

'You don't mean to tell me you didn't ?'

Juliet blushed furiously, partly from resentment: her father's ridicule seemed to her unfair.

'Where would I have learnt to?' she retorted.

'True enough! Well, it sure was time you were let out of school.'

Frith was amazed. He thought of girls of twenty in London, in films, on the stage, of girls who were in the forces in the war years, younger than that. Juliet was unbelievably immature. What was to be done about her? He looked at her searchingly.

Juliet swallowed and tried to call all her wits together. Now it was coming and she wasn't prepared: she hadn't the ghost of a plan. Her father spoke in a casual tone.

'I suppose you won't want to take up teaching again?'

'Not in a school.'

'Or nursing? You're scarcely hefty enough.'

'I don't want to be in a hospital – or in any shut-away sort of place.'

'Any idea what you *do* want to do?'

She looked into her own mind and replied thoughtfully:

'I don't think I care much what I do as long as I am out in the grown-up world. I just want to see the wheels go round.'

Frith chuckled.

'These Cunningham women! They are all alike: anything for experience. If you start out in that spirit, my girl, you may find the wheels going round a good deal too fast for you. Don't run about getting *involved*. The world is a whirligig.'

'Is it? Good! I adore merry-go-rounds. You feel you are in control of the fiery steeds.'

'Yes – but you are not, you know … Look here; let's talk sense. Just how much money have you?'

'Eight thousand three hundred francs.'

'About eight guineas? Is that really all?'

'Yes: you see, I had things to buy; but I have all the clothes I shall need for months.'

'I'll be able to leave you five thousand or so when I go and to send you a bit now and then while the filming lasts; but it can only be a stop-gap, you realise, Juliet.'

She said calmly, 'Oh, the gap won't be that big.'

Desperately she was hoping that he wouldn't worry; wouldn't get even the shade of a shadow of a notion that she might become dependent on him. That would spoil everything, as it had spoilt everything between her and her mother. She spoke with all the assurance she could muster: 'I'll be no time finding something to do.'

'How are you going to set about it?'

'Well, when I've seen you off, I'll go to the agents in Nice. Aunt Isabel used to try them for maids. And I'll answer advertisements. My Italian is all right and, with English and French … There are always people wanting companions or interpreters or someone to mind their children or push their wheelchairs or do housework. And if you could send me a little money regularly I could save it and give it back to you and, meanwhile, that would make it easy to get a permit.'

He frowned.

'Agents! Strangers! People we can't know a thing about … Your mother spent six years on this coast and do you mean to say you have no friends?'

'Friends!'

Hot colour flooded her face and a most unyouthful bitterness edged her tone.

'Those people Mummie called her "friends" were mean, treacherous worms. Nearly every one of them played those tricks with Swiss and French and Italian exchange; and they smuggled and gambled and everything. They never seemed to talk about anything else. Only they managed not to be found out, and when Mummie was in trouble … Oh, well, you know about it. Never, never, would I appeal to them.'

Frith nodded.

'I see; and now there isn't a soul in England to turn to; and I don't see where you'd fit in, in Donegal.'

'Gloriana!' Juliet exclaimed, laughing. 'Wouldn't they be startled if I walked in? Would I say I had come to be a farmer's girl?'

'We'll try it on, if you like.'

Juliet attempted the brogue that Frith sometimes employed to lighten a reprimand or get his own way.

'Is it go beg to your uncles? And they after black-sheeping you the way they did? Begorrah, I'd sooner break stones on the road!'

He chuckled.

'Stage-Irish! I'm ashamed of you.'

'Some day I want to go.'

Frith said nothing to that; if he ever went back to Carrowmore it must be as a successful man.

René Loubier appeared with a Neapolitan ice and a Pernod. He lowered a saffron awning outside the dining-room and moved their table and chairs into the shade. A tired-looking lady wearing a limp hat came out from the house; hovered and fluttered and then pulled the bell. An alarming clangour rang out. René hastened to attend to her, putting up a huge umbrella and placing a chair and table for her at a distance to theirs. He was busy, quick and precise, losing no time.

'This ice is thrilling,' Juliet told her father. She felt pleased. She thought she had sounded well able to take care of herself, but he was sipping his Pernod with a brooding look.

'Stravaguing alone all over the Riviera? I don't think a whole lot of your notion,' he said.

'Among the dope-fiends and white-slave traffickers?' Juliet suggested, trying to make him smile.

'Drunken sailors,' he added, 'and racketeers. But, no,' he declared seriously, 'it won't do.'

Juliet sighed. 'All right,' she said, with deliberation. 'We must simply sacrifice a whole day; go down to Nice together on Tuesday and fix me up in respectable lodgings and register me with a respectable agency before you go. Then you will leave with an easy mind ... Daddy!' she added, and was rewarded with a grin.

He tweaked her hair as he rose, but was still preoccupied, as he walked, hands in pockets, towards the garden steps.

'Well,' he said, 'we could do that, of course.'

Juliet walked with him down the garden towards the gate.

He gave her the crooked grin with a cocked eyebrow which had been effective in several of his favourite parts.

'And afterwards?' he enquired. 'When I am through in Corsica? Will you want to try your luck in England, or what?' Juliet waited. Her heart raced. He added, casually, 'You would find it a bit chilly, I imagine.'

Juliet did not reply for a moment; her throat had closed up; but before they reached the gate she gave Frith a good imitation of his own one-sided smile and quoted, in his own airy tone, '"Tomorrow is another day."'

Chapter III

UNDER THE SUN

ABOVE THE DAZZLING LANDSCAPE with its rich tints of ochre and burnt sienna, hot orange and rust, the forests spread pavilions of shadowy green. A restless longing grew in Juliet. Something – perhaps the fairy tales of her childhood or, perhaps, a single blissful day, her seventh birthday, spent in the New Forest, had left in her a nostalgia for the silence and mystery of deep woods. Exploring alone, she found on the road lined by olives that ran past the inn a sign-post that pointed to the gorge, nine kilometres away. She walked on, leaving the inn and the olive orchard on her left, uphill, then down again by a long slope that led to the old stone bridge. On the other side of the river was *la route* – fine, metalled motor road. On Tuesdays and Thursdays the bus went up to the gorge. Juliet wanted to take it but Frith refused.

'Is it waste weather like this in a stuffy, stinking, jolting, rowdy, rickety bus? Not on your life! You are here to spend your time in the open air.'

That was true and the weather was perfect. Every morning the sun rose in a cloudless sky, shone for more than twelve hours with a glorious warmth that rarely became oppressive and went down in a golden splendour behind the mountains. Nevertheless, Frith could not be persuaded to follow those alluring roads into open country. Nature bored him. '"The proper study of Mankind is Man,"' he quoted, and spent fascinated hours strolling about the streets.

Juliet enjoyed every minute of it. Nobody could be better company than Frith when he was in this amused, idle mood. He entertained her and himself by casting individuals as types. Of the couple who sat at the table beside them in a café, the husband was an extrovert and the wife an introvert, he declared; the German family at the inn were pachyderms, one and all; the mother and daughter from Dijon were the she-Moloch and the sacrificial virgin of all time; Martine Loubier was passive and René dynamic, and so on.

'And you?' Juliet demanded, and supplied the answer: 'Hamlet?'

Frith grinned. 'Every second actor thinks himself that.'

'Whatever I am,' she declared, 'I am certainly not a Juliet – little goose!'

'"We know what we are, but we know not what we may be,"' Frith quoted in hollow tones.

Exploring the streets, they dodged into as many of the dark little shops as they could invent pretexts to visit, relishing their smells of wine and tobacco, spices and onions, and listening to the excited exchange of family news, congratulations and condolences that were endlessly retailed. Frith's curiosity was boundless and irrepressible. Catching a phrase, he would make some sympathetic comment and elicit a dramatic story, his face registering solicitude, amazement, dismay, approbation so convincingly that no one would have guessed that he understood not one word in ten of the tale. Juliet would relay it to him afterwards and enjoy his sardonic comments. He had an extraordinary insight in to roguery of all sorts.

'Life seems to be eventful in St Jacques,' he remarked.

Juliet agreed.

'I suppose it's because they live one another's lives as well as their own. I am sure if a woman finds that which was lost she calls her neighbours in to rejoice with her.'

'Terrible, to live in a small, close, isolated community!'

'But why? They seem so friendly and peaceable.'

'The village is probably a seething cauldron of gossip and malice and censoriousness. Just look under the smiling surface,' Frith went on, in melodramatic tones, 'and you'd find all the superstition and cruelty of the Dark Ages.'

'You wouldn't. It is clean and honest and gay.'

The village delighted her, every corner of it. It rose in three tiers, like a wedding cake, with its church and belfry at the top. The buildings, though they had been erected at haphazard over centuries, were grouped and proportioned as if with a flawless instinct for harmony, and everywhere there was something to charm the eye. The Place de la Pompe had its fountain and stone trough shaded by pepper trees; the Place Centrale, its old archways and buildings rich with wrought iron and carved stone, its vines and chestnut trees; the Place du Marche, its cool arcades, its square marked out with plane trees, and trim cafés with plants grown in great earthenware jars. She would sit there at a table outside the Coq d'Or, drinking orange juice and watching a game of bowls, while her father visited a tavern under the arcades where they had a local wine that he liked. It was not until Friday that they decided the time had come to attempt the climb to the church. Taking a narrow street cut into steps at intervals they came to the Place Jeanne d'Arc.

This was the oldest and highest part of the village. The church and the two square towers were backed by rock and flanked by houses crooked from age. Opposite the church stood the war memorial, a four-sided column that recorded the names of sons of St Jacques fallen in three wars. One name was repeated seven times, another five, and many three or four times; Juliet turned from it, half sick at the thought of those families, and followed her father into the dark church.

The stained-glass was modern; there were the usual statues and pictures, in no way out of the common. They admired the fine chandelier, but it was not until they had turned to leave that something else attracted their attention. In a dark corner was what looked like a rough model of a mountain town.

'Put five francs in the slot and it will light up,' Juliet, who had found a notice, read.

The francs were put in and, in the agglomeration of pasteboard houses set up on a terraced rockery, lights appeared. Windows and lanterns shone. On the summit was an empty stable under an unlit star. Here and there, figures could be discerned – men and women in Provençal costume, with camels, donkeys and lambs, moulded in clay and painted; there were soldiers, a fiddler, a fisherman with fish in a net, women carrying fruit and a figure of a king. Juliet gazed at it, smiling.

'Had your money's worth?' her father asked, drily, as the light went out. He sounded irritable. 'I suppose it amuses the congregation: mental age eight,' he said.

'Is that my great-grandmother talking?' Juliet enquired.

'Maybe: she'd have called this a Papish absurdity,' her father answered, and then was silent – too late, for the priest who had just risen from his knees in an obscure corner must undoubtedly have heard. It was to be hoped that he knew no English. He moved towards them with a courteous salute.

'You like our Bethlehem, Mademoiselle? Monsieur?' He spoke in careful English, with the accent of the Midi.

'At Christmas', he said, 'it is very pretty: one sees the Holy Family, the ox and the ass, the shepherds, the Kings of the East and many angels with golden wings, and the star shines bright.'

'I should like to see it,' Juliet responded, unhappily. Frith was mute, for once.

The priest opened the church door and the three moved out into the glare of the day. The curé was an elderly man, small-boned and of less than medium height; he had a thin, pale face and grey eyes set wide apart under a furrowed brow. His lips were long and thin and he would have given an impression of austerity but for the lines that wreathed his face when he smiled. He turned a quizzical regard on Frith.

'Often we have English visitors here,' he said, 'and some of them do not like our Bethlehem. They find it infantile; and yet, do you

30

know, Monsieur, I believe they would greatly like to play with their own children at such a toy. There is in everyone a secret child who needs sometimes to play.'

Juliet was relieved: the curé was used to sceptics and his feelings had not been hurt. She was also amused: had her father ever allowed her to manage her toy theatre on her own? He and the priest were looking with a sort of friendly challenge into one another's faces. Frith said, with his most disarming smile, 'And it is not on their childish side that you like to approach people, is it not?'

The curé shook his head up and down slowly. 'A very Protestant question,' he commented and then said, quietly, 'But you are right. It is not, so much, to reason that we appeal as to inborn feeling and love, and these, perhaps, belong to our childish part.'

'I suppose, in these villages, marooned in the mountains, people remain simpler than on the coast?' Frith suggested, and the priest sighed.

'I do not think simplicity remains anywhere in Europe. But, perhaps …' He gave Frith a questioning look. 'In your country, Monsieur? Ireland, is it not? I had Irish friends in Rome and I know the voice.'

'I have not been home to Ireland for years. I doubt if the Irish people are simple now – they are making too good a hand of politics. There were some who believed in fairies when I was young.'

'But they keep their religious faith?'

It was evident that the curé desired conversation. He was probably a lonely man. 'You walk this way?' he enquired, moving towards the passage that led down to the chestnut trees. 'I, also: I like to meet the children when they come out of school.'

This alley, he told them, was one of the Roman streets. The belfry had been a Roman watch tower. He spoke of a time when St Jacques had been depopulated by plague and repopulated by order of the overlord; of the terrible religious wars that had raged within and around its wall; of revolution and cession and restoration; enemy occupation and the Resistance – a stormy history that had passed now, and left the place a haven of sweet peace. He seemed to know and love every stone.

31

School was out. There was a bench under the chestnuts and Juliet and her father rested there, grateful for shade, while the priest spoke with eager children who ran to him happily, each with something to tell him or some request.

'A new little brother?' they heard him exclaim with interest after a girl had whispered excitedly in his ear. 'Tell your mother that I will visit her in a day or two.'

Juliet watched the lively, slender, quick-moving youngsters with pleasure but her father's eyes were elsewhere.

'Ha!' he exclaimed in a stage-whisper. 'See who comes!'

She was turning up the rue de la Pompe, dragging after her a sort of rough sledge on wheels such as children use in their play; it was piled with old kettles and pans. In spite of the load, her movements were as easy and vigorous as when she had walked unburdened and free. The fringed shawl over her shoulders was of silk; its colours, faded now, had been rich and her worn-out shoes had once possessed high heels. She wore the black scarf round her head. Its corner concealed her left eye and part of the cheek but the chiselled beauty of the woman's lips and long throat made Juliet turn to her father to share her surprise.

'Egypt's queen!' Frith exclaimed under his breath.

A rope in either hand, she faced the hill and walked on as though alone in the world, heedless of the children who, as she passed, drew back, silent, some of them clustering close to the priest. Even when the ascent rose sharply and she had to stoop and labour to draw her load no one went to her help. Frith had moved into the road and was looking after her. The curé spoke to him.

'She lives in the high woods and must drag that truck the whole way. Her mule died last month,' he said, quietly.

'A tinker?' Frith asked, astonished.

'Among other things. A Romany. An unfortunate. They cast her out of the tribe.'

'She has the air of an empress,' Frith declared.

The priest's face saddened as he answered, 'Yes, she is proud.'

Julie knew just what would happen now. Bidding the priest a hasty farewell, her father went striding up the hill after the woman and took hold of one of the ropes. She turned her head with a move-ment so gracious that Juliet felt his chivalry was deserved. The priest said quickly, 'Avoid her, Mademoiselle,' and she glanced at him in surprise. He bowed to her gravely and walked away with a group of children and she went on up the hill, slowly, troubled by what he had said. Near the garden gate of the inn Frith relinquished the rope, received the woman's thanks courteously, and went in. Juliet saw the gypsy hesitate as though tempted to follow him into the garden. While she stood there René came out. He came so suddenly and with such a harsh exclamation that the woman recoiled. He spoke to her. His voice was low and Juliet did not hear his words but she saw the woman shrink from them as from blows. As suddenly as he had come he was gone and she stood erect again, facing the hill. Juliet saw her slowly, rigidly, lift her head and stretch her arms out, each hand grasping a corner of the shawl, and then fling the shawl across her breast and over one shoulder in a gesture expressing at once defiance and wild despair. She stooped to her ropes, took them up and went toiling to the crest of the hill, dragging her load again.

Frith was in the gateway, watching. 'My word! Cleopatra in person! Cleopatra when she hears about Fulvia,' he said. 'What a morning! It has given me an appetite. Is it nearly time for lunch? That priest is a fanatic, though you mightn't think it; young Loubier is a menace and that woman is, well, 'tis pity she's a … Well, never mind!'

2

THE LONG, HOT DAY brought drowsiness early and after dinner Juliet was content to sit on the terrace with her father, watching the light change. He smoked a cigar and a scent of richness and leisure and luxury hung in the soft air. From the streets below there came, now and then, phrases of tunes played on a flageolet. Most of the guests were playing cards in the dining-room and others were out. Their only companion on the terrace was the Professor, who was deep in talk with Frith about gypsies and their traditions and the curious cards some of the Romany tribes used in their fortune-telling. Their Tarot cards, he was saying, had a strange and ancient history.

'The gypsies claim that their race is the repository of occult knowledge which has been denounced as heretical and stamped out everywhere else. Rákóczi, in his book, declares he has heard them claim that the secret knowledge of the Chaldeans and the Egyptian priests, of the northern Druids and oriental Yogis have been handed down to gypsies, and to them only, and are all embodied in that set of symbols.'

Frith, who was fascinated by superstition, and delighted in making its absurdities manifest, was well entertained. Juliet listened with half her mind and pursued reflections of her own with the other half until Professor Goyet said 'Goodnight' and went in.

Colour had ebbed from the air and the light of the moon grew potent. Far off, along the crescent of coast, chains and clusters of lamps twinkled, while lonely lights appeared here and there among the half-invisible hills.

Juliet sighed. She had relinquished a dream; yet it was from contentment that she sighed, marvelling because the loss of it cost her so little pain.

Was it the sun that had given her courage? No, she told herself for the sun had shone just as brightly those other summers, when she had walked up and down by the sea in torment because of the way things were changing, forced, sometimes, to go into the dark of a cinema in order to hide her tears. No, it wasn't the sun. Was there, then, some magic in this village, in this inn, that made happiness seem a natural thing? Whatever the reason, she had begun to believe that she would be able to make her way and that all would be well. She would have to ask her father for very little and so would keep his affection. He had worried about her. She had been a weight on his mind. He had never expressed this in angry, stabbing words, as her mother had done, but Juliet knew. And now that she had managed to reassure him he liked their relationship; he would think about her with pleasure when they were apart. She had gained something real and had lost only a dream.

People came back from their walks, paused to say a few words, yawned, observed how soon one grew sleepy up here in the mountains, said 'Goodnight' or '*Bonne nuit*' and went indoors to bed. The dining-room windows were dark now, although it was only half past ten.

Frith asked lazily, 'Oughtn't you to go to bed?' and Juliet answered, sleepily, 'It's such waste of time to sleep.'

He turned his head and smiled at her.

'You are liking all this?'

'I'm loving it, Frith.'

'You have great powers of enjoyment, haven't you?' he said, reflectively. 'I dare say it's because, for six years, you have had a rather thin time. You're a plucky child.'

His praise so elated Juliet that she stood up. She moved along the balustrade, looking out, looking around, thinking, 'I will always remember this.'

She saw, then, that they were no longer alone. Somebody had come out through the dark house and was standing on the terrace close to the porch. It was a stranger: a man; probably somebody wanting a room. The street door must be open still. People wandered in that way and came out to the terrace or went down to the bar. Finding no one to serve him, he turned as though to leave again; it seemed he had not noticed the bell. That was fortunate for when you rang it it sounded all over the house and would waken people who had gone to sleep. The inn mustn't lose a client, all the same …

Juliet would never quite understand the impulse that seized her then; she must, she thought afterwards, have been a little intoxicated with the heady wine of her father's praise. Demure as a well-trained waitress, she advanced to the visitor and said primly, '*Monsieur desire?*'

She knew he was English as soon as he spoke French. Diffidently he enquired whether it was too late to ask for something to eat. She told him that she would see and, maintaining her impersonation, went into the house.

What next? The front door stood open and the lamps in the hall were alight still, but not a soul was about. Both the Loubiers must be downstairs.

The house dropped at the back to a lower level and the bar and back door and kitchen were down there. She went down and called quietly from the stairs and was invited by voices behind the door on her left to come in. She entered the kitchen. The husband and wife were there, sitting at ease by the open window under the light of a lamp with a red, frilly shade. They sprang to their feet, eagerly busy, as soon as she reported a customer. Chicken and salami, cheese, bread and wine were quickly assembled and René ran upstairs with the tray.

Juliet lingered. The big room, with its air of being both a cosy home and an orderly workshop, charmed her. Some white knitting lay on the table but Madame Loubier was occupying herself at the stove. Juliet thought that the smell of hot chocolate would forever make her think of this inn. She hoped intensely that her father, who was, doubtless, by this time, deep in conversation with the young man, would not give her away. She flushed to think of what she had done.

'Would you not like a cup of chocolate, Mademoiselle? It will help you to sleep,' her hostess said. She looked pleased as she filled the cup for Juliet, who sat down at the table, and another for herself.

'You were kind, Mademoiselle. And it might be important. You see, a little thing such as this – a meal served without complaint at a late hour – can make a new friend for an inn. Besides,' she said wisely, 'I have noticed it: a late caller often brings good luck, and one must not turn one's luck away.'

Juliet gulped her chocolate, not knowing how to reply to this funny mixture of childish credulity and mercenary good sense. The eyes looking across the table at her were large and serious.

'Yes,' Martine Loubier repeated. 'You will see. A man came just at this time one stormy night and next day René won five thousand francs in the lottery. Once – last April – it was only a beggar who came but I gave him bread and meat for charity and, do you know, Mademoiselle,' – her brown eyes widened and her dimples appeared – 'it was the very next day I knew for the first time that I was at last *enciente!*'

Juliet contrived to suppress a smile at this odd sequence of cause and effect. She responded, with sincerity, 'I would love to bring you luck because your inn has been lucky to me.'

'You go next to Corsica, do you not?'

So easy it was to talk to this girl, with her assured, happy, natural place in life; her friendly, gentle eyes and smile, that Juliet, before René returned, had told her a good deal. Martine was interested: she gave her the address of a hotel in Nice, cheap and clean and pleasant, for working girls.

René's vivacious face was full of mischief when he came down.

'That is an agreeable young man,' he said, standing by the table, 'and a hungry one. He is staying up on the mountain, at my uncle's, and has an hour and a half of climbing before him. He and Monsieur Cunningham entertain one another.'

He had more to say but his wife shook her head at him, warning him not to tease. Juliet thought with dismay that he knew what had happened; her father had given her away to the stranger and Monsieur Loubier had overheard.

'As for me,' she said, rising hastily, 'the chocolate has made me sleepy all of a sudden. Thank you so much, Madame: it was delicious. I will go to my room now. Goodnight.'

Presently she was lying, relaxed and drowsy, between cool sheets, taking a last look at the sea-green of the afterglow that lingered still in the western sky; telling herself that the day which was ending was the happiest since her childhood and, for some reason she was too sleepy to understand, one of the most important in all her life.

Chapter IV

PIPES AND TAMBOURINES

SUNDAY WAS NOT a day of peace at the inn and Madame Loubier apologised for scamping the upstairs work. A bus load of excursionists would invade the village at noon and, as well as strangers, regular clients – relatives of people on the farms, hill-climbers and 'Sunday painters' would come here for their midday meal.

An auxiliary appeared in the person of Madame Bonin, a local matron with a commanding presence, who accompanied Madame Loubier when she returned from early mass and who proceeded to take charge in the dining-room, instructing Marie with a resonant voice and large gestures, while René turned chef, leaving young Gatti in sole charge of the bar. Tables were set on the terrace and extra tables crammed into the dining-room. It reminded Juliet of visitors' day at school with the difference that, there, strain and agitation and short tempers made the occasion odious, while, here, everyone was in high spirits and the teamwork went like a dance. The rush signified growing reputation; ambitions being fulfilled.

Frith fidgeted. While he often sought crowds, he did not like them thrust upon him. The delays at lunch were endless and the noise of chatter, of jocular greetings flung from table to table, irritated him. The scene at dinner was equally lively and he declared he wasn't young enough to enjoy it. 'A week is just enough in this place.'

'Not for me,' his daughter retorted, then looked at him with an anxious smile, for from the streets below was rising, over all the chatter, a thin music of pipes and tapping of rums, as if of a marching band, and her feet were almost out of control.

'I do hope you're not feeling too venerable to come out and dance with me?'

'What!' he exclaimed indignantly. 'In the street?'

'Yes; that paved square in the marketplace, where they play bowls.'

He and her mother had gone to so many dances when she was little. Those exquisite, gauzy dresses! How adorable Mummie had looked!

'When I dance,' he said tartly, 'I like a good floor.'

'Oh, *Frith!*'

'You want me to shuffle about on pavements and elbow and shove and be shoved in a sweaty crowd?' Then he relented, unable to resist the appeal in Juliet's face. In spite of all the corruption that had surrounded her in her early girlhood, his daughter had essential innocence and her joys and desires had the wholeness, the freshness and intensity of a child's. He said, 'If you like, we'll go and look on. I believe some of them do the traditional stuff.'

She beamed at him.

'Frith, I am beginning to find you out. Your bark is formidable, but you don't bite.'

PROGRESS WAS EASY at first because the throng was all moving one way, but nearer to the marketplace and the music it developed currents and eddies and Juliet and her father were pulled apart. He was so tall, however, and she so easy to see, in her white jacket and buttercup dress, that they soon reached one another again. Friendly voices said, '*Ah, la jeune Anglaise!*' Stalwart men cleared a way for her and presently she found herself hoisted up on a bench from which the dancing place was in full view.

It was a gay scene. Dressed in the regional costume – striped skirt, black bodice, gaudy neckerchief, with flat straw hats slung on their back, girls were dancing with girls.

'It is rather like an Irish long dance,' Frith remarked. He stood by the bench, peering over heads. On a raised dais six young men dressed in white shirts and trousers and scarlet sashes made shrill, strongly rhythmic music. Each played two instruments, drumming on a long, narrow, barrel-shaped tambourine while he blew on his flageolet. Frith, looking up, said with amusement, 'They enjoy themselves under ecclesiastical auspices.'

From the tall posts at the corners of the platform wires had been stretched diagonally and lamps were suspended from them. Over the centre a gaudy lantern hung. It was an elaborate affair of fretwork and coloured transparencies: a model of the village church, stained-glass windows and all.

While strangers and old folks watched the Provençal dances, younger people were dancing in couples in the square and streets. Juliet, islanded on her bench, turned and looked at them a little enviously and her father's glance followed hers. 'They are romping, not dancing,' he said.

'Just one romp?' she pleaded and he groaned.

Suddenly his face changed. 'Hi there! Faulkner!' she heard him shout.

He was signalling violently and Juliet was too late with her 'Oh, please, no!' It was the young man who had come to the inn on Friday night; with whom she had made such a giddy fool of herself, and she was pilloried up there with not one inch of space into which to descend. Hot with dismay and with anger against her father, she had to stand there and accept the introduction.

'I am saved by a miracle. This is Mr Michael Faulkner. My daughter.' From that unseemly perch she had to look down into his face and say, 'How do you do?' like a well-brought-up English girl. The young man was preoccupied with the effort of holding his place in the shifting crowd.

'I would awfully like to dance, Miss Cunningham,' he said, 'but I doubt if it's fair to ask you to come down from your pedestal and face the scrum.' He looked serious, even worried about it; it would be quite easy to refuse; but Juliet wanted to dance even more than she wanted to escape. She accepted; he contrived a gap for her and she stepped down.

'All right, Sir?' He shot an enquiring glance at her father and said to him, 'If we lose you, I'll steer her back to your inn.'

He was an adept at working a way through a crowd. With gentle wangles, soft apologies and calculated dashes, he soon had her through the press and out into the comparatively clear Place Centrale. There they paused, gasping and laughing and looking round. From a balcony over the pottery works came light music played by four men with fiddles and pipes and people were dancing a sort of two-step, with improvised variations, in the paved space under it. Juliet found herself being guided and swung in and out among other smiling couples, lightly and easily, as irresponsible as if this were some Christmas party and she was a child. Soon, however, another influx of dancers made movement a battle and they stopped.

'I say, thanks a lot! That was better than I'd hoped for,' Michael said. 'I thought I'd be partnering farm-girls the whole evening. What luck, meeting you and your father!'

That remark broke the spell. All Juliet's confusion flowed back. In a moment of painfully vivid recollection her mad bit of play-acting was gone through again. She saw herself advance on the young man, raise a pert face to him, ask her pert question, as if seeking to make his acquaintance at any price. What a cheap little pick-up she must have seemed! No amount of composure and dignity would counteract the awful opinion he must have formed of her.

'Thank you: I, also, enjoyed it,' she responded stiffly.

'I am afraid', he said, 'we would have to choose between being crushed and dancing on cobbles if we danced now. Let's walk, shall we?' They turned down the rue des Arquebusiers. Juliet found nothing to say.

'Do you know', Michael said, 'when I saw your father first, I had that odd feeling of having met him before, but it wasn't until he said something about Oxford that I recognised him. We hadn't met but I'd seen him acting there; it was in that thing, *Ambrose K.C.* You saw it, I suppose?'

'No, I didn't.'

She hadn't seen her father act since she was twelve, but she couldn't tell him that. She just couldn't talk to Michael Faulkner, though he had the friendliest voice she had ever heard. He was long and agile and sunburnt. She was bitterly sorry that they had not met tonight, like this, for the first time. He was talking about his mother now.

'She really knows a great deal about acting and she thought he was much too good for the play.'

'That's very nice.'

They walked on. He was looking a bit frustrated, and no wonder. To make conversation she asked, 'Where are you staying?' although she knew.

'In the Loubier farm up in the forest. The people are relatives of the fellow who owns your inn.'

By the steps leading up to the ramparts there was a lamp.

As they passed up under it he looked into her face. His own, by its light, showed. Hollows under the cheekbones and deep-set eyes. It was rather a stern face, but she saw in it, now, the slow beginning of a smile.

They came out on the ramparts and turned to the right. He spoke casually.

'Jolly well he must run it, too,' he said. 'On Friday night, somewhere around eleven, I turned up starving. I'd been in Menton, and, although I thumbed a ride up part of the way, and walked for an hour and had eight miles or so more to do. You can't do the shortcuts through the woods after dark. Well, would you believe it, people were still on duty and they gave me a slap-up meal? Was I thankful! I was as hungry as a cormorant.'

Juliet laughed. She was laughing at herself, at her *gaucherie*, her ridiculous shyness and stiffness. What a goose she had been to suppose he had noticed and remembered and recognised her! He'd been thinking about food, not about the waitress; and anyhow, on the terrace, it had been half dark. All her confusion had been for nothing. For him, this meeting *was* their first.

She said happily, 'It's a dream of an inn.'

She was garrulous in her relief and chattered.

'It was such a lucky chance that we went there instead of the Coq d'Or.' She relayed René's comment about Madame Tissier's *cuisine*. 'Give her a lamb and she'll turn it into an old sheep in the cooking; whereas buy Martine the cheapest piece of meat in the market and she'll serve a dish fit for a cardinal.'

Michael laughed. 'I've just had a good dinner at the Coq … Camille Loubier and his girls', he told her, 'are forever talking about René. Is he such a fine fellow as they make out?'

'His wife thinks so.'

'René shoots up there in the winter, it seems, and there isn't a gun to equal him, nor was there a man to compare with him in the Resistance, and so on. I think the girls madly envy his wife. They say he ought to have married a woman with brains.'

'He has married a woman with a heart,' Juliet said, warmly, and Michael looked a little surprised. Why should he be? Probably he just didn't know how rare Martine's sort of goodness and kindness was. Probably his mother adored him and spoiled him – he was so good-looking; he had such an amused, understanding smile – as if he knew something about you that you didn't know, and liked it. Suddenly Juliet knew what he knew. He had recognised her. He had known at once but had guessed that she didn't want him to. And it was all of no importance at all. He had simply put it out of his mind, spun his little yarn, and begun all over again. Not many people, she thought, would have had the wit and gentleness to do that.

They paused at a place where the crest of the wall jutted out, making a little embrasure, and looked around. There was a pale half-moon in the sky and in the wide valley lay silvery wisps of mist. The air, flowing inland, had in it a breath of the sea.

'It is up there I am staying,' Michael told her, 'on the far side of the ravine.' He was looking up at the mountains, south-westward, where the road disappeared. 'It's a great place.' He turned to her and asked, a little diffidently, 'Would you come up by the bus on Tuesday and let me show you some of the forest tracks?' She told him that they were leaving on that day.

'Oh, that's too bad,' he said, and asked, 'Where will you be?'

'I don't know. Somewhere, I hope, in a job.'

'I see.'

He seemed to become lost in thought, as though he had forgotten that she was with him. They walked on to where the great gateway opened below them and the rue de la Porte ran out of the village into the motor road. A wall of rock faced them and they turned back. It was easy for them to be quiet together and they did not talk much while they returned by the *chemin* to the Place Centrale. They paused there, at the crossroads, standing just at the spot where Juliet and her father, when they first entered the village, had stopped, undecided which way to go.

'What would you like to do?' Michael asked her. 'Dance some more? Or look for your father? Or come to a bistro and have a *vin blanc?*'

The crowd had grown noisy and merry and she didn't want to dance again; nor did she want to go into a café or bistro or to look for her father. By this time Frith would have found someone to drink with; he was in one of those places; he might be in any of them and he might have drunk a good deal. He had been so good, so careful, nearly all the time they had been together, but this evening she had left him alone. She said, 'I think I would like to go back to the inn.'

'Good: that's my way home, too.'

The chestnuts stood like a dark mosque flecked with silver under the moonlit sky. Michael looked up at them.

'Those are well-tended trees … It is a pity you have to go without seeing the forest,' he said.

Yes, it was a pity, Juliet thought. It was the pity of the world she had not remained quiet, sitting by her father, Friday night. There would have been time to make friends. Michael Faulkner would be a friend to trust.

'Goodbye,' he said, when they stood by the front-door steps. 'I have enjoyed this. Thanks a lot.'

Should she … ? Could one … ? No, of course, a girl didn't invite a man, and order a drink for him, and pay … Perhaps he would suggest coming in? But he wouldn't, of course, when her father wasn't there. If he wanted anything he would wait until she had gone, and then come in and go down to the bar.

'Goodnight, Mr Faulkner: I enjoyed it, too. Thank you much. I'm sorry I can't come and see the forest.'

'I'm sorry, too. Goodnight.'

'Goodbye.'

He didn't wait; he turned and walked away, topped the hill and went down without looking back; down and round the bend, out of sight. It wasn't likely – it was altogether improbable – that they would ever meet again.

'It is a pity,' Juliet thought.

Chapter V

FEATHERS AND BROOMS

SO EARLY that she had the world to herself, Juliet was up and dressed and out on the terrace. This was their last whole day in St Jacques and she didn't want to waste a minute of it; besides, there was a good deal to think about.

As if by magic, strength had come back to her – and what was she to do with it? How was she to spend all this springing energy that was rising in her like sap in a tree? In trees it made leaves and flowers and fruit. There must be something life meant to use her for – surely, surely, she wasn't destined to waste herself in some worthless, mean- ingless occupation with no purpose in it except to earn money. What was she to do?

The terrace hadn't been swept yet: that meant that Marie hadn't arrived.

How enchanting everything looked gilded by the early light! Below the glossy green of orange bushes, one looked down over the acacias, poplars and tamarisks of the lower gardens and the domes of the – chestnuts, those well-tended trees – and then over the roofs, huddled at all angles, ridged with shadow, their rounded tiles glowing red, struck by the sun, and, beyond, the valley and hills and sea.

The gates would be locked still and the old front door always groaned when it was opened; Juliet stole through the house, down the stairs, and opened the little door to the yard. She could easily get over the low wall that separated it from the lane. The doves were sunning themselves; preening their cloud-grey feathers and putting their heads together with soft, secretive chucklings and murmurings.

What on earth had been happening in the yard? There were feathers scattered all over the place. Did doves quarrel? But these feathers were white. Had someone been plucking geese, and so carelessly?

She was over the three-foot wall in a moment, watched in sleepy surprise by Mireille, across the lane, over the stile and among the olives. They were old trees, their thick trunks then from withstanding the *tramontana,* but still they produced their delicate foliage and their fruit. René, with two neighbours, owned this field, which was not terraced but formed a saucer-shaped hollow tilted to the south. It was fenced, but there was another stile at the far side and then a path over pasture where goats grazed which led out to the road near the bridge. In the field one could always find quietness, shade and air. Michael Faulkner would like it, she thought.

There he was – intruding into her mind. She wouldn't have that. She would return to her room and find something to do. The dress she had worn last night was all rumpled and needed laundering. She could wash it herself in her basin, but Martine would take it to dry and iron and already Martine had too much to do.

The gate was unlocked. René was vigorously at work in yard. He had a broom and was sweeping the feathers up as if his life depended on it. He saw her, exclaimed with relief and, in an urgent undertone, implored her, 'Help me! I beg you to help me, Mademoiselle!'

The broom was in her hands; he had another, and she was raking with concentration like his own before she had time think. René's anxious glances up at the attic window, tension in his sinewy face, the silence and swiftness with which he packed feathers into a sack infected her with a sense of urgency; but it was not quick work. Damp feathers had to be scraped from the ground; downy feathers chased. Feathers lodged in her hair and attached themselves to her clothes. It was not until no feather remained visible anywhere that she handed back her broom and asked herself whether she had wandered into some Hans Andersen tale.

René hid the sack in the toolshed and locked the door, came and stood over her then and she stiffened herself against the fury that burned in his eyes, although she knew his anger was not against her. His voice had a note in it that would have made it difficult to argue or disobey – Juliet wanted to.

'My wife must not hear about this: promise me you won't tell her.'

'I promise.'

'I thank you. I cannot thank you sufficiently. You do not know what harm you have prevented. And now, please, go in.'

He held the door of the kitchen open for her; she went through the room, which was so tidy that it, too, might have belonged to a fairy tale, and up two flights of stairs to her own room. There she sewed and meditated, in deep puzzlement, until her chocolate was brought by Martine – Martine, with her sweet air of peace and security, who must not know that white feathers had lain about in her yard.

LAUNDRESSES WERE ALREADY at the rinsing-trough when Juliet peered out through the little window beside the front door. She ran up for her dress and carried it over to them. It was seized by a stout, laughing woman with muscular arms who shook it out and promised that it should be returned, in all its perfection, early next day. There were many exclamations over its heart-shaped neckline and small cap sleeves.

Frith was on the terrace. She joined him before his temper had mellowed. He preferred to breakfast alone. He had a headache and had sent his tea away and asked for a large pot of coffee, strong and black.

'Well,' he said, drily, 'I suppose you enjoyed yourself?'

'I did: very much.'

'Was your escort attentive?'

'Very.'

'Good-looking chap. A bit like his mother.'

'Goodness, Frith, do you know her?'

This was wonderful. He wasn't just someone who came and went, never to be heard of again. He had an anchorage.

'Oh, no: not personally, but she's always a hostess at garden parties for the theatre orphanage: Dame Alison Faulkner. I've handed round the tea she poured out.'

'Dame Alison?'

For some reason, Juliet's spirits sank.

'Her husband was a surgeon. Died of some infection he caught in Germany just after the War. It's lucky for her she's got an upstanding son. She probably thinks nobody's good enough to walk in the same street with him.'

'Very probably,' Juliet agreed. Dame Alison Faulkner: a well-known person; a hostess at big public functions; a widow with an only son. 'I suppose he's an only son?' she said to father.

'Why should you?'

'I can't imagine why.'

'He said', she remembered to tell him, 'that she saw you in *Ambrose K.C.* and thought you were too good for the play.'

That pleased him. He grinned and said, 'So did I.'

The odd thing was, Juliet reflected, that she had asked nothing about him. Now she wanted to know everything – everything Frith knew.

It wasn't much. Michael was going abroad in the Colonial Forestry Service and was taking a busman's holiday up in woods pursuing, among other things, some caterpillar that damaged pines. 'Queer job for a hefty young man, grubbing up grubs,' Frith remarked.

Juliet didn't want his comments; didn't want to hear his withering wit playing about with Michael and his career. To change the subject she said, 'A queer thing happened this morning. Will you swear not to mention it, even sideways, if I tell you?'

'Tell away.'

'But do you swear?'

'Ay, by St Patrick! Okay, I'll be mute.'

She told him and he was interested. 'I bet it's some local superstition,' he said.

That was a startling notion.

'How *could* it be?'

'Oh, like turning the stones in Ireland. If you want to put a curse on a man you go and turn the stones on his land. There are all sorts of ways; that's just one.'

'Cursing? How horrible!'

'Or it could be an animal sacrifice,' Frith went on. 'Professor Goyet told me that some of these mountain places are saturated with pagan beliefs and even pagan practices. He says that at Gorbio, not long ago, they slit the throat of a black cock once a year. I asked him what the Church did about it and he said he thought they had incorporated it into some Easter celebration – like St Patrick with the Beltaine fires. They are wiser in their generation than the children of Luther … White feathers?' he went on reflectively. 'To give them is an insult, in England. There may be some connection.'

'But that would be frightful,' Juliet exclaimed, with so much earnestness that her father laughed.

'It's not *your* headache! My dear child, do learn not to get all het up about other people's affairs! What's Hecuba to you?'

Juliet regretted having told him. One ought to remember that everything interested Frith but mighty few people concerned him.

'Here's Hecuba bringing your coffee,' she said.

Martine glanced with solicitude from Juliet to her father as she set down the enormous coffee-pot and a jug of cream.

'You go to the market, Monsieur?' she asked and promised him, 'There you will see all the animation of the region.' She warned him to go early before all the best things were sold. 'You will like some of the pottery, I think. Much of it is modern and ugly, but there is one man who uses a beautiful black glaze and, Mademoiselle, you will find ribbons. Your hat, if you will excuse me, should have a smart new ribbon for Nice. I go myself to buy something good for your dinner, but I will not tell you what it is. Your last dinner with us: it shall be one to remember, Monsieur. You will see!'

Frith gave her his charming smile, with a keen glance from narrowed eyes, and answered, 'But all your dinners are memorable, Madame.'

2

'IT IS LIKE a market in Italy,' Juliet commented, pleased by the colour and movement and noise. Swarthy vendors had started a mock war and were shouting eloquent abuse of one another and fantastic recommendations of their own wares while laughing, voluble customers egged them on. Trade was proceeding merrily but finding friends and joking and gossiping seemed to be the real business of the day. Sweets and cakes and highly coloured syrops sold rapidly and so did stuffs and garments of all kinds. The pottery was neglected, waiting for tourists to arrive, and so were the flowers. There were pyramids of them – roses, carnations, gladioli and huge dahlias – shaded by umbrellas and watered with sprays. Stalls of fruit and vegetables, set out with a nice sense of colour-contrast, made brilliant pictures in reds and yellows, orange and green.

Drawn up on the shady side of the *place*, beside tilted carts, were the mules and donkeys who had hauled produce from the valleys and down from the nursery gardens and mountain farms.

Frith bought plums from a stall kept by a small, wiry, grey-haired man and two girls who looked with the liveliest interest at Juliet. One of the girls was short and pink-cheeked and had bright, black eyes; the other, tall and graceful, had melancholy grey eyes in a regular, oval face. As Juliet and her father turned away the three were greeting Martine and enquiring anxiously whether René meant to come. They were his uncle and cousins, Juliet guessed. Animated chatter and consultation over the fruit and vegetables selected to fill Martine's basket went on until a shrill woman's voice interrupted it.

'If you would have the goodness not to obstruct the whole stall, Madame! Other people, also, might wish to obtain a few provisions, even if they do not get them below the price.'

'Oh, pardon, Madame Tissier,' Martine said quietly and turned to move on, but too late: a lanky youth who had come in the wake of her adversary – a lad with abnormally long arms which hung from his shoulders loosely, like a puppet's – had thrust out an elbow, tilted her basket, and sent purchases rolling in the dust.

Then it was bedlam. Martine, almost in tears, was helped and upheld by vociferous champions while the aggressor and his disconcerted mother wriggled and shoved their way out of the hostile crowd. Words of detestation were hissed after them: 'It is Ignace! Always this Ignace! This commences to be too much!'

So the Loubiers have an enemy, not only a rival, Juliet thought. Had the horrid trick with the white feathers been theirs? She and Frith would have offered to go home with Martine, who was pale and distressed, had not her friend Madame Bonin borne down upon her, relieved her of her basket and led her away.

Now the fortune-teller caught Juliet's eye, smiling and beckoning and spinning her wheel. Juliet joined the circle surrounding her and listened to the woman's patter that flowed in a breathless gush. The 'Wheel of Fortune' which lay on the table before her was decorated with the signs of the zodiac. Amulets bearing similar emblems were displayed on cards. Customers were confiding their birth-dates to the vendor and buying appropriate charms together with printed sheets on which fortunes and characters were described. Her own sign, for the ninth of October, was the constellation of the Scales – a pretty pendant – but Juliet hadn't the money for such frivolities.

'The malady that you must beware of is rheumatism,' a stout woman was being told, from a reading of her horoscope. 'Take good care of your feet.' The advice produced hilarious shouts from her three companions.

'Oh, so it's the stars, is it, not those high-heeled shoes?'

Frith was listening. 'Well, well,' he remarked. 'The bread of the wise is the folly of fools.'

'What great sage said that?' Juliet enquired. 'Confucius?'

'No. Cunningham.'

Making their escape from the ubiquitous Algerian pedlar with his carpets and leather pouffes, they collided with a grinning youngster who carried a tray of miniature dogs, wire-jointed, tremulous, too lively and expressive to be resisted. Frith bought one and began, by manipulating the base, to make the thing writhe and waggle from head to tail. The boy held out another and, with grave faces, the two made their dogs advance, inspect one another, cringe, retreat, wag and wriggle and nod until Juliet was aching from silent laughter and bystanders were shouting with uproarious mirth.

'I say you *are* an expert,' a young English voice said, admiringly. Juliet, instantly sobered, looked up into the amused face of Michael Faulkner. She dropped her handbag, stooped, groping, and had recovered her composure before she retrieved it and met his regard again. He was buying a couple of dogs. The boy's tray was almost cleared.

Inviting him to come and have a drink, Frith began to lead the way towards the tavern under the arcades but before they reached it Michael paused at a stall.

'I think wine would make me sleepy,' he said. 'I want one of those poison-coloured syrops,' and he asked Juliet, 'What about you?'

'I'd like a vermilion one, or that yellowy-green,' she replied. Frith muttered, 'Debased tastes – well, I'll leave you to it,' and went on his way.

Michael seemed thoughtful. 'I suppose,' he suggested, when the tumblers were in their hands, 'I couldn't persuade you to buy a broom?'

'What sort of a broom?'

'The sort that witches ride on.'

'I'm not a witch and it wouldn't fit in my luggage. Are you selling them?'

'It's that poor woman over there. Nobody buys from her and it goes to my heart.'

'Where?'

Juliet expected to see some dazzling young girl, but the broom-seller, standing beside her pile of baskets and twigs in the shadow of an arcade, was the woman with the bandaged eye.

'You know her?' Juliet asked with vivid interest. 'My father and I have been no end intrigued by her. Do tell me her story,' she begged.

It was fine to have something objective to talk about; it helped her to keep her voice light; her manner cool. He mustn't guess how happy it made her to meet him again. Today, in good grey flannels, he looked so very English, so assured and relaxed, with his easy stride. This meeting was mere chance; that must be remembered; she must seem casual, too. But it was natural to be interested in this gypsy with her tragic history.

'Do you know her name?'

'It is a queer name: Terka.'

'Hungarian?'

'I don't know. I only know she's a Romany. Her tribe wanders all over southern Europe, it seems.' He hesitated. 'It is a grim story, if the people up in the farm have it right. They say she was a sort of Helen of Troy. Men forgot their wives for her. And gypsies have no tolerance for that particular sin.'

'I thought they lived anyhow and loved anyhow!'

'So did I, but, it seems, that was a mistake. They have stringent laws and a court and trials and all and their final punishment is expulsion from the tribe.'

'And Terka broke the law?'

'Yes: she committed the unforgivable sin.'

Their drinks finished, they withdrew from the crowd and began to circle the marketplace while Michael continued the story in low tones.

'Some feast they were having – on Midsummer Eve, probably, with bonfires and torches, and she disappeared, and so did a married man. There was a furious hunt and the two were seen. They were chased. The man's wife and her buddies were savage. They attacked Terka with torches. The men saved her life but she was badly disfigured, they say.'

'Was the eye injured?'

'Nobody seems to know. The cold-blooded part of it is that afterwards, in that condition, the poor wretch was cast out of the tribe.'

'When did all that happen?'

'I gather, about three years ago.'

'So she came here? And here, people won't buy her brooms. Is it because they are intolerant, too, of that particular sin? René Loubier, even, was brutal to her.'

'I don't know why it is. Up in the forest – her hut is there not far from where I'm staying – they are forever whispering about her, not talking openly, and the women more than the men. I can't make head nor tail of their attitude. I guess a lot of them trade with her secretly but nobody will speak to her in public. Look at her now: it is to outsiders she's selling, isn't it? The locals just don't look her way. And yet they say she helped in the Maquis and did really brave and dangerous things.'

'That doesn't surprise me a bit. I think her right profile is beautiful – heroic and Greek, like a statue, don't you?'

'Beautiful, yes; but not Greek.'

Juliet was puzzling over the strange story.

'I can't understand it,' she said. 'These village people seem friendly and kind.'

'Are they? I'd be surprised – all cramped together and shut in by the wall. They must hear one another talking in their sleep. I bet every rumour and whisper goes round and round.'

They had arrived close to Terka's stall. Juliet said, *'Bonjour, Madame,'* politely and looked for something cheap enough to buy. The only small things for sale were bunches of sun-dried herbs and she paid a few francs for rosemary, thyme and wild mint to give to Martine. The gypsy, while she counted the change into Juliet's hand, stared into the palm. 'Mademoiselle', she murmured, 'is going away.'

'I am: tomorrow.'

Terka raised her head and looked into Juliet's face as if seeing more and comprehending more than time had yet written there. She held the girl's hand lightly with her fingers and said impressively, 'Do not go too far. Your luck is here: do not hide from it.'

She dropped the hand, but Juliet stood and gazed as if mesmerised into her face. The fine, long nose with wide, sensitive nostrils, the lovely sweeping curve of the eyebrow and lips, the dark lashes fringing the large, lustrous eye, perfectly set in its arched cavity, might have been engraved on an ancient coin; might have been the features of a queen. But she saw, too, lines and planes that marred their beauty. Suffering, knowledge and experience, as well as harsh weather, had left their marks. 'She must surely be wise,' Juliet thought.

'Do not remain ignorant of your fortune; do not walk blindly and lose it,' Terka went on. Her accent was curious; her voice deep and strong but kept very low. 'Visit me in my camp in the forest and I will advise you. I will tell you what your stars command.'

Michael Faulkner broke in abruptly.

'You heard her say she is leaving tomorrow.' His hand, compelling, was on Juliet's arm.

'*Merci, Madame,*' Juliet said to the gypsy and let him draw her away.

In a tone of disgust, he said, 'I suppose they fall for that crude gypsy patter up in the farms.'

Juliet nodded.

'I dare say they do. My father would want to hear her doing her stuff. He sort of collects superstitions and gnaws at them.'

'Superstition is what keeps millions of human beings degraded and cringing and miserable,' Michael said hotly, and then excused himself. 'Sorry! I've got a thing about superstition,' he said. 'But I say – there's something I want to buy but I don't know the name of it either in English or French: stuff you tack across a window to keep out insects.'

'Muslin? *Mousseline?*'

They went about looking for it.

'I like moths,' Michael explained. 'I'd go miles for a Painted Lady or A. Eupenoides, but I do *not* want them flying in by the score when I am trying to work at night and sizzling themselves to death against my lamp.'

'Are you studying up there in the forest?' Juliet asked. Sometimes he looked young enough to be a student, at others, too mature.

'Yes,' he replied, 'but not for exams. I'm through with exams, thanks be; but I'm collecting local stuff for myself about conifers – just these Mediterranean species with their diseases, fungi, insect enemies, and so on. We were given a course in les Maures last July and I wangled permission to hang on. I had a notion, then, I'd be going to Cyprus.'

Michael stopped with a one-sided grin and began to ask Juliet something about herself, but the word 'Cyprus' was raising a mirage of strange beauty in her imagination and, instead of answering, she said, 'And you are not?'

'No,' he replied. 'I'm for the Gold Coast now.'

It sounded deserts and aeons away.

'When?'

'End of October. I'm to have a couple of weeks with my mother first.'

He closed that topic very deliberately, giving Juliet a quizzical look that crinkled the corners of his eyes.

'And you, Miss Cunningham? Actress on holiday? Art student? Professional daughter? I can't guess.'

Juliet chuckled. 'None of them, so far. I'm nothing. I'm on the lap of the gods.'

'Which of them?' Michael asked and then gave her a slightly apologetic glance. The grin widened across his face. He seemed to think her remark much funnier than she had meant it to be. Presently he asked, soberly, 'Is it true that you've no notion where you'll be?'

'It's perfectly true. Exciting, isn't it?' She tried to sound pleased and thrilled by the prospect. 'I present myself at agencies in Nice tomorrow and in a day or two I may be anywhere.'

'While your father goes to Corsica?'

He had hazel eyes with a great deal of force in them, a rather square jawline and long, mobile lips. His mood showed with no concealment at all. Juliet knew instantly that he was thinking she should have been better provided for and she felt humiliated. Her voice was chilly as she replied:

'My father arranged for me to become a teacher. I tried for three years and I was not a success at it.'

His reply did not improve matters.

'Lord – you must have begun in your infancy!'

'I was seventeen.'

'I say, I am being inquisitive: I am sorry.'

'It's all right. There's no secret about me.'

'Isn't there?'

Again his slow smile lighted his face.

'*I* am being cross and there's no reason,' Juliet said, candidly. 'I'm sorry, too.'

'Well, let's both stop being sorry and find my muslin. The stalls are beginning to pack up.'

He found what he wanted. While it was being cut for him Juliet looked round for her father and saw him, some distance off, weaving a course in her direction rather aimlessly. He saw her and waggled a hand and began to move towards the stall. Her heart warned her, beating rapidly. She was alarmed. It had happened before, one evening at Marseilles, and he had become foolishly garrulous, crudely jocular, dreadfully indiscreet. Anything would have been better than this. She ran to meet him, stood between him and Michael so that Michael should not hear or see. Frith greeted her with reproaches, but smiled.

'Hello, so there you are, my one fair daughter. You got rid of me nicely, didn't you, you two? Well, it's natural; perfectly natural; I'm very pleased, as a matter of fact. He's a charming fellow, your Romeo. Don't you want to invite him to lunch? ... "Romeo, Romeo, wherefore art thou Romeo?"'

Rudeness, abruptness, couldn't be helped. She hustled her father away from the marketplace, out into the rue Centrale. She was afraid to look round for fear Michael should be following them – having noticed; thinking he ought to help. On the seat under the chestnuts Frith sat down. Juliet left him there and turned back. She had no notion what she was going to say.

It was ages before she saw Michael and, when she did, he was busy, preoccupied, as if he had forgotten her. He was helping Camille Loubier to harness his mule to the cart. When it was done be looked up and came striding towards her.

'I say,' he said gently, 'do forgive me for sprinting off without you like that. I'd forgotten I'd promised to help Camille. That mule of his is a beauty but it is a bit of a mule at times. Are you all right?'

'Yes, I'm all right.'

He stood looking down at her. He had seen. He wasn't trying, this time, to deceive her but only to give her a way out. She knew by the stern, concerned look in his eyes that he knew and was anxious for her but couldn't think of any way to help. And she had hoped … she had hoped that, perhaps, he would come to the Inn of the Doves for lunch.

'Goodbye, Mr Faulkner,' she said.

Michael glanced back at the Loubiers' stall.

'I've got to help them load up now; there are some heavy crates.'

He pulled some papers out of his pocket and handed her an envelope. It was one addressed to himself at the Ferme Loubier. His voice was as grave as his face.

'Juliet, please keep my address and let me hear from you,' he said. 'I'll be there for a while and after I've left my letters will be sent on. I don't sail till the end of October. If, ever, there's anything I could do you'll remember, won't you?'

'Yes, Michael, I'll remember,' she said.

He smiled.

'I'll always be sorry I couldn't show you the forest.'

'I'll always be sorry, too.'

He took her hand. Even his smile was serious. He said, *'Bon voyage; bonne chance; bon courage!'* Then he turned, went back to the cart and began to help the farmer to load it with crates. Juliet returned to her father where he sat, brooding and wretched, under the chestnut tree.

3

STRIPPING HER ROOM and packing her things did not take very long: it was just a bad quarter of an hour. Juliet looked in the glass, pulling a comb through her hair, brushing the ends up, then trying what a touch of powder would do for her telltale face. She didn't want Frith to know she had been crying. She felt sorry for him. He had been so proud of all he had done for her, and now he was angry and wretched and mortified. However, they still had twenty-four hours, and among all the distractions of Nice. She believed that if she could keep up her own spirits, and if he approved of her lodgings and the agency he would cheer up again and go away satisfied.

She put her brush and comb in her case, powder compact in her shabby handbag. Was there anything else? Someone tapped on the door and in floated her buttercup dress 'in all its perfection' suspended from a hanger, Martine carrying it like a banner before her. Martine arranged it tenderly on top of everything else in the case. She had brought tissue paper to lay in the folds. 'They charge too much – two hundred francs,' she said. 'I have put it on Monsieur's bill.'

'Oh, please, no! I pay these things myself.'

'But it is so expensive! Why did you not let me do it for you?'

'You do so much.'

Martine was pale and without her dimples, quite without her radiance, today, and Juliet missed her sweet humour acutely.

'It becomes a little difficult,' Martine confessed. She turned to Juliet's hat which lay on the bed.

'Still the old scarf?' she exclaimed, dismayed.

'I forgot to buy a ribbon.'

'What could make you forget a thing so important? For Nice, that is not possible. Let me think! … Wait, please.'

She went downstairs and returned very soon bringing a needle-case, a thimble and a roll of white satin ribbon. It had been intended, no doubt, for a baby's sash. Sitting on the bed, she worked with absorption and presently presented a transformed hat to Juliet; the ribbon was set round the crown at an angle and short ends hung just over the brim. It was more stylish, as Juliet told her, than it had ever been in its long life. René was calling his wife urgently but she waited to cut fish-tail ends on the ribbon before hurrying down.

Juliet was ready now: all ship-shape for Nice in green and white. She lifted her two suitcases out to the landing and went along the corridor looking for Marie. Marie emerged from a bathroom, received her *pourboire* with a quick 'But it is too much,' and an equally quick thrust of her hand with the money into the pocket of her skirt.

'Mademoiselle is sad to leave St Jacques?'

Juliet nodded, turned away and took one more look into her little room and then went downstairs, wondering whether when she was much older changes and partings would bring less pain.

A conclave was going on in René's office. It was a little room off the hall – the only room on the ground floor with a window on the street. She supposed that her father was paying the bill and went in to contribute her two hundred francs. The three stopped talking when they saw her. Frith seized her arm, steered her across the hall and shut himself up with her in the dining-room.

'Look here: you like these people, don't you? You trust them?'

'Of course I do.'

'Madame Loubier is a good little sort, don't you think?'

'She is as good as bread.'

'And René – in his way, he's a gentleman. I mean, he wouldn't exploit you.'

'Frith, what in the world …?'

'A half-time job and a nominal salary. You'd keep your room. I'd have to send you enough money regularly to make it legal – "Visible means of support" – and you could save most of it for your return fare … No time for dithering: the chap with the luggage truck's waiting and it's time to sprint for the bus.'

'I'm not dithering, Frith!' Juliet laughed.

'You could see me off and come back tomorrow and start. You want to take it on, do you? Sure you'll feel equal to it? You wouldn't let them overwork you?'

Juliet laughed again.

'Oh, I will,' she said, 'I won't.'

'Good!'

Frith's spirits had soared. Delight was on every face, warmth and pleasure were in every gesture as goodbyes were said on the steps. Frith whistled and chanted nonsense as he and Juliet strode down the hill.

'Will you, won't you, won't you, will you, will you join the dance?'

Juliet chuckled and said, but secretly, to herself only, 'I will; I'll do that, too.'

Chapter VI

THE BUBBLE

THE MUSLIN was too narrow but Claudette joined and hemmed until she had a piece to fit over the window of the hut. She even fetched a hammer and tacked it in place. These girls had the admirable idea that a man ought not to have to do such things for himself. Since their mother's death, the two had looked after their father and their bedridden grandmother, seeing little of the world outside, and to Michael they seemed ignorant, credulous children one minute and responsible young women the next.

Michael liked them. He liked everything about this place except the meals. He liked Camille Loubier, who was as honest as he was shrewd, and his malicious, garrulous 'Maman' – eighty if she was a day – and Rouge, the setter bitch who belonged to René and was cherished for his sake. He liked the warm, dark farmhouse kitchen with its antique furniture and garlicky smells. And he liked, after supper, to get out into the air, walk through the vineyard to his own timber hut, light the oil-lamp, and work in absolute peace. There was a quality in that profound silence, the breathing silence of multitudinous trees, that energised one's mind and set imagination to work. One caught the relations between seemingly unrelated effects and sometimes began to suspect a common cause: guesses were confirmed or eliminated and new roads of speculation opened up. It was more than he had hoped for. His intention had been merely to inform himself a bit more about the effect on conifers of long, hot summers, sea-winds and dry, shallow soil. His notebooks, specimens and photographs were intended only for himself. In these quiet nights and solitary days, however, a larger ambition had spread roots in his mind: there were lines it would be worth while following up – the natural regeneration, for instance, of the Aleppo pine and certain methods of nourishing young trees; then this material could be worked into reports and monographs. Meanwhile, after years of working under direction – vacations and travel, even, under direction – to be a freelance was fun.

The Gold Coast! By no means the pearl of colonies. Still, Africa had always fascinated him and trees were trees everywhere. But if his mother's prayers had worked it would have been Cyprus. Old Sir Hughenden would have died of his stroke and Hughie would have had to take over at home. Michael wondered, chuckling to himself, whether she'd had the nerve to pray for the old boy's death. He wouldn't put it past her.

About midnight, sleep began to weigh on his brain ... This was – what day? – Tuesday? And, he realised with remorse, he hadn't written to his mother this week. Better do it now.

He dated his letter 'Sep. 16th–17th' and wrote on the paper at hand.

DEAREST MUFF,

Sorry about squared paper again and not having written on Sunday. There was a fête in the village and, obeying your orders not to go native, I took myself down there to dance. The farm-girls, who were my only acquaintances, were a bit weighty as partners but then I had a stroke of luck. Do you remember the actor, Frith Cunningham, who, you said, had let you down as a prophet? (I see why: romantic-looking and lively and clever, but looks upon the wine when it is red.) He was down there with his daughter and she is as light and airy as spun glass – but, I imagine, as brittle, too. You remember the Bird of Paradise you used to put on the top of the Christmas tree and how I pestered you to let me play with it and how, when you gave it to me, I just stared and stared at it, afraid to touch? One feels a bit like that with her.

Don't worry! They've both gone off into the blue and nothing got cracked.

Grand that you fixed your escape from the mag., but why do section-editors only get one month? I bet your chief takes three a year.

About plans. Paris on Oct. 13th will suit me fine and I don't expect to sail till the 30th. Yes, I'd certainly like the west coast and swimming, after getting dehydrated here. Of course, your mark for your furniture-snooping is the Rhône Valley, and you can go back that way and have a week in your adored Arles and Avignon. By the way, I tried to take the bread-cupboard and kneading-trough but couldn't get good light.

I brought no flash-lamp, like an idiot. If you think you could use them I'll haul them out of doors.

Gorgeous weather. I'm tramping from dawn to dusk and sleeping out and am as fit as Samson. My only complaint is that I'm sometimes wakened by the nightingales. I don't like to think of you stuck in London. Cheers for the 13th! I'm looking forward ravenously to our spree.

Bless you!

Your loving,
MONKEY.

P.S. Do get Our Liz decarbonised. Driving her as she is now is too much like work.

NUMBER ONE, two coffees and rolls; two, two teas; three, two coffees; four, chocolate and croissants; five, orange-juice and toast Melba; six, chocolate; me, chocolate ...

It was all written up on the slate in René's clear writing; the times too, except the blessed old lady in number five who had said, 'Dear child, what a rush you must have! Bring mine any time you like after eight o'clock.'

Breakfasts, from first to last, took nearly an hour. René carried up the double-room trays and the Professor's. He had strict notions of what it was *comme il faut* for Juliet to do. Martine didn't have to be down, now, until it was time for the rooms to be done.

Helping her was a pleasure and also an education. Martine, who had helped to bring up her stepmother's six children, treated Juliet as if she were a younger sister learning to keep house. Herself, she seemed a born housewife. She worked as if it were her hands, not her brain, that reacted, but, confronted with any situation that was new or complex, she would pause, her head on one side, and then go to it with precision; no muddle; no lingering. She made one think of a bird building its nest. At times she would philosophise about an inn-keeper's problems – the art of keeping clients contented; of being generous yet never extravagant, indulgent without upsetting routine.

'You sometimes talk as if you were fifty,' Juliet commented, amused.

'It is René who taught me. He is experienced. You know, he is thirty years old.'

'And you?'

'Twenty-four last March.'

'Only three-and-a-half years older than me, and you know a thousand things I haven't even begun to learn.'

'You learn quickly; there are brains in your fingers; all that you do is nice. When you have your own home it will go easily: you will see.'

Juliet would have liked to spend more time in the kitchen.

The low-ceilinged room fascinated her with its cleanliness and completeness, its families of canisters and coffee-pots, its hierarchy of shining saucepans, its gadgets and contrivances. She liked to watch while René and Martine concocted delicious dishes, working with such perfect coordination that they scarcely needed to exchange a word, but Juliet had some of the marketing to do and the tables to lay, and she helped René with the waiting. She had a free hour or two after lunch when she lay down on her bed and then, when teas were over, she could go for a walk. Martine was sent her to her room, firmly, at nine every night. When René observed, conscientiously, that she was supposed to do only a half-day's work, she told him that she preferred to be busy. That was true. Besides, Martine really needed the help.

'You don't know, Juliette,' René said on Saturday morning when he had checked her purchases and approved them. 'You cannot imagine what good fortune it seems to us to have a little assistant like you. I would have been forced, this week, to find somebody, but, you see, our young people – the intelligent ones – go for the season to the hotels on the coast and it will be mid-October before they come home. To instruct the stupid sends the blood to my head, and for Martine, who is as quick as a squirrel, it is misery to work with one who is slow. Do not leave us, please, until our son is born – it is less than two months now. You save Martine's peace of mind.'

He spoke earnestly and the words were balm to her heart.

Juliet admired René but was not entirely at ease with him. One felt he had fierce energies held in leash. Except with Martine, with whom he was invariably gentle, he showed himself somewhat moody and unpredictable. Good-humoured and kind when he had his way, he was capable, when vexed, of explosions of temper, abrupt behaviour and terribly scathing remarks. Young André Gatti, who helped in the bar, was afraid of him and Marie would redouble her elbow work, scrubbing, washing and polishing, when he was near. With Juliet he had two manners: in public he gave her his orders politely and addressed her as 'Mademoiselle,' but in the yard and the kitchen he would tease her, scold her mockingly, call her 'Juliette' or 'Giulietta' or – a word that baffled her for a moment – 'Bellop'.

She tried very hard not to be a 'bell-hop' but, uncontrollably, whenever the terrace bell rang, her feet carried her fleetly upstairs. She would pull herself together in time to walk sedately across the hall – to find some perspiring and thirsty excursionist in need of a drink.

Her father, over their last meal in Nice, had given her bits of advice. If things had been just a little different she might have followed them.

'Don't go putting so much imagination into everything: nothing ever works out the way one imagines it will, so it's waste of time, and it only breeds disillusionment.' And then, 'Send a postcard to young Faulkner. He'd come down on Sunday evening and take you dancing.' And then, 'Don't be such a blighted crustacean! Where's the danger in coming out of your shell? A girl has to, you know. Nobody's going to bother to winkle you out.'

'And if I did come out of my shell,' she reflected. 'If I did send Michael a postcard, imagining he would want to come for me, and if he didn't come – how should I feel then?'

When she was not occupied, thoughts that were very painful, memories full of bitterness and mortification, would often well up into her mind.

… Girls without any position or any *dot* whose chatter the whole day long was about how to attract young men! She had known them. Her mother and aunt had joked about them, naming them 'man-hunters' and 'man-eaters'. Sometimes the two had abetted such girls, enjoying the comedy, and sometimes tried to protect a male friend. It had frozen her to listen to them … That ghastly afternoon in the Hotel Victoria, when Madame Beuque burst into their salon, red-faced, railing against her own daughter because she had let Paul Groute 'escape'. Germaine had come in, weeping tempestuously, and Aunt Isabel had said to her, 'The fact is, my girl, you over-played your hand.' Juliet thought she would rather die than be taken, by anybody she cared about, for a girl like that.

If things had been different – if she could have met Michael on his own level, as a girl of his own secure, privileged world whom his mother and friends would have welcomed as a friend, she would have written to him. But she couldn't, because he knew. He knew, now, that she had no home and no training and that her father wanted to be rid of responsibility for her … To *force* Michael to dance with her! And then to talk in that awful way in the marketplace … Michael hadn't heard: she was almost perfectly certain he hadn't. And if he had, he wouldn't misunderstand her. But just well, as things were, it would be a thousand times happier if their meeting should come about by chance. It was a thing to wait for and pray for, but one that she could do nothing to bring to pass.

'Do your job,' she commanded herself severely. 'Look after Martine. That is important. Only eight weeks now before her baby should be born, and nothing must go wrong.'

It was over their bed-making that Martine confided to Juliet the story of her long anxiety: how two years of married life had gone by without promise of a child; of René's gradual loss of spirits and her own desperate distress.

'He made me go to the doctor, but the poor old man was ill and despondent. He gave us no comfort at all. So then,' – Martine smiled and her eyes brightened – 'then, René went up to the forest and brought down Henri Bonavera who, you know, is a *marcou.*'

'A healer?' Juliet was not sure what the word meant. 'Is he a *guérisseur?*'

'Oh, yes, he is, but so much more! A *guérisseur* like César, you know, can only cure this or that and has to use herbs. Henri is a *panseur de secret,* more powerful even than the famous woman who lived near Draguignan and whom they called *la Médecine.* He has only to touch. He is true *marcou,* although, I have heard, he is not a seventh son.'

Juliet listened, baffled, as always, but rather touched by Martine's childish credulity which so oddly accompanied her mature, wise ways.

'And what,' she asked, 'did Henri advise?'

'He made me go on a long, long journey. We made a pilgrimage to the shrine of the Black Virgin, Notre Dame de Bonne-garde. It was too far for me to go alone so René came too. It was Christmas and his father could not come to replace him, so we had to close the inn for three days.'

'And the pilgrimage helped?'

Juliet wished she had not sounded like her father when she said that. Not for the world would she hurt Martine's feelings. But Martine was not hurt. Her face was lit up, sparkling with thankfulness.

'Is not our son to be born in two months?'

'Does the Black Virgin always send boys?'

Martine laughed.

'How busy she would be if she would do that! No: but the moon was waxing when he was conceived.'

In spite of herself Juliet would not have been able to help laughing at Martine's logic had not a look of the utmost gravity come over the girl's face. In a low voice Martine said, 'So you understand, don't you, Juliet, how terrible it would be for René if anything went wrong now.'

Yes: even though it seemed a mere routine of shopping, and serving meals, and tidying rooms, Juliet knew that her work was important. It was the only important thing she had ever had to do, and she intended to do it well.

The night after that conversation Juliet had a curious dream. All the morning, although its images eluded her, its strange tensions remained, but it was not until the hour of the siesta while she was lying down, half asleep, that she caught the bubble again.

It was a most exquisite bubble, with all the colours of life reflected in it, and it rested between her hands. There it swelled and grew until it was so fine, so fragile, that at every second she thought it must burst. It was in danger from the feathers, white feathers that were falling all around like a snow-storm. One of them would touch it and break it, or her hands would contract … In her fear for it she woke herself up and then she lay wondering drowsily what it could be – the frail, beautiful, menaced thing that the bubble symbolised.

3

MARTINE, WHO, during the first days of Juliet's companionship had recovered her spirits, seemed to lose them again before the end of the week. It was on Tuesday that Juliet began to feel worried about her. There was more than depression in her friend's manner: there was tension, nervousness, strain. Martine was watching René anxiously and when, as he usually did on Tuesdays and Fridays, he took possession of the kitchen, she went a little furtively out of the house. Juliet saw her cross the terrace clasping a sack to her breast – a small sack in which something struggled; go down the garden and come back without it, bringing lettuces. Later, when lunches were just over and Juliet was clearing away in the dining-room, she saw Martine come up by the path, rarely used, that ran under the tamarisk hedge, and busy herself on the terrace with one of the umbrellas that needed no attention at all. She looked so white that Juliet went out and spoke to her quietly.

'Martine, are you not feeling well?'

'Where's René?' The question was whispered. The empty bag was crammed into her apron pocket. She glanced nervously at a pigeon which had perched on the balustrade and was busily grooming his ruffled feathers.

'He's with André in the bar.'

The brown eyes that looked into Juliet's were doubtful for a moment. Juliet said, 'Can't I do something to help?' Martine nodded.

'Yes; yes, Juliet, I believe you can.'

Martine looked round uneasily and then seemed to take courage again.

'You haven't seen our room yet; come and let me show it to you,' she said.

Juliet followed Martine up the wooden staircase from the yard into a room like the inside of an ark. The ceiling sloped steeply on both the longer sides and the little windows, which looked over the yard, were set low in the wall. The ventilation might have been better, Juliet felt, but the room was pretty.

'It is like a room in a picture,' she said.

'And look!' Martine opened a door at the gable end and displayed a water-closet and shower. 'American plumbing! René is very proud of it,' she declared. 'We are fortunate, you see, because, as well as piped water, we have our pump.'

Surveying the bedroom, Juliet wondered how the great bed with its carved posts had ever been carried in. Under one window was a fine old chest decorated with carving and under the other a wooden cradle that surely ought to have been in a museum. In spite of her uneasiness, Juliet could not help smiling at the contrasted characters represented on the walls. Between the windows was a rack which supported an important-looking, double-barrelled gun, while over the bed hung a holy-water font and reproductions of sacred pictures, and there was a bracket in a corner on which, before a statue of the Blessed Virgin, burned a small red lamp.

As if these surroundings soothed her, Martine relaxed, and Juliet sat down on the chest.

'Tell me,' she asked, 'what is worrying you? What is it you would like me to do?'

'Juliet!' The response came breathlessly. 'If you would take a message for me: a little gift and a letter?'

'But of course I will, Martine. Where to?'

'To the forest.'

'The forest!'

'Yes. You will like the forest, Juliet, and up there the air is so pure; it will do you good. One day a week you must be quite free. It was René who said it, and Thursday will do. On Thursday, at a quarter past eleven, there is a bus to the gorge. I will give you a picnic. Oh, Juliet, if you will please, please go for me!'

'I would love to go to the forest, Martine.'

'Oh, thank you! I will make a little map for you. You must take the road on the far side of the gorge, pass the farms and then ... But I do not know how to tell you, for I, myself, have not been. You will see a little rise, all pines, and go round it and on the far side is the hut.'

Then the message was not to the Loubiers' farm.

'It is the camp of a gypsy,' Martine said.

'Of Terka!'

'Yes: Terka, from whom you bought those herbs ... Juliet, it is a dreadful thing but I am afraid ...' She seemed scarcely able to get out the words. 'I know that René has offended her.'

Juliet knew how true that was. The woman's gestures of humiliation and despair recurred vividly to her mind.

'Does that matter so much?' she asked.

Martine was sitting in a low chair by the cradle, twisting her hands. 'You see', she went on, deeply agitated, 'every week, usually on Tuesday, I give her something. I leave it for her at the foot of the garden, in that broken, dusty frame that is not used. She likes a pigeon best, or a chicken, but sometimes it is only a piece of stuff or an old pair of shoes; but something, always. I leave it in the morning and in the afternoon it is gone. But for two weeks now she has not taken it, and that means – it *can* only mean – that René has stopped her ... He doesn't understand; doesn't believe ...'

Martine was stammering, half incoherent.

'It is because of her I persuaded him not to keep a dog. He doesn't know why. A strange dog bit Mireille, and I pretend that I am afraid ... I have been told – Madame Bonin told me – that some of the men have made a conspiracy to drive Terka out of the district and that René is the leader of it. He is afraid of nothing and he would despise me if he knew how I am afraid.'

Bewildered, Juliet asked, 'But why? Why is Terka to be driven out, and insulted, and feared – that poor, helpless, mutilated creature?'

Martine was silent a moment then shook her head. 'Do not ask me to speak of it, Juliet. Even thoughts can harm an unborn child.'

Juliet hesitated. She was tempted. She wanted to go to the forest and she wanted to console Martine, but stronger, even, than this double temptation was her sick revulsion from deceit and her longing to rely on the integrity of these two and of their relationship.

'How can you bear to deceive René? Oh, Martine, you must tell René and trust him,' she implored. She added, gently, 'I can't help you to deceive him, you know.'

Martine's disappointment was pitiable. She pleaded but Juliet would not give way. At last Martine bowed her head on her hands and spoke chokingly.

'Go, go,' she said. 'He will miss you and ask questions. And now you will betray me! You will tell him! And I thought you were my friend.'

'I won't tell him. I won't betray you. It is because I am your friend that I can't help you to spoil your own happiness to break your lovely marriage, Martine.'

She was herself half incoherent with distress. She had to go and leave Martine weeping there.

4

'WE ARE tiring you, Juliet,' René said. 'You are quite pale. It will not do to make you faint again, like the first day.'

Martine, confessing only to fatigue, had stayed in her own room; the guests moved about between the bar, the terrace and the porch where, at the hour of the apéritif, some of them liked to sit, and Juliet was helping René to lay the tables for dinner. Compassion and perplexity dragged at her mind and her efforts to seem light-hearted had failed.

'I have quite, quite recovered; there will be no more fainting,' she assured him.

'Please sit down a moment. There is something that I wish to say to you,' he said, and she obeyed.

Working rapidly, carrying stacked plates and setting each in its place with a movement of the wrist, neat as a juggler's, René completed his job, then stood over her.

'I think you worry a little about Martine?'

'A little, sometimes.'

'I think you are her friend, and mine also.'

'Yes; yes, I am.'

'What I ask you to do for us is not an order: it is no part of your duty. I ask because it is for her peace of mind and because you are discreet. About the feathers, you kept your promise, and, about this, you will be secret, too.'

Juliet frowned and protested.

'But I don't like keeping secrets. I don't want to *know* secrets.'

'But this is important.'

With an air of urgency he lowered his voice, pulled a chair close to hers and sat down.

'There is a person who comes here secretly, when I am occupied elsewhere,' he said. 'She comes, and she frightens Martine. So much

73

Martine is afraid of her that she disobeys me and speaks to her, even gives her money or gifts. I have threatened the woman, but still she comes.'

Juliet's heart sank; what impossible request was coming now?

René, fixing his eyes on hers, said, 'I want you to watch for this woman. You will know her: she is a Romany and wears a scarf covering one eye. Tell me at once, or, if I am out, watch what she does. On Tuesdays and Fridays, while I am in the kitchen, please watch Martine.'

Juliet laughed. She heard the bitterness of her laugh, and detested it. Wheels within wheels! This was like a comedy by Molière, yet it might easily turn to tragedy. She tried hard not to let the force of her anger show. She spoke, after a moment, quietly.

'I know Terka,' she said, 'that unfortunate woman! How can anyone be afraid of her, René? What harm can she do?'

His jaw tightened; she did not like the expression on his face.

'She will indeed be unfortunate,' he said tersely, 'if I find her here again.'

'I have heard her story and I know she was sinful, but so many people … I think it is wicked to be so hard on her,' Juliet declared, and added, 'Surely, she has been punished enough?'

René's eyes opened wide so that all round the dark, large iris white showed. He could make one feel foolish when he looked at one like that. He said quietly, 'You know very little about her, I think, and it is not necessary that you should know … What I wish you to do is this: if you see her in the garden or the yard – if you see her anywhere speaking to Martine, I want you to find me and tell me at once.'

Tears of anger stung Juliet's eyes.

'You have no right to ask me to do that!' she exclaimed. 'I think you ought to be ashamed, René. You are asking me to spy on your wife.'

To her immense relief René's face changed; his smile flashed, he shook his head and laughed.

'You English! The things you will never understand! The things you will not even believe! … All right,' he said with a shrug, 'I will see to it myself.' The look he turned on Juliet, now, was friendly and kind.

He rose to put finishing touches to the tables and spoke lightly while she busied herself, helping him.

'Something much nicer, I will ask you to do. On Thursday, you may spend the day in the forest. That will put colour again in your face. I will ask you to take a letter for me to my uncle at his farm. They will be charmed to make your acquaintance, and they will give you supper.' He laughed. 'It will not be a good supper. You shall have another, however late you return ... Will you, perhaps, do this for me?'

'Yes, René,' she answered, 'I will.'

Chapter VII

INTO THE FOREST

HER TOES CURLED every time the bus swung round one of the hair-pin bends with rocks above and the ravine below. The edge looked as if it was not an inch from the wheel, but these drivers knew exactly what they were doing and the roads were kept in perfect repair. The illusion of risk added to the exhilaration of the adventure on which she was bound. Before she returned in the evening, walking, probably, by short cuts that Michael knew, so many things would have happened. She smiled to herself, recalling her father's warning against imagining things, and the English couple from the inn who had the seat next to hers smiled at her in return. Like most of the guests they were friendly and nice to her but just a little inquisitive. That was because of her dresses, she supposed. This green and white was too dainty, really, for country walking, but her plain ones were four years old and she had spent too much on her shoes to be able to buy anything else. They were nice: good shoes to walk in, both on stones and on grass.

The bus stopped with a jolt at the Relais du Cheval Mort.

There was nothing romantic about the Relais except its name. Juliet saw an old stone house around which had been built a petrol station and a big timber shack that served as restaurant, shop, and *Bar Américain*. In an open shed stood an old car with a placard on the windscreen proclaiming that it was for hire. The Langs decided to take it for the afternoon and invited Juliet to drive with them. Her explanation that she had an appointment at the farm widened their smiles. Truly the village was a whispering gallery, as Michael had guessed.

To her relief, when she had crossed the bridge and turned left along the road on the south side of the gorge, Juliet found herself alone. A man who overtook her on a bicycle to which were tied a new rake and hoe soon vanished round a bend. A sign nailed to a tree gave warning that there was no road here for automobiles and, indeed, this farm track would not have been safe for them. A precipice covered with scrub and brambles fell straight to the river, while the forest, marching down the mountains, seemed scarcely to have checked itself at the brink. Trees overhung the path and roots had heaved up the soil on one side, making the surface slant towards the edge and raising ridges to trap one's feet. One understood why the farmers used mules. However, when she heard hooves behind her and stood aside, it wasn't a mule that came trotting, briskly and carefully, drawing a light, trim cart; it was Eldorado, the Tissiers' little mare, and that was young Tissier sitting beside Dr Gompert. The lad grinned and waved as they passed her, proud to be perched up there on his father's *charrette*. Ahead, where the road turned sharp to the right round a bluff of rock, the doctor pulled up and Ignace dismounted and led the mare round the bend. Those small mountain carts took the sharp turns easily, as Frith had observed, because the front wheels were small. By the time Juliet had rounded the rock they were driving away again.

Now the road left the gorge and turned south, climbing a little, with old trees on both sides. Nearly all the trees in sight were pines or firs without weeds at their roots or birds in their branches; upright, aspiring, majestic, but much less alluring, Juliet thought, than a mixed English wood. Of all the varieties to be seen, she knew only one by name: the stone-pine which the French call *pin parasol*. Four beauties grew out of the bank on her right, leaning over the road, and a solitary giant, a little farther on, made a great arch over the path, shading it with so thick and heavy a canopy that the high sun was quite shut out. Seen through that tunnel, cleared spaces beyond shone like a pictured page illuminated in gold. She saw fields, won from the forest and cultivated, with fences, vineyards, one immense round water tank and a house. She was close to the three farms.

Juliet paused there, in the shade. She felt like Red Riding Hood, with a basket of goodies for Grandmother Loubier on one arm and her own lunch in its wire carrier dangling from the other hand. She decided to eat here and found for herself a fine chair framed by roots and cushioned in mast.

Her strategic plans were exact. She would not present herself at the farm at dinner time, when Michael would be there, as if coming to take him from his work and be entertained on her free afternoon. He should find her there when he returned for supper, surrounded by the family, whose amusement at his astonishment would help her to keep her poise ... And in between?

The cold coffee was a good thirst-quencher and the sandwiches were delicious. It was like Martine to insist on making them herself and to put in a mixture of minced chicken and salad and mayonnaise which the richest client would not have despised, as if anxious to console Juliet for the pain of being forced to refuse to help. Tired and subdued, Martine was all kindness, still.

Well, there was one thing Juliet could do. It had been no more than a notion when she started, and a rather alarming one; but up on this height, where the air and light and the scent of the trees had the very essence of courage and strength in them, she had no more fear. She was free. She was free of dull, heavy, down-dragging memories. They *were* memories now, nothing else: they belonged to the past. The thing she could and would do was visit Terka. She would make her acquaintance, get some understanding of the inexplicable dread that she seemed to create. Probably intolerance, mixed with superstition, accounted for it. One could not imagine that Martine had in her life anything that anybody could blackmail her about, or see Terka as a blackmailer, either. Very likely, all the trouble was the shadow of a shadow and had no real cause at all. To make sure of that and prove it to Martine would be a useful and sensible thing do.

In the white purse slung from her shoulder Juliet had half her week's wages – five hundred francs. As a pretext, she would go and ask Terka to tell her fortune. That would be amusing, and something lively to write to her father about. Her problem, since she didn't want any Loubiers to know what she was doing, would be to find the way.

That solved itself. Today she was lucky. She passed the first farm where three men, working among the vines, paused to follow her with black-eyed, embarrassing stares and then she came to the second – the Granerols': a place fit only to be burnt down, René had called it. A starved-looking dog, chained to a post, barked at her and was answered by the shrill whinnying of animals somewhere behind the house. A vile smell of manure hung in the air. The vegetable beds before the house were invaded by grass and weeds and the house-front lacked plaster as well as paint. Waiting at the gate was young Tissier in charge of the mare. She had heard that Ignace spent half his days idling in the forest; he would tell her the way. He told her so eagerly and with so many repetitions that she wondered whether she would become confused, but she repeated his directions about the hill, the felled trees, the juniper and the heather and rock. While they talked there, a woman came out of the house followed by the doctor, who scolded her ruthlessly. She looked as if she deserved it. She was dirty; her face was bruised and blotched and unsightly and she wore broken shoes.

'Empty that filthy stock-pot,' he growled at her. 'It's a breeding-pot for germs. Scour it with sand and boil water in it. *Boil* – do you under-stand? You have no one to blame but yourself for your husband's condition and bringing me up here is an outrage.'

The woman began to blubber and Juliet fled.

A TALL WIND-BREAK of cypress separated that farm from the Loubiers', and, at the Loubiers', one was in a very different place. Their vineyards and tilled fields stretched to the edge of the forest. The homestead was an old house with shallow roofs on different levels, deep eaves and a cave-like entrance. It looked solid, homely and secure. Juliet walked between lines of washing hung where the breeze flowed, entered the porch and tugged on a bell. She smiled when an old, cracked voice croaked, 'Step in, child: push the door and step in,' and again directed her to a room door, calling, 'This way, this way!'

The old lady was sitting up in bed, close to the window, where she had a fine view of everyone who approached. Her long nose, alert little eyes in a brown face, framed by a white cap with goffered frill, were so very appropriate that Juliet failed to repress a laugh. The grandmother laughed in response and held out claw-like hands for the basket, which was loaded with Martine's gifts. These were pulled out and examined with cackles and grins of approbation. The old woman broke off a piece of *pâté de campagne* and munched it then and there. Juliet arranged the packages on the great table in the order dictated from the bed. This was the living-room of the home and generations had enriched it; it was filled with massive pieces of furniture, noble in form and decorated with carving, on which common-place pottery and cheap utensils were incongruously set out.

Juliet was striving to make sense of a vehement discourse when a beautiful red setter came in, and then Camille Loubier entered and welcomed her.

The sturdy little man received René's letter with thanks and interest and, while he searched the place for his spectacles, told Juliet what his old mother was talking about. His eyes twinkled under shaggy eyebrows while he interpreted.

'She demands that you should tell Father Pascale it is time he came up and heard her confession!' The man shrugged. 'What sin she can commit, lying there, one cannot imagine, but she desires him to come. I think she invents sins in order to have a gossip with him.'

He was smiling but his countenance changed when the old woman, after much groping among boxes on the table beside her, produced a small article sewn up in a soiled chamois-leather bag. Her excited mumblings were translated with sceptical grimaces by Camille as she pressed the object into Juliet's hand. It was a blood-stone, she said. Because Martine had been born under the sign of the fishes it would bring her good luck and an easy delivery. When Camille asked his mother, suspiciously, where she had obtained the stone she stubbornly refused to reply. Instead, she began to gabble about 'Monsieur Michel' with such wicked glee on her crinkled old face that Juliet was thankful that she did not understand and that Camille did not translate.

Did she mean to take the bus down at four o'clock, he wished to know. Juliet told him that she wanted to spend a long afternoon in the forest and walk down.

'Then come back and eat with us,' he said cordially. 'My daughters will be here then. We have supper at six o'clock.'

While he read the letter he compressed his lips and nodded emphatically.

'You may tell René,' he said, looking up at her over the rims of his spectacles, 'that he is perfectly right. I am in accord with him, and I will do whatever I can.'

As Juliet left the house she could hear the old woman complaining that René would make trouble for everyone.

2

THE SMOOTH FLOOR of the forest monotonously strewn with mast, the evergreen canopy that diffused the light, the reiterated symmetries of the pines, conspired to prevent one from finding the way. Very soon, Juliet realised that she had lost the north. In what quarter was the sun? Under these thick interwoven boughs it was hard to guess. However, one had only to climb a knoll and look for the farms. But there, a little way off, were the felled trees. Yes; four of them; and there, too, was a pile of sawn logs. You left those on your right. A noise surprised her – a loud noise that had just started up: she heard a drone and a thudding, as if an engine of some kind were at work. Walking towards it, she found the ground sloping down and trees becoming scarce. There in a cleared, sun-lit hollow was a sawmill; a little open-air workshop with a lorry-engine driving the belt. The piles of sawdust and the newly cut planks shone yellow and the men who were working, stripped to the waist, were as brown as statues of bronze. Beyond, up on the hillside, two men were cutting down a small pine, swinging their hatchets in turn; the sun glinted on a lifted blade while the other bit into the trunk. The picture was an idyllic one in its setting of evergreens. Juliet sat on a log at the brink of the hollow to watch. She saw a shudder run through the tree and caught her breath, afraid for the men; then saw them stop and skip quickly aside. The tree toppled and groaned aloud and flung itself, as if in despair, on the ground.

Out of the shadows, now, came a horse. He moved to where a couple of trunks, stripped already, were lying, and stood there while the men attached one of them to his harness with iron bars. They rested while the horse, without their guidance, followed the easiest path down to the saw and stood beside the men who were working it. The trunk was uncoupled and hoisted onto the slide that lay between two circular saws. One man started the engine, the other set the wheels, and the trunk, passing between these, was stripped of its bark and its curved surface along two sides. It was brought back, turned and stripped on the other sides and then, changed to a square column of timber, was lifted on to the criss-cross pile.

There was something in the simplicity of the equipment and the strong, easy rhythm of the action; in the fragrance of the air and the rich colours, that brought Juliet one of those moments in which one longs for time to stand still.

She watched the two men by the saw wiping their foreheads and stretching their arms and backs. The smaller one moved like a boy but had white hair. The other was tall, finely built, and not burnt such a dark brown. He looked around and her heart gave a startled throb. It couldn't, *couldn't* be Michael? But it was. He stared at her, drew a hand in bewilderment over his forehead, stood still and gazed again. He started to run, then turned back, pulled on a shirt and, in a moment, was standing below her, laughing incredulously.

'I don't think I believe it,' he said.

'I didn't know you were you. Why didn't you tell me you were a wood-cutter?'

'I'm not: I'm a silviculturist.'

'Are you a hungry silviculturist, by any chance?'

'Hungry? When am I not?'

'I've got two marvellous sandwiches left from my lunch.'

Michael ate with enthusiasm, sitting at her feet.

'Tell me about you,' he demanded between mouthfuls. 'I imagine you on the Promenade Anglaise pushing some old chap's bath-chair, and you appear before me suddenly, like a dryad, all mixed up with the trees. Are there two of you or what?'

Juliet explained and the story delighted him.

'You appear to be one of the people fantastic things happen to,' he commented and added, 'But Juliet, this is fun!'

He lay, completely relaxed, on the ground and she asked whether he was supposed to be working. No, he told her; he gave Henri a hand now and then because Henri was valuable to him.

'He knows things you'd not find in any book: things about plants and insects and trees.'

'Is he Henri Bonavera?'

He was, and she told Michael about the strange powers Martine believed him to possess. Michael laughed.

'"A white witch," in fact! Honest Henri! He's a dowser, all right: finds water. I've known others. But he never told me nonsense like that. He wouldn't. He is full of sense.' He added, meditatively, 'All the same, the Loubiers, particularly Marie-Louise, have a sort of veneration for him.'

He drank water from a flask that he drew from a pocket of his workman's jeans and asked whether he should go to the spring and get water for her. Juliet told him she wasn't thirsty except for sensible talk.

'There are things I would like to consult you about – extremely confidential things.'

'You look serious! Not trouble, I hope?' He was sitting up.

'I don't know, and that is the trouble,' she replied.

She told him about René's harshness to Terka and he listened. His listening was different from her father's, and the little air of flippancy she had tried to assume, because it was what one produced for Frith, was quickly dropped. When she described Martine's uneasiness, her frightened plea and her weeping, he said vehemently, 'It's damnable, this sort of thing.' When she spoke, a little distressed, of how she had refused that plea and René's request, also, Michael said firmly, 'There was nothing else you could do.'

'I thought of going to visit Terka,' she told him. 'In fact, I was on the way.'

'Were you, indeed?'

He looked at her and that gradual smile, as though something he saw in her pleased and amused him, came into his face.

'In order to scotch the nonsense?'

'I … I suppose so. To try to understand her, first.'

'You know she is supposed to possess the evil eye?'

'Is *that* it? Gosh, I am stupid I never guessed!'

'That, and a whole crazy jigsaw of other things of the sort. Colette and old Emma have been solemnly warning me.' He looked at her quizzically. 'Do you still want to go?'

'There is all the more reason to.'

'I think that's an awfully sound idea.'

He didn't much like her notion about the fortune-telling but she told him how it would amuse her father and how perfectly immunised she herself was from any danger of being impressed, and how hard it would be to find any other excuse for seeking Terka out in her camp – since she definitely did not wish to buy brooms.

'So that is who you were looking for?'

His voice sounded flat and sulky, like that of a small, disappointed boy.

'Yes. I just turned off because the noise made me curious. I never thought of there being a sawmill.'

'Nobody told you you'd find me here?'

'Well, you see,' Juliet responded gently, 'I didn't happen to ask.' And, to her dismay, she blushed.

84

Michael chuckled: 'I certainly asked for that.'

He heaved himself up, helped Juliet to her feet and detached a long burr from her skirt. 'Seems this is my lucky day,' he said lightly.

'Mine, too.' Juliet gave him a candid smile.

'I hope I won't be crossing our luck, leading you into the witch's den.'

'"We defy augury,"' Juliet replied, as she followed Michael down the narrow path, among the entangling briars and weeds.

Chapter VIII

THE TREE OF LIFE

JULIET HAD NOT been so foolish as to expect to see a gay garden and a painted caravan, but never would she have imagined this. It was a slum. How could Terka, with her fine air of pride, live in such ugliness?

The hut was no more than a derelict timber shack; its roof, a piece of corrugated iron, patched with an old carpet. There was no glass in the windows and no chimney. The ground all over the clearing was scarred by fires. Under an iron tripod, on which a cooking-pot hung, was a pile of ash. Skinny cats were prowling around a refuse pit. A cart stood with its shafts in the air; bundles of bamboo and willow rods were stacked in it and under it. Wooden boxes and tubs lay about everywhere. Some scraggy hens were squawking and scratching in a cage made crudely with wire netting and in another a huddle of rabbits crouched. A yellow dog lay asleep, looking as if he was dead. Terka was not to be seen.

'What horrible, sordid poverty!' Juliet exclaimed.

'It has got worse since her mule died, of course,' Michael said. 'She used to go trading all over the place – across to Roquebrune and over to St Agnès and Gorbio, Henri told me, and she did better in those villages than in St Jacques. I can't imagine how she carries on now.'

'Couldn't she buy an animal and pay for it gradually?'

'She wants to. She has been pestering Camille and Granerol, who have both got old mules they'd be glad to get rid of, but they won't sell to her.'

'That seems cruel, doesn't it?' Juliet said.

'Superstition can be hideously cruel,' was Michael's reply. They said no more; Terka was coming, a bundle of kindling poised on her head. She still wore the black bandage, but no shawl, no earrings, and her feet were bare. When she saw them she laid down her load, stood erect and still, as if a little incredulous, then gave Juliet a radiant smile. If the girl's visit had been a longed-for event, an honour, expected and well-timed, her welcome could not have been more warm. For Michael Terka had only a formal bow but she took Juliet by the hand and gazed into her face.

'So you have come to Terka, my sweet English demoiselle!' she said, in a satisfied tone. 'Ah, you are wise! So much good fortune awaits you, so much happiness; but where? That is the question: where? Here for a little while; there for a little while; never, I think, for long in one place. Perhaps you must stay or maybe you ought to go. The cards will tell.'

Terka had taken control of the situation and Juliet could only pick up her cue. She said diffidently, 'I could spare two hundred francs; will that be enough?'

Terka shook her head regretfully but then, again, came that brilliant smile.

'I cannot refuse you. It is too important. Yes! ... I will even, for you, do what I do rarely; I will read the Tarot.'

She disappeared into the hut and Michael came over to Juliet. His distaste for the business was unconcealed. 'Look,' he said, 'I'll go back a bit the way we came and wait for you. Don't stay too long. This is a filthy place. The whole thing is a bit nauseating.'

Juliet promised and he took himself away out of sight. She felt a moment's nervousness when he had gone.

Terka returned, transformed. She had brushed her hair, put on earrings and a fringed scarf and even a pair of red high-heeled shoes. She set a long board between two boxes and a piece of green baize over it, and on that laid a thick pack of cards. Boxes placed on either side of the improvised table made seats for Juliet and herself. Sitting there, in the shade of a tree, obedient, Juliet shuffled the pack. The cards were unlike any that she had ever seen.

'The Tarot will not spare you,' Terka warned her. 'It reveals everything. You will see your past and something of your future; what is good for you and what is dangerous; what you must seek, and what you must avoid ... Now cut the pack in three with your left hand, to your left.'

Juliet did this. The mood in which she had approached the reading was a little rebuked by the gravity and dignity that the woman brought to it. As Terka set the cards out in three long columns, her finely shaped head was bent over them. Her long fingers turned them face upwards, one by one, and she stood looking down at them. Wavering light, sifting down through the boughs, made the pictures seem to move.

Juliet wondered at the richness and art of the coloured designs that every card displayed. There were men and women, horses and monkeys and skeletons, wheels and towers; a woman driving a chariot; the Throne of Judgment; a bludgeon and discs and cups; sun and moon and stars and flames of fires – a bewildering medley of emblems and stylised figures cunningly interwound.

'Now,' Terka said, 'I have set out your Tree of Life.'

She stood brooding over the curious images as though they could speak to her. When she spoke, it was in a low voice which took on, now and then, strong modulations; her gaze, even when she lifted it to Juliet, seemed oblivious of everything but her mystery, as if no listening girl sat there.

Her finger hovered over the picture of a throned woman. 'Look! There she is, the *Impératrice,* sceptred and crowned! The woman who ruled your heart. She was close to you.'

Juliet's heart missed a beat ... 'She was close to you.' Yes, yes, when she was little, truly her mother had ruled her heart. Indeed,

indeed, they had been close. They had been close until Aunt Isabel, who didn't like children, who hadn't invited her, began to find fault …

Terka's gaze was resting on her, waiting, patient. Juliet nodded. This, of course, was mere coincidence.

Now the voice flowed evenly on.

'Ah, she had the world under her feet! There was money and company; much company.'

Too much company, Juliet reflected with a sigh. Parties for dinner at Monte Carlo; parties for lunch at Beaulieu; dances at Cap Ferrat. Mummie was so pretty, so popular. One couldn't ever see her alone … But how – how in the world did the gypsy know?

Terka's finger rested now on the gaudy figure of a man with a golden disc at his feet and another lifted up on his hand.

'There he is – the *Valet de Deniers* – the Knave of the Discs. Gold! He commands much gold. You are separated from her. There are tears.'

Gold! Money! Yes: it was about money, always, that Signor Frozelli had talked to her: about 'systems' – Every evening they were at the Casino; and about how you could wangle with exchange – All those visits to San Remo. And she needed money, often quite desperately. Frith couldn't have helped, even if he had wanted to. He was touring and not earning much …

Terka glanced at her and then looked down, her hand moving over two other cards.

'Opposite to her, see, the Strolling Player, with his staff and his bag and the dog tearing his clothes, and, above him, the King of Cups. I think those two are one. He is both. With him, money comes and goes; cups overflow but love is given to him. You must not give him too much love.'

With a lurch of her brain, as if the direction of the earth's revolution had been reversed, Juliet felt that she had been wrong. Nobody, no stranger, in this remote place, could possibly know so much by natural means. There *were* unnatural powers and this woman did possess them. Dizzily, Juliet listened, while the monologue went on and on. Every emblem, every combination of emblems, touched a live nerve or conjured up memories. It was true – the school had been a prison; and it was true – someone she loved had gone over the sea … Now, much more deliberately, in a voice so low that Terka appeared to be thinking aloud, talking only to herself, forecasts of the future began. There were a crowned woman and many bent staves.

'You see, she comes between you and him: the Queen of Wands. The wands are crossed between you already; but never mind; you are under the Sun.' She turned a glowing smile on Juliet and pointed to a card, lavishly coloured, in which were depicted a great sun shedding his beams on two little figures who stood, side by side, against a low wall.

'*Le soleil!* It shines on you,' Terka said happily. 'You have friends.'

'Yes, I have friends,' Juliet thought. She was tired. Terka was erect, now, staring, recoiling a little.

'But, see, the Wheel, your Wheel of Destiny! It is turning! The fates turn it; friends become enemies; safety turns into danger. You have stayed too long in one place!'

Two odious little figures, dressed-up monkeys, were spinning the wheel, while a crowned monkey sat above. Juliet wished Terka would end, but the voice went on.

'You are in danger there.'

A tower, not a house, it was, in the picture. Its summit was toppling; figures were tumbling out of it, while flakes of fire fell on it from the sky. Terka's voice was urgent and stern as she said, 'Leave it! That house is accursed!'

Now her eye was fixed on the second column where, about the centre, lay a dreadful picture representing death. A skeleton held a scythe and was mowing; around him lay severed feet and hands. Terka's fingers circled this card and moved to one near it which showed a hermit carrying a lantern in his hand. As if she scarcely wanted to be heard, she muttered, 'He, too, brings danger. The priest has to do with death.'

Juliet's heart was pounding; she didn't think she could stand much more, but it was at a gay picture that Terka was pointing now. A knight in blue and golden armour was riding a lively charger and holding his drawn sword in his hand.

'There he is!' she said: 'The Chevalier of the Sword.'

The fiery sword? That was St Michael … Michael … The Chevalier.

'Ah! Take care!' As if danger were imminent, Terka jerked out the warning and followed it with vehement words: 'Look look! The swords are pointing downwards and the moon is dark! He is leading you into darkness! He throws himself against Powers about which he knows nothing; Powers that he has not the sense nor the knowledge to measure. Keep far from his path.'

Juliet had not recovered her breath before the cards had been swept up and packed together and Terka was standing still. Her large eye had a wild light in it. She said, harshly, 'I have told you too much. Give me my money and go.'

Bungling, with clumsy fingers, Juliet groped in her purse and put the notes down on the table.

Terka took up the cards and the money and turned away.

She went into her hut and shut the door. Juliet moved away from the dreadful place, slowly, her heart beating out of time, her thoughts in confusion, to the sun-lit track where Michael was waiting for her.

2

MICHAEL HAD BEEN court-martialling himself. This wasn't fair. Juliet wasn't, apparently, engaged to be married or taken up specially with anybody and she had no one to look after her. He had felt a bit too pleased at meeting her again and, what was worse, had shown it. In less than four weeks he would be leaving. This would be just the briefest holiday comradeship and he would be a lout if he let her think, or wish, for a minute, that it could be anything more. He'd got to keep himself in hand and be a bit more casual, that was all.

So, when he saw her coming, he called out, cheerily,

'Well? Did you get your money's worth? Are you all armed to slay the bogey?' Then he saw Juliet's face. It had gone small and white and her eyes looked enormous, and her breathing was all out of control.

'My dear girl, what has happened? Come here and sit down!'

She refused. She shook her head and walked on, staring in front of her.

'What in the world has happened? You're all upset.'

'I'm all right. Give me time.'

He steered a course for the farm. She walked quickly, as if eager to get away from that place. Terka had frightened her.

'Damn and blast all fortune-tellers!' Michael exclaimed, only half under his breath.

'No; she isn't wicked; she means well.'

Juliet spoke as if her mind were focused on something far off. He couldn't stand it. He caught her wrist.

'What is all this? I've got to know.'

He could see she was having a struggle – wanting to tell yet afraid of saying something that she thought she ought to keep to herself.

He pleaded. 'You know you can trust me, Juliet.'

'Yes, Michael, I know that,' she replied. Slowly, she said, then, 'I think I know why people are afraid of her; but it isn't her fault; she can't help it; she shouldn't be blamed.'

'What do I care whether she should or shouldn't? The question is, what has she done to you?'

'It is just that she knows things,' Juliet answered, still walking on and not looking at him. 'She told me things nobody knows.'

'But, Juliet, you can't possibly ...'

She looked up at him, shaking her head.

'It is no good, Michael. No good telling me it is nonsense. I know you won't believe it, but Terka *has* some supernatural powers.'

'And you swore to me you were perfectly immunised.'

'I know I did.'

'She has impressed you, the charlatan.'

Juliet's high spirits were gone. To recall the eager pleasure, candid as a child's with which she had greeted him, and now to see her like this, made Michael hot with anger. This racket ought to be forbidden by law. He said, 'She foretold catastrophe, I suppose?'

'Yes.'

'To you?'

'Yes … No … I suppose I could escape.'

'This is insufferable! But, Juliet, you don't, you can't take her seriously? You can't believe that she, or anybody, sees into the future? It's against nature and reason, isn't it? Haven't we free will?'

She rested her eyes on his, longing for reassurance. 'How can I be certain? I mean, when it's proved that she knows my past, and by some supernatural means?'

'Supernatural my hat! That's an old trick.'

He was scoffing; he couldn't help it; but scoffing, he realised, wouldn't console Juliet. He must try another tack.

'Juliet – if you understood just by what means Terka knew things about your past would that ease your mind about all the rest?'

'You mean, if I knew it was just a trick? Oh, how I wish I could think it was!'

He said deliberately, 'Remember, your father is a rather well-known man.'

'Not in St Jacques.'

'St Jacques brews gossip.'

'Nobody here could possibly know the things she told me.'

Michael made his decision. Surgery was necessary. This would hurt her, but she had got to be hurt. This poisonous root of superstition had got to be cut out.

'Come and sit down – here on this hummock,' he said.

Juliet obeyed.

'Will you tell me what she told you?'

'I can't, Michael.'

'Why can't you? Aren't we friends?'

'Yes, yes, we are. But, still, there are things I can't talk about to anyone.'

'Listen, Juliet; and do understand that I wouldn't tell you this if it didn't seem important for you.'

Her eyes were on his face and he reddened, but forced himself to go on.

'During the last couple of weeks I've spent two or three evenings in the Coq d'Or. What do you suppose they gossip about in the bar?

When they've exhausted the prospects of the vintage and prices and politics and local feuds they start on the visitors. Every shred of gossip is scraped up. Young Ignace is an expert at it. It seems to be his function – to attract custom by picking up bits. He's not half such a fool as he looks. Well, I heard, there, just where your father was going to and for what purpose. I heard what kind of reputation he had in England, and … and so on. I heard where you had spent the last three years and about your fainting the day you arrived at the inn. It's a marvel I didn't hear you had stayed on. And I saw them handing round a cutting from a magazine.'

Juliet flushed. 'About my mother?'

'Yes … Are you angry with me for having heard?'

'I don't like secrets, Michael. I'm glad you know.'

'I told you', he said gently, 'only because I want you to realise that Terka could easily have learnt a great deal.'

Juliet was frowning, still unconvinced.

'I see that she could, yet I can't believe, somehow, that it was trickery. I feel sure she *thought* she was reading it all in the cards. She seemed to be *feeling* it.'

'You ought to know acting when you meet it.'

'But she knew even what I had minded; how I had felt.'

Smiling, he asked her. 'Have you never been told you have a transparent face? And Terka watched you, I bet, out of the corner of *her* eye. She saw every shadow, every contraction of a muscle, and heard every little change in the rhythm of your breathing, They are clever, these gentry. They have their technique. It's hereditary. But it isn't supernatural.'

Juliet bent her head, reflected, then relaxed with a sigh and gave him a look of measureless gratitude. 'You *are* a friend, Michael,' she said.

They walked on and Michael talked about himself – about his mother and his sisters and childhood memories.

'There was one rotten time when I was six,' he said. 'I'd like to tell you about it, Juliet, because I suppose it explains why superstition is a thing I'm apt to go out of bounds about.

'My mother was very ill and I was at my grandmother's in Yorkshire for months. She had this Highland lassie to look after me and her idea of keeping me under control was to talk about ghosts and bogies who'd carry me off if I didn't obey her, all mixed up with the flames of hell waiting for bad little boys. She nearly drove me off my nut. Fortunately for me, my father cared more about intellectual honesty than anything else. He made me take science at school and that quashes superstition double-quick. You've just got to learn what is and what is not proved and to recognise the laws of cause and effect. And when you do that, life begins to make sense.'

Juliet was listening in a way that was, he thought, more a boy's than a girl's way – oblivious of herself and of him, absorbing new ideas as a plant absorbs sunshine and rain.

'And that's why', he told her, 'when I see a girl like you, with your fine, honest mind, getting yourself all messed up in these myths and superstitions, I just can't take it ... Will you give me a promise?' he asked.

'I will if I can.'

'Promise to put that fortune-telling clean out of your head.'

She walked by his side for a while without answering and then looked up, troubled and serious.

'I couldn't keep that promise,' she said, 'but I will promise this: I won't let Terka's forecasts change anything; I'll *behave* as if it was all nonsense, even when I'm not sure that it was. Will that do?'

He responded with gravity equal to hers, 'I think that is a very brave promise, Juliet: it will do fine ... And now, after all that, aren't you beginning to feel hungry? I am, in spite of your sandwiches.'

Juliet laughed, 'Next time I'll bring a picnic for two.'

'Goody! And, do you know, we'll just be in time for supper if we hurry. You'll see what Marie-Louise's onion soup can do for body and soul.'

Chapter IX

THE GOAT

DEAREST FRITH,

Thanks for the gaudy postcard. It's nice that you are having 'pastime and good company'. So am I. It will be a thrill to see you as a double-crossing Secret Agent. Don't work your eyebrows too hard.

Sorry to have sent only scraps but the days go skeltering by. Yes: we're full. Two in all the doubles except three Poles in one who make litter enough for a dozen. They have a card pinned up with a white eagle on a red shield. 'My soul for my God; my sword for my country; my heart for women.' Nice of them to warn one, especially as they think waitresses are there to be flirted with. René, who is all propriety and consideration, has taken over their table himself.

Most of the clients are nice, but one, Miss Clements – she is all nerves, upset the whole place by losing a ring. Finally, she called me into her room, closed the door and, with tears in her eyes, implored me to give it back! You wouldn't have believed it *was me, saying in a smooth, cool voice, that she must repeat that in front of Madame! (Would it be Grandmother Cunningham popping out?) And you'd never have believed Martine could be so formidable!*

Miss C. *I demand that this young person's room be searched.*

Martine *(gently) And mine, no doubt? And those of the other guests?*

Miss C. *(shakily) It was my mother's: the only thing of hers that I possess!*

Martine *(firmly) You may recollect, Mademoiselle, that you twice left your bag in the dining-room all night, and nothing, I think, was missing? And did you not leave a parasol in the bus? I suggest one should commence by searching your own room.*

The ring was in the drainer of the wash-basin! But suppose it hadn't been found. Never, never, will I accuse a hotel servant of theft.

Later. Sorry! There is more to do every day but every day I'm able for more. I feel as if I were living on champagne. Can you imagine, after the squabbles and sulks and fault-finding and artificialities of that school, how lovely it is to be doing real things and making people enjoy themselves, and to see them smiling and pleased? I do bless you for fixing this.

No: I'm not overworked. Yesterday René gave me a free half-day and sent me up to his uncle's by bus. The Camille Loubiers invited me to supper and I walked in the forest. Michael was there. And I called on Terka and had my fortune told. It was a good two hundred francs worth – strolling player, and the house under the sun, and fire that's to fall from heaven and all. Michael says it is a mixture of spy-work and guess-work and watching my face. Isn't that beautifully rational? I'm becoming a rationalist. Do you like the creatures?

Time to go and do the beds for the night, 'with the sheet turned down so bravely, O!' I do think that is the limit of luxury, don't you?

Goodnight and happy dreams,

Your loving and happy
Juliet

P.S. The money has come. The postman came upstairs while I was lying down and spilled it out all over my bed. Thousand thank-yous.

Juliet fell asleep pleased with her letter; in the light of morning, however, she knew that it was far from being the spontaneous outpouring it seemed; in fact, it was camouflage. She had written like that to conceal from her father, and, perhaps, from herself, the change that had taken place in her. Those episodes of inn-keeping that, a week ago, would have filled the foreground of her world mattered not a bit to her now; but by recounting them in detail while writing in so casual a way about Michael she had been telling her own unbelieving soul that Michael's reassuring, protective friendliness was just that, and no more. For the glitter and tremor that filled those hours with him in her memory, the hush in her heart when she glanced at the future, were not permissible, not to be confessed to, even in her inmost mind.

She had tried, also, in that disingenuous letter, to exorcise a small, haunting dread; to diminish the shadow that the figure of Terka was casting over these radiant days. She was ashamed of her own preoccupation with Terka. Even on this busy Saturday morning in the crowded streets, with an immense basket slung from her arm and a long list of commissions to do, she found herself looking here and there for the tall form, the black bandage and the swinging purple skirt.

In and out of the shops Juliet passed, exchanging greetings, explaining about the special lunch that had to be prepared for tomorrow and collecting the carefully chosen vegetables, the spices and herbs and flavourings it required. All this was sweet and enlivening to her spirits; here she was no schoolmiss but a responsible woman with a woman's proper share of the world's work. It was queer, how every action, everything she thought and saw, had new and far-reaching significance to her now. She found herself looking at children with an interest that they had never stirred in her before and she knew that the smile with which she returned their greetings was a grown-up's smile.

The rue de la Pompe, when she returned to it, was loud with excited laughter and cries and she crossed the road to look through the railings of the school playground to see what game was producing so much noise. Was it blind man's buff? No; it seemed to be something new. The big, black-haired girl in the middle kept a hand over her left eye; whenever she twirled round and removed the hand the child she glared at would fall with a shriek. The dark girl was ugly and rough. She found a hair-ribbon trampled into the dust, snatched it up and tied it over her eye amid yells and cheers from the rest. Ignace Tissier dashed down from his favourite post near the washing-trough, ran to the railings and began scolding angrily:

'I'll tell her! I'll tell her you made a mock of her! Cécile Proux, you devil, you will be sorry for this!'

Cécile's answer was to snatch up a handful of dirt and fling it at Ignace shouting, 'Tell-tale! Spy!' and a fine variety of words of abuse. Juliet hurried on, disgusted. These were polite and civilised children as a rule. What had come over them? Was fear of Terka infecting them, too?

'I won't let it infect me, whatever happens,' Juliet vowed to herself.

This was a matter, now, of loyalty to her promise to Michael; of coming up to his standard and deserving his friendship. She was resolved that, although moods would certainly come in which Terka's warnings would seem portentous, would frighten her, she would act as though she had never heard them. Tomorrow she would visit the priest and give him Grandmère Loubier's message.

'The priest has to do with death.' How silly to have been impressed by that! Naturally, he had. He read burial services and administered the Last Sacrament. She would stay at least two months longer at this house under the sun and the sun's rays would be all the fire that would fall on it from heaven. As for the Chevalier of the Sword ... Well, she couldn't very well warn Michael that he was the knightly horseman and that he must not go out against occult powers!

'Forget about the gypsy,' had been Michael's parting advice. It would have been easier to follow if other people had not seemed obsessed with her. She could not forget Camille Loubier's angry growl when he heard about the fortune-telling, nor his mother's excited, voluble questioning, nor the nervous glances and silences of the girls. 'René will not be pleased,' the serious Marie-Louise had said. There wasn't much hope that René would not hear of it.

Claudette's story, told in a low voice while she walked to the forest's edge with Juliet and Michael, clung to one's memory, too.

'René loathes Terka now, but once he defended her,' Claudette had said. 'You see, when she first appeared in the forest – it was in Autumn, three years ago – she seemed to forget her misfortune sometimes. She was so full of life. She would come up to the door to sell things or exchange them for eggs and milk, and sometimes, walking about, she would laugh and sing. It made you shudder when she laughed and smiled and glanced coquettishly out of her one eye. It made you shrink from her. The Vial boys were at home then. They were not very civilised, those boys, and they made a sport of chasing Terka: they would screech at her and hunt her and throw stones. Well, René, you know, often came up here to shoot; he would be all day out in the forest with the Domenicos; and René is such a magnificent shot that we girls would often follow to watch, and Terka would creep after them, watching too. Somebody – I forgot who, said, once, that she and René – that they had known one another in the Maquis, but I don't know if that is true, Well, one day those Vial lads saw her behind a bush, watching, and they started to have some fun. It was only fir-cones they were throwing, but they cornered her and she couldn't escape. She began to shriek wildly, as if she would go mad, and René ran up. He caught Jules and gave him a beating there and then and the two made off and Terka flew at René and kissed his hand. Have you ever seen René in a fury? He can be terrible. I don't know what he said to her. She flung herself on the ground and we left her there, and that was the end of her singing and her laughing looks.'

One couldn't forget a story like that.

AIRLESS AND HOT though it was in the kitchen, it was good to spend the afternoon there, doing practical things. Maître Philippe Daniel, who had commanded, for Sunday, a *déjeuner a quatre fourchettes*, was a person whom it was important to please. Not only had he and René gone to school together but he was the most promising young advocate in Menton and a highly popular fellow. It was chiefly in order to advertise René's inn that he sometimes invited friends to eat there. The luncheon of four forks would cost him a good deal and it must leave nothing to be desired. The puff pastry must be made and the stuffings prepared this afternoon.

Martine, immersed in her craft, became her tranquil self again. With light, precise fingers and lips compressed, she chopped veal, pork, beef, garlic, sausage, parsley and onions and mixed them in the traditional quantities, proper for the stuffing of the courgettes, baby marrows, golden as custard. By rising early tomorrow she would have everything ready in good time. Eagerly she instructed Juliet, showing her the wrong and the right way to do this and that, 'For I know', she said, smiling 'that your Romeo likes good food.'

'Please, please, Martine, never call him that!' Juliet begged. 'If you knew what confusion I suffer because of my name! And we are friends, no more.'

Martine gave Juliet her wise, elder-sisterly smile and pinched her cheek.

'Never mind! We tease you only when we are alone … Do you not want, now, to iron your yellow dress with the little pleats? I am sure you will go dancing tomorrow night.'

Juliet shook her head.

'No, he is not coming tomorrow.'

Martine was obviously disappointed. She asked, tentatively, 'Is it not true that in England a man and a young girl may enjoy themselves together as friends even if they are not affianced?'

'Yes, oh, yes; they can; they do.'

'Why, then, will he not come?'

Michael hadn't said why, but he had been disconcertingly decided about it. If she would come by the bus on Thursday, he would meet her, he had promised; he would wait for her by the stone-pine that arched the road. About Sunday, he had said not a word.

Martine looked quite troubled about it and Juliet smiled as she answered her question.

'Perhaps because we are not in England,' she said.

2

JULIET WANTED to laze a little next morning but remembered that it was Sunday and that Martine and Marie both had to go to mass. She had just risen from her bed when she was startled by a cry from the yard. It was repeated – a long, grieved, 'Ah-ah!' Then she heard René shout and saw him bounding, half dressed, down the outside stairs. Martine was rumbling at the padlock of Mireille's stable and failing to pen it. By the time Juliet reached her, René had the key and was unlocking the door. Inside, the white goat was lying etched out and stiff on the straw. René lifted her head.

Martine, her fists against her mouth, struggled not to cry out but Marie, running out from the kitchen, flung up her hands with loud exclamations, asking whether Mireille was dead.

'She's dead; dead as a stone,' René answered brusquely as he came out of the stable. Something black ran out after him from among the straw; Marie uttered a shriek and René kicked at the creature which darted away, limping, leaped the wall and was gone. It was a black cat. Martine stared after it and her face became so white that Juliet caught her arm.

'She's been dead for hours', René declared, 'and there wasn't a thing wrong with her yesterday evening when I locked her in. I don't know how to account for this.'

Martine was asking in a shaky whisper, 'How did it get in? Oh, René, how did that cat get in?'

He did not answer; he was testing the padlock and key and his jaws were clenched. Marie and Martine gazed into one other's frightened eyes.

'The Devil knows how,' Marie said, and repeated, 'Yes, the Devil knows.'

Women were calling down from the bathroom windows, asking what was wrong, and Marie stood shouting answers to them until René ordered her roughly to hold her tongue. Martine went with Juliet into the kitchen and sank down, laying her head on the table, sobbing convulsively. When René came in she looked up at him in despair.

'What will happen next? This is a warning – only a warning. Oh, René, what have you done?'

He stood holding her, trying to soothe her with protective murmurs and gestures, but black anger was in his face.

Juliet wanted to escape to her room. She had only a coat on over pyjamas; her feet were in mules and her hair was tousled, but a bunch of agitated women in bath-wraps and dressing-gowns waylaid her in the hall. What was wrong? Marie had been incomprehensible. Ought one to telephone for the doctor, or the *sage-femme*?

Juliet heard herself answering calmly. 'It is nothing of importance: a small misfortune: Madame's goat ate something that disagreed with it and had died in the night ... I will bring the breakfasts in a few minutes. On the terrace, Mesdames? And yours? Certainly; perfectly; yes, at once.'

She hurried upstairs. It was twenty minutes to eight and the church bell was ringing for early mass.

Chapter X

THE DOG

IT WAS ONLY JUST POSSIBLE to keep pace. The news of the mysterious death of the goat seemed a magnet to draw people to the inn. The bar, which did little business as a rule, was so popular that the gabble of talk from it penetrated to the kitchen. Every table on the terrace was occupied, soon after the last mass, by people who came for apéritifs and lunch. Martine worked in silent concentration while René advised her, carried trays, gave orders to Marie and Gatti and Juliet and kept the wheels turning smoothly. If he had been conducting a military operation his discipline could not have been more strict. This quiet efficiency was shattered for a while, however, when Madame Bonin, fussing and bustling, her full, good-natured face set in a solemn expression of solicitude, arrived to assist. She had been an employee of René's father; had met at the inn the wealthy client who afterwards married her, and now, a well-to-do widow, lacked scope for her energies except when she was called upon by her married daughter at Antibes. She loved to reign for an afternoon where once she had served, patronising and instructing Martine.

If a close relative had died suddenly the good lady could not have been more full of exclamations, questions, and condolence. Martine's self-control began to break. The olive oil that she was pouring, drop by drop, into the wooden bowl, was nearly spilt.

René and Juliet had a *ratatouille* to prepare: bacon, onions, tomatoes, red and yellow peppers, aubergines and courgettes had all to be cut *en paillette*, fine as straws, and simmered together. The work demanded concentration.

'Listen, Madame,' René said firmly, 'Mireille is dead. She is also buried. A good neighbour has seen to that for me. She was a nice goat and gave good milk. Naturally Martine is upset. That is normal. I shall buy another goat, less delicate in the stomach. That is all.'

But Martine broke in, her voice tremulous.

'Mireille always knew what not to eat, and René himself examined the patch where she grazed and pulled the greens for her supper. Besides there was the ...'

Martine stopped, checked by a glance from her husband, but Madame Bonin, who was filling the water-jugs at the sink, completed her sentence.

'There was the cat.'

'We will not speak about this,' René ordered. 'One must not think about other things while one prepares food. In less than an hour Philippe's party will arrive ... Juliet, the round table in the corner, for five.'

Juliet, for her part, tried to shut out thoughts about goats and cats and go quietly about her duties. An inn, she perceived, was like a theatre: the customers' pleasure must not be shadowed by anything that happens behind the scenes. The show must go on.

THE SHOW WENT without a flaw. Maître Daniel and his guests, at their corner table, seemed wholly taken up with themselves; they were hilarious and either knew nothing of the Loubiers' loss or were deliberately ignoring it. The *poulet au vin* was cooked to perfection and extravagant compliments were sent to Martine. René was summoned to sit and drink toasts with them and did so with apparent enjoyment. When it was all successfully over Juliet felt exhilarated as well as very tired.

'You were magnificent, Juliette,' René said, making her feel like a trooper praised by his officer. 'And now,' he went on, 'as soon as you have had a little siesta I will ask you to take a message for me. I want Gaston Brocard to come; and please do not tell Martine.'

'I'd like to go out,' Juliet responded. 'I'll do it at once, before the rain comes.'

A storm threatened and the overcast sky diffused an oppressive heat. There would be thunder sooner or later, she thought. It was as well that Michael hadn't planned to come. She went to her room for her raincoat and when she came down again met Martine coming up to look for her.

'Oh, you are going out, Juliet?'

'Yes, just for a little, before the rain starts. Can't you lie down for a while, Martine?'

Martine's face was drawn and a hand was pressed to her side.

'Yes, yes, I will ... Please be very kind and take a message for me. It is to Father Pascale.' She caught Juliet's hands in hers, intertwining their fingers nervously. 'Tell him I implore him to come. Ask him to remember something I told him once that a good priest did in Flanders. Just say that.'

Juliet sighed with relief.

'Certainly I will tell him and surely he will come. He is the right person. He will make you see, Martine, that what you think is all foolishness, all a nightmare. The curé will convince you, even if nobody else can.'

JULIET KNEW the Garde Châmpetre, who had been helpful in the matter of her permit to work. Red-cheeked, double-chinned and portly, in his dark-blue uniform, wearing, as a rule, a small beret on his large round head, Gaston had been a popular figure in the neighbourhood for years. His home outside the village was a villa set back from the road that led from the Place de la Pompe to the old, high bridge which was called 'The Bridge of the Sheep'. It was on that bridge that Michael, having brought her down from the forest by the woodmen's path, had turned back and left her go home by herself. Gaston Brocard's round-eyed stare from the bench by his little gate where he sat, smoking, had made their goodbyes rather abrupt.

Gaston was not at home, nor was his dog, a famous fellow whose acquaintance Juliet had desired to make. The guard trained him from puppyhood to assist him and boasted he was the first police-dog in the Alpes Maritimes – a hero and a pioneer. René's message had to be entrusted to Madame Brocard, a wisp of a woman, who tried every wile to engage Juliet in conversation and educe the whole story from her. Juliet replied in accordance with René's instructions and made her escape.

She did not like this weather. The village was not a good place today. The close little streets shut the air out while clouds made a leaden lid over the roofs. Even the children seemed listless and nervous, sitting about, whispering, huddled in groups. Ignace Tissier was lounging with other youths at the corner of the chemin Jeanne d'Arc. When he saw Juliet he grinned, limped a few steps, and miaowed like a cat. The raucous laughter of his companions resounded in the narrow street. An old woman sitting at the foot of a flight of steps plucked at Juliet's skirt and mumbled some question, while others leaned out of upstairs windows listening for the reply. Juliet repeated the formula and passed on, feeling scores of eyes fixed on her back. The village which had so charmed her had grown sinister.

The priest's house was a minute and very ancient one squeezed in behind the church. His suspicious-looking, squint-eyed housekeeper left her to wait in a small parlour whose only window looked out on to a mass of rock. The dark room smelled of damp and mildew and the ceiling was stained. She heard the priest come down the creaking staircase. He knocked on the door and waited before entering his own room.

'Ah, it is you, Mademoiselle! How are you? And how is Monsieur Cunningham?'

His welcome was cordial. He sat opposite her at the narrow table, facing the window, and waited for her to speak.

First of all, lest she should forget it, Juliet delivered old Madame Loubier's request for a visit. A smile wove a mesh of wrinkles over the priest's face.

'Old Emma', he said, 'leads me into temptation. She knows well how I delight in a drive into the woods behind Monsieur Tissier's mare. Well, well, she is old. I must go to her before long … And the young Madame Loubier? Good little Martine? She was not at mass. I am sorry to hear of her loss. Is she well?'

'No, Monsieur le Curé: she is much distressed.' Juliet repeated Martine's message carefully.

The priest nodded. 'I remember very well. Tell her I will do as she desires.'

He bent his head, brooding as if in perplexity, then raised troubled eyes to Juliet's and asked, 'Does Martine blame the gypsy for this?'

'Yes: she thinks it is sorcery,' Juliet replied.

'There is a rumour about a cat: something their Marie told my Thérèse.'

'Unfortunately it is true.'

'Terka comes here to mass, sometimes, for her own irreligious purposes, although the forest chapel is nearer to her hut. This morning she did not come.' He paused, reflecting.

Juliet asked, diffidently, 'Do you think, Monsieur le Curé, that someone can have been playing a trick? Some mischievous boy, perhaps, like Ignace Tissier?'

The priest shook his head. 'Poor Ignace is a gossip and a mischief-maker; he loves to spread rumours, start squabbles, and so on and, out of mere contrariety, he has made a friend of the Romany. They call him her "Familiar" – a monstrous term. But he would not have the intelligence to play an elaborate prank and I do not think he would poison an animal.'

'I see … The worst of it is that Martine looks on the death of the goat as a warning and is frightened,' Juliet explained.

The priest sighed deeply and moved his shoulders as though some accustomed burden were beginning to grow too heavy to bear. Juliet thought that she understood and her own distress and perplexity overflowed suddenly into words.

'All this superstition', she exclaimed, 'making a happy girl like Martine sick with fear; driving kindly people into acting like brutes! And that poor Terka, who has been so dreadfully punished already – making people persecute her! I should think they will end by driving her out of her mind … Isn't it cruel and wrong and … and … and absurd?'

Juliet's vehemence faded away – Father Pascale had fixed on her such an astonished gaze.

'Poor Terka,' he repeated. 'You pity the woman?'

'Why, yes!' And Juliet added, forcing her courage a little, 'Don't you?'

His voice was quiet as he asked, 'How much do you know of her?'

Hesitantly, Juliet confided to him the story of her enterprise in the forest. She thought he would understand her motive but would tell her that she had been childish, and she wanted nothing more than to have the clinging shreds of her superstitious dread torn away. She was dismayed by the shocked look that stretched the priest's eyes when he understood what she had done.

'I know it was foolish of me,' she confessed.

'It was much worse than foolish, Mademoiselle.'

'Do you mean', she asked, 'because one may become impressed?'

He leaned across the table towards her and spoke with intensity: 'I mean because those cards are accursed.'

Juliet was astounded. The priest's face was that of a fanatic.

'My daughter!' He checked himself. 'Pardon me, Mademoiselle,' he said. 'You are not of the Faith, but I cannot, for that reason, refrain from warning you. Listen! Not only do those cards perpetuate the emblems of odious heresies – they are, I am convinced, the cards that Father Bernardine of Clairvaux denounced – but they contain, also, the symbols of occultism in a most base and dangerous form. There is no fathoming the harm that may come of meddling with them – the evil that may be evoked.'

Juliet heard herself protesting in a faint voice.

'But surely, surely, it is mere superstition? How can anyone fore-tell the future? Are we not to believe in free will? It isn't rational, is it? You can't, surely you can't believe ...'

'You are an educated Protestant. Have you not read the Bible, Mademoiselle?'

'Yes, but those Bible prophecies, that witchcraft, belonged to past ages.'

'And are you so sure that the spiritual laws governing us have changed? Beware of over-rating the power of our pitiful human intel-lect, Mademoiselle. The limits of what we can know by means of reason are narrow. What is to be "rational"? Is it not, with the presumption and arrogance of the sceptic, to despise wisdom garnered through centuries?'

His grave, clear eyes held hers; his pale face was illumined by the ardour of his convictions. 'Believe me,' he insisted, 'the forces of evil are potent, and we cannot know whom they may use as their instru-ment when they are seeking the perdition of souls.'

'Do you mean', Juliet asked weakly, 'that you believe that Terka's prophecies will come true?'

'As to that, I can say nothing, because I know nothing,' he replied.

'And do you believe', she asked with a sinking heart, 'that she has the evil eye?'

The priest sighed and leaned back in his chair. She could see that the whole question lacerated his sensitive temperament but she had no impulse to spare him. He was a man of learning and experience who had given deep thought to these obscure regions of belief and she could not go without an answer from him.

For a time he sat silent, his eyes half closed, his lips compressed but twitching a little at the corners, and when he spoke he was answering some question in his own mind, not Juliet's.

'They say she casts the *jettatura* – the evil glance; there are some who would swear to it. Whether they are right or mistaken, the belief does infinite harm. In countless ways, the evil sinks in.'

He looked towards Juliet and spoke half to her, half to himself.

'This was a sound Christian community only three years ago. Families were united; young people respected their parents; all, except very few, attended to their religious duties faithfully and obeyed their priest. Now, our young girls sneak away to Terka, purchasing her love-philtres and amulets and paying her to foretell the future. Wives placate her with gifts, furtively, deceiving their good husbands. They suffer secret fears and a burden of guilt, shrinking from confession ... And, in the men – in some who believe that she is a sorceress and also in those who refuse to believe it, smouldering fire of anger begins to burn. To cause that to burst into flame would be wrong ... yet what could be weaker than to allow this dark, creeping evil to go on increasing with impunity?'

There was a long silence. The troubled man brooded, his forehead on his hand, forgetting the girl who sat opposite in the darkening room.

'Father,' Juliet murmured at last and he stood up.

'Do you pray, my daughter?' he asked gently.

'Sometimes,' she answered with honesty.

'Pray for faith. Against such forces as these, the Church is the only refuge,' he said and added, looking at her compassionately, 'I will pray for you.'

'Thank you, Father.'

She was out in the street; out in the failing light and the falling rain, her doubts like a sodden garment about her, her courage lost, and her longing for Michael grown so intense that Thursday seemed an unbearable age away.

2

HILLOCKS OF DISHES lay about the kitchen; an armoury of cutlery; caterpillars of cups. Madame Bonin was wiping and talking, asking rhetorical questions, awaiting no answers, while Marie pattered about in enormous felt slippers, mumbling and nodding and putting things away on the shelves. Outside, in the rain, René was examining the wire-mesh door of the stable with Gaston Brocard whose big German sheep-dog, black and shaggy, nosed about in the yard. Martine, sitting at the table, polished knives with mechanical movements, watching her husband and listening unhappily to her neighbour's monologue. Her taut face relaxed when Juliet came in. She lifted cloths from the chair beside her; Juliet sat there and began polishing spoons and forks. The low room was half in darkness and the rain drove straight on the window panes. She saw René bring Gaston indoors and heard the two go in to the bar.

'What is an occasional pigeon or chicken', Madame Bonin demanded, 'if it will buy you peace of mind? She never asks very much – an old pair of shoes, or a bag of flour, or even a stale cake. I have never refused her – why should I? To do so would be false economy. As you know, Martine, there is scarcely a street in the village in which you will not hear of some misfortune falling on those who have crossed her – yes, and up in the farms, too. What, I ask you, happened to Antoinette Castelli, who threw a jug of water in her face? Her daughter and her son-in-law both drowned! And the Vial boys, who stoned her there in the forest? Jules killed by the land-slide, and Jean crippled. While all St Jacques', the widow boasted, 'knows that I have fabulous luck.'

Juliet tried to interrupt. She wanted to stop this outrageous tirade which was agitating Martine, but Madame Bonin swept her protests aside.

'And do you know what I hear now?' She approached them and leaned over the table. 'You remember how André Leclerc went to Menton, to complain about her to the police? He swore she was trapping rabbits on his land. Fool that he was! The police could do nothing and told him so. Terka pays rent for that cabin and has her rights. And what are a few rabbits beside the health of a beautiful young girl? That daughter of his – although he's on his knees for her night and day and spends a fortune in lighting candles, the doctor declares she'll never walk again. They say Terka followed her, called her, lifted that scarf and looked at her, and the muscles began to wither from that hour. And now little Cécile Proux! The girl will probably lose the sight of that eye.'

Juliet, whose temper was rising beyond control, recognised that name. She broke in. 'What is this about Cécile Proux?'

'Yesterday', Madame Bonin answered, heavily, 'Cécile made a mockery, in her play, of Terka's affliction and today the girl's left eye is a hideous sight – sore and swollen and oozing pus.'

'So it should be! That is easily explained.'

Overriding all interruptions, Juliet told the story of the trampled rag and the handful of dirt. Anger and bitterness edged her voice. It was with ignorance like this, such lunatic talk, that these women had worked up the whole witch's brew of terror and hatred, to persecute an unfortunate outcast and torment gentle souls like Martine. At the moment she loathed Madame Bonin. In her need to refute the curé and his warning she was rude to the woman. Martine looked at her in surprise.

'Don't you see, Martine?' she said, pleadingly. 'Can't you understand that all those stories have no more sense or meaning in them than this one? That this is the sort of thing that started them all?'

'Ah, Juliet, not all.'

Madame Bonin seemed in no way put out. She shrugged her large shoulders and remarked, 'That is very interesting. But it was not dirt that paralysed poor Angèle Leclerc.'

'Paralysed?' Martine echoed the word, appalled. Her hands lay still among her knives and cloths. Suddenly compassionate, Madame Bonin sat down and began to advise her to leave the village, to have her baby in Menton, in the maternity hospital. She, herself, would come and sleep at the inn; would take charge. Martine, however, shook her head in helplessness.

'How can I leave René?' she said.

Juliet rose, crossed the passage, and stood in the doorway of the bar – a thing she had not done before. René, seeing her, gave a sideways nod of his head to Gaston and the two men joined her, the dog at their heels.

'Get rid of Madame Bonin,' Juliet said, 'she is upsetting Martine.'

The dog's entry, dripping and muddy and with a laughing expression on his hairy visage, entirely changed the atmosphere of the kitchen. He was exclaimed over, scolded, wiped down, given tit-bits to eat and then took his place on the hearth-rug, definitely centre stage. The grandfather chair groaned under Gaston's bulk and the smell of Gaston's Sunday cigar added its savour to those already permeating the air.

'Madame,' René said, 'it rains. Upstairs there are eight guests who doubtless bore themselves. Will you have the goodness to engage them in games of cards?'

Juliet rejoiced to see that even that dominating personage had to obey René when he asserted himself as master of the house. Madame Bonin left the room with a good-humoured smile and a stately inclination of her head. There was stillness in the kitchen when she had gone. At length René spoke: 'There is nothing wrong with the lock.'

'Or with the wire mesh,' Gaston said.

'A corner could have been lifted and fixed down again, couldn't it?' Juliet suggested and René nodded.

'In any case,' Gaston said cheerfully, 'we are going to pay a visit to the gypsy; myself and Scoot.'

'Scoot?' Juliet repeated. That was how the name had sounded to her. Then illumination came and she exclaimed, delighted, 'Oh, he is a Boy Scout!'

'I present my distinguished colleague to you, Mademoiselle.'

He waved his cigar; the dog raised a floppy paw in a sort of salute and Juliet laughed.

'Yes, we are colleagues, almost equals I may say,' the proud owner boasted. 'Scoot has never known whip nor chain.'

Martine's eyes were fixed on her husband's. In a low, imploring voice, she asked him, 'René, what are you planning to do?'

'We are planning', René replied, 'to give Terka a wholesome fright.'

'The rain has destroyed scents; nevertheless, the dog will know if she's been up to mischief; and if she has he'll bark to shake the soul out of her body, if she has a soul,' Gaston declared. 'A bad conscience, you see, has a bad smell. Scoot always knows … But, we will need a witness,' he added.

René was looking out of the window.

'The rain is stopping. If it isn't too heavy up at the farms it will swell the grapes nicely,' he said. 'I'll borrow a motorcycle and go with you tomorrow if you'll leave it till three o'clock.'

He swung round at Martine's cry: 'Oh, no! Not you, René! Not you!'

René was standing beside her in an instant, his hand on her shoulder.

'Don't cry, Martine,' he implored. 'It is so bad for you.'

He hesitated, but not for long. His tone was conclusive when he said to Gaston, 'Get someone from my uncle's to accompany you. Thank you, Gaston. You are very good.'

Gaston heaved himself out of the chair, accepting dismissal, and murmured words of consolation to Martine. The dog was reluctant to leave; he looked into René's face, wagging his tail; raised sympathetic eyes to Martine, nuzzled her skirt and licked her hand, but, finding her unresponsive, followed his master out and across the yard.

'Martine, listen to me,' René insisted, then. 'There are two ways of dealing with Terka: your way has turned you into her slave. Now we are going to try mine.'

His wife was in tears.

'You don't know what you are fighting against, René. You can't know what powers are protecting her …'

As Juliet went upstairs she was thinking that if Michael were asked which of the two ways of dealing with Terka he would prefer his choice would not be appeasement: it would be war.

IT WAS PAST nine o'clock, and René had made his wife go to her bed, before Father Pascale came. When he left, nearly half an hour later, René accompanied him down the street and Juliet went up to Martine.

In the attic two candles were burning and Martine, her hair in plaits over her shoulders, looked, in the flickering light, like a sick little girl.

'Oh, Juliet,' she said, thankfully, 'you are good to come. Look, there is something I want you to do.'

She put her hand under her pillow, drew out a clean handkerchief, and, opening it, showed Juliet a ball of melted tallow or wax.

'Do you know what this is? It is a thing I talked about long ago to the curé and he remembered all this time. My stepmother told me about it. In her village in Flanders there was a witch. If she entered the kitchen when they were churning, the butter wouldn't come, but nothing would keep her from coming in. They were educated people, however, and knew what to do. They got blessed wax from the priest. One day, when the witch was in the kitchen, they put a piece over the door and she wasn't able to go out; when she tried to, she cried out and cursed and went frantic, like a bird beating against a pane of glass. At last they took it away, and she ran out, screaming, and she never returned. This is wax from the Easter candle. I am going to put a bit over every door. Put it up on the lintel for me, Juliet; put it where René won't see.'

So that was what the priest had done for Martine. Now the poor girl was confirmed in her dreadful belief that diabolical powers were threatening her. Juliet wanted to refuse but she looked at Martine's exhausted face and thought, 'She must sleep.' She pulled a chair to the doorway, stood on it, and pressed a bit of the wax into the lintel, far back, where it would not be seen, then returned the chair to its place.

'Goodnight: sleep well, Martine!'

'Juliet, Juliet!'

Martine's hand clutched hers.

'Promise me, Juliet! Promise you won't go away! You won't leave me until my baby is born? Just a few weeks more ...'

'Oh, Martine, don't ask me to promise!'

The protest sprang out and Juliet felt selfish. But all this was becoming too much. In three weeks Michael would have gone and she didn't know how she could stand it without him. She wanted to escape.

The word, as soon as it formed in her mind, shamed her.

What was she doing? Letting herself be infected by Martine's infantile superstition; allowing Terka's fortune-telling to control her, and betraying her promise to Michael as well as deserting her poor little friend.

She made an effort to conjure up more courage than she possessed and when it failed to come she acted from a reckless mingling of pity and pride.

'Yes, Martine,' she promised, 'I'll stay until your baby is born.'

Chapter XI

THE PENDULUM

SEEN THROUGH the square window, the vineyard glistened and Michael, who had been forced by the threat of more rain to sleep in his hut, went barefoot out into the lustrous world and ranged the heavens with his gaze. There was cloud, but a north wind was blowing it out to sea. The day would be fine. His spirits rose like a lark springing into the sky. The tune he was whistling as he douched himself from a bucket of rain water belonged to some song, he imagined, about a lark.

> And winking Mary-buds begin
> To ope their golden eyes:
> With everything that pretty is:
> My lady sweet, arise!

That was it. Michael grinned. The old subconscious giving itself away. But, right enough, a wet day would have been a blight. There was just no place where they could meet in rain. And it had been a week.

A squabble of birds was going on in the hazel copse. In the dewy air the scent of the pines was superb. What a place! What a life! There was Camille out already, coming slowly up among the vines, scanning the grapes with infinite solicitude. Was this the day? Yes. Seeing Michael, Camille beamed, flung both arms up and wagged his hands in a boyish gesture of joy. The rain, then, had been just enough and not too much. Picking was to begin. Michael decided, while he shaved and dressed, that he would give token assistance until eleven-forty precisely. Then it would be time to start for his rendez-vous at the *pin parasol*.

He chuckled as he glanced at the letter from his mother that lay on his shelf. He could just see her writing it, very thoughtful, very deliberate, walking to the window to seek inspiration by looking down at Regent's Park, and then choosing casual phrases with great care.

I can't help feeling relieved that the dancing daughter of that playboy, Frith Cunningham, and the silly unprincipled gambler he married, has changed her sky. As to the Bird of Paradise – don't forget dear Monkey, that you broke its wing and cried your heart out, and that crying was no use. Be a good boy.

She was a funny Muffin, he thought, smiling; so wise and consultable about most things but absurd about her only son – convinced that every girl he met wanted to snare him into matrimony. A man bound for the wilds wasn't all that much of a catch. 'Good?' he reflected. 'I've been a positive prig. Too good to be true. I've wasted a week. It just can't go on.'

A pity things had gone wrong down at the inn, but Juliet wouldn't be terribly agitated, he imagined. He believed he had managed to deal with that little attack of superstition: to quiet her heart and mind. He had never had a sweeter experience.

Work went cheerfully in the vineyard. The light rain in the night had been good. The vintage might be the best for six years. Georges Castelli, son of the family who owned the Relais, arrived on his bicycle and took his working station beside the vivacious, blushing Claudette. He brought the morning's news: the police-dog was still missing and Léon Granerol was still a very sick man. Michael was sorry for Gaston. He thought the clever Scoot would turn up but he remembered what it was like to lose your dog. Marie-Louise said serenely, 'If the dog is alive Henri will find him. He is coming to seek on the map with his *pendule.*'

The sun climbed, scorching the backs of the diligent harvesters with his potent rays. Michael left them at work, clipping steadily, filling the deep baskets with small, purplish grapes. He waited under the arch of the pine, grateful for its shade. He had time, while he waited, to take control of his exuberant mood: to remind himself that he was bound for the Gold Coast, where an Assistant Forestry Commissioner might not, during the whole of his first tour of duty, bring a wife – where, perhaps, conditions might make it unfair ever to bring one; and that Juliet was as loyal as she was sensitive, so that to trouble her peace would be utterly inexcusable.

She came round the bluff of rock, gay as a buttercup, with a big white hat on her head and pleasure alight in her face. Michael's cautious thoughts dissolved, were forgotten; he started forward but checked his pace when Gaston appeared in her wake, peering to right and left as he walked. He was a changed Gaston – ill shaved, untidy and dull-eyed, either from too much drink or too little sleep.

Michael's optimism was lost on the guard. He would accept no consolation from him or from Juliet. He was convinced that the siege of Terka's cabin – Terka cursing from her window, the dog barking enough for twenty – which Michael had enjoyed mightily, had sentenced the gallant creature to death. Scoot had vanished during the night of Tuesday and no trace of him had been found.

'Look here,' Michael argued as they walked towards the farm, 'even police-dogs have their private affairs.'

But no, Scoot had been above such divagations, it seemed. Every theory Michael advanced was rejected. No bait of poisoned beef, no trail of decoying aniseed, no drugged water, would for one moment have deceived that super-dog, nor would female wiles have seduced him. He was the victim of sorcery, fallen in the line of duty – a martyr deserving of a monument.

When Gaston had gone on to the Loubiers' for dinner, Michael said commiseratingly, 'His spirit is broken, poor chap. He'd rather never know what happened than prove Terka had broken the law and be forced to prosecute her. I hope it turns out to be only a case of "the dog he would a-wooing go". I sure wouldn't care to be any sort of a guardian of law and order in that lurid village of yours … I say, this basket is good and weighty! Let's see.'

In the centre, a bottle of wine poked up its head. They sat on a shadowed bank where the air was spiced with the perfume of sun-warmed rosemary. The wire basket, when opened flat, revealed within the napkin sandwiches of three sorts, salad and oranges.

'And Martine is so unhappy,' Juliet said affectionately. 'Well, she doesn't mean us to be – and I'm not …'

'Are you, Juliet?'

Juliet shook her head.

'Not now, but I have been – perplexed.' She selected the word with care.

'Is Terka supposed to have killed the dog and the goat?'

'She is, Michael, and even what happened about Cécile Proux didn't make Martine see what nonsense it all is.'

That story delighted Michael. In return, he entertained Juliet with a lively account of the contest between the guard and Scoot and himself of the one party and Terka of the other, with her tied-up, yelping yellow cur. 'Scoot had the last word,' he declared. 'Terka's threats sounded terrific but the hound's voice out-howled and out-lasted hers.'

Juliet laughed, but then an expression of worry shadowed her face. Michael thought with vexation: 'They are getting her down with their backyard tragedies,' and, to divert her thoughts, began to talk about himself – his years at Oxford, his three years before that in the Air Force, his forest vacations under tuition in three countries, and the formidable house-party at which, finally, the personalities of candidates for the Colonial Forestry Service had been appraised.

'Glory!' she exclaimed, aghast. 'Don't you all turn into porcupines? I would.'

He looked down at her. His lips remained straight but the smile that began in his eyes travelled all over his face just the same, and a chuckle showed in his throat.

'I bet you would,' he said. 'No,' he went on, 'I don't think most of us did. They really handle the thing awfully well.'

When he had finished his second cigarette and extinguished the stub with the utmost care, he asked Juliet whether she wanted to see 'the white magician doing his stuff', and they walked to the farm, talking about Henri.

'I like him,' Juliet said. 'He looks good.'

'He *is* good,' Michael responded. 'He's first rate. With his eyes shut, he can identify a tree's species by passing his hand over the bark or by the sound its leaves make in a breeze.'

He wondered what thought was dinting Juliet's cheeks. Oh, that wasn't what she had meant by 'good'!

'He's sound, too,' he went on. 'Completely sincere. He won't accept money for healing and he prepares for it by fasting and meditation. He lives alone, poor fellow. As Grandmère Loubier says: "What girl wants a husband who can see her thoughts?" No one will marry him.'

Juliet was surprised by a certain respect and thoughtfulness that had come into Michael's tone.

'Then you don't dismiss it as superstition?' she asked.

'I've been cogitating. They swear by him up here, and he doesn't use herbs or even manipulation. I imagine he brings a cure off by setting auto-suggestion to work. Auto-suggestion can kill, so why shouldn't it sometimes cure?'

'It can kill?' Juliet exclaimed. The thought shocked her.

'Fear can kill,' Michael replied. 'Do you know there are some places – Haiti is one – where men of magnificent physique will die if their medicine-man tells them that they have broken a taboo?'

A little shiver passed through Juliet. 'Even thoughts', she remembered Martine's saying, 'can injure an unborn child'; but then her mind took a leap. There was something she had been half afraid to ask Michael, but she saw now that it wouldn't incur his scorn. She said, 'There is a thing I wanted to ask you, but please don't be cross with me if you think it is foolishness.'

Michael smiled at her. 'When have I been cross with you?'

'You were, rather, over the fortune-telling, and it is about that. I wondered whether telepathy is a real thing, because, if it is, mightn't Terka have taken memories out of my mind? You see', she went on hesitatingly, 'that would account for her seeing things out of the past, but still, all the rest – her prognostications, and the evil eye, and cursing people – all that might be nonsense.'

'I'm afraid telepathy's a question I've given no thought to,' Michael replied. 'I'm certainly not in a position to be dogmatic about it, for or against. But it's a nice piece of reasoning. I think it's quite possible you have got something there.'

So Juliet felt she might cling to her theory. She was relieved.

2

OLD MADAME LOUBIER was alone in the kitchen, propped up in the bed that she occupied all day, for she would have died of melancholy isolated in her little room. Henri Bonavera had come but had been sent off by her to try what he could do for Léon Granerol, who, poor wretch, had been ailing for a fortnight, couldn't keep his food down, and was as weak as a cat.

'That wife of his is a slut and a shrew,' the old woman declared. 'She pretends to be jealous of him – as if any girl would look at that pink-eyed rabbit of a man! Claudette occupies herself with something better than that, but Agnès has to have her grievance to squeal about. A week ago, I told her to send for Henri, but she wouldn't, for reasons of her own. She got that new doctor from the village who is so young and raw he couldn't smell mischief when it was under his nose. I've sent Henri along, now, in spite of her, and when he returns we'll know what we will know.'

'You are a scandalous old woman,' Michael told her, and she cackled with delight.

Juliet had to submit to a volley of questions about the goat and the dog until, to her relief, Camille came in with his daughters and Henri and Gaston followed them. Henri greeted Juliet with his extraordinarily attractive, confiding smile. Grandmère Loubier clamoured at him. 'Well? Wasn't I right? Did you find out the truth?'

'I found out the truth and I think Léon will recover, but he needed no help from me.'

Henri turned to the elder girl, whose grey eyes rested on him all the time and who flushed when he spoke to her. 'Marie-Louise, will you, this evening, go in to Léon and give him his soup? Agnès is taking the bus to the village but she will have to walk back.'

'Ha, ha!' the old woman cried triumphantly. 'She is scared to death! She runs to the priest to make her confession! I was right.'

'Be quiet, Madame, or I must leave immediately.' Henri's blue gaze quelled her. Although his hair was white, he was a man still in his thirties and had force in him. 'Can you be still and neither chatter nor ask questions? If not, I must work elsewhere,' he said to her. Calming himself with an effort, he asked gently, 'How, if peace is not in me, can I give peace?'

Her walnut face was creased in a hundred wrinkles by her grin. 'Oh, I'll hold my tongue,' she said.

A roughly drawn map was spread on the table, the corners held flat by knives and set by Michael's compass. It represented the course of the river and the country on either side of it between lines drawn south of the sawmill and north of the Bridge of the Sheep. The legendary spot which had given the gorge its name was marked with a thick cross. Juliet recognised the forest track by which she had walked down with Michael a week ago. It ran steeply down from the sawmill to below the waterfall and came out on the motor road, just where the *route* cut through the woods.

Henri was restless; he prowled about.

'It is not good to attempt so much in one day,' he said uneasily. 'I fear very much that I shall fail to help you, my poor Gaston.'

Marie-Louise took a chair near her grandmother while the rest, standing a little back from the table, watched Henri's pendulum. It was a globe of metal about the size of a walnut which hung on a chain five or six inches long; at the base of the globe the metal came to a point. Henri stood with his right arm extended over the map, so still that the pendulum, suspended from the chain held between finger and thumb, hung motionless. Presently it began to oscillate. Moved to another point, it vibrated in the same way, describing a line at an angle to the first. This seemed to give Henri his indication – a spot just east of the cross. The *pendule* held over that point, began to gyrate, and soon it was swinging out in a wide circle. Vigorously, the motion went on, and Camille sighed.

'Anti-sunwise,' Henri muttered unhappily, and the old woman exclaimed, 'I knew it! … My poor Gaston, your dog is dead.'

The guard was silent.

Michael spoke drily. 'You got the result you expected, didn't you, Henri?'

Henri showed no resentment. He sighed and sat down, pressing his hands to the sides of his head, as though he felt pain there.

'It is possible that my powers are failing,' he said quietly. 'I am not a seventh son, you understand. We were seven, but one of us was a girl.'

'You have never failed in healing, Henri, never,' Marie-Louise said intensely and Henri gave her a smile that sent colour flooding over her face.

'She is in love with him,' Juliet thought, 'and Henri wants a wife. Is she afraid that he would read her thoughts? She doesn't look as if she had anything to conceal. They would be happy together; they are good.'

That was the end of the quest. Gaston declared lugubriously that his brave comrade lay murdered in the depths of the ravine and would never be seen again by mortal eyes. Sadly, he thanked his friends and left, to return to St Jacques by the afternoon bus. Camille and his daughters went back to the vineyard and Michael took Juliet far into the woods where not even the sound of the sawmill could be heard.

MICHAEL LOOKED DOWN at Juliet's thoughtful face. He had gambled, taking her to see Henri at work. But had he won? Juliet looked up and knew, by indefinable sighs, just what was in his mind. She asked gently, 'Suppose he had traced the dog?'

'I would think', Michael answered, 'that Henri had made a good guess.'

'But not that it was trickery?'

'No. He wouldn't know it, but I imagine the muscles of his finger and thumb respond imperceptibly. The *pendule* would simply enlarge the microscopic movements in them.'

'Respond, do you mean to his *wish?*'

'Not even that: to his anticipations, as they form themselves in his brain. He's what they call a *radiesthésiste.*'

'Couldn't it be to *knowledge* of some kind – like in water divining?'

'What? Over a map? I'd be surprised! Anyhow, it's not sorcery, Juliet.'

Juliet revolved all this, walking in the soft, lovely hush of the evergreens, in and out of sunlight and shade. Michael had set his heart on reassuring her, on ridding her of the dread Terka had left. She knew that and felt she could almost bless the cause of his solicitude. Now he was talking about trees. In no time Juliet had learnt to distinguish several of the conifers that grew on these slopes – to know the Maritime pine, erect and symmetrical, from the stone-pine with its heavy umbrellas of foliage massed at the end of the bough, and the Aleppo pine, with its rounded top, small cone and supple needles. Michael taught her to identify firs and pines of many species by noticing how the needles were bunched, and by the bark. He drew sketches for her. He talked about the diseases and the enemies of trees.

'These are natural woods and regenerate themselves naturally,' he said, 'but man has to help. The Aleppo pine, for example, needs soil kept free from weeds and needs sunlight and air. It has to be watched for heart-rot, and protected from goats – then there's the procession caterpillar.' With a smile, he asked her, 'Have you seen the blighters moving across a road?'

'I have, and I've taken such pains not to tread on them.'

'Next time, squash the lot.'

'Must I?'

'Yes; not with your hands, though.'

'Ugh!' Juliet grimaced.

'The brutes will strip a pine white,' he told her. 'All the fault of a monk of Cimiez,' he went on, solemnly. 'They damaged the crops, so he went out with bell, book and candle and cleverly ordered them to confine their depredations to the trees.'

'And they obeyed?' Juliet asked in a voice as grave as his own.

'Naturally, or they'd have been excommunicated.'

She said: 'Go on telling me *true* things,' and Michael described for her some of the countless intricate devices by which plants defend themselves against draught, frost and pests, protecting their health and their fertility. Juliet listened as if under a spell. She thought how, around them, leagues beyond leagues, beautiful trees were growing and spreading their branches, nourishing themselves with earth, sun and air; and of how, since the world began, the cycle of birth and life and procreation had gone on in accordance with strict, mysterious laws. She began to feel the urge of it in herself; to feel overcharged with the excitement of being young and alive and destined to pass life on.

Then she thought of the little haphazard chances that combine to bring something about – something which, when it happens, seems to have been inevitable: predestined for you when you were born.

Michael stopped talking because Juliet's eager responses and questions had ceased. He was aware of her withdrawal, as though some imagined distance were operating between them. They walked on. He was filled with a sense of wellbeing, and so, surely, was she? Her quietness puzzled him.

Chapter XII

THE HOUSE OF GOD

RENÉ HAD MADE the coffee before Juliet was down. Martine was asleep still after a bad night. Marie would come straight from early mass and Martine would go to the half past ten.

'It's a pity that you're a heretic, Juliet,' René said, with a slight smile.

René had altered. Gay and vivacious as ever with the clients, in the kitchen he was preoccupied and morose and, at times, when he looked at his wife, there was something like fear for her in his eyes. Martine, he had told Juliet, had taken refuge in endless praying; in their own room, her rosary was never out of her hands.

Martine did her work faithfully, nevertheless. She was down and had drunk her coffee by the time Marie arrived, bringing her usual budget of rumours and news relayed in the toothless mumble of which Juliet understood only an occasional word. The old woman was flustered and garrulous and did not seem able to deal with her apron-strings. Juliet and René went up and down stairs with trays. As Juliet came down after delivering the last she heard Marie say something about Terka and saw Martine start so that a jug that she had been holding was smashed on the tiles. René came in and caught his wife by the elbows. It was the Castellis, Marie repeated; driving down in their car they had overtaken Terka in her Sunday finery on the road. She was evidently coming to late mass. 'And she limped,' Marie whispered, as if this appalled her. 'She limped.'

'And would I regret it,' René said savagely, 'if she tumbled into the ravine? If her bones rotted there till the Day of Judgement while her soul rotted in Hell?'

Martine was clinging to him, distraught, and he was scolding, teasing, trying all means to quiet her, when Marie and Juliet went upstairs to tidy the dining-room. Marie was quite useless from agitation. '*He* did it; that is what is so terrible; he lamed her; I saw it with my own eyes; you saw it, also. He kicked her,' she babbled.

Juliet gasped. This had become a tale out of Grimm – no longer from the gentle Hans Andersen.

'Marie,' she exclaimed, 'you can't mean – the black cat?' Marie's head shook up and down but she spoke slowly, so as to be understood.

'They change themselves into cats and hares. People know it, up in the mountains. If a man shoots a witch-hare, the witch has the injury, and she takes her revenge. But it is through the poor little Madame that Terka will have hers. You will see; you will see, Mademoiselle. Her baby will be born with a club-foot …'

The gruesome prognostication went on but Juliet contrived not to listen or understand. The thought of what Martine must be suffering, utterly needlessly, through mere folly and ignorance, filled her with pity and something not far from contempt. A little later contempt melted away and amazed admiration took its place. Martine, in her old-fashioned black coat and hat and tight black gloves, was waiting in the shadows at the back of the hall, prepared to go to mass. She kept herself out of sight of the clients and she did not want René to go with her, yet she looked as if she did not know how to go out alone. René signed to Juliet. She went with him into his little office and he closed the door.

'Why don't you keep her at home, René?' she asked.

'She doesn't want to miss mass again. She would feel she had sinned. And inside the Church she knows she will be safe: the Devil himself couldn't harm her there. If you would go with her and make a little reconnaissance, Juliet: make sure Terka doesn't waylay her in the street. I know you are not afraid.'

'You are speaking as if *you* were.'

'What I am afraid of is Martine's fear.'

'But it is fear of nothing! You know that. Oh, can't you make her see?'

'*Do* I know that? How do we know?'

He paced up and down the small room, tormented; wrestling with doubt; thinking aloud.

'We pray to God and sometimes our prayers are answered.'

'How can we know others do not pray to Satan and that their prayers are not answered, too?'

'You can't believe these absurdities. You can't believe Terka changed herself into a cat!'

'No, no, I do not. That limp is a coincidence. But I know she puts curses on those she hates and that misfortunes happen to them.'

Juliet sighed, baffled. 'And yet you have insulted her?'

'I have. I have defied her. I don't see what else a man can do. Are we to prostrate ourselves? But if I have brought her malice down on Martine ...'

He rocked on his feet, his clenched hand beating his head, then crashed his fist on the desk.

'If only there were enough who had courage we could rid ourselves of the witch.'

'Martine is waiting,' Juliet reminded him. This outburst had chilled her. René, it seemed, was no more rational than the rest.

'If you would go with her? You are her good angel. Please go with her, Juliet.'

'Of course I will go.'

She ran to her room, made herself neat, put on her hat and unearthed her one pair of gloves, then went out with Martine to the sun-lit street.

THE CONGREGATION WAS a small one and very mannerly.

Footsteps were quiet, genuflections slow and complete, all movements subdued. The glances cast at her and Martine were brief. The pews at the rear of the church had been left empty and when, just as the curé and his acolyte came to the altar, someone was heard taking a place there, the wave of movement and whispering that passed over the people was no more than a breeze stirs in a field of wheat. Juliet looked around. Martine, who was kneeling, had not moved.

'Is it Terka?' she whispered, and Juliet answered, 'Yes.'

The priest, Juliet thought, looked very ill, as if he had prayed and fasted too much. She recalled their talk and how greatly it had troubled him. And indeed, he must be troubled, she reflected – a shepherd whose flock was distraught and threatened: who believed that their very souls were in danger from diabolical powers. Devotion and wisdom shone in his face. Was it possible that such a man could be so profoundly deceived?

Gradually the tension within her and around her relaxed.

The calm, ordered movements before the altar; the clear note of the bell; the rhythmic prayers and responses in sonorous Latin – all the power of that ancient, sanctified ritual, enfolded the congregation in an atmosphere in which they felt safe. Juliet grew less conscious of her separateness, more aware of the mood which united the worshippers. There was a sense of surrender, and, with surrender, release; an illusion, too, as the mass proceeded, that the flaunting, defiant presence in the shadows at the back grew dim, shrank and weakened, losing its potency.

She knelt with the rest while the priest, in a fervent voice, prayed that the blessing of the Lord might be in his heart and on his lips; she rose and stood while he read the Gospel of the day, and sat still, looking up, while he ascended to the pulpit slowly, as if with reluctance.

In an abstracted tone he read announcements about changes in the hours of mass; mentioned a collection for a chapel to be built in a mountain parish; read the banns for an affianced couple. A long pause followed. With troubled eyes he searched the faces of his congregation, as if seeking reassurance from them. When he spoke it was in a low, impressive tone, as though he were weighing each word.

He spoke of charity and patience; of tolerance and self-control, urging his flock to remember that vengeance lay not with them but with God; that theirs was a Christian community on whom the blessings of civilisation and education had been bestowed.

'I have taken the decision to trust you,' he said. 'It is because I lacked the – courage to trust you sufficiently that I hesitated to take a certain action which I should otherwise have taken more than a year ago. I hoped that it might prove unnecessary. I have sought, by private warnings and admonitions, to avert the danger from your souls, but, by many of you, my warnings have been disregarded. Your simple Christian duty has been overruled by greed and ignorance, by folly and fear. But, now, matters have come to my knowledge which forbid any more delay. Evil is among us and it must be cast out.'

It was as though a wave passed over the congregation, causing a cowering together and leaning over; a whispering and a sigh. Martine's hand groped for her friend's and Juliet gripped it in a hard clasp.

'There is a woman in this church', the priest said, full-voiced and erect, 'who wills evil. You are forbidden all dealings with her. You will neither sell nor give to her nor aid her in any way. I command her to rise, now, and leave this church, of which she has made use for unholy purposes. She is to walk out through that door.'

Very slowly, heads were turned. People near the back of the church stole from their places and gathered against the walls. No one remained between Terka and the door. Without haste, Terka rose to her feet and moved into the aisle. She stood there, erect and vital, a woman in the prime of her life, and looked straight in the priest's face. For a throbbing moment Juliet thought she was going to lift the scarf and she held Martine close; but Terka did not raise her hand. She turned, without genuflecting. She did not limp. As if going to some proud rendezvous, she walked to the door, opened it and went out.

The woman left a hush behind her such as is laid on a field by frost, then a great commotion spread over the congregation and all faces were raised to the priest. Martine, although she was pale and lay against Juliet's shoulder, neither fainted nor made a sound. mass was resumed and concluded; the priest told his congregation to go in peace. He spoke in an exhausted voice as though virtue had gone out of him. Outside the door was an excited throng which increased every moment.

'She walked away down the street', someone said, 'with the air of a bride.' When they learned what had happened many were aghast but others were relieved and even triumphant. Martine declared in a joyous voice, 'We are safe from her at last; she will never dare to come to the village again.' An old man who had heard her shook his head. 'The Devil does not give up so easily,' he said. 'Father Pascale is a brave man.'

2

MARTINE, WHO RETAINED, all the long, busy day, her mood of tranquility, turned to Juliet when nine o'clock struck and urged her to go to bed, but René, coming in from the bar at that moment, suggested, 'Perhaps fresh air would do her more good.' His eyes were twinkling as he said to Juliet, 'Put on your coat and take a turn in the orchard.'

She pelted upstairs for her coat, ran down again, but walked sedately across the kitchen and stood still outside in the shadowed yard. All day she had been fighting a tide of grief that was beating against her, threatening to overwhelm her, and that was yet the strongest joy she had ever known. She was in paradise, but in two weeks – two weeks from this evening – she would be alone again, her happiness at an end. She did not know how she would go through the rest of her days. Never would she regain the ability to depend on herself and be contented in loneliness. That had gone, and there would be no other man … When she saw Michael waiting for her under the olives beyond the lane, she knew this. She loved Michael; there was no part of her, mind or body or spirit, that did not love him and need him. But he mustn't know: she had a part to play.

He threw his cigarette down and stamped on it and helped her to cross the stile; then his hand closed on her arm.

'I just had to tell you,' he said, in his strong, quiet voice. 'I've had good news. It came yesterday. I'm going to Cyprus. You just can't imagine how much it means.'

Nor could Michael imagine how much it meant to her, to bring him back from dark African jungles and to place him in Europe, in a Mediterranean island, a place her imagination could reach to and wander in. Her joyous response made him smile at her, half surprised. He guided her down the chard slope towards the lower field where the river ran.

'It's nice of you to be interested,' he said. 'I'm a bit of a spoilt boy, wanting someone to shout with. My mother's to blame. Gee, she'll be so pleased!'

'And your sisters?'

'Oh, they're taken up with their husbands and kids; but it will be the world and all to my mother,' he said.

'Have you sent her a telegram?'

'I've got it with me, written out. Send it for me in the morning, will you?'

'Indeed I will, first thing … Oh, Michael, how enchanting Cyprus must be!'

'Gosh, yes – marvellous. Wild and civilised, sunny and European; the Mediterranean to swim in and hills – hills where the climate in summer is all you could wish …'

He paused, gave Juliet a startled glance, as though afraid she would think he had said something he had not meant to say; strode on alone, then waited for her and began, confusedly, to tell her about the man who was leaving the post.

'I met him after his first tour of duty when he came back for the refresher course. They won't like quitting; the big campaign against forest-fires has been won, but there's no end to be done. They have their house in the forest and a car and go to the capital every fortnight, and the Cypriots are fine colleagues. The Aleppo pine is extremely important and …'

Michael was talking about the increase of conifers while Juliet was wondering why he had said 'they'. Now he was talking of the nearness of Crete and of the journey out – Venice and the Greek Islands and the Acropolis. She couldn't find one word to say.

'It sounds like a dream.' She heard herself murmur that flat, inadequate phrase and saw Michael's face change. He looked at her a little repentantly. When they reached the brink of the steep drop to the river they stood still.

Darkness was falling but faint light survived. The thread of water that was the river shimmered in its deep bed. Everything had colour still but all the tints were dim and overlaid by a silver patina shed by the moon. It was a scene of peace.

Now Michael was asking about Terka, about the fantastic story that had travelled up to the farms. Juliet told him, briefly, that it was true and that Martine believed the danger over but others thought that Terka would take her revenge. 'I want not to think about her,' she said.

'Fine! Let's chuck her into the river.' He took up a stone and flung it. It sank. 'Goodbye to Terka and all her works!'

Juliet wanted to let her thoughts live in Cyprus; visualise those forests; see Michael there, at work. He was going to be important. She imagined his mother acting as hostess for him, pouring out tea for administrators and diplomats. She was thankful there wasn't much light.

'I'm terribly glad for you, and for your mother,' she said, and asked whether he had to go home. He imagined it wouldn't be necessary. He'd been back and got his equipment in August. If anything had to be altered his mother could probably be able to see to it. It would all be shipped Marseilles or Genoa. He'd sail at the end of the month, probably, on a Greek ship. His tour with his mother wouldn't be cut short. He took the wire he had drafted out of his pocketbook and gave it to Juliet.

'I'll send it first thing,' she promised. She wished her voice hadn't sounded so small.

Michael turned and they walked up the hill and into the shadowy dip of the olive field. When Michael spoke it was casually.

'I have to pack my notebooks and specimens. There's a biggish job to be done – mounting and labelling. I wonder if, on Thursday, you'd come up and give me a hand?'

Juliet did not know how to answer. She did not know how, now or ever, to let him go. One should fight for one's life; yet nothing mattered so much as that Michael should not find out. She decided to refuse.

'I would like to,' she said.

'Of course, I mean if it's fine.'

'Of course.'

They crossed the lane and paused at the little gate in the wall that bounded the yard of the inn.

'Goodbye then, till Thursday, Juliet.'

'Goodbye, Michael.'

But he didn't go. He stood there, looking at her, not smiling, not, even, like a friend. It was a stern, almost angry look. He didn't put out his hand. It was Juliet who moved. The kitchen was empty with one lamp burning. She went in and locked the door and when she looked out of the window Michael had gone. She closed the curtains and put out the light. She thought, 'He is going; and when he has gone my life will be like an empty room.'

Chapter XIII

THE CUPS

DEAREST MUFF,

You should get my wire some time today.

I've made three attempts to write tactfully but it's no use. I can imagine how happy you are about Cyprus but you can't begin to guess how much it means to me.

The snag is, I can't, now, meet you in Paris or Amiens. We can't have our tour. I want you to spend those two weeks somewhere near here, instead. And please, like the Senior Wangler you are, do fix it that I don't have to come home.

Now you'll have guessed, because you know there is only one thing that would make me let you down. Your letter, my dear Muff, was nonsense – the most enraging nonsense that ever dripped from your learned and fertile pen. Just how far out you are about Juliet I won't waste time trying to say – having torn up three attempts.

She is at St Jacques and I have to see more of her. There's just about a month left before I sail and I think it might be enough.

I am almost quite certain about myself and I don't think there is anyone in my way. The trouble is, Juliet is so sensitive and so lacking in self-confidence; so incapable of coming halfway or even quarter-way, that one has to be as wary as a bird-watcher – a Bird-of-Paradise watcher, if you like. The timing would have to be right. And you know what a clumsy mutt I have always been. So I need the whole month. I know you will understand.

Meanwhile, a rather grim situation is blowing up in these parts – a vent de crise – and the inn where Juliet is working is in the middle of it. Actually, it has helped a lot, but now I'm afraid it is making Juliet ill.

Please – what are you doing about my room? Keep it free for the autumn, would you, for a bit? If the gods are with me I'll be getting a home ready in Cyprus and my girl will be wanting somewhere to wait, and very, very much needing a friend.

Bless you, my blessed, forgiving Muff,
your loving MONKEY.

P.S. Don't forget amber lamps. Let me know where to book a room, and for when. Driving, you can't arrive till the Wednesday, I suppose – the 15th. Terribly sorry you'll have that long drive alone.

It wouldn't have been so hard, Michael thought, as he read and stamped his letter, if only his father had been alive. Getting this alone, being alone with all the anxiety it would cause her, wouldn't be too good. But it couldn't be helped.

The grape-picking was finished and that was as well, because a dull sky threatened rain. Glad to be spared the temptation of sunshine, Michael set to work in his hut. There was quite a biggish job to be wound up: his memo on the Aleppo pine to finish; specimens to be sorted, ready for mounting, with his sketches, and photographs. When all that was done he would have the beginnings of a handy file of his own about Mediterranean conifers.

It had been a brainwave to ask Juliet to help, because ... well, because this was the side of forestry work that could have no romance or fascination about it for a poetic temperament, and if she took to it – if she was happy, grubbing indoors with labels and paste and dead moths and things – well, it would make one easier in one's mind.

Satisfied with his personal dispositions, Michael spent a long and profitable afternoon oblivious of all problems unconnected with trees, until ravenous hunger sent him down to the house, and after supper he shut himself up with his notebooks and collections again, working by the light of his lamp in the silence that he loved.

2

THAT WAS NO MOTH knocking against his window. Startled, Michael dropped his magnifier and the dry leaf beneath it was crumbled. However, it could be replaced. Pulling the muslin aside he saw, staring in, the pale face of Marie-Louise. When he opened the door she caught at his arm.

'Please come, Michael,' she panted. 'They are talking so wildly – all of them, all have come. They pretend it is to ask my father's advice, but it is really to make him responsible too. Some of them have knives and César Domenico has a gun.'

As a rule, the farmhouse was silent by nine o'clock, with lights out and door and shutters bolted. Now, through the half-open door, lamplight and raucous sounds poured out. The clamour ceased as Michael entered the kitchen and Camille called out a welcome to him.

He was not welcome to the rest. No one rose to shake hands and their nods were belied by sullen, distrustful looks. There were eight seated round the table: Granerol, yellow-visaged and emaciated; the three Domenicos – swarthy fellows whose faces looked congested with anger; the Vial boys, both under eighteen – Paul flushed and Pierre very pale; Georges Castelli, scarcely recognisable as Claudette's gay suitor, and his long-faced, responsible brother, Anton. Camille stood behind Georges. With a jerk of his head, his daughter was ordered upstairs to her room. She obeyed, casting a glance back at the small door beyond the cupboard from which the shrill calls of the grandmother could be heard. The men paid no attention to them, but it was not until Michael had withdrawn into a shadowed corner that their discussion was resumed in muttering, guttural tones.

Michael, who knew every one of these men, was astounded by the alteration in them. Most of them were young; the sons of wine-growers and agriculturists; good workers and skilled: types of the stable element, he had thought them, in the economy of France. Now, in the light of the oil-lamp that burnt on the table, their eyes seemed to smoulder under drawn brows; nostrils were dilated and jaws set taut; they breathed like men overwrought. They looked vengeful and frustrated and afraid.

'I swear I will face her,' a young voice declared. 'I am not scared.'

Much that was said Michael could not comprehend, but he understood a phrase now and then.

'Then you are a fool!'

'It must be at night.'

'A night without moonlight. Tonight there is thick cloud.'

Those were older men speaking. Young Pierre raised his voice again.

'Yes, it must be tonight. How can we face our mother tomorrow otherwise? It was her curse that destroyed our brothers and Maman has waited for us to be men. And now the curé has given the sign.'

A chorus answered him.

'He has denounced her from the pulpit.'

'He has said it in public.'

'He has denounced her as a sorceress.'

'I don't believe it. Who heard it?' Michael said, thrusting himself among them.

'My wife heard it,' Granerol answered. 'She was there. The curé had expressly bidden her …'

'You ought to know, Léon!' Anton Castelli cried with a harsh laugh.

César Domenico silenced him with a snarl.

'I have a plan,' he said and the rest listened.

'Is not her name "Fontana"? She is Italian. Anton – your car is in order? We will seize her tonight, tie a sack over her head and smuggle her over the frontier. That will mean an Italian prison for her and …'

'Seize her?' impatient voices demanded. 'Easily said! How is that to be done?'

'While she's asleep.'

'That yellow bitch of hers yelps to wake Hell.'

César gave in.

'True, I forgot the bitch.'

A moment of brooding silence was ended by Paul Vial, thumping the table with his fist.

'She must be shot!' he declared. 'She is a murderess.'

Heads were nodded but no one spoke until Granerol muttered, 'Ay, and she tried to make a murderess of my wife; ay, because I refused to sell her a mule. Agnès, the fool, went to her for a philtre. She swears it was for my stomach but I know better ...'

A burst of ribald laughter relieved the tension but Granerol's grating voice went on:

'I nearly retched the soul out of my body. That's why the priest denounced her. That's what made him do it at last.'

Michael asked sharply, 'What has become of the stuff?'

'I threw it on the weed fire, bottle and all. It made a sulphurous smoke.'

'Shooting's the only way,' Pierre urged. Neither boy wished to be outdone by his brother. 'Shoot her', he said, 'in the back of the head.'

Camille put his hands on the lad's shoulder.

'So that your mother may lose two more sons, and this time to the guillotine?'

He spoke quietly and there was a restless stir. Georges muttered: 'No court would condemn a man for killing a witch.'

'But they would,' Camille replied. 'There are laws. Do I want an assassin for a son-in-law?'

'What is your own proposal, then, Camille?' Marcel Domenico called, and his younger brother cried, jeeringly, 'Where's your brave nephew? Why is René not here? He is the one who is always talking about getting rid of the witch.'

Camille answered firmly:

'René is a civilised man and what he and I propose is a civilised process. Isolate Terka. See that your womenfolk and that idiot, Ignace, cease aiding and feeding her. Starve her out of the district ...'

He was shouted down. That, they declared, had been tried and had failed and had brought curses and disaster on those who had attempted it. With a shrug Camille turned away.

César, who seemed to exercise a kind of leadership, now said in heavy, impressive tones: 'There is only one thing to do. It must look like an accident. We must all be in the attempt: every one.' He bent a suspicious look on Michael. 'The Englishman also, lest he should give us away.'

'I'll be no party to an attack on Terka. I believe she's an innocent woman, and in any case ...'

Michael's words were drowned by shouts of fury. 'Innocent! She?'

He had so enraged them that they lost all caution, and disregarding his presence, proceeded, heads close together over the table, to devise their plan. Camille left the room, disappearing into the cellar by the ladder that was reached by a trap-door. The bitch was to be poisoned; boards were to be nailed over the window and door of the cabin and its timbers set on fire.

So outraged was Michael that he lost control, seized Georges by the shoulders, pushed him aside and stood at the table, blazing at the men. His indignation gave him fluent if crude French.

'Idiots! What is it that you are going to do? Will you start a conflagration among firs and pines, dry after the summer? Is it your wish to burn the forest?'

With respect, they listened. Some of the men assented: 'C'est raisonable,' these agreed; but others declared that some risk must be taken; the sorceress must be destroyed. Michael turned to Camille, who had returned with bottles and who signed to him to set glasses before the men. Puzzled, Michael obeyed. He hoped that the colourless liquid Camille was pouring out was as innocuous as it looked. He took none. He needed a clear head. While the men, placated and quieted for the moment, drank and exclaimed with appreciation, he had time to think.

The atmosphere they had created was dangerous. He had been infected himself. He'd listened to plans to burn a woman alive and excited himself only about the trees. What black spell had come over the place? César, he was sure, would not stop at crime, nor would those Vial boys, and the rest would not have the courage to stand out. Now, one by one, they seemed to be consenting to César's horrible project. They were discussing how to deal with the bitch.

Camille joined in, to Michael's amazed disgust, while filling glasses generously again. He even discussed the matter in detail, showing the difficulties about his method or that, himself suggesting another, and then deciding that it would not do. It was not until Michael caught a glance, followed by a wink, from the crafty old man, that he understood. Then Michael sipped the drink. It was as potent as brandy – Camille was sacrificing the most treasured produce of his vines – his Marc.

The discussion mounted, grew excited, fantastic; grew infused, incoherent, quarrelsome. Camille's conclusion that the whole plan needed long and careful preparation was acceded to, after a while. The Castellis remembered that they had a dangerous walk before them along by the gorge and the Vial lads, who had drunk less than the rest but were sad and subdued, offered to accompany them. Granerol fell asleep over the table and the Domenicos, who were his neighbours on the west side, hauled him up and said they would see him home. Rain was falling. They would all get a wetting – and it would do them good, Michael felt.

When, at last, all were gone, Camille stood regarding his littered kitchen, that stank with the fumes of strong tobacco and oil from the smoking lamp. The floor was filthy. There was a shot-gun under the table, also a broken glass.

He inverted two empty bottles and smiled ruefully.

'I'd saved them for Claudette's wedding,' he said. 'Perhaps,' Michael reminded him, 'it has saved her fiancé for her.'

Camille nodded.

'Georges is not usually a fool.'

'What about tomorrow?' Michael asked him and Camille replied, thoughtfully, 'They will not attack Terka in cold blood. Their fear of her is too deep. But she should leave.'

'Surely she will, after what the priest has said – whatever it was.'

'I wonder', Camille said, between enormous yawns, 'just what the good curé did say.'

Walking through the darkness up to his hut, Michael thought of the strange dilemma the gentle priest must have felt himself to be in if he truly believed that Terka was the instrument of diabolical powers, and of what he would feel if he guessed at the vile reaction that his words in the church had produced. Poor Father Pascale!

The wet earth and the trees were giving out fresh scents. Michael breathed them gratefully, and lifted his face, receiving the cleansing grace of the rain.

Chapter XIV

THE COACH

THE SAWMILL WAS QUIET, and Henri, who was working alone with a plane in the shade, heard Michael's whistle and looked up. With quick and precise gestures he signified that he would finish what he was doing in five minutes and would come along. Michael lit another cigarette and waited for him. At all times, Henri seemed ready to walk and talk. He was a man who read books, observed the stars, contemplated the habits of plants and creatures, had swarms of questions in his head and nobody to discuss them with. Michael found it a bit embarrassing, sometimes, to be regarded as a learned and travelled man with whom it was a privilege to converse. Actually, he enjoyed Henri's companionship just as much as the lonely fellow liked his.

The morning was young and the sun had not yet dried up the moisture from last night's rain; drops from weeds and branches spattered the two as they made their way round the knoll towards Terka's camp.

'You do right to warn her,' Henri said when he had been given an account of the meeting at Camille's. 'I agree that they are not likely to organise an attack on her now, unless she does something new to enrage them, but if a man were out with a gun, for example – and there is much scaring of birds just now – and saw Terka, I think he might be tempted to shoot.'

'That is what I'm afraid of,' Michael told him. 'They seem to have interpreted whatever the curé said as a license to kill. They were barbarous, Henri. Why is it that people seem to change, as soon as they even speak about Terka, into something entirely unlike themselves?'

'It is from fear.'

'Fear of witchcraft almost bewitching them? … Yes,' Michael went on slowly, 'it is a case of fear of an unreal danger creating a real one. I suppose that is happening all the time. I suppose it causes wars.'

'Why do you say "unreal"?' Henri broke in. 'I ask myself if it is possible for men like you, Michael – Protestants, sceptics – to comprehend how terrifying the threat of witchcraft is? There is no way to combat it, no way to escape, no way to end it except by the witch's death.'

Michael was astounded. This from Henri!

'But *you* are not afraid of her!' he exclaimed.

'I do not wish, just now, to confront her. She will know that it was I who persuaded Agnès Granerol to confess to the curé.'

'She will know? How?'

Henri did not answer and Michael realised that argument would be useless and insistence unkind. At the brink of the clearing he paused and asked Henri to wait for him. 'By the way,' he said, smiling, 'I'm to tell her that if she swears that she'll leave this district immediately, Camille will sell her the mule.'

Henri's eyes stretched incredulously.

'But,' he exclaimed, 'Camille must not do that!'

'Why on earth not? It is surely the one sensible, practical thing. Without an animal, how can she move her gear?'

'He would be disobeying the priest.'

'I am certain Father Pascale would agree.'

'It would be felt he was betraying his neighbours. They do not discriminate. They will take it, if Camille trades with her, so may they. It would spoil his good influence.'

It was really all very difficult, Michael thought. Wheels within wheels. What on earth was to be done? While he stood, perplexed, he saw Henri's face light up with his childlike, innocent smile.

'It does not matter what I do,' Henri said. 'I am outside – alone. It will be all right for me to sell her the animal – Camille has only to sell it to me. If you will negotiate?'

Michael's outburst of laughter surprised him, but his own smile broadened. Michael clapped him on the shoulder, saying, 'Okay! I'll negotiate – you wily old casuist!'

HE CAME ALONE to the clearing and looked down at the ugliest sight that had met his eyes since the War. The door of the hovel hung open; smoke and ash drifted from piles of charred rubbish – rags, pots and tins. The rabbits were very dead; not a living creature was to be seen; a stench of destruction hung in the air. His first thought was thankfulness that Juliet would not see this.

Joining him at his call, Henri went forward with him, appalled. On a rough gibbet, five rabbits hung strangled. The mule-cart was there, its shafts tilted up, and near it a swarm of flies and bluebottles buzzed. The slab of stone they hovered over was red and the object that lay on it was a cock: a black cock without a head. When Henri saw that, he turned away, all the colour gone from his face.

They went into the cabin. It was no more than one room with a dirt floor. Beside the hearth of stones was an iron grill and in one corner a pile of straw and rags had evidently served as a bed. They saw a pestle and mortar but no tools. Twigs and bamboo-canes and a half-made basket lay on the floor; there were also a soldered kettle, a pair of broken boots and a piece of leather; a torn petticoat with a needle, threaded, stuck in it, and a ragged coat. A pitiful fight for existence had gone on here.

Curious odours permeated the cabin. They were accounted for by bunches of herbs that hung from the rafters. These, they took outside and examined. Michael recognised, besides wild mint and thyme, box and savory, myrtle and rosemary – common herbs of the Maquis, some harder to find – hyssop and fennel and marjolaine. There were twigs of the bush spurge which, Henri told him, were sometimes thrown into water to stupefy fish. There were others that he did not know.

'Are any of them poisonous?' he asked Henri, who seemed to have identified all of them and was separating them into piles.

'These are narcotics,' he answered, 'and that is said to be aphrodisiac. This is the "squirting gourd": it causes vomiting. At one time winegrowers used to spray grapes with it – a few tempting clusters – to stop thieving ... I do not see anything that would kill: there is no oleander ... but this, I think ...' He lifted a twig with small opposite leaves and examined it carefully. 'Yes, it is what they call "ubbriaco" – that is, "intoxicated". Animals eat it and begin to stagger about. They fall. It is not common in these mountains. I wonder where Terka found it.'

'And I wonder', Michael remarked grimly, 'what she wanted it for.'

He had regarded Terka at first as a harmless and persecuted pauper; then as a gypsy charlatan, driven to making a living in mischievous ways. Now – he began to wonder whether he had not been very obtuse.

Henri said: 'Whatever she used these for, they are better burnt.'

In the centre of the clearing, they piled some twigs, flung the herbs on them and set them ablaze. Henri threw the dead rabbits and cock on the fire and, to the aromatic smoke from the herbs, was added the smell of burning flesh. Sickened, they turned away from the polluted place.

'I suppose', Michael said after a while, 'all that was meant to impress her enemies. The rabbits and cock were a warning, no doubt.'

'They were animal sacrifices,' Henri said. He was still looking pallid and shocked.

'Sacrifices?' Michael exclaimed, startled. 'Sacrifices to what? To whom?'

'To the Evil One,' was Henri's quiet reply.

'Do you mean that she's crazy enough to pretend – to *want* people to think she is a sorceress?'

'Terka *is* a sorceress,' Henri said.

2

RAIN-CLOUDS ADVANCED from the east, shutting out the sun from the village, spilling showers that refreshed the gardens but wetted the sheets and garments hung out to dry. Juliet ran out to the yard and helped Marie to take down her washing and carry it in.

'The weather has broken; our fine summer is ending,' Marie said.

Both Juliet's frocks – the white and green one and the white and yellow – were still too damp to be ironed. She hung them on a line in the scullery, left Marie to deal with the rest of the laundry and went up to her own room. René was at his Tuesday stint of work in the kitchen, making the *bouchées* and *quenelles* and *mousses* of which he was so proud, and Martine was resting. The weekend rush had subsided and number two was empty – a great relief. Juliet decided to seize the hour for a realistic review of her clothes, her financial position and … and everything.

'Our fine summer is ending.' How ominous Marie had sounded! What mournful words!

She opened her drawers and wardrobe, pulled her suitcases from under her bed and laid her belongings out, one by one. They did not make up a trousseau …What a silly word to come into one's head! … But the fact was, if Thursday should happen not to be warm and dry, she just could not go up to the forest, because she would have nothing to wear. She had no respectable cool-weather clothes.

She almost hoped it would rain on Thursday – rain so hard that Michael would not expect her. And not only because, except her light white jacket, she had no coat. Because … well, because things had changed. Sunday had changed things between her and Michael. Their fine summer had ended. Their lovely, lighthearted friendship, which, she had thought, would go on all their lives, no matter how far apart they might be, had without one word or touch, come to an end. It had changed into something that couldn't continue. It had changed for Michael as well as for her.

Four years old, her suit was. She had let it out and turned it and worn it last winter at the school. It was a disgrace. And the taffeta skirt was cracking with age. Two good white blouses; two good pairs of shoes; the cheapest of underwear; the awful old raincoat for which she had swapped her mother's lace blouse with Yvonne. That was practically all. Her own earnings would be just enough for a skirt and stockings and gloves. When she needed a coat she would simply have to beg from her father or spend the money which he'd saved for her fare. She wondered if in case … well, an emergency, how much Frith would help. Because, in the sort of post she could hope to get, one wouldn't, even in a year, earn as much as some of the girls had been given for pocket-money. You couldn't hope to earn nearly enough to, for instance, travel on a ship … You couldn't dress like a schoolgirl or a waitress in … in the outside world.

To her shame and dismay, tears splashed down on the black taffeta skirt. What a thing to cry about! Money! As if she was going to let such things matter. As if they *did!* It was only … only that one didn't want to have to be *rescued*: to have nothing to give, nothing to bring, no way of pulling one's weight. And she hadn't even skill or experience or anything. She wasn't much more than a schoolgirl, after all. Once you let yourself cry, you weakened. Now, putting her wretched things away again in their places, she had no courage left at all. She was almost praying that Thursday would be wet.

She looked out of her window at the bills. By leaning out and looking south-westward, one could often see Michael's forest. Now it was visible, floating, like a wooded summit in a Japanese print, out of a silver haze. The rocky peak stuck up behind it and against that the knoll stood out. It all looked far-off, enchanted, a place in a dream. She wondered what Michael was doing up there in the sunlight. She wondered what he was thinking about.

Chapter XV

FIRE FROM HEAVEN

PLANKS WHICH, with Camille's help, had been carried in and laid on the trestle, changed the bed into an extra work-table and on it Michael set out his material: index cards; boxes of tree-samples – root, bark, foliage, flower and seed; his sketches of timber harmed by pests or disease; boxes that Henri had lined for him with agave, into which insect specimens had been pinned. He added mounting-papers, photographs, diagrams, paste-pot and scissors, and strips for mounting and labelling.

With pleasure he viewed the neat, symmetrical set-up, which would make the job a straightforward and enjoyable one. He smiled, guessing with what delighted, self-forgetting absorption Juliet would immerse herself in it, and how clever her delicate fingers would be at the task. It was raining, but he did not suppose for a moment that a little rain would put her away and by twelve o'clock he was waiting within the tunnel made by the leaning pine. Juliet did not come.

It did not help that the whole family knew. An extra large bowl of soup served by Claudette and sympathetic looks from Marie-Louise only made him feel more aggrieved. He imagined Juliet was the sort of girl who would pull on gumboots and a sou'wester and brave any weather rather than break a promise to help a friend.

Working alone while rain streamed down his window and finding it hard to keep his mind on the job, Michael began dually to realise that he had been unreasonable. The rain was probably heavy in the village and, both coming and returning, she would have been drenched. And he *had* said something like 'only if it is fine'. And how could Juliet be expected to know what importance he had attached to this afternoon? He had asked her with a carefully casual air. Indeed, he hadn't realised the whole of it himself. He'd cheated himself a bit about his motives. The simple truth was he had wanted her here; and he'd wanted to have her handwriting on the labels – so that, in the future, in solitary places, whenever he used this collection, her smile, her voice, the soft brightness Juliet had about her, would be evoked, with the memory of today. Now the day wasn't worth remembering. There was nothing to it: a lot of dead moths; dry twigs; withered leaves.

He stood looking down, perplexed, at his collection. What had happened to it? What had happened to him?

Up and down his cramped, narrow cell. Michael took prisoner's paces while he tried to understand his own mind. How had he been such a slow, dull-witted clod? Was it because, facing the African post; feeling it wouldn't be fair to ask Juliet for a promise, he had guarded himself from knowing how profoundly he needed her? So that all these four days and nights, during which he had known himself to be free, he had still resisted and wasted time?

He flung his door open and shouted for Rouge, René's setter, the only companion he wanted. Rouge answered rapturously from the stable and bounded beside him as Michael walked through the copse into the wet woods.

'I'm free!' he said in a loud voice to the dog. 'Do you realise it, you chump? I am free!' Rouge flourished a congratulatory tail and Michael laughed. Drops fell from the trees so that you didn't know whether it was raining or not. And who cared?

She was not a girl to be taken by storm, Michael reflected, so it must be a siege. There must be no more lost days. One would have to make certain that no hint of compassion, no protective impulse, revealed itself, to hurt Juliet's bruised and sensitive pride. Gently, gradually, her diffidence must be overcome. It could be done.

It was a great pity, he felt, that his mother had ever heard of her parents; but if she was going to be so blind and prejudiced as not to see the sweetness and beauty of Juliet, then, poor darling Muff, she would be the one to suffer for it.

What about going down, now, at once, by the afternoon bus? Too late! And, anyhow his stuff couldn't be left laid out like that. No – the thing was to get the job finished tonight, pack up tomorrow and run the lot down to Menton in Castellis' hack car. From there it could be shipped at the word 'go'.

An inspiration of the most supreme brilliance came to him out of the blue. He could afford it. He'd hire that car for a week, book a room at the good old Coq d'Or, take up his quarters there, and see Juliet for at least an hour or two every day. They would drive and walk in the hills. When he sailed he'd take with him her promise to follow him.

Michael whistled to Rouge and swung on his heel. Knowing his heart, believing in his star, buoyant with joyous purpose, he ran the whole way back to his hut with Rouge, ecstatic, sharing his jubilation, barking and racing him.

2

THUNDER WAS NOT ENOUGH to wake Michael. What brought him to his feet was a scream – the hideous screaming of panicking animals. He was tying his shoelaces when he heard shouts. Camille was shouting 'Fire!'

That cry, ominous in a pine-forest, sent him dashing to the farm-house, through the yard, among the barking dogs, and round to the far side of the house. There was not a gleam from anything but his torch until a viper of lightning spat in the sky; then, above the wind-break of cypresses, he saw smoke. The fire was at Granerol's.

Men were roping the frantic and plunging mules, hauling them out of danger and tying them up, while women splashed water from buckets against the stable whose timber roof and doors were ablaze. Agnès, crouched at the tap in the huge tank, was wasting the water, letting it overflow. Marie-Louise pushed her away. Thunder broke close and the mules tried to stampede. Their teeth bared and their eyes rolling, they reared and whinnied piteously, but the ropes held. César Domenico ran up with two buckets of water and Michael, grabbing one of them, flung as much as he could on the roof. His reach was good but not much could be done. Inside, the manger and the stalls were on fire. Behind him a chain of workers had been formed and, one after another, the handles of buckets were thrust into his groping hand. He scarcely knew what he was doing in the deafening din, the blinding and choking smoke, but as pieces of roof fell, blazing, he sluiced them with water and quenched the flames. Girls yelled at him not to go too near and he sprang back, but too late to save his left foot from a beam that fell on it, flaming. He escaped with a scorched instep, and one of the Domenicos pulled him back and took his place at the head of the chain. Michael crouched on the ground, painfully sucking air into his lungs. His eyes were stinging and watering. Someone was crying through the growls of the thunder that the water was giving out. He thought of the hay in the open shed; the cypresses. It ought to be raining. Why didn't it rain? … He sprang to his feet and yelled and waved his arms about as wildly as the others when a spatter, and then a torrent, of rain fell. The scene was farcical, men clashing empty buckets together; Claudette weeping and laughing hysterically; Camille and Léon hugging one another; everyone lifting smoke-grimed faces and hands to the welcome rain, while the smouldering timbers sizzled and subsided into a black, smoking, ill-smelling mess. Rubbing their sore eyes and coughing, the men staggered about in the deluge. The trembling mules were dragged off by the Domenicos, who had stabling to spare. Léon pushed his sobbing wife into the house and, without a 'thank you' to anyone, followed her in and banged his door. Michael, to his own surprise, when he was safe with the Loubiers in their kitchen, realised that he was full of such vigour and exhilaration that he almost wanted another fire to fight. He could understand the criminal passion for arson. Fire seemed to release and revive the primitive man whom civilisation forbade to draw breath.

Marie-Louise, alone, was calm and efficient. It was she who quieted the grandmother, who was calling from the bedroom in a rage of frustration and inquisitiveness and complained about having been left alone. Claudette was shuddering and blubbering like a shocked, frightened child. Her sister soothed her and sent her to bed. Camille was disturbed. He could not understand how and where the fire had started. There had been no metal near the stable, he thought. Marie-Louise reminded him of the strange things lightning was known to have done and succeeded, or so it appeared, in satisfying him. It was she who warmed water for the washing of soot-begrimed faces, and who dressed and bandaged Michael's foot. The rain, she declared, had been an answer to prayer. When the water in the tank gave out, she had knelt on the ground and prayed to the Little Flower.

'Well, it might have been worse, certainly,' Camille admitted, philosophically, at length. 'One feels safe for a time after such a thing has occurred, for accidents must happen, and, every two or three summers, the lightning has to strike.'

'Yes, surely, it might have been worse,' Michael agreed, and left them and hobbled back to his hut.

But he was annoyed. He had hoped for long walks with Juliet, and this foot would be a nuisance for several days, and his good English shoes were a total loss.

Chapter XVI

THE PRIEST

THE POSTMAN WAS TELLING René something that pleased him. As Juliet passed through the hall with her tray she saw them in the porch, and they were talking still when she came down. The *courrier* earned his name, she thought: very often, as well as the letters, he brought news from the farms, relayed by the busman or postman from the Relais – which, also, deserved its name.

'A letter for you!' René called, when she came up with the next breakfast. It was from her father. René, smiling, stuck it in the pocket of her overall. There it had to wait until all the *petits déjeuners* had been served. Juliet opened it then, sitting on the bench in the yard.

MY DEAR JULIET,

What fun you do have in that village! I look forward to the sequel in which The Boy Scout will, of course, unmask the guilty one. She should be buried at a crossroads with a stake through her heart.

Good for Father Pascale and his wax! Counter-suggestion! That's the stuff!

We go up Corte tomorrow and wipe out a family – the Black Hand do, that is to say, while I rescue the beautiful maiden. Fortunately she is beautiful. Have you seen Wanda Lloyd in films? She starred in Green Carnation *and* Billy Girl. *Did you know that she and I were great friends?*

Here it comes. Hold on to your hat. As soon as we're through with this film we are getting married. Probably in Rome.

I don't imagine you and she will have a whole lot in common and there's no reason why you should. I have told her there is another girl in my life with whom I'll disappear on a holiday now and then. She positively declines the office of stepmother.

Write soon and tell us the rest of the village drama. Meanwhile keep your fingers crossed – that is the charm against the evil eye.

Love,

FRITH

Wanda Lloyd. Juliet had seen her face on posters: a brunette with a broad smile and a fringe. What an extraordinary thing for a man of fifty to do! But probably he had been terribly lonely, and that might account for a lot. Perhaps, with a wife to be ambitious for him, he might do a comeback. This was a good thing.

For a shaky moment Juliet was a small, tearful girl again, watching the train that was taking her father away: she was scolded for forgetting to wave. Well, she would wave this time. She would send him a telegram ...

There was a postscript scribbled along a margin and she turned the page to read it. She could scarcely take in its full meaning at first.

I've been getting the length and breadth of W's tongue for expecting you to earn your living without diplomas. We can stand you a year's training at anything reasonable if you can face living in a Young Women's Club. Can you? Think it over and say when.

Martine had come down and was laughing at Juliet, who was smiling and frowning over her letter. They drank coffee together in the kitchen.

'You won't leave me yet? You won't break your promise?' Martine pleaded when the news had been told.

'If things are all right with you I might ask you to find someone else and let me off, but I won't go if you can't,' Juliet answered. 'You'll train me meanwhile! I'll take some sort of course in domestic science – cooking and dressmaking and everything. Do you think I could be a really good cook? To be good at practical things, as you are, must be marvellous.'

Martine was laughing again.

'What a child you are still!'

Juliet laughed too but she was thinking, 'That's just the trouble. Martine doesn't understand. To have the ignorance and inexperience of a child and want the life of a woman – that's what she doesn't understand. Martine has always been worth her keep.'

'That postscript has changed everything,' she told herself, almost incredulously. 'If this letter had come yesterday morning I would have gone to Michael. I wouldn't have been stopped by rain or thunder or my frightful old mackintosh.'

René was calling Martine. Bringing dusters and brushes, the girls went up. He was in his office working at accounts. René did endless calculations. He knew how much it cost to splash tea on a tray-cloth or wash your hands. Fortunately, he seldom talked about it. He was making out the bill for the American family. The season was ending, and that was just as well for Martine.

'I have good news for you,' he said. 'It came down with the bus yesterday. Terka has gone. Her cabin was found deserted. I'd like to give the curé a case of champagne!'

René's vivid satisfaction was not reflected in his wife's face. After a moment's silence she asked nervously, 'Where has she gone?'

'The Devil knows!' René replied lightly.

With a sharp intake of breath Martine turned away.

'I'd rather know where she is,' she murmured. She was quiet and slower than usual in her movements while they made the beds and tidied the rooms.

JULIET WROTE her telegram in the post office – just affectionate wishes, and salutations the most distinguished to Mademoiselle Wanda Lloyd – and sent it off. She finished her shopping quickly, avoiding gossip, and returned to the rue de la Pompe.

The sky was clearing and the mountains had drawn so close that you could see hundreds of separate trees, and chinks and hollows and ridges of rock. The rain had laid the dust and freshened everything. The village was at its brightest and so were the smiling faces of the people who greeted her as she passed. St Jacques, she thought, was celebrating.

Young Tissier startled her out of her pleasant thoughts. Had he been ambushing her – hanging about outside the garden gate? A grin was wavering all over his face. He asked her whether she had heard the news and she told him that she had. Obviously he hoped to question as to where Terka had gone, but Juliet wouldn't ask. He repelled her, with his little malicious eyes and his high voice.

'You've heard they've been struck by lightning up there?' She clung to the ironwork of the gate. The world lurched and darkened. It wasn't until she had implored him that Ignace told her the rest. So it was nothing. Léon Granerol's stable. Nobody killed; nobody hurt; the animals safe.

Ignace was chattering on and on; boasting. What was there to boast about? Oh, the poor fool thought Terka had done this. It was Terka's revenge – Terka had pulled the lightning out of the sky.

'You ask *Monsieur le curé* if *he* can do that! Go on and ask him! He's going up to the farms in my father's yoke, and he turned me off. He won't take me.'

'Why should he, you wicked, hateful, odious boy?' Juliet cried, childishly.

Sure enough, there was the *charrette* with Monsieur Tissier's mare, outside the door of the inn, with André in charge. Juliet sped up the garden to the terrace and sank down on a chair there beside Martine. René and the curé both spoke at once, gently, telling her that Michael had not been hurt. Her heart was battering and in the wrong place. She wondered why Father Pascale looked so drawn and ill. As they talked, she soon understood. Madame Castelli had driven down from the Relais early, called on the priest and told him about the fire and, far more distressing, about the wild state of mind of the young men of the district, including her own sons.

'Her sons and their neighbours and even old Granerol have wholly misunderstood me,' the curé said wretchedly. 'They have given a fearful, unchristian twist to my words. They would use them as a license for violence, and, now, for regarding the gypsy as responsible for this fire. May God give me strength and eloquence to enlighten them!'

He was on his way up to visit every house in the region of the gorge. He very much wanted René to go with him, but Martine clutched René's wrist and with tears in her eyes begged the curé not to ask him to go.

'You are afraid for him?' the priest asked her reproachfully. 'Even in my company?'

Martine's throat was constricted. She assented with a nod.

'But what harm could come to him?'

'Harm comes to everybody who crosses her path. And nobody knows where she is hiding now.'

'But, my child, I go to try to save her from harm.'

'You denounced her, Father; and Agnès Granerol was the cause – and this has happened to them.'

'Only the good God controls the lightning, Martine.'

Martine moved her head uneasily. She said, 'Do not bring her curse on us. Not now ... not now when I ... when we ...' She broke down, sobbing.

René held her and soothed her, saying he would not go. 'You will excuse me, Father, I know!'

'Certainly I will excuse you, my son.'

'If you go to my uncle first he will accompany you. Those fellows listen to him.'

Martine controlled herself, ashamed and grateful, and rose, leaving the priest and René to finish their wine. She took Juliet with her to the kitchen and there a basket was packed with delicacies for the grandmother and tied up in a linen cloth. Juliet snatched a minute to write a note to Michael – a thing she had never done before. It was short:

DEAR MICHAEL, I'm glad you are all right. I'm sorry about yesterday. I would have liked helping to pack your specimens.
                                                                    JULIET.

The curé put the note in his pocket, settled the basket carefully in the back of the *charrette* and took his place on the high seat, whip in hand. He drove off alone and did not look back. They watched from the steps and René was frowning. He said, 'He usually drives off like a boy, joking and flourishing his whip. He is taking all this too much to heart.'

'He would sacrifice his life,' Martine said in a grieved voice, 'to save one of us from committing a sin, and what has he done? Poor Father Pascale.'

3

THERE WAS nothing else for it. One couldn't go barefoot in St Jacques. Michael slit his canvas shoe to the toe and, seated on a packing-case, tied it with caution and ingenuity over his bandaged foot.

If he had to get a foot disabled the affair had timed itself nicely, he reflected. Now, with a snow-white conscience, he could hire the Castellis' car for a week and drive Juliet all over the place. What could be better? The monstrous outbreak of virtue and circumspection which had kept him from the village since Sunday was having its reward. The only snag was that the foot was sore.

He stood on one leg and surveyed his cases, all padded with shavings and packed up. Henri had spent a morning helping him to pack and Granerol to clean up. Henri would take the cases down by the shortcut, some day soon, on his flat cart and Michael could take them to Menton from there in the car. Everything was under control.

He was hungry after all that and was disconcerted to find, at the farmhouse, a cold snack being eaten instead of a proper midday meal. The place, which they had messed up last night, was transformed

– the windows had been polished and adorned with white curtains, and clean white cloths had been spread on the tables. As for Madame Loubier, she lay propped up against snowy pillows, with a shining white quilt over her and a crisp frilled cap on her head. The curé was expected, it appeared. Georges had come on his bicycle to give warning. The place smelt of soap and beeswax and piety and was, Michael felt, no place for him. He ate hunks of cold mutton and bread and drank red wine and then explained his general plan.

'We shall miss you, Michel,' Marie-Louise said. 'Come sometimes to dinner and bring Mademoiselle Juliette. It is a pleasure only to look at her.'

Michael liked Marie-Louise.

Claudette, too, was a good sort when she wasn't declaring that Terka had directed the lightning and that their own time would come. Knowing that Michael meant to go down to the village, she had asked Georges to leave him his bicycle. That would spare him a slow and painful hobble as far as the Relais. He took himself to his hut and busied himself there, brushing soot out of his pyjamas, packing his rucksack, changing into his good suit and attempting to make himself look like a respectable citizen. That took a lot longer than he had expected. It was past three o'clock when he locked the door of the hut behind him and went to the farmhouse to return the key. The curé had come and gone. Grandmère Loubier was sitting up in her bed saying her rosary – the picture of a religious old lady.

'She has received a fine penance that will spare our ears for a while.' Camille said with his shrewd, humorous smile, as he helped to fix the rucksack on the back of the bicycle.

Michael said grateful goodbyes. Claudette was teasing, her sister very earnest, and Camille heartily confident when they wished him *bonne chance*. They knew all about his purpose in going down. As he pedalled along the sun-dappled track Michael thought what a splendid summer he had spent up here with these friendly people and how sorry he would have felt to be leaving it all but for the years that lay before him. It dazzled his imagination, just as the sun was blinding his eyes, to think of years in Cyprus with Juliet.

He smiled as he passed under the arching stone-pine that had been their first chosen rendezvous. The noble tree deserved that honour, he thought. About the others, that grew on the bank just before the sharp bend farther on, he thought with regret. Their roots, lifting the track, had given it a very dangerous camber towards the unfenced edge of the deep ravine. Even for cyclists it wasn't safe. The trees would undoubtedly have to come down. They cast a heavy shadow, too, on the path.

Michael dismounted just where the shadow began; otherwise he might have failed to notice the black, inert figure sprawled against the myrtles that grew along the lip of the gorge. It was Father Pascale.

At first Michael could find no pulse at all, then he felt it, feeble but regular. The priest's breathing was shallow and he was cold. Anxiously, Michael examined the pupils of the half-closed eyes. He sighed with relief. There was no sign of injury to the brain. The left forearm was broken – a Colles fracture. The blow near the left temple would have caused the concussion and there were abrasions on both hands. There might be broken ribs and internal injuries, and the man was probably bruised all over, but the immediate danger was shock.

He rolled up his sweater, put it under the priest's head, laid his rucksack on the road a few yards farther along, to force any mule-cart that might be coming to stop, and prepared to cycle back to the Domenicos for help. There was nothing else he could do. It was with relief and astonishment that he heard, from beyond the bluff of rock at the bend, the hoot of a motor-horn. He shouted, left the bicycle on the road again and ran back. Two women appeared and they were kneeling beside the injured priest when he came up to them. They were the widow Castelli and her sister-in-law. The run-away animal had stopped at the Relais, trailing the broken cart, and, in extreme anxiety for the curé, they had risked bringing their car as far as the bend. Their one idea now was to put him into it and take him to their own house. They were offended with Michael when he insisted that the place for him was the secluded *ferme Loubier* and that he must not be moved one centimetre except on a stretcher.

Michael was not prepared for the violent reactions that his news produced among the Domenicos. The brothers, while they wrenched an out-house door off its hinges, uttered more imprecations and oaths of vengeance than expressions of solicitude for the priest. Their shrill-voiced sister ran by shortcuts to warn the Loubiers and when the slow procession, that had the air of a funeral, with two black-clad women following the stretcher and Michael limping beside it, approached the farm, Camille was waiting at his gate.

As the injured curé, whose hollow, colourless face wore the look of death, was borne through the kitchen to Camille's bedroom, the old grandmother broke into a pitiful outcry – lamentations and wild denunciations mingled with prayers, while Claudette crouched, sobbing and crossing herself, on the floor by the bed, of no more use than a terrified child. Marie-Louise never ceased trembling but she provided all Michael required to bathe and disinfect cuts – there were lacerations on both Father Pascale's hands – fix a splint on the wrist and a bandage over the ribs which, though they did not seem to be dislocated, were probably broken or cracked. There was no sign of returning consciousness. The sooner Dr Gompert could get here the better, Michael thought.

'How did it happen?' Camille asked him quietly, but in deep perturbation, as he was leaving.

Exasperated, Michael replied, 'An extremely obvious accident – and there'll be more of them if that road isn't levelled. I suppose a bird or a squirrel startled the mare.'

Camille nodded his grizzled head slowly. He said, 'Tell them that in the village, Michael.'

Chapter XVII

THE BLUDGEON

JULIET WAS in the grip of a whole *mistral* of self-pity. Why couldn't Martine have collapsed at any time except now! For a few days Michael would be in the village, wanting her company, waiting to drive her to wild, glorious places – and then he would be leaving to join his mother and if things went wrong she might never see him again. And things were going miserably wrong.

She stirred and stirred but the sauce was lumpy. She just couldn't manage sauces: she would never be any good as a cook.

If only he had come to stay here instead of at the Coq.

'I don't want you waiting on me.' What an *English* thing to say! It made her smile in spite of her woe to recall it. 'Besides,' he had said firmly, meaning, of course, 'Besides, we are in France.'

Snatching the casserole off the flame, she splashed sauce on her overall. There wasn't time to go up to the linen-room. A clean one of Martine's hung on the door and Juliet put it on. It was too short and wide for her, but it would have to do. She would have to start the sauce all over again, wasting butter and flavouring and eggs. If Michael came, as he had said he would, at a quarter past eight, he would find her looking as much like a dishrag as she felt. It would probably end with his helping to wash up instead of taking her for a drive.

It had been this time yesterday when the car appeared in the lane and Michael came hobbling across the yard, half smiling, half grimacing from the pain of his foot. Martine had made him sit down and eat in the kitchen and at first he hadn't told them the awful news. He'd told René when Martine had gone.

Juliet had never seen René lose control of himself before. He'd been like a savage in his fury – so distraught that he blurted it out when Martine returned.

'Now it's the curé! Thrown out of the *charrette*. Unconscious, perhaps dying, at Camille's.' Michael's insistence that it had been a very natural accident did not seem to reach their minds. Martine had gone slowly as white as chalk. She hadn't cried out; she had said, in a low, breathless voice, 'Then the Devil is stronger than God.'

René had taken her up to her own room and there she still was, afraid to leave it, and Juliet had to do two people's work.

Being in love always makes girls selfish, she had heard Aunt Isabel say … 'Certainly,' Juliet thought, 'if selfishness is a sign, I am in love.'

She had forgotten about heating the plates. As she shut the oven door on them, she added, 'And now I'm a coward, too.'

It was all she could do to stay on in this house. She had to. She couldn't call on Michael to rescue her and she couldn't abandon Martine. She hadn't sunk quite so low.

But – 'Fire falls upon it from heaven'; and 'The priest has to do with death'; and 'See, she comes between you, the Queen of Wands!' … 'Wanda' is not such a common name. And then, 'Leave that house: it is accursed.' Promises held her: her promise to Michael as well as her promise to Martine. She had to stay. The only comfort was that if any of it meant anything it seemed now as if the Chevalier, who went out against the Powers of Darkness, was not Michael, but the priest.

René came in, hurried and sombre and purposeful, gave her his orders crisply, saw that the dinner was properly served and, himself, took a tray up to Martine. 'He would grind my bones to make her bread,' Juliet was reflecting with rueful smile when he returned in an altered mood.

'Martine is eating the fish!' he said happily and gave Juliet his brilliant, disarming smile.

'Now you must eat, Juliette, or you will be ill – and then, think, the house would fall down.'

They had eaten and were stacking the dishes at the sink when the bell on the terrace rang twice. Juliet started up. René said quietly, 'Ask Monsieur to come down. I will explain.'

Father Pascale, Michael told them, was better – almost out of danger, although very weak and in pain. Michael had gone up to see him but they had not talked. He did not remember his fall and, the doctor supposed, never would. He was being quite perfectly cared for up there.

Michael's enquiries about Martine were polite, but no more. He finished his coffee and stood up.

'And, now, is Juliet ready to come?'

René stood up also, gestured towards the great pile of used crockery and began, 'I regret ...'

Michael did not appear to have heard. With a sympathetic shake of his head, he said, 'Who would be an inn-keeper?' He went on, cheerfully, 'A half-time job, like Juliet's, no doubt, is amusing. It seems to please her. But for you, Monsieur, it is a whole-time one – night and day, is it not?'

René's black eyebrows performed an odd contortion; His head was thrown back, then, and he laughed.

'Go then, Juliette!' he said. 'The air and the moonlight will do you good. But before you go, say goodnight to Martine.'

2

WHEN JULIET HAD LEFT the kitchen René turned to Michael, eyes sharply focused and muscles taut.

'What do they think up there about this – this "accident"?'

Michael shrugged.

'They talk a very great deal of nonsense. It is not the first of its kind and won't be the last. The miracle is that he didn't go over the edge.'

'And at the Coq?'

'Crazier nonsense still. When I suggested that a bird or a rabbit might have startled the horse, a man shouted, "Or a hare." The others applauded him.'

'And the fire?'

'There was lightning.'

'Why should the lightning strike just there?'

Michael looked incredulously at René, and the dark, intense eyes returned his stare.

'My wife is sick from terror,' René said.

'And can you not convince her that it is absurd?'

'What is absurd, Monsieur?'

'To attribute two absolutely natural accidents to witchcraft: to a gypsy's curse! To believe that a woman ...'

'Do you not believe in prayer?' René broke in.

'That is a completely different thing.'

'But it is not, Monsieur! It is not! What is a curse but a prayer to the Evil One? Are we not taught that the Devil exists and goes about amongst us? Why should not curses have power?'

He paused while Juliet entered from the yard, bringing Martine's tray.

'Look! She has eaten everything! Now she will sleep! ... I won't be a moment changing,' she said lightly, and ran upstairs.

'I think, Monsieur,' René went on, 'that Terka has cursed the curé, and cursed the Granerols, and that her curse will be turned, now, on me. And if she wants to destroy me she knows how to do it: it will be through my wife ...'

'What an appalling, crazy, outrageous idea!'

René went steadily on, keeping his voice very low.

'That is why Martine is afraid; and there is only one person, besides myself, who does not agitate her and share her terror and make her worse. That is Juliet. Martine clings to her. I implore you do not – at least until our baby has been born – do not take her away!'

Michael struggled to hold back a furious declaration that he would take her away from this damned place, this foul, superstition-ridden village, tomorrow. He would scarcely have succeeded had not Juliet come in, in her light Coolie-coat, hatless, her face irradiated with happy anticipation. He said an abrupt 'goodnight' and hurried her out to the car.

3

THEY SWITCHED-BACKED DOWN, up and down again, crossed the bridge and turned left. The car moved neither smoothly nor quietly, but it moved. It did fifty.

'Is that too fast for you?'

'The faster and farther the better.'

'What is lock-up time?'

'I have Martine's key.'

'Good. Anywhere special you'd like to go?'

She responded thoughtfully.

'Yes … yes, there is. That Roman place with the beautiful broken columns. It should be over there, somewhere.'

'I was just thinking about it.'

Now they were on a ridge and the road zig-zagged, twist after twist, in sharp-angled descent. Michael's caution could not have been surpassed.

'Does driving hurt your foot?' Juliet asked.

'Not unless I brake suddenly … What luck to have such a night!'

There were clouds in the sky and the moon was riding among them. It was full and turned a rippled cloud into a silver fleece. When it drew clear the long rock-face shutting the valley in on their left became a glittering wall. Their road and the opposite mountainside were shadowed and the headlamps turned shrubs and tree-stumps and boulders into theatre scenery, cutouts for some fantastic fairy tale. Above them, the crumbling village of St Agnès appeared and vanished with its rock. The road turned westward along the Col de Madone and a wide valley, stony and barren, opened below. The surrounding Alps rolled away, fold beyond moonlit fold. Michael stopped. His coat was in the back of the car and he made Juliet put it on. She flapped the ends of the sleeves that came down over her hands. 'It would hold two of you,' Michael said. His voice was as light as his heart.

'I drove up to the farm before dinner', he told her, 'to screw down my cases and clear the hut for Camille. Father Pascale was awake. He doesn't seem to remember what happened.'

'Do you think he'll recover, Michael?'

'The doctor wouldn't give an opinion. He seemed very weak to me.'

'In the village it is as if he were dead; it is as if they had lost their father and were too frightened to speak.'

Her voice was a little shaky and Michael turned to her.

'I have something to tell you, Juliet. I can't leave you alone in that witch's kitchen. I'm not going north to my mother. She's coming south. I'll be around for another three weeks.'

The way she looked at him, lips parted, made him believe she was going to say, as she had said before, 'Michael, you *are* a friend!' but she said nothing. He laughed to see her blink tears out of her eyes. He, too, said nothing, yet, but drove on. He couldn't help teasing her; she was so sweet. Recovering, Juliet began to chatter about a letter from her father, who, it appeared, was about to console himself. Wanda Lloyd? Well, well. Ought to suit one another, he thought, but did not say it aloud. He was quite conscious of an irrational prejudice against the said Frith. He tried to listen gravely while Juliet confided in him her proposal to study dietetics, home-nursing, cookery and all the domestic crafts. It wasn't until, in reply to a question about where, in London, she would live and she answered, 'Oh, I suppose in some sort of club or hostel for working girls' that his amusement exploded.

'Holy smoke!' he exclaimed and drew the car to the margin to have his laugh out.

'Why is it so funny?'

'I don't know.'

'I think it's exceedingly sensible.'

'So do I ... Tell me, Juliet, what did you mean to be when you were very young?'

'An opera-singer.'

'That's much more like it!'

He chuckled; Juliet giggled; he recovered his senses and drove on.

Presently there was a glimpse of the ruined, moon-blanched Trophy of Augustus erect on its hill. The vision, its beauty and ancientness, changed Juliet's mood. She quietly, 'Tell me about your mother.'

'She's a funny Muff,' he answered, smiling. 'She's just a man's favourite sort of mother, I suppose. But you never know what she'll do. She hates to seem bossy but likes to get her own way and her methods are sometimes devious. She likes work, and motoring, and travel and old furniture, manages so that they earn one another, somehow.' He told Juliet about the post she had more or less invented for herself on the art periodical, *New and Old,* after his father's death and about her ambulance-driving during the War. Perhaps he had made her out a bit overpowering? Juliet sounded nervous when she asked, 'How soon is she coming?'

'Oh, in ten days or so, I suppose.'

Michael was completely happy. His only problem was to keep his exuberance from communicating itself to the engine as they levelled out and ran into La Turbie.

They stood on the little crescent-shaped platform, leaning against the balustrade, looking down. In the sky, which held the tint of wild violets, a few pallid stars shone, but the moon dominated air, earth and sea. The maze of lights that sparkled below, climbing a cliff, embracing a harbour, spilling out eastwards along the coast, belonged to Monte Carlo and Monaco. To the east lay a headland.

'That must be Cap Martin,' Michael said; 'and beyond it is Italy, isn't it – that glimmering line? And, beyond Italy …'

'Cyprus,' Juliet said.

There was peace between them. Michael marvelled at it. The girl beside him was in some incomprehensible way different from the Juliet whose young, brittle, childish pride had imposed on him so much caution and vigilance. The shy restraint of that night in the olive orchard had vanished, and so had the air of distance in which she had wrapt herself during the last hour of their forest walk. She stood beside him at ease, relaxed, letting the wind play with her hair, the shadow of a smile on her cheek.

He let the peace deepen in silence, and Juliet, too, was still.

Then he turned his face to her and asked, 'Have you ever walked in a forest at night?'

'Never, but I would love to,' she answered, and moved with him back to the car.

Juliet scarcely spoke while they covered the miles; when they reached the Bridge of the Sheep and Michael, instead of crossing it, drove on, she smiled, without surprise. As the road entered the forest she watched for the gap on the left where the woodmen's mule-path came out. The trees, in the dark stillness, looked unfamiliar. Erect on the steep mountainside in their thousands, they had taken on an aspect of immortality that made her feel weak and confused. They had gone a good deal too far before she murmured, 'I think we have missed the gap.'

Michael slowed down, looked up and exclaimed, in a startled undertone, 'What's happening up there?'

Small lights were bobbing about, high up, among the pines.

'People with lanterns,' Juliet said.

The lights were moving, coming nearer, passing above them, now held high, now near the ground; clustering, then strung out apart. A man shouted suddenly, 'The other way!'

Michael turned the car.

'They are looking for something. They are hunting for … someone,' Juliet gasped.

Michael drove back, keeping pace with the moving lights. He did not believe they were lanterns – not all of them. Suddenly there was a blaze and a cry. With shouting and commotion, the fire was put out. Michael sprang out of the car and tore up the bank. He heard a yell that had hate in it, as he ran.

'You fools! Are you trying to fire the forest?' he cried, his voice was drowned by a howl like the baying of hounds. He saw lanterns and torches in wild motion and heard a high, agonised shriek.

'A witch-hunt,' Michael thought and cursed his stiff, clumsy foot as he tried to break into the mule-path. He was on it, running up, hoping to intercept the men, when he saw Terka rushing towards him, bounding down, fleeing at incredible speed.

Terka looked like a maniac as she passed him, and so did he who pursued her, his eyes glaring out of a blackened face, his mouth stretched like a wolf's. Michael hit out and, the man reeled, wrested his torch from his hand. Reaching the road, Michael flung the thing down where it could do no harm and leaped into the car. He was hunted himself, but it was only a moment before the car was well out range of the stones and sticks and torches flung after it.

'Stop, stop! Look at her!' Juliet cried.

Ahead of them, Terka was staggering along the road, like a great, flapping bird with a broken wing. Michael stopped car and Juliet ran to the panting, stupefied woman, opened the door at the back and pushed her in. Michael drove on, telling himself the danger was over, but his hands were tense on the wheel and he could not speak. He had let Juliet do a reckless thing.

There were men ahead: two: one on either side of the road. The one on his side was swinging a lantern; the other, a club. As he tore past, the club was flung at the car. He had barely time to pull Juliet's head down. The club struck the metal bar of the windscreen and rebounded, scattering splintered glass.

Crouched over the wheel, Michael drove on at the utmost speed he could get out of the car. He felt Juliet's heart beating and heard her muffled voice asking him whether he was all right. They were off the main road and across the bridge before he pulled up.

'It was my fault. Your eyes! You might have been hurt, my darling, my darling,' he murmured, pulling the coat away, scattering fragments of glass.

That pale face that was lifted to his, that he cupped in his hands, was unscarred, and what he saw in Juliet's eyes was neither terror nor pain.

'My darling,' she said, under her breath.

Neither of them was aware of the moment when Terka slipped out of the car. When they remembered her and looked round, she was gone.

Gaston's cottage was shuttered and silent; the road was empty; the river flowed without sound; the leaves of the olives sighed and the moon shone.

Chapter XVIII

THE EYE

FATHER PASCALE WAS regaining strength. The danger of pneumonia was over and Dr Gompert, who had stayed with him all night, had left him asleep. The guests of the inn brought the news back from mass. The visiting curé had announced it to the congregation and prayers of thanksgiving had been said. Martine's heart was eased.

She had not gone to mass; René had forbidden it; but had come up to the bedrooms in time to do her share of work. Now she slipped into Juliet's room and was there a few minutes alone. When Juliet came in Martine rose from her knees and turned dark, questioning eyes to her.

'Do you think,' she asked, 'that I shall be forgiven for the terrible, blasphemous thing I said?'

Juliet could hardly help smiling at the swiftness with which Martine's view of the universe changed; but Martine needed a scolding, she felt.

'It *was* terrible: terrible and foolish and childish,' was her reply.

Martine blinked away tears, then her face relaxed and the shadow of a dimple even appeared. She said peacefully, 'Yes, it was childish and I do not imagine *le bon Dieu* took it seriously.'

She was very repentant; very much ashamed of having, in her weakness and panic, thrown extra work on Juliet.

'Especially now,' she said.

Juliet had wanted to keep her secret, but Michael, when she'd said, 'Of course your mother and my father will have to be told before anyone else,' had laughed at her for her French conventions and said, 'There just isn't time for all that.' And Martine was longing to know. Martine, whom one couldn't help at all by argument, was easily influenced by a mood; so Juliet, who felt in herself, this morning, such abounding happiness, confidence, strength, that it was as if she floated above all fear and trouble, smiled at Martine.

'Michael and I are going to be married,' she said.

If Juliet had been her sister, Martine could not have shown sweeter pleasure and pride in the news.

'And it was here you found one another! We have brought you good fortune. I am enchanted, enchanted!' she exclaimed, and insisted that René must immediately be told.

René, however, was preoccupied. He was in the kitchen with Marie and was sending her harshly about her business. 'Remember! I have warned you!' they heard him say. Marie irritated him a good deal. Martine and Juliet exchanged signals: 'Not now.' For his wife, René had a task waiting – elaborate *hors d'oeuvres* to be prepared. For Juliet, he had a reprimand and a note for five hundred francs.

'I forgot this. The Americans left it with me for you. Why were you not at hand when they were leaving?'

This was the one aspect of her employment in which Juliet could not and would not acquiesce. She reddened and answered stiffly: 'Do you not add the service to the bill? Do you not pay me, always; my share?'

'It is understood that there are *pourboires* also: especially from Americans.'

'I don't wish for them.'

'I can pay you no more and you work all the time. You are not receiving sufficient, and so I am told that I exploit you.' His eyes smouldered.

'No one has said that!'

'You heard Monsieur Faulkner.'

'He didn't mean that, René!'

It was wretched; almost a quarrel; their first. Must there be a clash between Michael and René? Juliet was upset and so was Martine. What had come over René? He looked haggard and spoke jerkily and he did not, in his usual charming, disarming way, end the little dispute with a jest. He went on sombrely with his work. It was not until half past two, when Martine was sleeping and Michael arrived, that Juliet understood.

With formal apologies René requested Michael to come down and speak with him in the kitchen. The three sat at the table. Michael smoked. He put his bandaged foot up on a chair saying, with a grin to Juliet, 'The scramble last night didn't do it much good.'

'I have heard about this,' René said.

So that was the trouble! Juliet had meant to warn him but here had been no opportunity. Michael grunted.

'So has the Coq d'Or heard of it – or heard some crazy version,' he said.

René said tensely, 'I think if my wife learns that Terka is in the neighbourhood she will become exceedingly ill.'

'Then get your wife out of the neighbourhood,' was Michael's retort, 'for the whole place is beginning to buzz and I'm sure rumours can't be shut out of an inn.'

Madame Bonin was in Antibes, at her daughter's, Juliet reflected. That was one small mercy.

'Will you please tell me what happened?' René demanded.

As he listened to Michael's story his dark face became the face of an older and a more ruthless man. The change in it was hateful, Juliet thought. He said heavily, 'So you let her escape?'

'What could I do?' Michael responded.

'You ought to have driven her over the frontier.'

'I had no earthly right ...'

'Right? Rights, Monsieur, where it is a matter of that—'

He checked himself, glancing at Juliet. Michael's lips were compressed. He looked half sorry for René and half disgusted with him.

'You could, at least, have refrained from interfering,' René said with bitterness.

'Man, if you'd seen them!' Michael exclaimed. 'The Devil only knows what they would have done.'

'They would probably have burnt out her other eye.'

Juliet felt sick. Terka's long, agonised shriek rang again in her ears. Was that what Terka had been fleeing from – her hunters' strength outlasting hers? It would be enough to drive her out of her mind.

'Thank heaven we saved her!' Juliet said.

René's rage seemed to leave him slowly, and to leave him in despair. He looked miserably at Juliet, saying, 'You do not know what you have done to Martine. Now I shall have to send her away.'

Michael said quietly, sympathetically: 'I think that would be wise,' and asked whether there was any way in which he could help – perhaps with the car.

The discussion became reasonable. Where was she to go? René knew that his sister, with whom his father was living at Fréjus, would look after her well – but that was too far away ...

Juliet's heart ached for Martine, who would not understand why René was banishing her or, if she guessed, would suffer untold lonely suspense.

There was the Maternity Hospital at Menton: that seemed the place, but would they consent to take her a whole month before the infant was due? Perhaps if one explained the circumstances and her state of nerves? Reluctantly, René decided to try. The decision deepened his ill-humour and he grumbled about every detail concerning it, as if seeking some pretext to keep Martine at home.

'One wastes half a day,' he declared, 'going to Menton. If I take the afternoon bus on Tuesday, and do not find someone to give me a lift back, I cannot be in time for dinner; and if I go early, with the carnation carts ...'

Michael intervened.

'That's easily fixed. On Tuesday morning my junk's to come down from the hut on the woodcutters' cart and be packed into the back of the car. I'll take it down to the station and fix things with the Customs at Menton. Also, I have to buy shoes. I'd have you back by six if you came with me, starting, say, about three o'clock.'

Gloomily, René agreed.

2

MARTINE BELIEVED that René's decision to run down to Menton with Michael was a sudden impulse. He said he would bring back pastries to compensate for his truancy and save work. He would also match her wool and buy the crochet pattern she wanted. She gave him a list of commissions and she stood on the front steps with Juliet to see the men set out.

The women at work by the washing-trough nudged one another, turned inquisitive eyes on Michael, and stared after the departing car, while Ignace Tissier grinned and nodded and clapped his big flat hands. The girls hurried into the house and, although the rule was to leave it open, Martine bolted the door.

A charming task awaited them in the kitchen. Martine, through all her troubles, had not ceased to sew and knit and now, laid out on the white table, were neat piles of minute garments waiting to be trimmed and finished and pressed. They worked at opposite ends of the table, stitching, running baby-ribbon through slots, confecting tiny bows and rosettes. Sunlight laid a widening swathe of warm light over the table and, outside, a soft breeze made the leaves of the olives flicker, silver and grey. When a few garments were ready, Martine would wrap them in silky paper, move to the window and add them to the treasure in the antique chest that stood under it.

'It was René's mother's marriage-chest,' she said with pride.

A marriage-chest was a first-rate idea, Juliet reflected. Why had she never thought of preparing one? Well, she had written her news to her father, and, with it, a very frank beg. How queer that she just couldn't guess what he would do. The work began to give her exquisite pleasure; entrancing dreams. Martine answered the smile on her face. Their talk was the talk of women. Juliet felt the wheel of life moving, most as if she were moving it with her hands. 'I will remember this always,' she thought.

Martine, when she was tranquil, was so wise.

'A wife cannot change her husband,' she said. 'And why should she wish to? Some women do. But I loved René for what he is. All you can do is find out when a man is at his best and try always to keep him so.'

The beam of sunlight stole from Juliet over the table to Martine. Not once did a bell ring from the terrace. They made coffee only for themselves. At six o'clock René should be returning. The breeze dropped; the olives were still and Juliet, lost in the golden hour, forgot on what mission René had gone and how brief Martine's peace was foredoomed to be.

It ended before he came.

The last rosette was stitched on the christening robe and it was wrapped up. Martine carried the dress, full length, across her arms, to lay it on top of everything else in the chest. Juliet, who was standing at the table behind her, saw all that happened, and there was nothing whatever that she could do. While Martine stooped, busying herself with arranging the long folds so that they should lie even, Terka moved out from behind the stable, moved along the lane by the yard wall, and stood there, staring in. She was black and wild and unkempt as an old raven, but she smiled. As Martine straightened up they were face to face and Terka's hand was raised to her covered eye.

The lid of the chest fell shut with a thud. There was no other sound. Terka pulled off the bandage and Juliet felt Martine's weight sag in her arms. Gently, she lowered her to the floor. When Juliet looked out again, Terka had gone.

The cape … cushions … Juliet failed to lift Martine into a chair, so wrapped her up where she lay, her legs doubled under her, close to the chest. Her face looked waxy against the red cushion. She was cold. Would it mean a miscarriage? It was wicked to be so useless, so ignorant.

André was probably in the bar and Marie in the garden; there were people upstairs. Juliet was obsessed with the idea that not a word must escape about Terka's eye. What should she tell them? To whom should she go?

Brandy! There was some in the cupboard. She forced a little between Martine's lips; then, as Juliet turned to run for help, Martine moaned and stirred.

'She has gone. It's all over. I'll call the doctor! It's all right: you didn't fall!' Juliet's words scarcely seemed to reach the mind of the shivering girl. All Martine could gasp out was, 'Don't go! Don't go!'

Juliet tried to ease her position, took off her shoes and began to rub her feet.

'Don't! Oh, the pricking! Oh, she has begun! Save me, Juliet! Juliet!'

Martine's terror was abject. There was nothing to do except crouch on the floor and hold her and murmur meaningless words.

It was there that René found them when he returned, alone, just before six o'clock.

Chapter XIX

THE HEALER

IT WAS EIGHT in the morning when René telephoned to the doctor but it was past eleven when he arrived, dusty and hot after visiting distant farms on his old, heavy motorcycle, which was always breaking down. He was out of humour, refused a drink and said he must see the patient alone.

'He seems to have heard what happened, although I didn't tell him,' René said gloomily. He was haggard and could not speak civilly, even to Juliet. He went out to the group of clients who were demanding his attention on the terrace and Juliet returned to the kitchen where Marie was washing artichokes and muttering her distrust of Dr Gompert.

'Do you know what he said to old Madame Proux?' she asked angrily. 'He said that St Jacques is a village of lunatics.'

Juliet remembered his harshness to Agnès Granerol and felt anxious for Martine. She wondered what version of her collapse he had heard. Somebody must have seen Terka leaving the lane, for Michael, eating his dinner at the Coq d'Or, had been told a tale that made him leave it unfinished and tear up in his car to the inn.

'Dr Gompert will bully her,' Juliet thought.

A quarter of an hour passed before he called from the outside staircase and Juliet went up with René to the attic room. Martine had drawn the quilt up and lay with her hair loose on the pillow, dishevelled, her dark eyes pleading for help. The doctor spoke roughly.

'Put a wrapper and slippers on her,' he said, 'and get her into that chair.'

He stood near the door. When René had placed his wife in the chair at the other end of the room the doctor, in a sergeant-major tone, ordered her to stand up and walk to him. Martine tried. She raised herself a little by pressing her hands down on the arms of the chair, but her legs would not support her and she sank down again. More and more imperatively the order was reiterated, and with greater and greater efforts Martine tried to obey. She tried until sweat broke out on her forehead and tears were streaming down her cheeks; then René stopped it. He lifted Martine in his arms and laid her in her bed and drew the quilt over her.

'Come down. I must talk to both of you,' the doctor said.

He was disgusted, antagonistic, and made no secret of it. In the yard he cross-questioned Juliet.

'You say she was all right until she saw Terka?'

'Yes.'

'And you, also,' he said sarcastically, 'saw this appalling sight?'

'I saw what Terka did.'

'And did you, too, see the "rolling, glaring, enormous orb"?'

'I saw an empty socket covered with wrinkled skin. Terka has no left eye.'

'Exactly! Precisely what I supposed!' He turned to René. 'The paralysis, in my opinion, has no more real existence than that eye.'

'Haven't you seen for yourself?' René retorted. 'She can't stand.'

'She imagines she can't – just as she imagined she saw Terka's left eye.'

'I tell you her legs are paralysed!'

'And I assure you they are not. There are certain infallible tests and I have carried them out. I tapped the knees and they jerked: that is normal. I stroked the soles of the feet and the toes turned downwards: that is normal, too. There's nothing, physically, wrong with your wife. She will walk as soon as she honestly wants to.'

'Nothing wrong with her!' René exclaimed, hot and red with resentment. 'How do you dare to say that?'

'I said "physically". People can make themselves ill with wishing, you know. Possibly Madame felt a desire to lie down and be waited on. Pregnant women grow fond of themselves. This is mere hysteria; but, I warn you, she had better wish herself out of it very soon or the outlook for the infant will not be good.'

At that, the blood left René's face, and his voice held only supplication as he asked, 'The remedy! What is the remedy?'

The doctor shrugged his shoulders. 'I have left sleeping-tablets, Give her two at about ten o'clock another later if necessary. Keep her in bed until she gets bored with it. That may not be long. Her physical condition is very good.'

René's black eyes were fixed on the doctor's as if they would pierce to some source of help in him in spite of the man's hostility.

'That will not cure her. What will cure her?' he demanded.

A one-sided smile came to the doctor's sallow face. His close-set eyes narrowed and twinkled. It was a pity he was hostile, Juliet thought: he looked as if he could fight when he wanted to. He said, 'We had a case in Montpellier very like this. The patient was a pregnant woman. She cured herself.'

'How?' René's question was like a shot. The doctor chuckled.

'She smoked in bed, set fire to her pillow and ran like a hare out into the corridor! I do not suggest ...'

His laugh broke the bounds of René's self-control. He raged at the man.

'A doctor of medicine! You a doctor! Cynic! Barbarian! You ought to have been in the Gestapo!'

Startled, Dr Gompert picked up his bag. He hesitated, shrugged again and walked across the yard. At the gate he turned back.

'In Nice there is an eminent psychiatrist. Perhaps you could consult him – or the medicine-man who lives in the woods,' he suggested, and walked away.

René was beating his fists together in fury.

'He pretends that she is mad! He proposes that I should set fire to her bed!' There came from him a torrent of abusive words which Juliet did not understand, then, like a man half demented with anger and misery, he stumbled up the stairs to Martine.

2

ONLY BY LETTING HIM join her in the marketplace could Juliet, all that crowded morning, have any talk with Michael.

He was unhappy, blaming himself for having persuaded René to go with him to Menton, leaving the girls alone.

'I never got myself to take the Terka thing seriously,' he confessed.

'And I was sorry for her,' Juliet said, incredulously. 'How could I be so blind? She is wicked; wicked.'

'I'm beginning to wonder whether she isn't a criminal.'

'I know; so am I. She *could* have poisoned Mireille and killed Gaston's dog.'

'The worst of that line of thought is that it leads into the whole slimy morass. It's no good going to extremes. The question is, now, what can be done for Martine?'

'I know what my father would say. He'd say, "Try counter suggestion. Tell her that Terka is dead."'

'It might work until she heard it wasn't true.'

'I wish it *were* true.'

'Don't say that to René, will you?'

'René is desperate. He hardly knows what he is doing. I've never known him to go all inefficient before.'

'He's blaming himself, poor chap.'

'Because it is against him that Terka is having revenge? But *could* that sort of hate last all those years?'

'Who knows, with a Romany?' Michael answered, and quoted, '"Hell hath no fury like a woman scorned."'

'Poor René.'

Michael nodded.

'He's had bad luck. Yesterday, too. They refused, you. know, at the Clinic, to receive Martine; then the police – I talked him into telling them about Terka – offered no help at all. He was sunk in anger and gloom on the drive home.'

For Juliet it was an ordeal to move about the streets, giving guarded answers to horrified questions, responding to expressions of shocked condolence. Michael went back with her up the rue de la Pompe. They walked up the garden and crossed the terrace. René was in his office, telephoning. He opened the door and signed to them to wait while he finished dictating a telegram. He was cancelling advance bookings and his face was seamed with the bitterness of defeat.

He came out and told them that he had arranged accommodation elsewhere for his guests. All were leaving. He was closing the inn. 'Oh, René,' Juliet said, 'I am sorry! I wish I could do more.'

'You do too much.'

'Madame Bonin would come back from Antibes if you telephoned.'

'She would,' he said grimly, 'and she would arrange a funeral for Martine! I want no Madame Bonins, Juliet. Try to keep the neighbours away.' He spoke to Michael, calling him 'Monsieur Michel' and asking what he was doing this afternoon.

'Drop the "Monsieur", René,' Michael replied. 'I'll do anything I can. It is hard luck, having to close the inn.'

René said, his face contorted, 'I would burn it down if it could help Martine.'

Michael asked, 'What can I do?'

'Go up to the forest and ask Henri to come.'

'I'll do that. And I'll make a few enquiries. I'll find out whether the curé has remembered what caused his accident, and whether any sense can be got out of Agnès Granerol and Claudette.'

René drew them both into his office. Clients were passing through the hall. He looked after them ruefully. They were probably going to lunch at the Coq d'Or.

'That will be useless, Michel,' he said.

'It won't if I can get evidence for the police. Wouldn't Martine be relieved to hear that Terka was under arrest?'

'Police!' René's tone was full of disgust. 'I told you how they received me yesterday! They shrugged their shoulders and spread their hands and demanded if I expected them to comb the whole forest for the gypsy.' He turned to Juliet, his indignation overflowing. 'One of them even said it was Terka whom they might find themselves obliged to protect. It seems she does not break the law. The law takes no cognizance of sorcery. Maître Daniel, on whom I called, also, tells me the same thing. There are no sorcerers in France, according to the Code! It is an absurdity, but it is the law.'

Michael persisted. 'But if we could prove that she has broken the law? Has used poison and forced locks? At least that would convince Martine that the evil eye business is all imagination, wouldn't it?'

René brooded for a moment then shook his head. 'It is too late. Today is not yesterday. Arresting her now would do nothing but harm.'

Juliet sighed. 'You believe that Terka has cursed her, don't you, René?'

He answered steadily: 'Terka has cursed her; she has cursed her to punish me, and if I were the cause of sending Terka to prison the curse would be doubled. Prison walls do not shut curses in. If we do that, now, Martine will die.'

'Shade of Jeanne d'Arc! What age are we living in? You *can't* believe that!' Michael exclaimed, outraged.

René did not reply.

Juliet said, 'The trouble is, you see, Michael, Martine would.'

'I suppose she would. It's hard to know what to do.'

'Tell Henri we need him,' René said.

3

THE FOREST FELT EMPTY. Michael was puzzled at first: he had never before been aware of this lack in it – only of beneficent quiet and space. He smiled to himself when he realised what was missing. So that was what being in love did to a man. Would Cyprus seem empty, too?

One thing he was determined about. Juliet was not staying on at that inn. She was his girl and he would not leave her there, devoting herself to Martine and René. Both of them were decent, except for their crass superstition, and both were fond of Juliet, but either would grind her to dust for the other if it seemed necessary. She should go back with his mother to London ...

This was the eighth: Wednesday. On Saturday night his mother would be in Paris – alone, poor darling, except for those stuffy friends of hers at the Embassy. She'd probably take four days on the road and turn up this day week. She had certainly made her reply non-committal. Useful things, telegrams:

OF COURSE WILL COME SOUTH LOVING WISHES MUFF

How would it go? Juliet would be on the defensive – scared and brittle and stiff, at least for a while. And Muff? She wasn't a snob, but she did like achievement, or, at least, ambition, in women as well as men and it wouldn't be fair to expect her to see, at first glance, under a shy manner and sensitive face, the metal of which Juliet was made – pure gold, tried in the fire ... Well, in time she would know. And she would look after Juliet, he knew that, whatever her own feelings might be; and then, if they saw a good deal of one another, all would be well.

His foot was alright and he needed a forest walk. He left the car on the roadside by the gap and made his way up by the steep mule-path which he and Henri often used, thinking what an unlikely mission this was for his father's son to find himself engaged on – calling upon a white sorcerer to fight against black magic. With surprise he realised that he had definite hope of results.

He came upon Henri alone, clearing the path with a mattock. The delight that brightened his face when he saw Michael paled as he listened; gave place to a recoil, a shrinking. He turned away, making the sign of the cross.

'At such a time!' he ejaculated, appalled. 'At such a moment! It is to kill!'

'It is just such a case, surely, as you will be able to help,' Michael said.

Henri turned to him, hesitant, saying, 'It is not like a sickness, you see.'

'I know. It appears there is nothing physical wrong. That is why I thought you have a chance,' Michael replied.

'I can sometimes cure illness,' Henri said, looking helpless and despondent, 'but to lift a curse is a different thing.'

Disconcerted, Michael realised that to talk about suggestion and counter-suggestion to this man would only confuse him and could do no good. Whatever Henri's method was, self-confidence must be the principal element in it – that, and the vocation of the patient's will and faith. He said, with sincerity:

'Henri, as you know, I'm fairly sceptical as a rule, but this thing I believe you can do if you will.'

'Naturally, I will try!'

'Can you go straight down now?'

Henri shook his head. His face, under its deep tan, was pale. There was a certain likeness between him and Father Pascale, Michael reflected: the tightness of the skin over the bone; the broad forehead and wide-open eyes. He answered, 'No, Michel, I cannot do that. I have soiled my mind with thoughts about Terka. For healing, one must be in a state of grace. It will be late when I come.'

With that Michael had to be satisfied. He felt that he was moving in a world of which he had small understanding and where he could do very little to help. It was with diminished optimism that he retraced his steps to where the path forked and then walked to Loubier's farm.

At the house he found an oppressive atmosphere. Claudette stole about like a scared mouse. Old Emma mumbled only to herself, her fingers plaiting the fringe of her counterpane. Marie-Louise was the least despondent. She said, gently, 'Good *must* be stronger than evil. God will not let Satan prevail. I am sure Henri will cure Martine.'

Before she let Michael go to the priest's room she warned him not to tell the invalid about Martine's stroke. He had been told nothing about Terka except that she had disappeared. 'He suffers,' the girl said. 'As the pain grows less he suffers more in the spirit, wondering whether he has done wrong. If our men commit sins of violence in consequence of what he said or of what has happened to him I think he will die. You saved him when you saved Terka from them.'

This warning made Michael frame his questions carefully, asking whether any recollection of the moments preceding the accident had returned.

'I do not remember either my fall or the moment before it,' Father Pascale said, slowly, as though it cost him an effort to speak. 'You can tell them I saw nobody on the roadside and that nobody threw a stone ... Why', he said, unhappily, 'should you all wish to think evil? Could not a bird or a squirrel have startled the mare?'

It was evident that his head ached severely and Michael saw that it would be cruel and useless to question him further. He told him a direct lie about Martine, declaring that she was well. There were times when it was a plain duty to lie.

A talk with Camille was equally unproductive. Camille did not believe that Terka could be proved to have violated the law. The Romanies had a great deal of cunning and informed themselves well as to what to avoid. They never professed in plain words to possess occult powers, knowing that such profession would break the law, and he had never heard of Terka's overtly claiming them, except for her cards and arms and amulets. 'It is her deeds that speak.' As to Claudette, the girl had a lively imagination, and her tale about having seen Terka, during the thunderstorm, calling the lightning down out of the sky would not convince a judge. For himself, he would like nothing better than to help clap Terka into jail.

Together they went to the Granerols' and sat in their filthy kitchen trying to discover whether the two could adduce any evidence, good in a court of law, to support all their talk about poisoning. The couple's attitude, now, however, seemed reversed. It was true that Terka had sold Agnès *tisane,* they said; such sales were legal and the Romany knew about herbs, but, as for Léon's sickness, that had been as bad before taking the draught as after; Dr Gompert would bear that out; besides he often had these attacks.

If Terka had committed breaches of the law it would not be easy to find witnesses with the courage to testify against her, Michael realised; and, indeed, in view of what René had said, what use could one make of evidence were it found? As he drove back to the village he decided that, next day, after he had returned the car to the Castellis, he would try something else. He would search certain likely parts of the forest for Terka and if he found her he would see whether bribes or threats could not induce her to cease her persecution of Martine – persuade her, perhaps, to make some gesture that Martine might interpret as a removal of the curse.

When he confided this project to Juliet she gave him such a sweet, laughing look that he asked her what she was amused about.

'Oh, my darling,' she answered. 'You, of all people, double-dealing and double-crossing in superstitions. And "all for Hecuba"!'

'My darling girl, it isn't for Hecuba. It isn't for Martine. It's for you. I want to give *you* peace of mind.'

'You want that very much, don't you?'

'Very, very much,' Michael replied.

4

THE AFTERNOON WAS warm and oppressive. Juliet was thankful when the last of the clients had gone. She went up to visit Martine.

The room, with the curtains closed, was airless and dim. So neat the bed was, as René had left it, and Martine lay under the white quilt so straight and still that Juliet found herself speaking in whispers. Everything – the subdued light, the quiet, the sacred pictures on the walls and the ruby lamp burning before the statue – gave warnings of mortality; and Martine was worse. The paralysis had reached her thighs.

'Let us move you,' Juliet pleaded. 'All the bedrooms are empty now and they are so pleasant and cool.'

'Henri will find it easier here,' was Martine's gentle reply. When René came he, too, urged the change, but Martine became distressed. 'I am safer in this room,' she said. 'This bed has been blest. It is here that I want my baby to be born. I want to die in this room if I have to die.'

'Martine, Martine,' Juliet cried. 'You *can't* die of this. It isn't a dangerous illness. Martine, how can you believe you are bewitched?

There are no witches. Terka is only a wicked beggar woman. She has no left eye, evil or good. How *can* she harm you, Martine?'

'She kills', Martine answered, under her breath, 'by making a little image of wax. She sticks needles in it. First she was pricking only the feet. I felt that. Now I can't even feel. Now it is the legs. It will be my heart in the end.'

Juliet could not find words. René said, desperately, 'Henri will save you.'

'He must save me! He must!' Martine cried.

René contrived to calm her, talking and talking about Henri and the famous cures that he and others like him had made – of the *pléiade* of great healers in the Terres-Rouges – Enco de Bote and Michel Puit and the rest. René's own faith in these men and their gifts was perfect and it strengthened hers.

Afterwards, in the kitchen, René said to Juliet: 'It is going to be a duel – a duel between Henri, who is no longer young, and the diabolical Powers through whom Terka works.'

It might have gone differently, Juliet believed afterwards, if the new curé had not come. He was the only person whom they admitted. He looked kindly enough, with his fresh country face and round brown eyes. He spoke in a hushed voice and walked on tiptoe into Martine's room. He did not stay long but he left her desolated.

'It is because I gave gifts to Terka,' she sobbed. 'He called it "trafficking with the Evil One". He said I knew Father Pascale disapproved of it; and I did know. He told me to repent as if I hadn't repented a thousand times! And he said I had disobeyed my husband and stolen from you – *stolen* from you. Oh, René, René!'

She was inconsolable. 'God has turned away from me,' she moaned.

She began to vomit and was in a weak condition when, at seven in the evening, Henri arrived.

'I could strangle that curé,' René said, while he and Juliet sat on the bench in the yard, waiting for Henri to come down, and he spoke as if he meant it. Juliet made no answer. She was thinking of the day when Martine had implored her to take presents to Terka and René had asked her to help him get rid of her, and wondering whether this anguish would have been averted if she had consented to one or the other of those requests. She started up when a voice called from the kitchen; she ran in and tried to hush the intruder; that wasn't easy: it was Madame Bonin.

Madame Bonin was flushed and panting. She had heard the news only this morning; had taken the first train from Antibes, and, all the way from Menton, had walked and ridden on jolting *charrettes* in turn. If only her warnings had been heeded! René came into the kitchen and managed to make her lower her voice but not to send her away. She was hurt and angry when he told her that she could not see Martine.

'But she needs me, the poor little one. Who can do as much for her as I can?'

'In a day or two, Madame. Henri is with her now. You must leave us to speak with him,' René said, courteous but firm.

'I, also, should consult with Henri. The curé does not end with his visit. Novenas will be required, also. And am I not to take my share? I must pray with the poor child.'

René lost all wish to placate her. Tersely he said, 'I ask you to go.'

'You ask me to go?' Her voice rose. 'You attempt to separate me from Martine?'

René's temper cracked. He retorted furiously, 'I wish I had done so earlier. Your chatter has done her nothing but harm.'

'I have harmed her? You dare to say that? You, who have brought the curse on her by your obstinacy! Whose fault is all this, René, but your own?'

Nothing could stop her. She sat at the table pounding with her fist, glaring at René, working herself into a passion by her own eloquence. All her devotion to the inn and all René's offences against the gypsy were flung at him. There was neither sequence nor logic in her tirade. Her charges went back seven years and more.

'And do you imagine,' she demanded, 'that I do not know why you loathe the sight of her? Do you suppose it is not known, how you used and misused the wretch during the War? Philandering with a pagan gypsy, a girl without religion or morals!'

To Juliet's amazement, René broke in with, 'A fine girl, a brave girl, Terka was in the Resistance!'

'Yet you threw her over, didn't you, when she'd served your purpose?'

'When I knew she'd become a whore.'

'When she was disfigured and outcast!'

'When she had sold herself to the Devil.'

It was horrible. Juliet shivered. Imploring the woman to stop, she drew wrath on herself.

'As for you,' said Madame Bonin, in a low but furious tone, 'I have heard how you and your Englishman rescued her! *After* she had been shown up for a witch; *after* her curse had fallen on the priest. When the men had at last found the courage to deal with her! You will be execrated!' The word came from her throat with a rasp.

Her illogical twist suddenly made René laugh. It was an ugly sound.

'They saved some heads from the guillotine, maybe,' he said.

'The guillotine! As if any court in France would condemn a man for destroying a sorceress! ... They were *men*, those! As for you, though you've plotted and threatened and goaded others to action, you haven't the manhood to go against her yourself! Our brave René! Our hero of the Maquis! A coward is all you are, where Terka's concerned.'

There was a bread knife lying on the table. Juliet snatched it, alarmed at the rage that congested René's face. Madame Bonin knew she had gone too far. Covering her retreat with throaty mutterings, she collected her bag and parcels and departed. They heard her bang the street-door after her. Juliet sat still, waiting for her knees to cease trembling. René ignored her. He went to the sink, drank water and splashed his head. Then he stood still, breathing hard, until, at last, Henri came down.

In the kitchen René filled a glass with *vin rosé* for Henri, who sank down, exhausted, in the chair Madame Bonin had left. He refused a meal but swallowed some dry bread.

'Leave her alone for a little,' he said, and sat still, collecting his strength. Presently he rose and shook hands, first with René and then with Juliet. They went out with him to the road. Before he left them he said, 'Her faith in God's mercy was not perfect, and I think my gift weakens. I have done what I could, my poor René. May God comfort you if I have failed.'

When they entered the half-dark room, Martine was almost erect, just supported by the edge of the bed and holding herself up by the great post at its foot. She fixed piteous eyes on René; drew a deep breath and, letting go her hold, stretched out her arms to him. Her legs failed to support her; she swayed and, with a heartbroken moan, fell against him.

Juliet could not control her tears. She fled downstairs and out of the house, out into the olive field, where the trees hung grey in the fading light. She left the house, with its curse, darkening behind her and ran straight to the quiet heart of the grove where Michael was waiting for her.

Chapter XX

UNDER THE MOON

MICHAEL'S ROOM looked over the marketplace and, as a rule, noise kept him awake for some time, but the long day in the forest and the walk back to the village had tired him. It had tired him because it had done no good. Terka had vanished. She had probably turned herself into a night-jar, a bat, or an owl.

Light from a street lamp made a pattern with a shape like a rose on his ceiling. At least, he told himself as he lay and gazed up at it, he'd been on hand to steady and comfort Juliet ... Juliet sleeping alone in that *maudit* inn ... Today had been even more ghastly than yesterday, with Martine's paralysis creeping up ... Juliet must go home ... He saw her on to a boat with his mother before he plunged into sleep.

When the church clock struck one he heard it. He was broad awake. He jumped out of bed and stood at the window. The moon in its third quarter rode high and a ghostly light fell on the old square with its toppling roofs and cavernous arcades. He had no notion what had jerked him awake. The silence and stillness were unnatural – as weird as the monstrous fears that haunted the place. Windows glittered like cold, dead eyes. He wondered whether anyone at the other inn was asleep. The thought of René penetrated his mind. Poor fellow, he had tried everything, and everything had failed. He imagined Martine and the child were foredoomed to die, and through his own fault. He must be in torment.

Michael asked himself what René, with his temperament, his fighting record and his passionate love for his wife was likely to do; then he dressed hurriedly, went out into the white silence and raced through the sleeping streets to the inn.

From the lane he looked up at Juliet's window and at the windows of Martine's attic. No light showed. There was no movement, no sound. He did not believe that René was in the house.

He crossed the stile and walked softly among the olives, his uneasiness sharpened by the stark, moon-blanched immobility of the trees. The trunks, grotesquely contorted, half-veiled by grey foliage, cast shadows like skulking creatures on the rough ground. Fantastic speculations visited Michael's mind; notions that had been stillborn, finding no credence by daylight, quickened and grew in this moon-struck scene. He believed that he understood Terka at last.

He believed she had never planned, deliberately, this monstrous career of hers. Some accident, more likely, had started it – a series of coincidences, perhaps: disasters that fell on some of the countless people who had rebuffed and despised the outcast Romany. Then, starving and desperate, she would have found a means of livelihood thrust into her hands – and a means, not only of living but of exercising power. In the past, her beauty had given her power. She could wield power through terror, now, and at the same time have her revenge. Perhaps, in three years of pretending to possess occult gifts – to punish with cursings, to live in league with the Devil – she had grown to believe she was really a sorceress. Her success was beyond what seemed natural, right enough; but, then, so was her equipment. Terka would have learnt many things in the Maquis – to fiddle locks; set a time-fuse and start fires; mix drugs; dispose of a dog; would have learnt, too, how to cover her traces, leaving no evidence.

'Hell hath no fury ...' René had scorned Terka. She had adored him, if Claudette's stories were true; and he had hounded her. She probably meant to burn down his house.

'She'll try to do it tonight, while Martine is helpless. She has her informers,' he told himself, and turned to dash back. 'Get Juliet out,' he thought, 'then find René, telephone Gaston and set a watch.'

He saw her before he was half way across the field. She was standing against the trunk of an olive and staring at the moonlit house.

He stood still, unobserved. His first impulse was to shadow Terka, watch her setting about her work and catch her in the act, but then it occurred to him that she might already have started her mischief; at this moment a fire might be smouldering in the empty stable under Martine's room. He had taken the decision to rush at her when she moved. She walked warily, slinking from shadow to shadow, and the course she was weaving was down to the inn. Cautiously, Michael followed. He knew that Terka could run like a hare. She would escape him if he showed up now. Better let her get into the yard.

A twig snapped, but not under his feet and not, he thought, under hers: the sound had come from below, to the right, beyond Terka, not far from the house. She crouched where she was and Michael moved quietly to the right, peering down. He saw the gleam of moonlight on metal – on the double barrel of a gun. It was no surprise. René was moving stealthily from tree to tree, stalking his prey. He had Terka within sight and range.

'Don't shoot; we'll corner her!' Michael cried. Both figures were motionless for an instant; then Terka started upright, swerved and remained standing immobile, but she had the tree between herself and René now. René had advanced and was taking aim. Terka saw Michael rushing towards her and ran. The burst caught her. It was a short burst, very loud. René had stopped before Michael wrested the gun from him, but Terka had been hit in the legs. Scream after high scream shattered the quietude of the night.

Michael gave an order: 'Look after her. That is absolutely neces- sary. I'll see to Juliet and Martine.'

To his relief, René spoke no word of protest but gave him a startled look and then went to where Terka writhed on the ground, thrashing about with her arms.

Michael, because the ground was wet with dew, placed the long, heavy gun against a tree; then he ran and in a few minutes was in the yard.

The only light shone from Martine's window and it was out of her bedroom that Juliet came. She saw him and rushed down the staircase into his arms. Footsteps and shouting could be heard from the lane. Juliet whispered, trembling, 'What has he done?'

'He has wounded her. Tell Martine carefully,' Michael replied.

Juliet stood away from him for a moment, searching his face, her fists clenched at her breast. Then she did something so unlike her that Michael was astounded. She turned her back on him, went to the foot of the staircase and, lifting her face to Martine's window, shouted with all the power of her lungs:

'Terka has been shot!'

The cry rang wildly and Juliet repeated it. 'Martine, Martine, René has shot Terka! Come to René, Martine!'

It was scarcely a minute before Martine appeared, wrapped in a trailing sheet, at the top of the stairs.

'Is he safe? Is she dead?' she cried, in a frenzy of anxiety, oblivious of herself. Juliet did not support her, but stood ready. Martine did not need support. She repeated her desperate question: 'Is Terka dead?'

Michael answered.

'René is safe. He is perfectly safe, and so are you, Martine, She's lying helpless, out there, on the ground, shot in the legs.'

There was a brief silence, then Martine laughed.

'Go back to bed,' Michael ordered.

She laughed again. 'It has gone! Look at me, Juliet! The malady has gone from my legs – into hers! Look, I can walk!'

She would have stumbled, tripped by the sheet, but Juliet caught her by the shoulders. Martine's hysterical laughter eased and she began to weep. Juliet spoke with no note of compassion in her voice:

'Go in and get dressed. You'll be needed. Come down and help.'

They went in and Juliet came back with a key. She was trembling from head to foot.

'Good soldier,' Michael said quietly. He was immensely proud of her courage and sense. 'First-aid things, quickly, and water,' he added. She nodded, unlocked the back door, found what was needed and put coffee to heat on the stove.

There were men in the yard. Michael collided with Gaston, who wanted to telephone. Martine called joyously from her window and René, with a wild shout, went bounding up the staircase to her.

'She's bleeding from both legs,' somebody said. Half a dozen people accompanied Michael and stood around while he bound up Terka's wounds. Some held torches while others tried to quiet the unfortunate woman, who never ceased to struggle and rage. She was like a wild animal, hurt and trapped. She was still conscious and still lamenting an hour later when the ambulance came.

2

MICHAEL FINISHED the night in the bedroom Frith had occupied at the inn. He was wakened at half past seven by René: René in a good brown suit, smiling and debonair, bringing razor and towels and soap.

'I will bring breakfast in a few minutes,' he said. Michael had scarcely had time to wash, shave and collect his wits before his host reappeared with breakfast for two. Martine, he reported, had slept like a good child. She was well and happy and no trace of the paralysis remained.

'You see now, how right I was, do you not?' René demanded and Michael did not know what to reply.

René was going at once to Menton.

'You see,' he explained, 'it is necessary that I should report to the *police judiciaire*. There will be an enquiry. I may be detained some days. This is why I disturbed you, Michel.'

Michael asked, 'What cartridges did you use?' René's eyebrows shot up.

'*Des cartouches de chevrotines.*'

'Have you a permit?'

'But naturally! They are what one uses to shoot fox; wild pig, also. Is not that a magnificent gun? To buy that, I sold two litters of setter pups ...'

'René,' Michael interrupted, 'you realise that you will have to engage a capable advocate?'

'There is none better than Maître Daniel. He is my good friend. He will be interested ... But it is not to talk of all this that I have disturbed you. I wish to ask a favour of you. Will you, until I return, please take up your quarters here, for the protection of Martine and Juliet?'

'No: I am taking Juliet away – that is, the moment my mother arrives. You must see ...'

'But until then? I beg you: until then?'

He was vehement; distressed.

'There are difficulties,' Michael insisted.

'As to that, Martine will also invite a lady: it will be *comme il faut.*'

Michael laughed and gave in.

'Right: till my mother comes.'

'I thank you, Michel.' René seized his hand and pressed it. 'I thank you for everything. I do not know what it was that made you come at night to the field, but if you had not, Terka would be dead and I ...' René paused; his eyes were stretched wide and the muscles around them twitched. He said: 'I do not know why I lowered the gun, Michel.'

Michael spoke sharply.

'You never intended to kill her.'

'But I did. How could I guess that merely to wound her would cure Martine? That is a miracle, is it not?'

'If you meant to kill her, forget it, René.'

René, for all his vivacious air, had grown pale and his jaws were taut. Michael looked with dismay at the young fool who was taking himself to the police to tell them that he had, with premeditated intent to kill, shot and wounded a woman.

'How are you getting to Menton?' he asked.

'I will walk to the Bridge of the Sheep. The carnation carts go down at this time and somebody will give me a lift.'

'I think I had better come down with you,' Michael said. 'Then I shall be able to bring back the news. You know, you will certainly be detained.'

'Do this, please!'

René was relieved. He disappeared to leave a message with Marie and Michael scribbled a note to Juliet and pushed it under her door. René returned wearing a smart brown hat at a jaunty angle and carrying a leather *serviette* in which he had packed all that he thought he would need. He went down his front steps in a sober mood, but his appearance was the signal for a shout. Washerwomen waved and called, beaming upon him; in the houses all about the Place de la Pompe *volets* were flung open and heads were thrust out. René waved his hat in acknowledgement of the smiles, the cries of *'Brava!'* and *'Bonne chance!'* He shouted, and his words were echoed in joyous voices: *'À bas la sorcellerie!'*

Michael, striding ahead as fast as his legs would carry him, wondered what would happen next in this unbelievable village, and how long it would take him to extricate Juliet from its toils.

Chapter XXI

THE CHARIOT

'IT WILL BE a fine drying day,' Martine declared. 'The wind is veering with the sun; the evening will be beautiful, you will see.'

Her voice had a singing lilt in it and her eyes sparkled.

She shone with a sweet confidence in which Juliet's anxiety for her melted away like an icicle in the sun. Her recovery was much more than the end of illness or even than release from the fear of death; to Martine it was a sign that her sins had been expiated and that she had been received again into Divine Grace. And not herself and René only, but the whole region, had been liberated from over-shadowing dread by her husband's bold and devoted act. Her mind, more childlike and simple than René's, was as free from his vision of evil influences operating without concrete means. To Martine, Terka, ill in bed, prevented from using the sinister eye that could appear or vanish; from scattering feathers and pricking wax images – Terka, with her own legs rendered helpless at the moment when her victim recovered, was a sorceress overthrown. There was nothing more to be feared from her. Good had prevailed over evil and the prowling Devil had been banished from St Jacques. It was no wonder that, since early morning, people had been coming to the house with solicitous enquiries and gifts.

Perhaps because she had not slept enough, Juliet could not bring the night's events into realistic focus in her mind. They had an inconsequential, dreamlike quality. She had been wakened at about one o'clock by cries from Martine ringing across the yard; had found Martine sitting up in her bed, trembling, staring at the bracket between the windows from which René's gun was gone.

'Go out and bring him home!' she had implored. 'Terka will strike him down before he can shoot!'

Martine had looked so ghastly that Juliet had thought she would faint and refused to leave her. And nothing would stop René, she knew. They had been sitting there, side by side, straining to hear any sound in the silence, when shattering burst of fire came from the fields.

René, in his ecstasy and pride over Martine's recovery, had seemed to feel that heaven was rewarding him. Glorying in his success, he had not had a thought to spare for any other view that might be taken of what he had done. He had poured out his treasured *fine* and made Gaston drink with him, laughing at the guard's lugubrious face, until the ambulance had come and gone.

Until that moment, when she was left alone in the kitchen, Juliet had been too busy to think, and then Michael had come to her, and she had been most sweetly comforted. This morning her reason told her that Martine's peace could not last, but, with Michael's note in her pocket, Michael's cherishing to remember, she felt anxious for nobody. She was unfathomably in love.

Happily, the two girls went about their work in the empty inn. Sheets and towels were bundled up to be washed while Marie prepared her copper in the scullery and set up her in the yard. Marie, too, felt that the inn was blessed.

'I think', Martine said, 'that even if René returns tomorrow we should keep the inn closed for a while. We all need a rest. Perhaps we should lock the silver away.'

Juliet thought Martine looked exhausted and ought to lie down, and offered to transfer the silver to the safe in René's office herself. She was a little relieved when Martine declared nothing was wrong. It was only that Henri-Martin was restless.

'We have excited him, poor little one.'

With a return of her habitual eager interest in her young friend's affairs, she asked Juliet when Michael's mother was likely to arrive and whether, before their meeting, Juliet was not going to buy some new clothes. Should she not take a few hours in Menton?

Juliet crinkled her forehead. This had become a serious problem. No reply had reached her from Frith but, even if he failed her, her poverty must, somehow, be covered up.

First of all: gloves. Long gloves, half way to the elbow would, she thought, do more than anything that she could afford to give a touch of elegance to her *toilette,* and a touch of elegance she *must,* somehow, acquire, before Dame Alison came. Martine agreed with her: gloves and a new handbag would do a great deal. But there wouldn't be enough for a handbag if she had to buy either a suit or a coat …

With a small twinge at her heart, Juliet wondered whether she had been unwise in begging Michael not to give her a ring yet. He had agreed because he wouldn't buy a cheap ring and hadn't francs enough for a good one, but Juliet's reason had been the fear that Dame Alison might feel hurt if the engagement were made formal before she and Juliet had even met. To put the faintest shadow, the least chill, between Michael and his mother would be terrible. But her hands did look a scullery-maid's, she thought.

Martine was asking whether Dame Alison would perhaps stay at the inn if it were reopened in time. 'Or is she very rich? Is she accustomed to *hôtels de luxe?*'

Juliet did not know. Her mental picture of Michael's mother was dazzling, variable and incomplete. She was an elegant Englishwoman; a well-known hostess. She was 'an intemperate motorist' and a lover of hills. She had driven an ambulance during the Blitz and saved lives in a fire and had been created a 'Dame', but it was as much as your life was worth to mention it. Old furniture had been her hobby and now she wrote about it and photographed it. As for the rest, one could only guess by the little smile with which Michael talked of her. He wasn't good at description. He'd said, 'She's just any man's favourite sort of mother, I suppose.'

'And Michael,' Juliet thought, 'is any woman's favourite sort of son; and he'll be an important man, and his mother will want an important wife for him, not a half-educated girl with no *dot* and no background who has found nothing better to do with her life than work as a waitress in an inn.'

These thoughts alarmed and depressed her sometimes; but not today. She said to Martine, 'Anyway, she is a person Michael likes.'

Martine did not answer. She was leaning on a table, her head bent.

'You're not well!' Juliet exclaimed.

The answer came breathlessly. 'I'm not sure, but I think … I believe … I believe it is time to send for the *sage-femme*.'

The midwife's number as well as the doctor's were written large in the office. Juliet telephoned. A light voice answered, became pleased and excited when the name was given said, '*O la la!* It is not strange, is it? The eighth month! The room must be very warm. The doctor should be told. I come without delay. *O la la, la la la!'*

'That doctor shall not lay a finger on my baby,' Martine declared.

She was *full* of courage. She had prayed so much. Now nothing would go wrong. René would be spared all anxiety and come home to a joyful surprise. When she was safely in bed and the midwife had come, she advised Juliet to go and take a long rest.

'We shall both have a broken night again, you will see.'

Juliet's courage quite ebbed away. Her ignorance about birth was complete. She had never so much as handled a newborn kitten. And this baby, this infinitely precious first child, coming a month too soon. Martine had been through a fearful ordeal and wasn't strong. She *must* have the doctor: she's got to, Juliet thought.

She felt her own efficiency dissolving in nervousness. 'By right,' she thought, 'I'll be good for nothing.'

She would make Martine send for some neighbour. Not Madame Bonin. But they would all be anxious about René and would talk … If only she knew where to find Michael on the telephone! She wouldn't be fit to be seen when he did come. Perhaps it would help her morale to have a hot bath.

It did help. When she had bathed and changed into a fresh dress – the green-patterned one Michael liked best – and brushed her hair until it was shining, she had collected the strength to insist on her own way. She would put herself under the *sage-femme's* orders, but Dr Gompert must be called.

As to the doctor, Juliet was defeated. The midwife supported Martine. He was too full of theories, that young man. 'He puts prematures in incubators, as though they were chickens.' Madame Millo had delivered babies by the score without him and Henri-Martin would not be too much for her. Time enough to send for him if something went wrong. Madame Millo held modern notions in contempt.

The woman was like a plump pigeon, strutting about, chuckling and boasting. Her lively, facile talk tormented Juliet. Surely those stories of difficult births and delicate babies and suffering mothers couldn't be good for Martine?

'Please, please, Martine, let me phone for the doctor,' Juliet pleaded. 'I'll be terribly worried if you don't.'

But Martine, with tears welling up in her eyes, declared, 'He's not lucky to me,' and, for the moment, Juliet had to give way.

It seemed that nothing would happen for a long time. What could she do to steady her nerves? The emptiness of the inn was unnatural. It made her feel useless and out of place. She decided to go down to the dining-room and finish collecting the silver, but as she entered the room she saw through the window that someone was sitting on the terrace. In spite of the *Fermé* placards, a client had arrived. Well, the poor lady would just have to be sent away. How still she was sitting, gazing out at the view through dark glasses; and how cool and at ease she looked in her grey suit and soft grey hat!

The face that was turned to Juliet as she approached was squarely modelled; the long, unsmiling lips were kind. Juliet spoke in English. 'Good afternoon. I am so sorry, the inn isn't open,' she said.

'Am I intruding? I hoped that, perhaps, the restaurant might be. I wondered if I might have some tea.'

Tea was a good idea, Juliet thought. The midwife would like some, and Martine, and she needed some, too.

'Everything is supposed to be closed really; but if bread and butter would do, I could give you tea.'

'That's very kind. I don't want to drive on.'

When she had carried a tray to the attic Juliet set out the finest tea things, cut very thin bread and butter, heated the pot scrupulously, used the blend containing a little China and brought the visitor her tea. The presence of the quiet Englishwoman was helping her to recover her nerve. She had a warm, very charming voice.

'I am so disappointed about the inn. Will it reopen soon, do you suppose?'

Juliet shook her head. A spasm of dismay closed her throat. 'René will be in prison,' she thought. 'He will be in prison for a long time.' She was remembering how worried Michael had looked.

'Is something wrong?' The question came gently.

Juliet nodded. 'You see, Martine – Madame Loubier, is having her baby – her first baby, and her husband is … detained.'

'Is she all right? You look dreadfully tired and worried, child.'

Juliet had a little struggle for composure but won it. 'She won't have the doctor and the *sage-femme* seems sort of old-fashioned and it is a month too soon and I …' Nothing could stop the blush mounting. 'I'm disgracefully ignorant.'

'Disgracefully!' Her smile was amused and kind. 'They don't teach these things at school … Where is Michael?'

Startled, Juliet hesitated to reply.

'I know you are Juliet.' The dark glasses were taken off and hazel eyes, so like Michael's that Juliet heard herself laugh with astonishment, looked into hers. 'A very worried Juliet, too.'

'Michael's in Menton. Or perhaps Nice. They've arrested René and Michael is standing by. He's all right. Michael's all right, I mean. We … he … he didn't expect you so soon.'

'The husband has been arrested? When?'

'Last night. He shot a woman and wounded her. She was … It's the craziest tangle. He thought she was bewitching Martine.'

'Poor, poor Martine!' Dame Alison hesitated, then asked: 'Juliet, do you think, if I took my meals out and promised to make my own bed and everything, that you could possibly let me stay?'

'Oh, yes. You could stay, you could!'

'I know a good deal about babies, you see.'

'Please, please stay! I truly couldn't think what to do – and then Michael … he wouldn't, without a chaperone …'

Dame Alison's happy laugh rang out.

'How like his father! He really is *too* like him at times. But, of course, he was perfectly right. Juliet, dear, do bring another cup and some more bread and butter. We must talk, and you look as if you needed lashings of tea.'

They had finished their tea and Juliet was receiving instructions about the care of an eight-months infant when Michael, all unsuspecting, came up the garden steps.

2

IT WAS NOT until the doctor had come and gone and everything was prepared for Henri-Martin that Alison had much time for her son. By then it was past seven and he was ravenous and nobody had cooked a meal. His mother handed him a small key.

'If you'll look on the back seat of the car you'll find something to your advantage.'

'Is it the scintillating Citroën?'

'That's it. I hired it at Nice for a month. Necessary expenses for an article on Provence.' Her eyes twinkled.

Michael whistled. 'My word! The Goddess in the Chariot if ever one appeared! But what a masterpiece of timing, Muff. How did you wangle it?'

'You said there was a crisis and it seemed as if Juliet might be involved and I thought I might come in handy.'

'But how? I mean, when? Who … ?'

'I bribed The Sheep to take over my proofs and I cut everything and flew to Nice. It was a glorious flight.'

'Come in handy: I'll say you do.'

He went out and returned with a picnic basket containing cooked lobster from Nice. They ate in the kitchen in order to be within call of the *sage-femme*.

Martine had been told that René would be obliged to stay in Nice during the enquiry and that it would take some time. She had tried very hard not to cry.

'The worst of it is', Michael said now, 'that someone will come along to interrogate her and then she'll find out that he's in the prison at Nice. Grim-looking place! Maître Daniel took me along and we tried to fix bail but it was flatly refused. Premeditation, you see, and the *fusil de chasse superposé*, and those murderous cartridges. Daniel doesn't like it at all.'

Juliet was silent. She couldn't swallow her coffee. Michael gave his mother a cigarette and they smoked without speaking for a while, then Alison put her cigarette out.

'The whole affair is so grotesque that I can't assimilate it', she said. 'All I have grasped is that Juliet has been trying to keep the wheels turning here while the inn-keepers were running about shooting and getting bewitched and you were hunting black magicians and white magicians in turn. A curious occupation for you. It seems to me that this child had to be manageress and sick-nurse and psychiatrist and messenger and everything – and that she was very nearly quite literally, left holding the baby.'

Alison put a hand over Juliet's, looking down with a smile at the girl's hands, bare of jewellery and roughened by work. Michael was looking at his mother, affection softening his eyes.

'She'd have managed that, too', he declared.

'I believe she would. How old are you, Juliet?'

Alison's tone was so gentle that Juliet ceased to think of Martine. All her awareness was of herself and the lovely softness and warmth that were being folded around her like a cloak. She sighed, nestling into it, drawing it close, and answered vaguely, 'What date is it?'

'The tenth of October,' Alison answered.

'Why, then, I am twenty-one.'

'Since when?' Michael demanded.

'Since yesterday.'

Alison shook her head.

'A twenty-first birthday, and nobody knew! Monkey, Monkey, aren't you ashamed of yourself?'

'It shall never happen again,' Michael declared.

'It can't, can it?' Juliet spoke with a singing heart. Alison was wearing a wristwatch; it was a pretty little thing: gold on a gold-mesh strap. She took it off and passed it across the table to her son. 'You are a good boy and that is for you to do whatever you like with,' she said.

'Many happy returns of your birthday, my darling,' Michael said, as he slipped the bracelet over Juliet's hand …

'What funny things she cries about, doesn't she, Muff?'

Chapter XXII

THE ADVOCATE

THE LAMPLIT KITCHEN was warm and misty with steam. Juliet, stupid from strain and fatigue, lost count, as the hours of the night passed, of the number of kettles that she had boiled. At a quarter to three the midwife came for another; hurried, she nearly forgot to hand over the empty one.

'It won't be long now,' she called back from the yard. Alison and the doctor were with Martine. Michael sat in the kitchen, in René's chair. He looked haggard. Juliet felt that this was no place for him and, at first, his presence had made her helplessly shy; all the same she hadn't protested much. Michael, a surgeon's son, would never, she knew, hide from life or death, nor would he leave her to face an ordeal alone. He had not spoken a word of commiseration and Juliet, who had all she could do to suppress her emotions and keep her efficiency, felt grateful for that. His presence had grown to seem natural, as the slow hours wore on, their thoughts enclosing them in a grave and quiet companionship.

Both started up when footsteps were heard again. Breathless, Madame Millo burst in. She looked at Michael, important and agitated, and asked him to telephone.

'A boy; perfect as a child on a tombstone,' she announced.

'He breathes but he does not cry. Call the curé,' she panted, 'so that he shall not wander in Limbo for all eternity, poor little one.'

While Michael was upstairs, Juliet heard the longed-for sound of the baby's wail.

Proxies were required for the godparents, who were to be Marie-Louise and the husband of René's sister. The curé, in the emergency, accepted Juliet and Michael, and so they stood side by side in the half-dark attic, and Juliet held the tiny bundle, swaddled in flannel, in her arms while, on the infant's behalf, she and Michael renounced the Devil.

If the young priest had beheld Satan himself, incarnated in the baby, he could not have put a more dreadful solemnity into the words of the ritual, commanding the Evil Spirit to quit the child; to leave the infant in peace. This might have seemed a service of exorcism. When it was over Juliet was trembling and Michael was full of distress. He hurried her down to the kitchen, made her drink brandy and knelt beside her, rubbing her hands.

'What a night for you! What an experience! Has it frightened you, sweetheart?' he asked.

Juliet answered him with a smile. 'Didn't you see Martine's face?'

2

PHILIPPE DANIEL TELEPHONED at half past ten in the morning. He was speaking from Nice. He changed from French into English when Michael replied. He said, 'René demands the news of his wife.'

'You can tell him she's well. Tell him he has a son, who has already renounced the Devil ...'

'Who has – What is it, please, with the Devil?'

'Renounced. And who is said to be the perfection of male beauty and the image of his father.'

'With pleasure I will tell him this.'

'It's a delicate infant, unfortunately, but Martine is okay.'

'Okay? Okay! Martine is okay. Good.'

There was a pause then the advocate said, somewhat heavily, 'René has need of good news.'

'Does it not go well?'

'No. Who is talking to the press?'

'The whole village, probably. Here, we refer all enquiries to you.'

'They make a hero of René and this is doing much harm.'

'It would.'

'The affair is black enough without this.'

The advocate's tone was bitter. Michael did not know what to make of the fellow. He looked as clever as the Devil; was most sincerely concerned for his friend, yet, from the first moment, he had taken this defeatist line.

'You sound pessimistic, Maître,' he said.

'You, also, would be pessimistic if you heard the talk here, in the corridors.'

'You think he'll be sent for trial at the Assizes?'

'I do.'

'And that will mean?'

'A delay of at least four months.'

'Four months! In prison?'

'But certainly.'

'And if he is convicted?'

There was a pause, then came one word:

'Réclusion.'

'Corresponding to our penal servitude?'

'Criminal prison: yes.'

'But surely ...Yes. Yes; I see.'

There was a heavy pause, then the advocate said:

'You and Miss Cunningham are being convened for examination here, at the Palais de Justice at Nice, on Wednesday morning at ten o'clock. I must have a talk with you both. This evening will it be convenient if I dine with you?'

'Yes.'

'At seven o'clock?'

'We'll expect you ... I say: you can tell René that one of the best nurses in England is here on the job. She'll pull his son through all right.'

'Excellent. I will tell him. *Au revoir.*'

Michael found his mother busy in the linen-room. She wore a white apron and looked highly professional. Inspecting a blanket, she asked, 'Have you heard Juliet sing?'

'Sing? No, I don't think I have.'

'She was singing to the baby just now. She has an enchanting voice: not strong, but so clear and full and spontaneous. You'd think she was making the song up while she sings. Some day you should get it trained.'

'Some day we will.'

His mother looked up sharply. 'Dear, what is wrong?'

'Look, Muff, you've got, please, to get Juliet out of this.'

'Now, Michael? She's needed you know.'

He told her what the advocate thought and said, 'The outlook's grim, and you simply can't imagine how deeply Juliet is involved.'

'I know. That is natural.'

'It is natural only because she had no one who wanted her and her father was letting her down. These people needed her and were kind. It puzzled me at first – a girl of Juliet's calibre and that sweet little simpleton, but then I began to understand: she was starving for honesty and sound values and an atmosphere of affection, poor darling, and those they had. She has simply immersed herself in their affairs.'

'Juliet has a great deal of love to spend.'

'Well, now this will all smash up, and she'll break her heart.'

'She won't, Monkey: not now.'

'Not now? *Now,* because ...?'

'Because nobody except you could hurt her much now.'

'Bless you, Muff – you really see it like that?'

His mother rounded on him.

'Look here, you mutt – why didn't you tell me? I was worried to flitters.'

'Tell you what?' He was puzzled. 'That she'd promised, you mean? I wrote. I posted the letter on Monday. I thought that was what had brought you flying. Wasn't it?'

'It wasn't. That letter missed me. I decided to come because … Well, Monkey, I knew you would never have washed up our tour if this hadn't been quite a different thing from … well …'

She laughed and he gave her a one-sided grin.

'Well, I'm glad you realised that.'

'And that nit-witted, obtuse letter of mine!' Alison said, with a groan. 'I wonder you didn't send me a buzz-bomb. But, you know, you didn't tell me a single thing! Not even that she is the loveliest child … That angelic little face, even when she is so tired! Like a sea-worn shell with light shining through.'

Michael looked at his mother admiringly.

'Perspicacious dame! … But, you know, I haven't got a vocabulary like that. How could I explain?'

'She's a diamond of a girl.'

'I *was* a clod not to know you would know.'

'Really, I think you were!'

They regarded one another with a half smiling, deep understanding, then Michael reiterated his appeal.

'Take her out of this. Let's just drive off on Thursday, Muff.'

'Ah, no, that wouldn't be fair.'

'What do you mean?'

Alison was padding a folding table with blankets. Michael helped her. A sheet went on top with tapes sewn to the edges to be tied underneath.

'We're preparing a nursery in room five. This is the baby's toilet table. You'll have to carry it in. We can't go on nursing them in that attic.'

'What *do* you mean: "unfair"?'

She sat on the table and tried to explain.

'For Juliet this is a great achievement, isn't it? And, also, a great trust. She was a child, lacking knowledge, experience, confidence, and she fretted about her own immaturity. This is making a woman of her.

It is important for her to go through with it even if it ends painfully. To ask her to quit now would be wrong; besides, I'm perfectly certain she wouldn't go.'

'I see. I didn't think of it like that … Oh, Muff, how you do *bore* me! You're always right.'

Alison replied politely, 'I can only apologise.'

3

DR GOMPERT CALLED during the afternoon. He approved of the clothes-basket in which the infant was cradled and the sips of glucose administered by Alison. The temperature of the attic he pronounced correct, but not its ventilation, and advised removal to the other room as soon as Martine felt able for it. If the mother's milk remained all it should be, he said, the child should have a sixty per cent chance.

To Alison and Juliet, down in the hall, he expressed a less optimistic view.

'Madame Loubier is in for a shock,' he told them, 'and what that will do to the nervous system of a hysterical woman who is besotted about her husband one can only guess. I imagine she won't be able to nurse the infant.'

'René had such extreme provocation', Alison suggested, 'I can't believe the courts will treat him severely.'

'Just *what* provocation had he, Milady?'

'The whole thing! Terka's horrible trick with her eye …'

'It was not a horrible trick. Terka has no left eye. She was aware that the young woman believed that she had, and had worked herself up into a condition of superstitious terror about the *jettatura*. She came to the yard and lifted the bandage for the sole purpose – a very humane and generous purpose – of proving to Madame Loubier that she had none.'

Juliet gasped.

'That is simply not true.'

'It is what Terka affirms.'

216

'It is a lie. I saw her. I saw the look on her face. It was malicious and horrible.'

'So *you* say, Mademoiselle … Please come in here. I want you to look at these.'

Picking up a bundle of newspapers that he had left in the hall, the doctor strode into the dining-room and spread them out on tables, one after the other. Michael was in the room with more newspapers outspread. Every one of the journals displayed headlines about the paralysed wife, the devoted husband and the wounded sorceress. The *Nice-Matin* was restrained but most of them presented a highly sensational story. One reproduced a photograph of René receiving a cup awarded in some shooting contest; another had a wedding group in which he smiled proudly at the world, one arm around his shy, pretty bride, and several had photographs of the inn.

'What a display!' Dr Gompert exclaimed. 'Not one condemns the savagery of the act. Not one has a word of pity for his miserable victim.'

'How is she?' Juliet ventured to ask, only to be battered by the hailstones of his wrath.

'How do you suppose she is? I had to take a bullet out of her right kneecap. She's lamed for life. Oh, yes, René Loubier is a famous shot! He has lamed her and beggared her. A pedlar, a vagabond, forced by our godly curé to live on the roads – how is she to support herself now? Loubier deserves to be forced to support her for the rest of her life. I hope they shut him up for ten years. He's lucky to escape with his head. If Terka hadn't the constitution of a wild animal she'd be a sicker woman than she is.'

Juliet was staring at him, aghast. Michael protested: 'You speak as if Terka were innocent.'

'She *is* innocent. What is her offence? Poverty? A blind eye? A limp? From first to last she has been the victim of ignorance: of fools like the Proux women; crones like old Emma Loubier; sluts such as Agnès Granerol; hysterical girls like that one upstairs. Upon my soul, except for the half-wit, Ignace Tissier, I believe I'm the first soul who has spoken a civil word to her for three years. She has been weeping and groaning and pouring out her story. It is sickening to listen to.'

'And that, I suppose,' Michael said, 'is the story that she will tell the police?'

'Naturally! The judge's deputy was interrogating her when I left. He is coming here, by the way, on Monday. I have asked him not to disturb Madame Loubier before that. I can't undertake to salvage that puny infant if anything goes wrong with her milk.'

With a brusque '*Au revoir, Messieurs-dames*,' he rolled up his papers and took them and himself away. It seemed easier to breathe when he had gone.

'The case for the prosecution,' Michael said grimly. And Alison asked, appalled, 'Do you think he will talk like that to the judge?'

'And how! And what in the name of earth and heaven are Juliet and I to say?'

4

MAÎTRE DANIEL WAS scarcely recognisable as the vivacious fellow who had called René to drink with his party three weeks ago. His dark, nervous face with its prominent nose and flying eyebrows had been a comedian's then, and his rich voice and gift of mimicry had won shouts of laughter for his anecdotes and *mots*. Today, he had a tormented look. That expression changed, however, the instant he entered Martine's room. Juliet remembered that René had called him an '*acteur manqué*' and indeed he showed talent now. He was brotherly, brisk and gay; admired the infant, said he had his father's forehead, told Martine that René was 'outside himself' with pride and delight, begged her to be brave and patient because the law was a tortoise; and he left before she had time to question him. On the stairs he exclaimed, 'How could the man have been so mad? He had so much to lose. He could have gone so far.'

Juliet had spent hours over the dinner, which was the first she had cooked for Michael, and had prepared his favourite *blanquette de veau*, with rice and lemon sauce, following Dame Alison's instructions with meticulous care. So that there need be no running to the kitchen, to worry Michael with the sense of being 'waited on', this dish was placed over little lamps on the buffet, and there also she set out her bowls of *mousse au chocolat,* the coffee percolator, cheeses and fruit, while the *hors d'oeuvres* were ready on the round table.

She had chosen that table in the corner because she wanted Michael's mother to have the pretty view of the terrace and garden steps in the evening light. Michael's place was on Dame Alison's right, and Maître Daniel's opposite hers. When the advocate sat down such a sudden twist of grief passed over his face that Juliet wished she had not chosen this table at which his gay party had taken place; but he quickly recovered himself.

'If you will be good enough to excuse my errors I will speak in English: in French I go too quickly for Monsieur Faulkner,' he said. He had studied English from a dictionary, he explained, while he was a prisoner of war. 'Tell me first,' he demanded, 'what is the news of Terka today?'

Their report of Dr Gompert's attitude dismayed him.

'A formidable enemy!' he exclaimed. 'And we have another – René himself! René is a client the most difficult! He proposes – can you imagine – to state that he had intended to kill Terka: that it was a civic duty to kill a witch! He even quotes Scripture, like your Shylock,' he said.

Michael nodded.

'That's why I went down with him and insisted on his calling, first thing, for you.' He turned to his mother. 'Can you believe it? He complained that his *hand* had betrayed him, refusing to kill a woman: that he had wished to aim at her heart.'

'However,' Maître Daniel told them then, 'because he is proud of his marksmanship, I have been able to persuade him to keep that to himself. He declares, now, "If I had wished to kill Terka, she would be dead." ... You realise, Monsieur, that this must be emphasised – he aimed only to wound; also the fact that he attended instantly to her injuries?'

Michael nodded.

'I won't forget that.'

'His whole attitude is most unfortunate,' the advocate complained impatiently. 'He is too *insouciant*. He believes everyone feels grateful to him!'

'So people do, you know,' Juliet said.

She served the *blanquette* and Michael ate with evident appetite, but he might as well have been eating boiled potatoes, Juliet said to herself. Not one of them, not even Dame Alison, had a thought to spare for their food. Maître Daniel had created an atmosphere of extreme anxiety. He kept looking from Michael to her, his dark eyes sharply focused, his voice full of urgency, striving to make on their minds an impression that they would not forget.

'The line of defence must be consistent. It must be concrete and simple,' he said. 'Above all, we must avoid introducing topics – such topics as you talked about yesterday, Monsieur – which would antagonise the judge.'

'I see,' Michael responded. 'Go ahead.'

'In the first place that olive field is private property. René had repeatedly forbidden Terka to trespass upon it. She was trespassing, and at night. A man has the right to defend his home.'

Michael looked dubious.

'All the same – a woman in trailing skirts and two able-bodied men!'

Maître Daniel held up two fingers.

'Exactly. And therefore the second point is this: – You, I think, can bear witness, Mademoiselle. René was distraught. This is the extenuating circumstance.'

'He was indeed,' Juliet said fervently. 'It had been a terrible time for him. Everything piled up.'

'Precisely. He fears for the actual life of his wife and the unborn child. Terror of Terka has made Martine critically ill. He goes out to guard his home against new intrusion and, in his distress, is unwise enough to take his gun.'

'And to load it', Michael interjected drily, 'with those deadly cartridges. That is what I can't get over, myself.'

They had ceased eating. Juliet removed the plates. Alison whispered, 'It was excellent, *chérie,*' but Juliet was beyond caring, now, about the reception of her food. She had become infected with the advocate's gloom. Alison spoke now, diffidently:

'Won't Terka herself be the vital question?' she suggested. 'I mean, just the degree of danger that she *did* represent? If it could be shown that René's fear of her was justified?'

'Yes,' Michael assented quickly. 'As I told you, Maître, I had the notion myself that she might be intending to set fire to the house; that she might have fired Granerol's stable, and so on.'

The lawyer responded coldly:

'But you did not, I think, adduce any evidence? Nothing was found on Terka, in the hospital, to suggest such an intention. Any vagabond might have carried such things as those you found in the field.'

Michael and Juliet had searched the ground together. They had found a long, rough cord with dirty little bags tied to it. These contained a candle-end, a cigarette-lighter and some pieces of cheese. That was all. The collection had been sent to the police.

'You should mention your notion, of course,' Maître Daniel said, 'but René had spoken of no such idea and I do not imagine that it will carry weight.'

Alison persisted in gentle tones:

'Surely the fact that the curé felt it necessary to denounce her indicates that Terka was a danger to the community?'

The advocate's mobile brows were drawn down.

'It indicates, Madame,' he retorted, 'that the good Pastor is no more free from childish credulity than is his flock. I cannot hear that he has supported his condemnation by a single concrete charge. What can a Court of Justice make of that?'

Juliet protested.

'If he heard it all in the confessional?'

Her feelings became too strong for her. She broke out impetuously: 'Terka is evil and dangerous, Maître. I *know* she is. We *all* know it.'

To her relief, Michael supported her, saying positively, 'In my opinion she is a dangerous malefactor.'

'Evidence: evidence!' was the advocate's plea. He was fiercely impatient with the rumours and guesses that were all Michael could adduce, and his bitterness over the weakness of René's case showed itself in irritability against those people whose suggestions were exposing it. Juliet repeated that René believed that Terka was cursing Martine; quoted Martine's cry at the moment of her recovery: '"The malady has passed from me to her,"' and pleaded, 'You see, Maître, it worked.'

'A most pernicious argument!' was the retort. 'You will destroy René if you talk like that to the judge, Mademoiselle.'

There was a long silence. Michael lit cigarettes for his mother and for himself. The advocate preferred his own. Juliet did not smoke. She poured out coffee and put the cognac and liqueur glasses on the table. The thought of the interrogation to be faced in a few days appalled her. Michael said nothing. He was annoyed because the advocate had been irascible with her.

'Forgive me,' Maître Daniel said at length. 'You are English. Your statutes differ from ours. Your psychological problems are not the same. You, perhaps, do not understand. You do not realise that here, in the South, it is necessary above all to avoid even the appearance of advancing superstition as a defence. Here the legal mind abhors superstition. It is a vestige of primitive paganism; a survival from the Dark Ages, a thing to be extirpated.'

He was addressing himself to each and all of them, as if they were a jury. They listened in stillness.

'We remember the excesses of the Revolution,' he went on, 'massacres; persecutions. We know what a fire smoulders in the southern temperament and how perilous is the aftermath of war. Acts of private vengeance must meet with exemplary punishment. Mob rule, popular clamour, trial by newspaper – the courts must have the integrity to ignore and suppress. The popularity of René's act will appear as a reason for extra severity.'

'*Advocatus Diaboli*,' Michael murmured with a wry smile as he paused. 'You make a fine case for the prosecution, Maître.'

'I envisage what we shall have to answer,' was the sharp reply. Daniel added earnestly: 'Believe me, I love René like a brother. I shall do my utmost for him.'

'Nobody doubts that,' Michael said.

'I attempt to enter the mind of the *Juge d'Instruction* to whom the case has been assigned. In him we are not fortunate.' A thin smile came to the advocate's dark face. 'Monsieur Charles Maurice Gaidoni is exceedingly able but, "Civilisation is God and Gaidoni is his prophet," we lawyers say. Superstition is anathema to him.'

'Just what is his function?' Alison asked.

'He is the examining magistrate who takes the case from the *Police Judiciare*. He interrogates witnesses, instructs the police to collect evidence, assembles the dossier and studies every aspect of the case. It rests with him to decide whether to send the accused forward for trial at the Assizes.'

He turned to Juliet.

'I warn you most rigorously, Mademoiselle, to refrain from speaking of curses to the judge. Shall I tell you how he could react?'

Daniel's gaze became glassy, his voice heavy.

'What sort of precedent, he would ask, would such a defence, if it were admitted, establish? What should we find occurring in the countryside? Cattle die; a child falls sick; an adolescent girl develops hysteria, and the relatives say, "Ha! Recollect! We have offended that gypsy, or that hunchback. This is witchcraft; we have the right to kill."'

Juliet sighed. The sun had set and twilight was making faces look strange and pale. She hoped that Martine was sleeping. Marie was sitting with her, but Marie was never encouraging company.

'I understand, Maître,' she said.

Alison, out of the heavy silence, asked a question. 'Haven't I read that in France, although there is no statute against witchcraft, it is forbidden to *pose* as a witch?'

'Perfectly, Madame. That *manoeuvre* is an offence.'

'Then Terka is an offender,' Michael declared.

'Even if we could prove that I do not think it would help greatly,' the pessimistic advocate answered. 'But, you know, there is a good deal of tolerance. The sale of philtres is permitted, in a measure, and so is fortune-telling, unless solemn asseverations are made. Did Terka advertise herself as a sorceress?'

'A thorough enquiry might prove that she did,' Michael replied.

'Terka is not in the dock,' was the answer, in a voice edged with exasperation. 'Unfortunately, you see, it is permitted to do these things of which she is accused. It is permitted to kill one's fowls or one's rabbits; or to lift a bandage from one's eye … It is even permitted to limp. The police are not concerned with Terka except as the victim of an outrage. I must beg you to keep this in mind. You will discredit yourselves as witnesses if you talk about limping cats and vanishing dogs to the judge.'

'Surely it is all part of the picture?' Michael protested.

'It would suggest credulity and prejudice. It would introduce the issue of superstition as a pretext for violence – the issue I most wish to exclude. It would weigh down the scales on the wrong side.'

Michael said, uneasily:

'I must say you make it very difficult. I can't see what line Juliet and I are to take.'

'I can only suggest that you speak for René's character. You know him to be neither a fool nor a brute.'

'He is kind and fair and patient,' Juliet said.

They talked on, but their talk made circles and figures of eight. Alison said at last that Martine would worry if no one went up to her, and as they were leaving the table Marie came in. Martine begged Maître Daniel to visit her again before he departed. She wished to show him a present that she had received.

They went up to the attic. On the table, beside the bed, was a basket decorated with enormous white satin bows. It contained a loaf, an egg, a phial of salt and an outsize match. Attached to the handle was an illuminated scroll.

'It is from Madame Lelong – the old doctor's widow. She is an Arlésienne. It is their traditional wish. Is it not charming?' Martine said proudly.

Her baby was curled against her breast, fast asleep, and making sucking motions with his lips. Blue veins showed in his forehead and eyelids and his skin had the pallor of porcelain. He had become beautiful, Juliet thought. She read the inscribed wish:

May he be as full as an egg,
As good as bread,
As sage as salt,
As straight as a match,
And the protector of his parents in their old age.

Martine smiled as she looked down at her miniature son.

'The protector of our old age! Is he not sweet? How kind people are! Even Madame Bonin sent a layette, although René quarrelled with her. Do you not think I am fortunate? Please, Philippe, tell René about this. Please take him the scroll.'

'You may tell him, too,' Alison said happily, 'that this afternoon the protector of his old age weighed nearly three kilograms.'

'Three kilograms: I will remember.'

'I believe,' she said, 'that he has decided to give the world fair trial, though he didn't think much of it just at first.'

'He was scarcely to be blamed, in all the circumstances,' the advocate replied in judicial tones.

'And tell René,' Martine said gaily, 'that I can be very patient, because I know my prayers will be answered. Tell him how I prayed for help yesterday and, just at the darkest moment, Dame Alison came out of the sky.'

It was a relief to laugh and their laughter filled the room.

Chapter XXIII

THE JUDGE

FORMIDABLE, THE VAST flight of steps that led up to the Palais de Justice; chilling to the spirit were the faces of the people who stood about, waiting, in the great hall. Apprehension dragged at Juliet's heart. Everything about the ugly interior warned her to abandon hope. After nightmare-ridden sleep and an early start she felt stupid and afraid of forgetting the all-important warnings of Maître Daniel. It was impossible to escape the illusion of responsibility, helpless oath-bound witnesses though she and Michael would be. There *must* be things that they ought to say, besides those that they must avoid.

'Remember, the *whole* truth is on our side,' had been Dame Alison's parting words. 'Terka was dangerous and René knew that she was. If you can only make the judge *feel* that.' But one knew the whole truth by means of the little things – a tilt of the head, a twist of the lips – incommunicable things which one wouldn't be able to make him see …

It did not raise Juliet's spirits to see Dr Gompert emerge from a room down the corridor. As he passed he saluted them with a complacent smile.

Michael spoke in a low voice to Juliet.

'Listen, honey,' he said. 'You're not facing prosecuting counsel. Get hold of that. Monsieur Gaidoni is just the examining magistrate. He will simply be asking for information; trying to understand the whole set-up – characters, motives, and so on, and he wants our help. I agree with Muff about Daniel. He's too clever. You and I have only to tell the truth. We haven't a thing to hide and there's no hurry, and the issue does *not* rest with us.'

FACING THE JUDGE at last, she felt better. He gave her a little bow and said, gravely, *'Je vous félicite, Mademoiselle.'* That was not explained until she had taken the oath, swearing to 'speak the truth, only the truth and the truth entire', and the clerk had retired to his corner.

The judge was a fatherly looking man with bristling iron-grey hair and a moustache. His face was short and broad; alert eyes peered out from under a ridged brow and Juliet felt that in one deep glance into her own they had discovered a great deal. His voice was low-pitched and sympathetic.

'I am told, Mademoiselle, that you speak French to perfection. That is excellent. I commence by congratulating you because it appears that you and Mr Faulkner have prevented a very odious crime. Will you tell me, please, by what sentiment was your rescue of Terka Fontana inspired?'

That was easily answered; 'By fear, *Monsieur le Juge.*'

'But you ran a personal risk.'

'Fear, I meant, of a horrible thing being done.'

'And by pity for the woman, no doubt?'

'I think I had stopped feeling sorry for her by that time.'

'Formerly, then, you had compassion for her?'

'Yes: I was stupid: I know that now.'

'What acquaintance had you with her?'

'Well, I went to her once to have my fortune told.'

'Indeed? May I enquire, do you believe in sorcery?'

'No, oh no! I never did. It was just curiosity.'

'Tell me: did Terka declare to you that she possessed occult powers?'

Doing her best to be accurate, Juliet answered: 'Not that I remember. She seemed to attribute magical properties to the cards.'

'The usual gypsy prattle? I understand. And were you impressed, Mademoiselle?'

'For perhaps half an hour.'

The judge smiled. 'It is a pleasure to have to do with a witness so discriminating. Now think carefully: the compassion that you felt at first for Terka – when and why did it alter?'

'I think it was when the curé denounced her as "a woman who wishes evil" – oh, and a day or two before, when he spoke in the same way about her to me. I felt that he wouldn't condemn her without cause.'

The judge nodded slowly, his lips compressed. 'And yet, Mademoiselle, when my deputy visited Father Pascale to take his deposition the good curé could advance not one single concrete incident as a reason for that terrible public denunciation. Not one. He pleaded the secrecy of the confessional. I ask you, now, whether you have direct knowledge of any action of hers that has broken the law. You understand me: Terka is not on trial, but René Loubier's line of defence makes this enquiry relevant. Direct, personal knowledge, Mademoiselle?'

Juliet hesitated.

'No, *Monsieur le Juge*; but I do know that Martine Loubier lived in terror of her, and that a great many of the people one met ...'

She was cut short.

'I said first-hand knowledge, Mademoiselle.' He gave Juliet a reproachful smile. 'It seems, does it not, that because of what you had heard others say you allowed yourself to become prejudiced. Is that not so?'

Juliet tried to gather her forces together. She was determined to put the human picture before this man, who looked as if he could be made to understand. She spoke earnestly.

'*Monsieur le Juge*, it is true that I hated her because Martine Loubier was sick with fear of her. It was dreadful to see Martine so changed. She's intelligent, Monsieur, and courageous and calm. No everyday worry agitates her at all. And she was looking forward with supreme happiness to the birth of her first child. She is religious and good. But as one disaster after another happened she … Monsieur, she became like a person sentenced to death.'

From the files piled neatly before him the judge drew a long document and read from it aloud. One by one he quoted stories of the recent incidents for which Terka had been blamed. 'Martine's deposition,' Juliet thought. Concerning each episode he asked Juliet, firmly, what reason could be adduced for supposing Terka to have had any responsibility for it. He made all those suppositions appear as ridiculous as the tale about Cécile's eye or the cat that limped. At last Juliet, who felt that she was being driven into a false position and made to deny her own conviction, burst out, childishly, with 'I *know* that Terka did wicked things.'

Every hint of sympathy disappeared from the judge's face and voice.

'That is a serious thing that you say. You accuse this woman of being a malefactor – but upon what evidence?'

'Monsieur,' Juliet responded, desperate, 'I saw it in her gesture, in her face.'

Patiently, he asked, 'In what circumstances?'

'I saw her when she stood looking in through our window and uncovered that eye-socket. *Monsieur le Juge,* she did it slowly and deliberately, with a malignant twist on her lips. I *know* that she did it to terrify Martine.'

With a quiet gesture the judge put his papers aside and, sitting back, relaxed, in his chair, asked, 'And did you, also, see the eye, Mademoiselle?'

'I saw that Terka had no left eye.'

'She was standing, I think, with her back to the light?'

'Yes.'

'And Madame Loubier had that hallucination?'

'Yes.'

'Do you realise what you have admitted, Mademoiselle? You declare that because of a gesture and a facial expression, half seen against the light, you have permitted yourself to credit a whole medley of grotesque charges which, as your own reason had already shown you, have been made without a fragment of evidence. Do you not think that the distress of your friend, her hallucination, the febrile superstitions and hysteria by which you were surrounded, have a little infected you?'

'Wheels within wheels,' Juliet thought. Was one not to trust one's own mind, one's own senses? She struggled against an overwhelming sense of having been discredited and defeated, but Alison's words flashed into her memory: 'Remember, the whole truth is on our side.'

'Monsieur,' she said, 'even if I am mistaken, and the curé is mistaken, about Terka's wickedness, it is still quite, quite certain that she made Martine dreadfully ill. Even if it was nonsense about the animals and the fire and the philtre, Martine's paralysis was real. She tried to stand on her feet: she tried so desperately! I saw her. And she failed, again and again. And her baby was expected in just a month.'

'Yet she made a strangely sudden recovery. May I have your account of this, Mademoiselle?'

Vividly, every moment of that night lived in Juliet's memory. She recounted each incident, trying to give a picture of Martine's anguish and helplessness. When she had described her own impulsive cry, 'René has shot Terka,' and Martine's response, Martine's instant recovery, the judge nodded gravely.

'Again, I congratulate you. Dr Frieden, the eminent psychiatrist whom I am consulting in this case, declares that although what you did was dangerous, because the patient might have suffered an injurious fall, it was undoubtedly effective. You cured the hysteria, it seems.'

'It was René who cured her, *Monsieur le Juge*.'

He emitted a vexed sound, almost a growl. 'René Loubier achieved his purpose: yes. But the fact that an assault achieves the assailant's purpose does not justify the assault.'

'René adores his wife.'

'The law does not permit him to kill or wound for her.'

'He is not a violent man; he's kind and considerate.'

'I am aware that his reputation is good.'

'But everything seemed to combine to make him frantic. Dr Gompert could not help – he was even insulting; and the *guériseur* failed, and a neighbour taunted René with doing nothing and made him feel it was all his own fault, and on Thursday the paralysis was much worse. So he went out, and, *Monsieur le Juge* ...' Juliet knew she was stressing her opinions beyond what was correct or even mannerly, yet she persisted: 'If it had not happened like that I don't think the baby ... I don't think it could have been born alive; and I think Martine would have gone out of her mind.'

The judge gave her a little bow.

'It is interesting what you suggest, although it is not evidence and you are not a psychiatrist ...You have endured much strain for so young a lady and, if you will permit me to say so, you have shown yourself a valiant and loyal friend. I will let you go now. I thank you, Miss Cunningham.'

He leaned across his desk to shake hands with her, then rang a bell. Juliet returned to the gloomy hall. She could do no more than give Michael a weak smile when he passed on his way to the judge's room. He was followed at once by Maître Daniel, whose face was set in hard, bitter lines.

2

THE LITTLE CAFÉ was redolent of hot bread. They had the place to themselves. It was not until chocolate and croissants were before them that Michael asked, 'Well? How did it go?'

Juliet could not swallow even the bread. She said miserably, 'I'm afraid I've done more harm than good. He thinks I'm just one more hysterical girl maligning the poor, innocent wretch.'

Michael nodded. 'And I am a callous ex-RAF type who doesn't mind women being shot in the legs.'

'I tried my best to make him realise how terrified and ill Martine was and he said I was infected by her hysteria.'

'He would! When I mentioned my notion that she might have started a fire in the inn he said, "Another unfounded suspicion, was it not?" I told him how fierce the feeling was against Terka: how dozens of men were out for her blood while René had been comparatively restrained. He said, "He was the one who shot her, nevertheless," in a voice like an ice axe.'

'It froze my bones.'

'Maître Daniel plugged for all he was worth that René had gone to Menton and put it up to the police to control her and that they hadn't let him think that they intended to act. Also that when he shot Terka he stayed by her and dressed her wounds; but the fact that he loaded the gun with those cartridges is damning him, poor chap.'

Juliet's spoon went round and round in her cup.

'I suppose Dr Gompert has prejudiced the judge.'

Michael shook his head.

'No: the irony of it is that Martine's own statement is what has done the harm. You could see that by the disgust on his face whenever he glanced at it. He's a fair-minded man and all the bilge he has heard against Terka has simply forced him to take her part, and, by gum, I'd react the same way in his place. I know Daniel feels that too.'

'Maître Daniel was looking awfully unhappy, wasn't he?'

'Yes: it seems that René has realised his position and has reacted badly. Can't take it at all. Who could blame him? And of course, he thinks it is madly unjust. He feels like a man who has saved his village from a man-eating tiger.'

'Poor René ... and poor Martine.'

Michael looked at her with commiseration. 'Do you think you could eat an omelette, Juliet? I'm having one.' He ordered two.

While they waited for the omelettes Juliet began, for the first time, to despair. From the moment when Michael had brought his keen, trained mind to bear on the whole problem she had believed that he would cut a way to the heart of it, as an ice-cutter cleaves through a frozen waste. If Michael admitted defeat there was no hope left; and what would become of Martine?

'I thought', she said sadly, 'you might be able to convince the judge that Terka was dangerous.'

'I tried – and do you know what he said?' Michael grimaced. 'He informed me in words of one syllable that twenty false charges do not constitute one true one. He kept asking me for one item of evidence – one concrete, incontrovertible fact. And I hadn't one.'

'Perhaps before the Assizes something will be discovered.'

'There won't be anyone on the job. Martine can't employ a detective, can she? No, if it comes to the Assizes I'm afraid René's sunk.'

'Among all those endless stories, going back over nearly three years, there must, surely, be something provable,' Juliet persisted.

'That's what's so tantalising. Somebody, somewhere, *could* throw light on the thing, and they won't.'

'Or can't. Father Pascale *can't*. I'm certain her victims often confessed to him, because all dealings with her were forbidden, but ...'

'Father Pascale is like a man with a dark lantern.'

'Michael!' Juliet was startled. 'How funny that you should say that! In the card of the hermit, the priest, in the Tarot pack, he is carrying a lantern.'

'So he is, but it is shut up and sealed and doesn't let one ray out: sealed with the seal of the confessional. I am sure', Michael said wretchedly, 'that Gaidoni is a just man and the curé is a saintly one but, between them, I think a terrible injustice is going to be done.'

A brooding silence, full of despondency, settled between them; then Juliet saw a gradual change, a tension, come over Michael's face, as though eyes and brain were focused on something – some memory or idea. He looked down at the table, frowning. She kept still.

'Michael's brain', she thought, 'is like a lighthouse. Sometimes he scarcely uses it at all but just lets things go on around him and is amused, and then, if you are worried, you may be left in the dark; then suddenly it sends out a flash that sweeps far and wide and lights everything up; then all's in darkness again. Now it is sending out flash after flash. I mustn't interrupt.'

The omelettes came and were eaten in silence and in silence Michael and Juliet returned to the car and started on their way home.

Chapter XXIV

THE LANTERN

MICHAEL PREFERRED the route through the mountains but, mechanically obeying an idea fixed in the morning, he started to drive by the coast. He had meant, earlier, to take Juliet to a film at Monte Carlo, by way of much-needed distraction, on the way home; but she was in no mood for a film now. Outside Nice he paused, drew in to the kerb and sat pondering, his arms at rest on the wheel.

'The trouble is,' he said, 'one oughtn't, really, to lose a day.'

He looked into Juliet's face and said reproachfully, 'Say, darling, it's not I who am going to be kept in jail.'

'I was thinking how I should feel if it were.'

'My sweet, blessed lamb, you can't go through life like that. What is to be done with you? You are tired to death. You're in flitters.'

'What does it matter now?' Juliet answered. 'It doesn't matter now, how stupid I am.'

'It does matter that you're tired, because there is something I want to do.'

'Oh, Michael!' She was suddenly irradiated with hope. 'I *knew* you would think of something! I *knew* you would!'

'Could you face the trail to the farm?'

'Of course!'

Michael turned the car and drove at high speed up to the Moyenne Corniche. He said, 'I want a talk with Father Pascale.'

CAMILLE AND THE GIRLS were devoted to Michael yet his welcome at the farm was a quiet one. Claudette's eyes were puffy from crying; Marie-Louise looked haggard. Emma's hands fluttered about, picked at her coverlet, fingered her rosary, and her old head shook as she muttered, 'It would kill him; prison would kill René in a month.'

Marie-Louise went to prepare the curé for his visitor while Camille went to Granerol's to bring in Henri, who was at work there, measuring planks for the repair of the burnt stable. Michael asked everyone present, including Henri, when he came in, not to mention this visit of his to the priest.

All promised, but every face lit up with a faint renewal of hope.

THE PRIEST LISTENED to Michael in stillness, his every faculty tense. His hands gripped the arms of his chair so hard that the knuckles showed white. At the end of the exposition of René's danger he drew a painful breath, lifted his head and turned it away. His skin looked cold and Michael thought that he was in physical pain. The priest denied that and said he was well. He bowed his head, resting his forehead on his right hand, withdrawn in thought or prayer. Michael waited. He looked out of the small window to the patch of scorched grass and the old walnut under whose shade five cats and René's setter lay companionably asleep. The priest uttered a long sigh and relaxed. 'What is it', he asked, 'that you wish me to do?'

Michael spoke diffidently.

'You may be angry with me, Father, for I speak in ignorance; but I hope you will forgive me all the same, because so much is at stake.'

'Go on, my son.'

'Father, when you denounced Terka from the pulpit you had reasons. No one knows them – not the police, nor the judge, nor René's advocate: no one who might help. What I want to ask you is this. Is it possible for you, in the utmost confidence, to communicate even one …?'

The priest's hand was raised in a gesture that silenced Michael.

'I have already given my answer to that question. The judge's deputy came here and asked it. The answer is "No." And if René were going to the guillotine it would still be "No." Now do you understand?'

'I understand.'

Michael paused, and then went on: 'What I had in mind was this: is there not one of your parishioners to whom you could write or speak? Someone who has the evidence that is needed, whom you could persuade to come forward with it?'

'That is equally impossible.'

The priest was very pale, but there was a light in his grey eyes. Michael looked directly into them.

'Then,' he asked, 'must René suffer? He stands accused of wounding a harmless woman. Is it just? Is there no way of helping him?'

'My son,' the priest began gently, then corrected himself: '"Monsieur", I ought to say. But they talk of you here always as "Michel".'

'If you will, please, Father.'

'Tell me, Michel: when you first questioned me about the cause of my accident, what answer did I give you?'

On fire with excitement, Michael looked at him. The pallor of sickness had gone from the priest's face; it was flushed.

'You said, Father, that you remembered nothing about it.'

'Are you sure? Did I not say that I remembered nothing about the moment before my fall?'

'Very possibly. I don't recall your exact words.'

'You seemed to think, my son, that perhaps someone had stood on the roadside and flung a stone at the mare. I told you that no one had stood on the roadside and that no stone had been flung.'

Michael assented eagerly: 'So you did – and you said that a bird or a rabbit starting up would have been sufficient to panic her.'

'I gave the same answer to the judge's deputy … Have I shocked you, Michel? Is your creed so rigid that it will not admit a little deception even to save life? I dared not tell the truth. Or perhaps I was too ill to discriminate. I might, perhaps, have been wise to confide in you. But the need of concealment obsessed me. I was in mortal fear for the souls of those angry men. Michel, it was of murder I was afraid. Of murder and the damnation of souls.'

He was breathless and agitated.

'I can understand that, Father. And you had good reason to be afraid. If they had known for certain that she had contrived your accident they would have wanted to tear her limb from limb. Suspecting it even …' He checked himself.

'I ought to have spoken,' the priest went on sadly. 'When Terka was safe there, in the hospital, I ought to have let the police know the truth. But I saw, in my ignorance, no need for it. I failed to realise that her misdemeanour could have a bearing on René's case. I thought that, before she left the hospital, I would be able to visit her, and perhaps persuade her … I committed the sin of spiritual pride. I presumed to take the scales of justice into my own fallible hands. What anguish my sin has caused! I am blessed, indeed, if it is not too late.'

Michael reassured him: 'I don't think it is too late.'

'It is quite true, you see, Michel, that I do not remember jumping from the *charrette*. That moment has gone into oblivion, but I remember making up my mind to do it. I said to myself that if I had not got the mare under control before she reached that dangerous bend – that narrow, sloping place under the pines – she would certainly plunge with the *charrette* into the gorge. I must have sprung out just before she reached it. Isn't that where you found me, Michel?'

'Yes.'

Michael retrieved the pillow, which, displaced by the priest's agitated movements, had fallen to the floor, and readjusted it behind his head.

'How did Terka do it, Father?' he asked.

'So foolishly! So savagely! Anyone could have seen her, as I did. You know the first; single, overhanging stone-pine? She had climbed up into it. She was there, clinging like some wild thing, out on a bough, crouching and reaching down, and she had in her hand a long, severed branch – a branch with a brush of green on the end. I saw what she meant to do and shouted. I tried to pull up but she threw it. The poor animal must have thought that some beast had its claws in her head and eyes. She bolted madly, quite out of control, rocking the *charrette*. I heard Terka laugh. She must have felt very certain that I would die.'

Appalled, Michael suppressed the exclamation that sprang to his lips. He said, 'And you kept this to yourself?'

'I will go to Nice, Michel, and tell the judge.'

'You're not fit for the journey. An affidavit or something could probably do.'

The priest's eyes were bright.

'No: a little hardship is no more than Brother Ass, this vain and foolish body of mine, deserves. If a conveyance can be provided I will go. There is at the Presbytery at Nice my old friend and confessor to whom a visit would be timely. It is also time that I relieved the good people here of the burden of attending on me. From Nice I will return to my home.'

'Then I will drive you. My mother has hired a comfortable car. But now, will you write a letter to René's advocate – Matîre Philippe Daniel? I will take it to him. It will save time.'

'My right hand is still a little unsteady. Marie-Louise is my kind amanuensis. Will you ask her to come to me, Michel?'

JULIET SPRANG to her feet when she saw Michael's face.

Marie-Louise hastened to the curé's room. The others waited; even Emma was silent.

'It was Terka who caused the accident and she did it deliberately,' Michael told them.

Henri's words fell with profound impressiveness into the shocked hush that followed. He said, 'It is from a woman possessed by a devil that René has delivered us.'

'If you are called as a witness,' Michael remarked, 'I hope you will say that to the judge.'

Henri accompanied Michael and Juliet as they walked beside the gorge to the Relais where they had left the car. The afternoon sun was lighting the ravine and the path. Birds twittered; the air was sweet and tonic; Juliet was no longer tired. When they reached the overhanging stone-pine Henri climbed into it, not without a hoist from Michael, because footholds on the smooth trunk were few. Balancing skilfully, moving with practised ease, Henri explored the great tree, looking for broken branches and damaged bark.

'Truly, she has left scars,' he called down.

Michael, in his one presentable suit, was grounded and had to contain his impatience. 'What on earth are you doing there?' he called up.

Astride of a bough, Henri was making sawing motions with his right arm. He stooped down.

'The mad one,' he said, 'she cut it here! Sitting here, in full view from below. Here, she sawed off her branch. And there, plainly visible, is the stump.'

He tore off a small bough, and, then, agile as a monkey, he reversed his position and, holding by his knees, began to travel along the thick lateral branch which grew right over the road. He lay along it, his right hand stretched out, and cropped the bough. It fell in the middle of the path.

Breathless, Juliet turned to Michael. 'Concrete evidence,' Michael said.

Henri rejoined them and they stood, looking up, puzzled.

Terka had taken no care whatever to conceal herself from either her victim or witnesses. Michael quoted the curé's own remark: she must have felt very sure he would die.

'Or perhaps', Henri said, 'she had gone out of her mind.' Henri was very quiet as he walked on with them to the Relais. Juliet wondered what he was thinking, now, about sorcery. When they were standing by the car, ready to go, he said thoughtfully, 'I have often wondered why the Devil was permitted to work so much harm through her to innocent people. I was very foolish. I ought to have known better. Terka is a sad, angry, much-tempted woman, no more.'

He stood looking rather wistfully at Michael, reluctant to part from him. He asked, 'Will you ever return to the forest again?'

'I wonder?' Michael replied.

Henri's face, with its far-sighted eyes and the quiet lips a solitary line, was turned to Juliet. 'I think that you will wish to return and will persuade your husband,' he said with plea in his voice.

Juliet smiled and gave him her hand. 'I hope very much that we shall come to the forest,' she said, 'and visit you and your wife.'

His clear eyes opened wide.

'You think? You truly believe, Mademoiselle …?'

'I think you have only to ask her, Henri.'

'*L'audace, mon Vieux! Toujours de l'audace!*' Michael cried, letting in the clutch.

'*Merci! Merci! … Adieu, Michel, Madame!*' He lifted his arm high in a brave salute as they drove away.

'Madame!' Michael chuckled. Then he said, thoughtfully, 'Henri's one of the best and Marie-Louise would make him happy. I'm glad you said that.'

Michael took the descent at racing pace, spinning round the hairpin bends and enjoying every minute of it. Juliet thought he looked like a boy – a boy of the Golden Age, driving his triumphal chariot. But at the turn which brought St Jacques into sight, its towers and houses and encircling wall gilded, its windows sparkling in the rays of the late sun, he paused. 'Yes, we'll come back,' he said. Then they drove down towards the Inn of the Doves as towards a dear and welcoming home.

Chapter XXV

THE WHEELS

OUT OF A LONG and dream-busy sleep Juliet awoke to the awareness of wellbeing and leisure. She had half an hour in which to philosophise, and meditate about those revolving wheels.

Her father's telegram lay under the clock. She smiled at the sight
of it and at the low *roucoulement* of the flirtatious doves. Returning
over-tired from the day's importance, she had been sent early to bed
with orders not to be seen in the morning until half past eight. Michael
would bring his mother her breakfast. It wouldn't be the first time.

The wheels were still turning. They spun faster and faster, as Frith
had warned her they might. He had said, 'Life is a whirligig.' But it
wasn't: it was more complex; much more inexorable.

Wheels you could see and others you never guessed at; big and
little, they touched, engaged and turned one another like the intricate
wheels of a watch. The curé's destiny and René's; Terka's and the baby's
and Martine's; Michael's and Dame Alison's and her own: wheels of
fortune: not one of them separate: all revolving and all interlocked.
'And yet,' she thought, 'we are all so curiously without curiosity; so
drowsily unconscious about it all.'

The sky was pale as mist still, but clear. It was going to be another blue day, and they would all live serenely under the influence of the lovely, golden October sunshine as if no bitter parting lay just ahead, no shadow of anguish lay over Martine.

Martine was irrationally happy. Every day the scales recorded her baby's increasing weight, and in her thankfulness and confidence she failed to realise how precarious was the balance of the scales that held René's destiny. She didn't even realise that something that might just make the difference had happened yesterday. Alison thought it better to tell her nothing.

'Don't start Martine reasoning,' she had advised. 'Leave her in her dreamy peace.'

Somebody was coming upstairs quietly, carefully. That was Michael, trying to make no noise: to leave Juliet in her dreamy peace. She got up.

His mother had opened her *persiennes* and sunlight, glancing from the edge of the hand-mirror, threw a rainbow on the ceiling. She was sitting up in an elegant bed-jacket. The rainbow, and her smile, and a scent out of childhood – lily-of-the-valley, her favourite still – made Michael feel that he was a good boy.

'This is a beg,' he confessed. 'Can I borrow the car?'

'Of course – but have you got to go down?'

'So it seems. I've dictated the Padre's statement over the phone. Daniel is absolutely up in the air about it, although I woke him out of his sleep. He *is* a temperamental bloke! But he says the signed original will be wanted today at Nice. I'm fed up. Do you realise that I sail today fortnight?'

'Indeed I do.'

'Could you *possibly* manage it? You and Juliet? Come with me and lunch at Nice?'

'We will, whether we can or not.'

'That's the stuff!' He was delighted with her.

'Juliet will adore it,' Alison said, with an amused little smile. 'She wants to collect her money and buy clothes. Poor lamb, she thinks fifty pounds is a fortune! However, it seems she has saved her fare home as well. If she takes my advice you will see a new Juliet.'

'My good Dame, she would take your advice if you told her to walk down the street on her hands!'

'What nonsense! But I hope you will see a Juliet transformed.'

'But I don't want her transformed!'

'My beamish boy,' his mother said gravely, 'Juliet is just twenty-one and when, can you tell me, has she known what it is to feel care-free and young and gay? She has been a bullied governess and an overworked Jill-of-all-Trades, and a terribly anxious, responsible nurse. It is time something was done.'

'Gosh, Muff – as to all that, I couldn't agree more.'

He gave her a wide, slow grin. 'Okay: go on and do your stuff ... I've got a bit of shopping to do, too.'

He hovered, turning over her books, *Venture into the Interior; Green Glory; Africa Drums* ... Books about forests, every one of them.

'I brought them for Juliet, but she hasn't a minute for reading,' his mother explained.

He lingered still.

'Worried, Michael?' she enquired.

'Oh, no. Only I'm wondering. When Juliet goes to London on this ridiculous, time-wasting training stunt ... By the way, I suppose she'll travel with you?'

'I certainly hope so ... Will this new evidence mean a hold-up for you?'

'Afraid so. Daniel has promised to put it up to the judge that I have to leave, but he says I'll be interrogated again.'

'I was hoping we could drive up to Chamonix.'

'There'll hardly be time, but, if not, let's take the Route Napoléon to Grenoble. It must be gorgeous. Then the Rhône Valley to Marseilles.'

'Stopping at Avignon?'

'Yes. Juliet wants to see Avignon. She's in love with the song ... But, look Muff, if things go wrong here, Martine's got to find someone, hasn't she? I mean, she ought to be thinking about it or Juliet will get trapped. This Fool's Paradise thing could go on too long.'

'I know, Monkey. It's hard to know what to say, and just when to say it. You see, if Martine gets upset, the baby could ...'

Michael exploded.

'It's becoming a tyranny, all this hush-hush business and fuss for the sake of the baby! Juliet's being victimised; so are you, and so am I, for the matter of that.'

'Monkey, you are being so good over the whole infuriating affair that Juliet's heart is just melted away. She's so proud of you she doesn't know what to do.'

He smiled at her.

'It's not fair to disarm a fellow like that!'

There was a pause, then Michael asked, 'By the way, when I am gone, what are you going to do with the car?'

'Run around for a few days with Juliet; do my article; send it back to Nice, and go North by train.'

'She'll enjoy that.'

'Will she, do you think?'

There was irony in her voice, and compassion. Right enough, it wasn't going to be gay for these two, at first, after he'd gone … Well, it was time to come out with his question.

'In London, where is Juliet going to live?'

'Take the tray, will you?'

He removed it to the table; gave his mother a cigarette and lit it for her; lit one for himself, and, sitting on the arm of the chair by the window, waited for her reply. It came in a casual tone.

'In some girls' club or hostel, I suppose.'

Michael scowled at the sun-washed garden and the bright, coloured roofs below. 'That sounds grim and grimy to me.'

'It will be for less than a year.'

'I thought perhaps, as there will be my room …'

'There will; but I am too often away.'

'She'd be all right with Bess Burns coming in.'

'Bess only cleans up and gets lunch. No, she would be too much alone.'

'I thought you'd like it.'

'That's not the point.'

'I imagined you'd wangle something.'

'They look after the girls well in those hostels. She would have a healthy, regular life.'

Michael couldn't believe his ears. His mother's tone was entirely unlike her: cool and indifferent. He gaped at her, but saw not the ghost of a smile on her face. She met his incredulous stare with a level gaze. Apparently there was no more to be said. He took the tray and opened the door, but paused to look back and say, crossly, 'I give you up.'

Juliet, hurriedly changing into her buttercup dress for Nice, read the telegram again and was again shaken with laughter at it. She hadn't known a telegram could be so long.

GREAT NEWS REACHED WILDERNESS LOCATIONING THANK MICHAEL HIGHLY CORRECT LETTER TELL HIM HE IS OKAY BY ME PLEASE COLLECT FIFTY THOUSAND FRANCS FOR HOLIDAY AND BEAUTIFICATION FROM WANDA AND ME CRÉDIT LYONNAIS MENTON AND WHEN LONDON CALL BARCLAYS COVENT GARDEN ALL THE BEST FRITH

Now Juliet hadn't a care in the world. In a kit chosen with Dame Alison's help she would be able to face Paris and London. How was she to find words with which to thank Frith? What a generous person Wanda must be! This was going to be a marvellous day and, to make it perfect, Martine didn't mind being left in Marie's care.

Martine was enjoying the luxury of the sunny room with its view over the terrace, where from behind muslin curtains, sitting in an armchair, she could watch the neighbours who came and went, making enquiries for her and leaving gifts. It was known, and Martine knew, that René was in prison and an aura of martyrdom was added to his fame. She imagined him proud and resolute and was convinced that he would come home, vindicated, before the end of the week. It was agreed that this afternoon two visitors might be admitted to keep her company and admire Henri-Martin, who, peaceful and fair as a cherub, now looked the miracle infant the village considered him to be.

Juliet wondered whether, if all ended well for this family, Michael would guess the heights and depths of the happiness that he would have helped to save.

'DON'T LET Juliet loose near the Casino,' Michael warned his mother when he drove into Nice and set his passengers down in the Place Masséna. With ten 5000-franc notes burning holes in the pocket of the coat she had borrowed from his mother, the girl was looking a bit dazed. Giving them a rendezvous at La Rascasse for lunch, he drove to the Palais de Justice, where he hung about in the crowded hall, dodging advocates and their clients and looking out for Maître Daniel. Presently Daniel collided with him, dashing out from the judge's room. He grabbed the curé's statement and vanished with it, leaving after him the illusion of a trail of electric sparks. When he reappeared he rushed Michael into a dingy room, full of desks and benches, clapped him on the shoulder and scolded and mocked him as though they had been old friends.

'*Eh bien, mon vieux!* How you have thieved my thunder! What impudence! In there, they are upside down! They have sent already the order that Terka is placed under arrest. The curé is convened for an interrogation and you also for Tuesday. I can tell you it is quick work. But you have all the audacities. To go like that to the curé and force him to confess himself to you! How have you dared?'

Michael grinned.

'I suppose heretics step in where the faithful fear to tread.'

That delighted the advocate. He repeated it.

'Nevertheless,' he said, becoming serious, 'your curé has made an obstruction to the progress of justice. To have dissimulated the facts! It is altogether shocking.'

'He had rather severe concussion, you know.'

'It is very unfortunate for poor René. If I had known this more early, imagine the defence that I could have presented! Now it will be more difficult. The curé has made the law an ass, like Shakespeare, and the law does not like to change his face.'

'But, like Shakespeare, we have "a Daniel come to judgement",' Michael said, and added, soberly, 'I would swear Monsieur Gaidoni is a just man.'

'I, too, believe it ... They wait for me. Excuse me, please.' Daniel wrung Michael's hand and was gone again, this time leaving a smile in the air like the smile of the Cheshire Cat. Michael, out in the glare and the din of the streets again, felt that he had wandered into Looking-Glass Land. Nonsense rhymes began to chime in his mind.

> *They took some honey and plenty of money ...*
> *But what shall we do for a ring?*

That was quite a problem. Luckily he'd lived economically at the farm; and René, before they had parted, had had the bright idea of telling him to pay at the inn the same as he had paid Camille. That was cheap living. He'd prowl about and see what was in the shops, and if he saw a few rings that were possible, Juliet should come and choose.

> *So they sailed away for a year and a day*
> *To the land where the Bong-Tree grows ...*

It wasn't going to be easy, Michael reflected, after this dream of a time with his girl and his mother, sailing away alone.

3

JULIET WAS CONTENT to let Dame Alison take charge of the shopping, which she did by means of some intuition or flair that Juliet did not understand. Without having any acquaintance with the shops of Nice, she would pass the most glamorous window-display with a shake of the head, dive into some small place with a less alluring exterior, and there discover exactly the right thing.

Juliet enjoyed it, although she could not help being stung by memories of her mother who, during that first joyous year in the South, had loved to choose pretty clothes for her little girl in these shops and in the shops of Cannes. Later, she had complained that Juliet grew too quickly out of her clothes: was becoming 'a gawk'; was going through 'the awkward age'. Surely, surely she would like to hear about the engagement? To write and get no answer would be chilling, and that might happen. Still, Juliet decided that she would write.

'I am lucky,' she told herself. 'Who could have a more darling *belle-mère*?'

They found a coat and skirt in a cool horizon blue which needed no more alteration than Juliet could do for herself; a small matching hat with a pearl-coloured feather, and a pearl-coloured blouse. When Juliet had acquired these and two pairs of gloves and a length of the softest lingerie cotton, Alison thought she had spent enough for one day.

'Now it is my turn. I want to give you a present, just to surprise Michael,' she said. 'And you mustn't let me down.'

The consequence of this conspiracy was that Michael, arriving twenty minutes late at their rendezvous, scowled to perceive that his mother appeared to have picked up a stranger and invited him to their table – some cheeky-looking schoolboy in sweater and slacks.

When Juliet jumped up and came to him, flushed and laughing, he rumpled her hair, said, 'Young, gay and carefree and ready for the mountains,' and smiled at his mother, admitting, 'You win.'

When they drove home there were dress-boxes piled beside Alison in the back of the car and on Juliet's ungloved hand there twinkled a tiny brilliant, set in a thin gold band.

Before presenting herself to Martine Juliet changed into her overall. She was startled by the effect her new clothes seemed to have had on her outlook and didn't want Martine to feel it. The truth was that she had become aware of an intense craving to escape. She wanted passionately to drive away with Michael and his mother, out of sight and sound of St Jacques. She did not know how she would bear it if their holiday should have to be given up. Nevertheless, she was dismayed when she entered Martine's room, to hear what Michael was saying, while his mother listened, looking perturbed.

'A week from today, you see, we shall be leaving: the three of us. Have you made plans? Suppose René hasn't returned by that time, what are you going to do?'

Martine was pale to the lips. She flung a desperate hand out and caught Juliet's wrist.

'Not in a week! You wouldn't! So soon!' she panted, and then she saw the ring. She released Juliet's hand and looked up at her, then looked at Michael and yielded with a deep sigh.

'She is yours now. You will take her,' she said.

Dame Alison murmured, 'It will be her last week, Martine.'

Michael answered quietly.

'Juliet is neither mine nor yours.'

Martine was weeping now.

'You have all been too good to me,' she sobbed. 'I am spoilt, like a selfish child, but if they keep René I don't know what will become of us.'

'You are not selfish,' Alison said persuasively. 'We all think so much of you, Martine. Making a plan won't hurt René's chances, and he, you know, would worry less if you did ...You told me his father had written. Would he come?'

'Yes, Papa Loubier would come,' Martine said with an effort at control. 'We would open the inn. But it's not only Juliet's work ...'

'I know it isn't,' Juliet said.

Her voice trembled. She knew that if René were committed for trial at the Assizes Martine would go to pieces. The anxiety would be too much for her. To go off on a holiday, perhaps just when that news had come – it wouldn't be possible. She sent a tormented look of pleading to Dame Alison, who looked at Michael.

Michael came round the bed, put an arm round Juliet and drew her out of the room.

'Listen, sweetheart,' he said. 'Nobody is giving you orders and nobody's going to tear you to bits. If things get so bad that you can't leave without feeling like a murderess, well, simply, we'll all stay till I have to go. Wherever you are, you know, I'm happy, and mother's in bliss wherever we are. So that's that.'

Juliet's heart turned over. She thanked him with a kiss, like a child. Presently he said, 'All the same, I'm going to find out whether Papa Loubier is on the telephone,' and returned to Martine. Alison was smiling when she came out of the room.

'When Michael goes into action!' she said.

Chapter XXVI

THE SCALES

RENÉ'S FATHER WAS coming early next month. He seemed shocked to the soul by the closing of the inn, and unable to comprehend it, since René would undoubtedly return soon. He wished, however, to see his grandson and the appeal for his help obviously gave him great satisfaction. No matter what happened, in two or three weeks he would arrive, and Juliet would be free to travel to London with Alison.

To have faced facts and provided for contingencies brought a sense of balance and steadiness to everybody concerned. Martine, though no longer so sweetly confident, no longer pretty and smiling, remained calm. She dressed herself and began to take a share in the work. On Sunday she brought out clean sheets and towels, helped with the beds, and finished the trimming of the baby's cot. Madame Bonin arrived, breathless, after mass, to expatiate on the tremendous news that was blowing through the village like the mistral – that Terka was under arrest in the hospital and that on Tuesday the curé was coming home. She was all satisfaction and benevolence, her quarrel with René either forgotten or, in her opinion, thoroughly justified.

She proposed to spend the afternoon with Martine, and offered to assemble a nursery lunch.

Michael at once swept Juliet and his mother out and into the car. To avoid the village with its thousand eyes, he headed for the route by way of the bridge.

'Got your passports?' he asked. The answer was 'No,' and they had to go back for them. He wanted a long afternoon in the garden at La Mortola and that was in Italy.

There was a wind from the south. Instead of wasting time on lunch they sat at a table on the promenade at Menton and had coffee and *brioches,* while long waves crashed on the rocks, sending up fans and fountains of glistening foam.

A seventh wave approached, portentous, but so sleek and magnificent in its motion that they watched, fascinated, instead of withdrawing. It broke with a roar, hung a great veil above them and left their *brioches* salted and their hair and clothes bedewed with spray. That didn't matter. Juliet was ready for anything in her new white jumper and navy slacks and so was Alison. She was wearing the grey suit and the dark glasses in which Juliet had first encountered her such an incredibly short time ago. The wild, swift turning of fortune's wheel had made them friends very quickly, Juliet thought.

Michael was saying something about its being rather a pity that the chariot was so posh. You dared not take it over the smugglers' roads that he would have liked to explore.

'Why do you call it "the chariot"?' Juliet asked. But she did not attend very much to his explanation about the God in the Car who, in ancient tragedies, descends from the sky to snatch the victim from an unhappy fate. She was seeing two of the Tarot cards. There was Fortune's Wheel with queer, impish figures turning it, and there was a woman driving a chariot, all gold.

Michael listened, amused, while she described them and, then, others that came with startling vividness back to her mind.

'There was a house with two little people in it; and the House of God; and a house with fire falling on it in big flakes out of the sky. And, Michael, there was a man with a bludgeon, and a priest, and … and, yes, there was a judge! Isn't it uncanny?'

Michael laughed at her marvelling voice and eyes.

'Not a bit uncanny,' he declared. 'They probably have symbols for everything. I bet nothing could happen without their being able to show that they had turned up a symbol foretelling it ... Besides,' he went on, amused, 'it wouldn't be chancing too much to prophesy an accident if you meant to do your damnedest to bring it about.'

Juliet agreed, her eyes on his face.

'But, oh,' she confessed, 'you can't imagine how frightened I was sometimes. Her whispers! Her warnings! "That house has a curse on it: leave it!" and "The priest has to do with death," and, worst of all, the Chevalier of the Sword – "Keep far from his path." I thought that was you!'

Alison looked from one to the other, in sympathy and distress. Michael laid a hand over Juliet's hand that was nervously crumbling bread. He said, quietly, 'Yet you stayed. You stood by.'

'I promised ...'

'And you kept your promise. You defied augury. I don't believe one girl in a thousand would have done that.'

Alison spoke in a low tone, half smiling: 'Your father would have wanted to give her a large medal,' she said.

Michael wanted to be off, but no one appeared with whom to settle the bill. He left them and went into the café. 'I'm not such a sceptic as Michael is,' Alison said. 'He gets that from his father. I would have been terribly frightened, too.'

Juliet did not believe that. She could not imagine Michael or his mother being frightened by anything, but she kept these thoughts to herself. There was a peaceful, reflective silence and then Alison surprised Juliet. Apropos of nothing whatever, she said, 'If I were you, I wouldn't bother about training. Why, instead, don't you take a post?'

It was a long jump from Terka's encampment. Juliet managed it, blinking.

'But, goodness! Surely I don't know enough!'

'It seems to me that you do, Juliet. You have grasped the principles and the rest you would soon pick up. There are excellent books. Think what an intensive training you have had at the inn! Cooking, nursing, baby-minding. You could make a home anywhere now.'

Michael returned and Juliet did not reply. Why in the world had Dame Alison said that? But she had said it and therefore it must be true: 'You could make a home anywhere, now.'

The words sank deeper and deeper, like reviving rain, into the roots of Juliet's heart and mind.

For Michael, La Mortola was a sort of Garden of Eden, where trees and shrubs achieved their ultimate state of wellbeing, protected from all their enemies, planted with forethought and knowledge, bred and protected with skill and devoted care. While Juliet and Alison wandered along the terraces, under pergolas fragrant with late roses, and enjoyed the lovely vistas made by foliage, flowers, and steps running down to the sea, Michael stood rapt before one shrub for ten minutes; made drawings of another, brooded over some low-growing plant and extracted information by means known only to himself from a gardener whose language he did not know.

At tea-time he began to follow them to the restaurant but they lost him on the way. They were hungry; the pastries piled with fruit and cream were seductive and they decided not to wait for him.

'Now you know your only rivals,' Alison said to Juliet smilingly. 'You need never hope to compete with trees.'

Returning, they found Martine more cheerful, but Madame Bonin's conversation seemed to have bored Henri-Martin. He was cross and restless and had a spell of wailing. It took a long time to get him to sleep. Alison was, therefore, not entirely pleased when, as they were finishing their late supper, strains of martial music were heard from the street. Michael and Juliet, however, reacted differently. They gobbled their ice-creams and hurried out.

'Tambourines and flageolets – I shall always adore them,' Juliet said. She ran with Michael down the garden and out at the little gate. The musicians were grouped at the lower end of the street, in front of the chestnut trees, and half the village seemed to be following them. There were eight or nine performers and their conductor was no less a person than Monsieur Marcellin, who was equally famous as a coiffeur, music-master and player of bowls. He was powerfully built and his gestures with the baton were as vigorous as if he had been conducting grand opera. 'The March of the Toreadors' came to a resounding climax and an abrupt end.

Now the performers went into a huddle. Somebody cheered and sounds of assent were heard. The band, behind the conductor, swung into the rue de la Pompe and advanced with purposeful steps.

'Sakes!' Michael exclaimed. 'Do you know what they're up to? They are going to serenade Martine!'

Juliet was too much alarmed to stop to think. As the beaming conductor saluted her she called out, telling him that the baby was asleep.

He stopped in his stride, turned and halted the men. The straggling, laughing crowd also paused.

'*Le bébé dort*,' he said in a loud whisper, and the news was relayed down the lines. *Le bébé dort*. There was more whispering and then, very gently, very slowly, the baton was raised again.

The piping was like the low notes of birds and the drum taps were as light as April rain. Softly, merrily, tenderly, came the sweet phrases of the old tune: 'Sur le Pont d'Avignon'. Juliet stood by the gate, smiling with pleasure and gratitude at the music-makers, and Michael stood smiling down at her.

2

THE CHARIOT'S GLORY was quite overlaid by dust. On Monday morning, in the lane, Michael gave it a thorough washing. Juliet was helping him to polish it when Alison came across the yard with a note for her which a boy had delivered. The envelope was not very clean. Juliet opened it, frowned, and read it aloud:

Terka is anxious to see you. I think you should visit her. It was signed by Doctor Gompert.

Michael's bucket was dropped with a clatter onto the cobbles and water splashed on their feet.

'Blast the man's impudence! Does he imagine …' he began, but stopped, seeing trouble on Juliet's face. His mother was looking at her.

'The thing is,' Juliet said reluctantly, 'she might say something that would be useful. I suppose we oughtn't to miss any chance – ought we? I'm awfully afraid that I'll have to go.'

MICHAEL DROVE THEM to the hospital after lunch. His mother was to be present at the interview: he had insisted on this.

The matron explained, as she led the two visitors up a flight of scrubbed, uncarpeted stairs and along a corridor where the smell of coal-tar disinfectant fought a losing battle with other, less cleanly, smells, that she had been obliged to place Terka alone in a ward. 'One of the cleaners, unfortunately, told the other patients whom we had taken in and their reaction was very bad. We have had to tell them she has been sent to Nice.'

The long room had three dusty windows, high up; three beds and three wooden stools. At one end a black iron stove sent its flue crawling across the whole wall. The woman sitting up in the middle bed with a red flannel cape over her shoulders, her hair hanging in thick, black plaits, and a white linen bandage over one eye, was Terka. She lifted her head and turned a face glowing with eager welcome to Juliet. Alison was given a glance and a cold bow, then ignored.

Juliet said, 'I hope you are getting better.' The words sounded less cool and detached than she had meant them to. It caused her a pang to see the fine, free-striding gypsy reduced to helplessness, and she had not expected that affectionate smile. Composing herself, she sat on a stool some distance from the bed while Alison remained standing on the far side of it near the stove. When the matron had gone, shutting the door, Terka stretched out a hand, palm upwards, in a gesture that compelled the girl to draw her stool closer, and spoke in a voice so low and confiding that Juliet had to lean towards her to hear.

'I knew you would come. You are sweetness in an evil and cruel world,' Terka said.

She spoke in Italian, a language that Juliet loved, and it was in Italian that Juliet heard herself answering, saying, again, that she hoped Terka would soon be quite well. The battering of her heart

255

had subsided. Terka was no longer formidable, and the hard, calm tone she had practised was not required. Simply, one was visiting the sick.

'I sent for you', Terka went on softly, 'because there is something I want you to have. Mademoiselle, there are fearful days coming: a terrible vengeance will fall on the whole parish of St Jacques, and I do not wish that it should fall on you. You took pity on me: you saved my life ...' Terka's voice broke off in a gasp and her hands, clenched and trembling, were pressed against her brow.

'Do you know', she whispered, 'what those savages would have done?'

Juliet's voice, too, was shaking a little as she said, 'It is all over now.'

The woman nodded and laid both hands over Juliet's hands.

'Yes, it is over, and soon, very soon, punishment will begin ... Soon! Soon!'

The word was hissed and hatred tensed every muscle of Terka's throat and face. Recoiling, Juliet wrenched herself out of the mood of pity into which she had fallen and dragged her hands out of Terka's implacable clutch. Pulling back her stool, she looked straight in the gypsy's face.

'Terka, why did you do it? Martine had never hurt you', she asked.

As though in hurt amazement, the deep, vibrant voice protested: 'But I have done nothing to harm Martine.'

'You did a thing that you thought would destroy her. I saw you. I was there.'

'You didn't understand what you saw! Oh, my bright angel, don't be a cruel fool like the others – you who are so wise and kind! ... Look: I am going to give you the dearest treasure I have ever possessed.'

It was a small ring in the shape of a snake – a silver snake, coiled three times, with ruby eyes. Terka caught Juliet's left hand in hers and slipped it on to the little finger murmuring as she did so – murmuring some words in a strange language. Then she looked with a smile into Juliet's eyes.

'Now you are protected,' she declared. 'Neither fire nor air nor water will ever harm you as long as you wear that ring. Terka's enemies will be overwhelmed but neither wood nor metal nor poison, wild beast nor evil spirit will harm you.'

Juliet's head drooped and she gazed at the bright silver, bewildered. These changes were incredible, like a dream. This sick, hurt woman who seemed to love her and the malicious wretch who had paralysed Martine and tried to murder the priest – could they be the same? Lifting her head suddenly to stare at Terka, she saw a triumphing glint in the narrowed eye and a twist on the lips.

'You meant to destroy Martine, and you tried to kill Father Pascale.'

Juliet had spoken firmly. She stood up. Terka wrung her hands in agitation and her voice rose up, high-pitched and shrill.

'Not I; not I! It isn't true! These things happen: can I prevent them? My enemies suffer, always, and they always will; but I do not bring it about. They blame me, but – I am not to blame.'

Juliet said: 'You flung the branch down on the mare.' Terka gasped and shrank back against her pillow. Her face crumpled; the firm lips slackened; the chin trembled and sagged. When she spoke it was in the patois and with a whine.

'I am innocent. I have never done anyone any harm. Everyone is against me; they wish me to starve; I am a poor, homeless vagabond.'

Juliet sighed. She looked across the mumbling creature at Alison who was standing, anxious and vigilant, near the bed. Juliet drew off the snake-ring and left it on the stool. Terka pulled the blanket over her head and did not turn or speak or move as they left the room.

The corridor was empty.

'What a strange, strange person,' Alison murmured.

'She isn't!'

Juliet's voice sounded in her own ears abrupt and rough, like a petulant child's, as she went on: 'She's a wicked, smarmy, disgusting hypocrite, and a ham actress, that's all.'

Juliet did not understand why her friend looked so deeply pleased. Terka hadn't admitted a single thing. A tactful person would have got something out of her, but the visit hadn't done one scrap of good.

'Come and tell Michael that,' Alison said.

FATHER PASCALE LOOKED OUT from his cushioned corner with delighted eyes, and Juliet, who sat in the back of the open car beside him, felt her own almost aching sense of the hour's beauty quickened and released by his. It was years since he had enjoyed these scenes.

They had started early so as not to have to drive fast and the young day was flowering and opening as they drove. Its pale tints, suffused with a sunny haze, deepened slowly, while the wreaths of mist that separated the summits thinned and vanished. They drove through La Turbie, whose *Trophée* shone, raised like a huge shield, in the sun, and then, crowning a tower-like crag, the ancient town of Èze loomed up on the left, its clefts and plains and angles sharply defined in black shadow and dazzling light. The Mediterranean gleamed with a crystalline blue, more radiant than the sky. Juliet named headland after headland, town after coloured town. At the height of the road, where there opened, inland, a wilderness of valleys and hills and Alps. Already autumn had rusted the dwarf-oaks, and the crimson fires of sumac smouldered among them on the upper slopes. Michael stopped the car and leaned back to ask the curé whether the motion was causing him any pain.

'Only my conscience suffers,' was the smiling reply, 'to think my misdeeds should have gained for me such a pleasure as this. I had forgotten that France held such splendours. "*Tous les royaumes du monde avec leur gloire.*"'

He became subdued and quiet as they descended into the straggling streets of the port of Nice and made their way through the flower-market to the Palais de Justice.

Parked below the immense flight of steps were innumerable polished cars, while *camionettes* loaded with flowers blocked the streets. It was with difficulty that Michael found a place at which the curé might conveniently descend. There was no sign of Maître Daniel, but he had kept his promise: two sturdy porters were at hand with a canvas carrying-seat slung on poles. As these approached the car a white-haired priest, also, came forward, a smile of affection creasing his tanned face. He was Père Sylvestre, the curé's old friend. He showed where an old-fashioned car stood, close to the steps, and said he would wait in it to drive Father Pascale to the Priest's House, where Michael was to call for him: but not, it was agreed, before four o'clock.

After the radiance outside, the gloom seemed even deeper than before in the great hall: *la salle des pas perdus*. '"The hall of wasted footsteps,"' Michael muttered. 'I believe the League of Nations had one too.'

There was a chair for the curé. As the only person seated he was an object of interest and advocates pointed him out to one another as though knowing or guessing his mission there. His thin, pallid face became paler still as he waited, and Juliet began to feel the beating of her own heart, like the ticking away of time. She knew that if this effort for René failed there would be nothing that anybody would be able to do for him until he was tried at the Assizes.

At last Maître Daniel came out of the judge's room.

He greeted the invalid with reassuring gentleness and conducted him within. A moment later, threading his way hurriedly towards the same door, came the long, stooping figure of Dr Frieden, the psychiatrist, who had spent an hour yesterday with Martine. Juliet flushed, recalling his reprimand, rendered more impressive by the solemnity of his sallow countenance with its longer upper lip and cavernous eyes.

'In future, Mademoiselle, I trust that you will leave the administration of shock-therapy to the qualified practitioners. The young woman might have had a most injurious fall.'

Now, to her relief, he seemed absorbed in his thoughts and he passed into the room without having noticed her.

'Humourless-looking blighter,' Michael remarked.

It was nearly half an hour before Father Pascale came out with a clerk, who conducted him to the top of the steps where the porters were waiting for him. Long minutes passed and then Michael was called.

His welcome was not only courteous but cordial. Philippe Daniel's face could be inscrutable and it told him nothing, but the judge and the psychiatrist seemed relaxed. Monsieur Gaidoni, instead of putting specific questions to Michael, told him that they were endeavouring to envisage the accused woman's state of mind, asked whether he felt he could throw any light on it, and advised him to take his time.

Recognising his opportunity, Michael made his answer a narrative, long and detailed. All three listened intently but he found himself aiming his points chiefly at Dr Frieden because of the psychiatrist's appreciation of subtle suggestions which won little response from the legal men. He repeated Juliet's observations about the fortune-telling – the burning house; the house 'under a curse'; the priest who 'has to do with death'. The advocate's face wore a little, derisive smile and the judge pursed his lips, but Dr Frieden took rapid notes and said, 'Very, very interesting.'

Next, Michael described the stone-pine, of which some photographs lay on the desk, and declared that Terka must have been utterly heedless of concealment when she took her place on the bough. He told again in what state she had left her encampment, describing, without any softening of the picture, the hanged rabbits and butchered cock. Dr Frieden, hunched over the desk, looked as though he were visualising the scene.

'Then that night of the pursuit,' Michael said. 'I saw a complete change in her then. Before, she had looked composed, even commanding: had had her own sort of dignity. That night she shrieked and raved like a maniac.'

He stopped there. Daniel flashed him a rather Satanic smile. Dr Frieden and Monsieur Gaidoni made notes. There was a pause, then the judge looked at him very directly and put a question in a judicial form:

'In your opinion, Monsieur, did a large number of persons living in the village and parish of St Jacques believe this woman to be a witch?'

'A very large number. I know for a fact that they did.'

'Do you think that she herself believed that she possessed occult powers?'

'I have formed no opinion about that.'

The judge nodded. Dr Frieden looked up and cleared his throat.

'Monsieur,' he said, 'when I asked Terka this morning why she had refused to avail herself of the services of an advocate, she gave me a somewhat enigmatic answer. You may be in a position to interpret it. What she said was: "I do not need one. They cannot harm me. Let them try. I have powerful friends." Now to whom, do you suppose, did she refer?'

Keeping his tone as dry as the doctor's, Michael answered: 'To Beelzebub and his legions, I should think.'

'That was my own conclusion,' Dr Frieden said. Michael took care not to meet the advocate's eye. The judge coughed, closed his notebook, and turned to the psychiatrist.

'Doctor: apart from the question of her sanity, on which you do not wish as yet to pronounce, can you tell me this? Given the fact that a large number of people held this belief and that the woman herself appears, finally, to consider herself an agent of dark powers, did she, in your considered opinion, constitute a danger to the community?'

'A very grave danger,' was the reply.

'Do you believe that, had she remained at liberty, serious mischief might have ensued?'

'Yes, indeed: I would have expected an outbreak of mass hysteria; accidents; illnesses. I even consider it highly probable that young Madame Loubier would have died.'

Michael stared at the man: that long, solemn face; that dry-as-dust manner, and a fine, clean-edged, fearless mind! It was exhilarating.

They stood up. Michael received thanks and handshakes and was dismissed, but not before Monsieur Gaidoni had desired him, with a paternal smile, to convey his compliments to Mademoiselle Cunningham. '*Ravissante, ravissante,*' Michael heard him murmuring before the door was closed.

He waited with Juliet, hoping that Daniel would appear, and in a moment he joined them, mischievous glee in his eyes.

'If that doesn't shake Gaidoni,' he said, excitedly, 'nothing will! Frieden knows how to speak out, doesn't he? As to you, Monsieur Faulkner, you are wasted on trees!'

Michael asked him what would happen to Terka if she was pronounced insane.

'Undoubtedly she will become a resident of Dr Frieden's open-air clinic, for mental cases,' Daniel replied. 'She will probably preside over it, to the age of a hundred, in the character of Pope Joan.'

'Have you any guess how it will go for René?'

Daniel moved his hands in an elegant, delicate gesture to describe the slight fluctuation of balanced scales.

'*Comme ci, comme ça*', he answered. 'Monsieur Gaidoni has terminated his cases for today. No doubt he reflects. Let us piously wish for him an excellent lunch … And where do you propose to lunch, if one is permitted to ask?'

Michael did not want him to join them. It wasn't often that he and Juliet had a meal to themselves. He said, 'We hadn't decided,' and Daniel smiled.

'It's only this,' he explained. 'René is excessively eager to have a visit from you. He desires to hear the news of his wife and the inn, and to discuss finance. This is not the regular visiting day and I doubt very much if I shall be able to arrange it, but if it is convenient to you I will try.'

'I'd like to say goodbye to him,' Michael said.

'Good! Meet me outside the prison, then, will you, at three o'clock? *Au revoir. À bientôt, Mademoiselle. Bon appetit!*'

Their appetites were fine, especially Michael's. They enjoyed large bowls of *bouillabaisse* with a bottle of white Côte de Provence, and then strolled about on the Quai des Ponchettes where the fishermen were drying and mending their nets. Juliet's big hat flew off at a windy corner and chasing it proved good sport for some idle lads. It was retrieved and returned to her with smiles and compliments – to lose one's hat here was, it seemed, the classical thing to do, and she thought it was just as well that she possessed another one now. Then she and Michael lost the way to the prison and arrived five minutes late. Michael parked his car and they were contemplating the great shut gates when these were cumbrously opened and a black car was driven out. In the back seat sat Monsieur Gaidoni, alone. He recognised them and lifted his hat with a very pleasant and kindly smile.

'*Mes félicitations*,' he said.

Michael, who was hatless, saluted. He grinned and said to Juliet, 'I say, do we look all that engaged?'

The courtyard was empty except for gendarmes. The iron door at the top of some steps was closed. After a while it was opened and Philippe Daniel came out.

'You can see René,' he called. 'Please wait.'

Juliet was glad that it was not she who had asked for this visit. How sad and unsatisfactory it would inevitably be supervised; limited as to time; with so many things to be remembered and such urgent emotions to be suppressed! She said nothing except, 'Tell him that I love the baby and that your mother is very fond of Martine.'

'I'll tell him,' Michael said.

They were watching the door. It opened again, and again Maître Daniel came out. On the steps he paused to let someone else precede him. Then René came down: René in his brown suit and smart hat with his *serviette* under his left arm.

'Parole,' Michael said. He scarcely had breath for the word. Juliet, with René's eyes laughing into hers and René crushing her hand in a fierce grip, had not breath for a word at all.

'No, it's not parole,' the advocate said proudly. 'The case has been dismissed on a *non-lieu*: no grounds for an indictment. This dangerous type is a free man.'

Chapter XXVII

OVER THE HILLS

'BAGGAGE READY?'

Michael stood in his mother's doorway, all impatience. 'Just a second.'

Alison ran a comb through her short hair, pulled on her grey beret, fixed it carefully with a silver pin, then put the brush and comb in their bag, put the bag and her powder-box into her dressing-case and snapped the clasp.

Michael was regarding with extreme disapprobation the cardboard boxes and bulging rug-straps waiting to be taken down. His mother's baggage was usually the last word in *chic*.

'What the dickens is all this? Where's your new suitcase?' he demanded.

'I've given it to Juliet.'

'You have?' His face cleared. 'Well, I'll buy you a new one at Marseilles ... My papers have come,' he informed her. 'There were no letters for you.'

'Are they all in order?'

'Fine. The office is doing me proud. She's an English boat chartered for a gaggle of archaeologists. But it looks as if, with collecting my sterling, seeing the consul, and checking my gear and the customs business, I'll need a whole day in Marseilles – the twenty-ninth.'

'That means cutting out Chamonix, I suppose?'

'I'm sorry about that.'

'Oh, we won't have to be sorry for ourselves! The Dauphiny Alps; Valence; Orange; Avignon! ... Is the car ready?'

'She is. Have you sent off your telegrams?'

'I have ... Has René been amenable about accounts?'

Michael grinned. 'A very nice calculation. Juliet is to have her salary, if you please: full time instead of half time since the ninth. I pay in full – I insisted, naturally. You pay nothing, solely because you've acted as cook. René was explicit. He says you have saved the life of his son and "a man cannot pay for that".'

'Sensible and sensitive,' Alison commented. 'Very French ... Where's Juliet?'

The terrace was empty.

'Probably in her room.'

She was not there. The room was neat and impersonal; the bed was made up for its next occupant. She was in the yard, the baby held firmly against her shoulder, while Martine and René carefully arranged a rug, the cradle, a chair and a table under the feathery shade of the pepper tree. When René took his son the baby jerked his limbs in protest and cried. Quickly he was placed in his mother's arms and he was at once quiet again. Martine said something that made René throw back his head and laugh. Seeing Michael and Alison, he called up:

'You see how it is, Madame? I have been two weeks absent and already the inn has a new master,' he said.

Juliet told them the picnic basket was ready. 'You never saw such a feast!' she declared. Basket and all were a farewell gift from Martine.

'All set, then? ... You two women,' Michael complained, 'am I never going to extract you from this inn?'

At last Alison took her place at the wheel of the car, the picnic basket and wine on the seat beside her, and Michael fitted the luggage in at the back. Juliet said goodbye to Martine and the baby in the yard, and to René in the entrance-hall. He was not smiling. He looked an older man than he had looked two weeks ago. He took her hand in his strong grip and pressed it.

'You will return to us, Juliette. Always, there is a home for you here. How can I say all that I wish you? I will say this: may your own happiness be as measureless always as ours is today, *grace à vous.*'

'I hope yours will last always,' was all Juliet could find to say in reply.

She was in the car with Michael, hatless. Alison let in the clutch and the car slid away. René stood on the steps, waving. They were over the crest and down. He was out of sight. They drove between olive orchards and over the bridge and then uphill under the shade of the pines. Juliet told Alison that if, after crossing the river again, she would stop, she could look back at a lovely view of St Jacques.

'Tell me when to slow down,' Alison said.

The sky was immaculate and the air so clear that their road could be seen in white arcs and loops climbing among the mountains ahead.

'I wish it would never end,' Juliet sighed.

'It will end,' Michael said, 'exactly a week from today.' The bitterness in his voice dismayed Juliet. It was a note she had never heard from him before. Her own elation had been so heady that she had failed to notice his gloomy mood. She realised now that Michael was acutely miserable and, like a flood, his pain invaded her. But his mood had resentment in it. She withdrew a little into her corner, saying nothing.

'I suppose the idea is', Michael said gruffly, 'that one might have an accident, or somehow or other let you down. Then you'll be all set up with these diplomas. I suppose it's all perfectly sound.'

Juliet was hurt and indignant. She stiffened. She said, in a voice so cold that she herself hardly knew it: 'You know quite well that that isn't true!'

Michael opened wide eyes at her and shook his head. 'Of course I know it isn't,' he said. 'You haven't two grains of calculation in your whole make-up.'

That was enough. She gave him a smile. 'Was there something worrying in those papers?'

'Not a thing. Everything's fine.'

There was still a bitter edge on his voice. 'It's a special boat. We call at Naples and the Piraeus; we'll see the Parthenon, probably, and then go among the islands.'

'The isles of Greece, the isles of Greece,' Juliet chanted, with all the longing that lives in those syllables. Then she looked at Michael with troubled eyes.

'You sound bored with it, and you wanted it all so much.'

'In those happy days', Michael answered grimly, 'I was my own master; I was self-sufficient. There was no little chit of a honey-haired girl I wanted to show things to.'

Juliet managed to turn on him a solemn regard.

'And I,' she said, 'in those happy days, would have thought going to London no end of a thrill.'

'And isn't it?' He was alert now.

Juliet shook her head.

'Do you mean?' he asked sharply. She nodded.

'Darling, my darling, what idiots we have been!'

No one told Alison when to slow down. No one remembered about looking back. Now the woods had been left below and the road ran level between slopes of stone and scrub. Michael leaned forward.

'Pull up, Muff. We have a surprise for you.'

As soon as she came to a wider stretch, Alison stopped the car. Michael and Juliet got out and stood beside her, smiling at her, one on each side. Michael said, 'Juliet's coming with me.'

'I'm going with him to Cyprus,' Juliet said.

Alison sighed.

'So,' she remarked. 'Michael has come to his senses at last.' She looked with commiseration at Juliet. 'Isn't he the slowest old mole? He scrabbles and scrabbles away underground ...'

Juliet chuckled.

'I nearly had to ask him myself.'

'*Would* you have?' Michael exclaimed.

'I was just making up my mind to.'

'Of course you were,' Alison said.

Michael stared at his mother with puckered brows.

'Is that why ... Is that why you refused ... Is that why you gave her the suitcase?' he demanded finally.

'Well,' was the rather apologetic reply, 'I did feel worried about you, going all that way alone.'

Michael's head was shaken gravely. He said, 'I warned you, Juliet ... Perhaps,' he said to his mother, 'you've arranged about our wedding and all? Have you a special licence in your pocket, by any chance?'

'Can one get a special licence in France?' she asked.

'I doubt it,' Michael replied.

'I dare say if we phoned the Embassy, and the English clergyman at Avignon, and Maître Daniel, and if Juliet wired to her father ...'

'We can try all that,' Michael said. 'And supposing it doesn't work?'

'Oh, she can go all the same.' Alison put an arm around Juliet, who was listening, a little bemused. 'The captain will find some motherly soul.'

'Who will see that she leads a healthy, regular life? ... And suppose there isn't a berth left on the boat?'

'I'll see her off by the next one. Juliet would manage all right ... But actually, Monkey, I wired to the consul at Marseilles yesterday asking him to secure one. He'll just think, of course, that it's for me, and if ...'

Michael's shout of laughter stopped her. When he could speak again he enquired, 'Just how long have you been plotting all this?'

'Darling, there's no plot.'

'Oh no, Muff, there never is!'

Alison looked from one young face to the other. She saw in Michael's serious eyes a deep smile of amused admiration, so like his father's that it pierced her heart, and saw Juliet's blue eyes alight with happiness and trust and love. But Juliet's voice shook with laughter.

'I daren't marry you, Michael! I won't! I can't have a witch for a mother-in-law.'

Michael did not want to drive. He and Juliet settled in the back again.

Alison drove on over the hills, her eyes on the road, easy hands on the wheel, in the clear, warm light of the autumn day.

Dark Enchantment is part of Tramp Press's Recovered Voices series, which includes two other novels by Dorothy Macardle: *The Uninvited* and *The Unforeseen*. These are available from tramppress.com, or your local bookseller.